D1446272

*T*hree decades ago Cape Coral was a pup, the path of Interstate 75 still grew pine and palmetto and a creaky old swing bridge dictated whether passage to Fort Myers Beach would be a breezy jaunt or a miserable crawl.

Those were the days when the land grew flowers instead of condos, when Lee County was the Gladiolus Capital Of The World and fortunes were made in the fields a few miles south of Fort Myers.

There were fascinating tales baking beneath the harsh Southwest Florida sun. Brady Vogt unearthed his on Gladiolus Drive, a short stretch of highway jumping off the Tamiami Trail on its way to Fort Myers Beach. Digging in the sandy soil which nurtured the colorful gladioli, Vogt uncovered racism, exploitation, cruelty, and greed.

He spins a grisly tale involving a brutal pig of a man, a stupid deputy sheriff, a kind whore, four itinerant boys and a man and his wife longing to return to their Mexican homeland.

Vogt has lived on Gladiolus Drive and herein tills its fields of intrigue with a skillful hand. If you were in these parts thirty years ago, his story will take you back to familiar names and places. If you were somewhere else, or yet unborn, here's an opportunity to soak up some historical flavor in this gripping yarn about what could have happened in those days gone by.

—Joe Workman

GLADIOLUS
DRIVE

GLADIOLUS DRIVE

a novel

by Brady Vogt

Everglades Books, Inc.
Fort Myers, Florida

Gladiolus Drive is a work of fiction.
Except for real persons named and real
places also named, the characters and
the events portrayed are imaginary.

Gladiolus Drive
Copyright© 2000
by Brady Vogt

First Edition
Printed in February of 2001

ISBN: 0-9708677-0-0

Jacket design and typesetting
by Digital Blacksmith, Inc.

ghulseman@bigfoot.com

Special thanks to Miss Lori Austin
for editorial assistance.

Now the world's full of trouble,
everybody's scared,
landlords are frownin,
cupboards are bare,
people are scramblin
like dogs for a share.
It's cruel and it's hard,
but it's nothin compared
to what we do to each other.

—The Waterboys

Prologue

*I*n the early Seventies Gladiolus Drive was still a two lane black-top road built on crushed shell. It curved sharply from the highway one mile, straightened out for most of the rest of its length, then twisted as it entered Harlem Heights. From there it was a short sandy shot to the corner, to Roy Miners Grocery, where McGregor and San Carlos and Gladiolus meet. Harlem Heights was where the colored people and the Puerto Ricans lived. The community created itself. Farms filled the open land along the river, toward town, toward the beach, along Gladiolus. The farms wanted workers, at Fort Myers Beach there was a need for people in the fish houses, the motels, and the restaurants.

Harlem Heights was a village of cottages and shacks. They were hidden, unsteady dwellings perched on concrete blocks, sheltered from the sun by banana and papaya, mango and avocado, and coconut palms. There was yellow guava in every yard, the rutted trails that ran through the guava to the wood dwellings were poorly announced by ramshackle mailboxes and loose gates. The houses were randomly placed under the trees and palms. They had sprung up from the land beneath a green canopy that shivered with the breezes.

Along the first big curve on Gladiolus there was an abandoned quarry called the rock pits. They were a group of man-made lakes. Decades before, lime rock and shell had been dug excavated, pulverized, and used as a base for the asphalt roads being built throughout Lee County. Some

1

of the lakes were very big across; they were all very deep, the depth of the water along the sharp rock edges dropped quickly. Its color was a light blue, almost clear, but in the middle of the lakes the water looked like it was a bilious yellow-green. No one recalled having seen the bottom. The digging had ruptured sulfur aquifers, the water flowed continuously into the lakes as if from a freshwater spring. The offensive smell of sulfur hung in the air.

The waters were ruled by garfish, alligator gar, only the brave went swimming or diving there. The fish were long, cartilaginous spotted-green predators, like barracuda and northern pike, only meaner, hungrier, half-body and half-teeth. They cruised the yellow-green water in pairs and threes or remained solitary and motionless, suspended in place like underwater logs, waiting for something to come along. Some were five feet, forty pounds, the first two feet a pointed, ripping mouth of razor sharp teeth, the rest fiber and bone. They devoured bass, mullet, tarpon, pan fish, frogs, turtles and small otters. They hit at spoons, rubber worms, plugs and shiners. When a man or a boy was fishing at the rock pits and caught a gar, he would cut it in half just to be mean, or slice it into parts, bait the hook with the pieces to catch more. All that were brought from the water were destroyed. They were hammered with clubs, shot, smashed with rocks, stabbed, or kicked away into the sand to bake alive in the sun, because they ate everything that the fishermen were there to catch. There was hatred for the gar in the hearts of the men and boys who fished at the rock pits, and fascination.

Around the lakes, Australian pines had been planted for windbreak, to keep the sand from blowing away. The pines crowded the sand trail that led in from Gladiolus, they kept it in darkness. When the sun moved from east to west, the towering trees threw long shadows across the water.

Across the road was Coca Sabal Lane. It had been the main passage through an encampment built for a cypress mill. The camp cut cypress logs into planks. Big cypress trees, hundreds of years old, were ox-carted in from the swamps and strands, sawed into boards, and ox-carted out to Punta Rassa. The raw lumber went by boat to Key West where it was used for houses and stores and fences and floors. The sawdust at the mill was picked up by arborists and mixed with gray sand for seedling vegetables, crotons and grafted citrus. Just off the lane, close to the little road, one of the original buildings remained. It was kept up and repaired by Mister Congdon, whose place was right nearby. A rusted tin roof sloped down on weathered pine trusses, the paint on the thin cypress boards was a faded red, the doors and window frames were white, or gray where the paint had chipped. Behind the old shack Mister Congdon had built his glass orchid house. Broad mango trees and reclinata palms filled the space above the shaded yard.

The shell lane that ran past the weathered cypress cabin ended abruptly at the old fishermen's house. The narrow road had been planted with Washingtonia palms, the tops were eighty, a hundred feet up. The palms angled into each other, they had been blown that way by Hurricane Donna. The sprawling wooden house where the fishermen lived tottered on the stacked bricks and concrete blocks that were its foundation. A wide screen porch enclosed never painted lumber.

The house backed up on Hendry Creek. The creek was narrow and dark there but widened after two sharp curves, opened up, joined the Gulf at Big Carlos Pass. Two old brothers, one with an old wife, lived in the house. The brothers had been commercial fishermen in the Twenties and Thirties, had netted mullet and pompano, permit and jack-cravalle. They said they had brought in whiskey during the Prohibition. In the Forties and Fifties they had been guides and boat captains, had taken sport fishermen to Big Carlos and Little Hickory Pass, out in The Gulf for tarpon and sailfish. Their charters, they said, had included President Eisenhower, Clark Gable, and Al Capone. By the Seventies they mostly loafed or fished from the small dock where they kept one old skiff. On either side of the creek, as far as could be seen in either direction, salt-water trees framed the brackish water.

The only other resident on Coca Sabal Lane was Edith Potter. The ancient woman doctor had been a pediatrician, she had been an innovator in providing medical care for children. She was an expert regarding bromeliads. She bought the house and grounds when she retired, she made it incredibly beautiful.

3

The estate was planted with reclinata palms, royal palms, Canary Island date palms. Bamboo clusters framed reflection pools, lily pad ponds, tumbling waterfalls and bubbling fountains. Bromeliads and tilandsias from all over the world perched in her oaks and mahoganies. Terra cotta Indian maidens, clay porpoises, cherubs and urns stood singly or near mossy concrete walls set with hand painted ceramic. Soft grass grew in the speckled sunlight where the blue sky peeped through the treetops. The house was of Spanish design, two stories, heavily stuccoed, thick-barreled tiles for the roof, iron balconies, carved doors and windows. It was completely surrounded by a salt-water moat. The way had been diverted from the creek, impediments removed. The water in the moat rose and fell with the tide, it flowed in and out with the waters of the bay. Thick trunks of bougainvillea twisted over the walls on the south and west sides of the house, the branches reached past the balconies onto the tile roof. The bracts were brightly colored, purple, red, and orange.

Between U.S. 41 and Harlem Heights, after the rock pits and the old cypress mill and the Potter estate and the old fishermen's house, where the road straightened out for that first long stretch, that's where the flower farms were.

Chapter One

A Saturday in September. Overhead the sky was a deep, cool blue, but with the heat and the wet sand, the air was oppressive, more than humid. It was morning break at Royal Glads. May had her head down sideways on the horsehair seat cover. She was naked. Chug was behind her on the seat of the truck. Bent over like that, on her knees and elbows, her ass was raised up higher than her shoulders. Her black hair had fallen forward, it stuck to her face and neck. She pushed the hair away and held it with one hand. Big beads of salt sweat rolled down her sides, from her belly and breasts into the horsehair. Chug had stiffened up enough to where he could get a rubber on. He pulled at his dick with one hand and rubbed his other hand over the woman's upturned ass, then down into it.

"Chug, don't touch me there. You do that again and I'm going to turn around and slap you," she said.

The man pulled his hand away, he put it high on the woman's swayed back and scooted himself up behind her, closer. He reached out with his other hand and pushed a Hendrix eight-track into the slot. He leaned over the woman and spoke directly into her ear.

"I want you ass, May. When we gonna reach a agreement?"

"Chug," the girl lifted her head off the seat to twist and look back at him, she could see nothing past the dusty dashboard. "You can have me there, but it's five hundred dollars, you know that. You don't want to spend five hundred dollars, don't touch it."

She put her head back down. The seat cover scratched at Chug's knees. He wondered idly about May's knees, elbows, tits pressed into the horsehair. Tough shit, he thought. He smacked the girl, just getting ready. His jeans and underpants and cowboy boots were in a cluster around his ankles. The pointed toes of his boots dangled off the edge of the seat, the truck doors were open for the faintest of a breeze. He leaned way over to the floor and pulled another beer from the cooler. He popped the top, took a long drink from it, and set the beer down in the small of the woman's back. She flinched at the touch of the cold can.

"Stay still till I tell you," he said. "I don't wanna lose my beer."

He pushed himself in as deep as he could go, fucked her fast for a couple of strokes and then slowed it down, then slower.

"Now," he said. "Move it around."

The girl had drawn in air when the man slid into her. She squeezed muscles and tendons and lips, she moved her hips backwards and forwards on the big thing inside her. She thought about trying to reach down between her legs to touch herself while he was back there but decided she might lose her balance, she needed her other hand to keep the hair off her face. It was furnace-fire hot. The horsehair was sticking into her cheeks, her breasts, her knees. She pushed out a wide foot, struggling for a grip with her toes on the hump in the floor of the truck. She turned her face back and forth on the seat.

Chug held onto his beer and sawed away slowly at the woman beneath him. He was in no hurry, he wanted his fuckin money's worth. He looked out over the woman's shoulders. Right up close to the peppers. Thicker than shit, them peppers, he thought. He looked to his right. Inches away from his face were his rifle, mounted in the rear window, loaded. In his glove box there was a .38 Special. Under the seat in an alligator skin holster was a .45 automatic, the handle clip filled with fat bullets. Next to the pistol in the holster there was a hollowed out wood baton that had been refilled with lead. The floor of the truck was thick with litter, trash, and refuse. It was the detritus of a life of dissolution. Chug looked out the front window, toward the little lake, his cooler was full of beer.

6

"Everythin a man could want. Almost," he said.

He swallowed down the last of the can and threw it out the window for the Mexicans to pick up. He put a hand on either side of May's ass. He began to pummel her, running with the rhythm of the woman, racing for the pleasure of an instant. May got up on both hands, got her breasts off the seat cover and let her hair fall forward over her face. She pushed back against the shanks of the patrón and shifted the gears of the thickest part of her body to a high speed. Her fabulous bottom was in command, she brought him along quickly. They were connected. Break time was almost over.

When he was finished, he peeled off the rubber and flung it out also, into the weeds, hoping the Mesicans would see it. He wiped himself off with his shirttail. His skinny chest and flat stomach were white as milk, white as his loins and legs. He was dry and reached for another beer.

"That was good but I'm still gone have you ass, May. I could have it now, you know I got the money. Five hundred ain't shit to me, but for a piece of ass? That's bullshit. I can go up to The Hill and buy me ten for that," he said.

"That's all the difference right there, jéfe, mine is the whole thing, not a piece. Mine has never even been touched by a man. I am not everybody's puta."

"Maybe not, but you Chug's sure enough," he said.

May looked at the pepper trees while he swung his legs under the steering wheel. He stretched, pulled up his underpants and jeans, fastened his belt, left his shirt open. A moment later the woman reached to the floor for her shorts and blouse. She buttoned up the blouse and slipped her cotton underpants into her pocket. She wiped the sweat from her face with her hands, wiped her hands on her khaki shorts. The bones in her face were high, her nose was wide and flat, her eyes were dark brown. Her teeth were white, square, perfect, and she had never been to a dentist. She slipped her big feet into a pair of ragged tennis shoes she called sneakers.

"I'll be glad when it's cool," she said. "Why don't we have the air-conditioner running next time? Let's don't sweat while we're making love. We can fit."

7

Chug looked at her and almost smiled. He pulled off his dark sunglasses.

"What we doin ain't makin love, May. That's for pussies. It's makin you money though and makin me annoyed cause you holdin out on me."

He reached into his jeans pocket and pulled out a roll of tens and twenties. He peeled off a wrinkled bill and dropped it in May's lap. She folded it once and put it in her blouse pocket.

Chug ejected the Hendrix, fumbled with the tapes on the floor. He found *Idlewild South* and stuck it in the slot.

"Now listen," he said over the music, "we get up front an my old man's there, don't say nothin, don't engage him in no conversation about vegetables or flowers or any of that bullshit. You got me? I don't need him suddenly interested in what we doin money-wise."

"He's never here," she said. "If he was, I'd have nothing to say to him. Do you think your father is going to talk to a field hand?"

"He knows you run the market. Just don't be runnin you mouth."

He started the big Ford diesel and turned on the air-conditioning. In the back of the truck a brown pit bull jumped to his feet. The dog's range was held in check by a leather collar and chain, the dog's nails dug into the plywood that covered the metal. Chug drove around the field and to the front. The truck bounced a little on the ridges. Sand spurs crowded the sides wherever there was sunlight, fennel and grape ivy filled the shady space under the pepper hedge.

"Anyhow," said Chug, " if he was here, he just be wonderin why you ain't eatin breakfast with the other beaners."

"Let's just get up front, Chug," she said, " I want to wash you out of me."

Chapter Two

When the truck stopped at the door of the barn the woman got out. She walked in front of the truck, away from where the dog stood in the back. She walked into the airless shade of the building where other women sat, chewing food. It was greasy stuff they were eating, meat and potatoes, rice, corn, peppers and onions in thin tomato gravy, spooned from plastic containers onto soft tortillas. The women sat at wooden tables with lunch pails and buckets beside them on the narrow benches. They drank water from the spigot. The well water smelled like rotten eggs and had iron in it but they drank it anyway, from fruit jars and plastic cups. It was cheaper than soda. They had accustomed themselves to the taste but were still offended by the smell so they drank quickly. One of the big fans that was used to dry the wet leaves, the stems, and the buds of the cut flowers, roared at the end of the deepest table. The fan moved the stifling September air past the women and out the doorway. It kept flies and gnats and mosquitoes away from them and away from the wet food, but the noise of the motor and blades made it impossible for the ones nearest it to be heard. Speaking and listening and answering took energy and effort, so they all just chewed and swallowed and drank. The women chewed placidly, like cows at a table.

All of them except May wore men's clothes, long sleeve shirts buttoned at the neck and the wrists, cotton pants tucked into thick socks pulled up over the cuff, and sneakers or leather shoes. Black hair was tucked up under bandanas, under straw hats and baseball caps, shirt collars were turned up against brown necks. Underneath the clothing they were oiled, smooth and soft, but their hands and faces were becoming wrinkled, coarse. The women didn't want to look like women, they wanted to look like laborers, field hands, which was what they were. They were afraid of the sun and of the patrón. They wanted him to remain not interested, so they appeared to be sexless, unidentifiable as women. They stayed away from Chug. They knew, everybody at the farm knew, Chug was fucking May several times a week. They hoped she was getting paid enough for it. They dreaded the possibility of the white devil touching them.

"God, that gringo is a bad one," said one woman into the ear of another, looking into the side of her friend's face, away from where Chug sat in the truck.

"They are all bad," said the other back at her. "They have no morals."

The two women who had spoken looked down at their laps. They continued to eat breakfast.

Chug rolled down the window. The fumes from the diesel were mixing with the air and making the women sick. The dog was panting on his chain. Suddenly Chug whistled. He caught the women's attention.

"You all," he said loudly. "After you breakfast, you get out there and pinch them crown buds on them first twenty rows of flowers. You got all day, but I want them buckets full or you can skip you afternoon break. Leave a bucket in the office for me. I want to look for thrip. You all make sure you dump the rest of em in them barrels for burnin and get them buckets back in here. You all got any of you greaser meal left that you don't want? Save it for Hitman. He's hungry," Chug laughed and gunned the truck.

At the sound of his name the dog stiffened. He smelled deeply at the air. It seemed to the women that he was scenting them instead of the food.

The truck bucked forward twenty feet, it clouded the space in front of the barn with blue smoke. He stopped where the men and boys sat together, chewing on the same food, drinking the same smelly water.

"Jesus! Jesus! Goddamnit, boy, whatever you name is. Boy, you need

10

to start listenin closer to me. Has any of you all seen Enrique? Goddamnit, this pisses me off. Just because he ain't here don't mean you can sit on you asses all day. Breaks over. You," he pointed at the young man whose name was Jose and who was dressed like the women were. " Take you fellow Mesicans over to where we gassed yesterday and git that plastic up and into rolls. Bundle em up and put em in the road for the tractor to get. They too heavy to drag very far, especially for you all pitiful creatures. Whatever you do, Goddamnit, don't be kicking the shape outta them new beds. They perfect. I don't wanta see one fuckin footprint in them flower beds or I'll be bustin some Mesican ass. You peckerheads understand all that?"

Jose looked blankly at Chug, the patrón, el jéfe, the boss. He had never been given instructions by him before, he had no idea what the man had said. Enrique had told them Friday afternoon, when he handed out the pay, they would be pulling plastic today. He hoped that was what the man wanted but he wasn't sure. He would ask May. If they did the wrong thing the worst the man could do was beat him, he decided.

"After you got that plastic up we gonna raise the wire where them women been workin. Tomorra I want to git them rooted plugs out of the mist house an stuck. They is three thousand of em to stick by Tuesday, by God, stuck and watered and growin by Tuesday, or I'll turn my fuckin dog loose."

May had come out of the dirty bathroom. She stood in front of the barn, between the groups of women and men. Chug saw her in his side mirror. He twisted his head around and called to her.

"May, comere," he hollered.

The woman walked out of the shade and around the front of the truck to avoid being close to the dog. Her shorts and faded blouse were wet with sweat and the water she had splashed on herself. Her great breasts shook, they bounced under the damp cotton.

"May, you gonna need to get these people started," he said, "you hear what I told em?"

"Yes, patrón, we all heard it. We're just not real sure what all those nasty words mean," she said.

"Lookit, Enrique ain't here. I don't have no idea where the sumbitch is but I'm gone find out. My old man ain't gonna be happy his number one Mesican ain't here the first Saturday of season. I need you to tell these folks what I said an git em goin. Once they started, go on over to the mist house and make sure them plugs is good an wet on the bottoms. Get one of those there to water em. We gone stick flowers in the ground tomorra. Sunday or no."

He looked away from the woman then pointed his finger at the man he had called Jesus, or Jose, he didn't remember. He dropped his thumb like he was cocking the hammer on a pistol and yelled bang. The frightened little man backed up, tripped over a pile of shade cloth. He fell to the concrete floor.

"They God," Chug laughed, "what a fuckin group."

The people had stood up and were clearing away the tables and benches, putting the old jars and scratched plastic containers into the pails and buckets. They began to move from within the barn toward the door, toward the blinding light of the tropical sun.

"May," said Chug, " when you got these people in the right places you go on back up to the fruit stand. I'll check with you later an git my money. Lookit all the stuff an have one of these boy Mesicans bring you up some barrels of ice. Tell im to spread it around on the watermelons and cantaloupes. Check the vegetables an fruit in every damn bin and let me know what I need to pick up for tomorra. You gone be busy, earnin you money the hard way," he laughed. "Get these movin. I'm gonna see my old man later. It'll give me another hard on to tell him his top greaser is a no show."

"Are you coming back later?" May asked him. " To help us?"

"Fuck no," he said, " it's Saturday. Me an Hitman is goin fishin."

Chug pressed the accelerator and spun the truck away from the front of the barn, punching it hard, sliding on the sand. The people watched him go, then began moving together toward their places in the field. The women walked slowly, deliberately, like upright cows, the men discussed half-heartedly what the boss would have them do.

Chapter Three

*T*he creeks cut in from the bay, into the low land, leaving the wide expanses of green water behind. They become narrow and twist then straighten then twist again. They end altogether miles from where they started, in shallow pools of black water or as spots of muddy beach.

Sabal palms, mangrove trees, red, white and black, and green buttonwoods bordered the water. The trees were dense, they crowded each other and narrowed the creeks. In a few places where they had not grown or had died from disease or lightning, the consistent green mass was interrupted. Salt grasses grew there, along the water's edge. Behind the salt-water trees, as far as man could see, was coastal marsh.

The water appeared to be still although it was almost constantly moving in and out. Leaves and bits of bark floated on the surface. Sometimes the water was violently disturbed from below, sometimes it was pelted with heavy rain. Its color changed from green to brown as it moved inland, its level rose and dropped with the tides. In September the sky was clear and blue in the morning, the air above the water was faint of movement. In the afternoons, gray clouds and stiff winds preceded the rains, the trees above the creeks shook loose the yellow leaves.

The water was alive with fish, the air was alive with birds. The fish eaters perched in the tops of pines, and oaks that had been struck by lightning. There were eagles and osprey, red-shouldered hawks, big, powerful, hungry birds that floated on the soft currents and then aimed down. They dropped through the air at impossible speed and flattened into a glide, they reached out with sharp talons to snatch a living fish from the top of the water. The birds carried the struggling underwater creatures to the tall trees on higher ground where they would not be interfered with, and devoured them.

Fish came into the creeks and channels, to escape predators in the deeper water, because in the winter the Gulf waters were too cold, because in the summer the bay waters were too hot. In September the rain cooled the passages back to the Gulf, mangroves shaded the whiskey-colored water. Fish came to spawn in the brackish mixture.

The food cycle began for all the fish predators and the great birds with mullet. The composition and taste of the mullet's flesh is desirable to humans also. The flesh is changed, along with the fish's color and size according to the salt content of the water, according to what bottom green they eat. The mullet were never alone, they swam in small schools of one hundred to five hundred fish or in huge fish clouds. Thousands of the timid fish moved through the bays, up and down the inlets, like tremendous flocks of birds move through the air, curving, circling, darting, doubling back in various directions for reasons unknown. Snook and tarpon and big redfish came in from the Gulf, followed the mullet into the creeks. They cornered them against the mangrove roots and the grass banks. The game fish were cornered in turn as they entered the bay, by big rays, nurse sharks, and patrols of hungry porpoises.

The creek was not crowded with broad beamed boats that didn't move much, it was not lined with houses and docks and seawalls. Many weeks would go by and no men came in skiffs up the creek to cast-net for mullet. The gentle fish were left to themselves except for the birds, the robalo, the tarpon and the others. They swam up the creek in numbers so great that when they were close to the surface the whole top of the water moved, acres of water sometimes, where the creek was very wide. As the channel narrowed the water became choked with mullet, especially in the curves, under the mangroves. Old-timers said they had seen them so thick a man could walk across the water on top of the fish and only be wet from the splashing.

The mullet fishermen worked hard, mullet were cheap. They sold the mullet whole to the fish houses where they were headed, gutted, split and iced, they are eaten smoked or fried. The fishermen did not need to come into the creeks and corner the mullet, the numbers in the bay were abundant. The men fished between the south end of Fort Myers Beach and Black Island. A new bridge crossed over the wide pass, causeways continued to Bonita Beach.

The mullet men let out long nets from behind their boats, half-mile long nets, and ran the boats in loops around the spinning schools of mullet. Within an hour the nets were full of the club-headed, soft-lipped fish, heavy with healthy flesh and prodigious roe. The nets were pulled in or winched in, the men violently jerked the fish through or back out of the mesh of the nets and tossed them into piles in the bottom of the boats. Thousands of mullet moved in nearby circles that had not been part of the drama.

At the fish houses the men tossed the mullet on the dock. Pelicans and seagulls floated in the dirty green water, the birds clamored for the guts. When the boats were empty, the men went back to the bay again.

Chug parked his truck on Coca Sabal, next to the old cypress building. He didn't expect any trouble from old man Congdon. He let the dog out of the back and picked up his heavy rod. They cut through the Potter Estate, Chug thought about stealing some of the clay pieces as he passed by them. He climbed through the tangle of mangroves and buttonwood, he worked his way along the edge until he found an opening in the trees. He stood on the bank in the high grass next to the water, he moved the rod back and forth, testing for clearance. He readied himself in the shallows. He held the thick casting rod and the big Mitchell reel in his powerful right hand. The line was heavy-test. At the end of the monofilament there was a steel leader three feet long. At the end of the leader, next to a quarter-ounce of lead shot, he'd tied a big treble hook. The hook was new, the points were as sharp as they would ever be. Hitman stood beside him in the water, his eyes were slitted down against the glare. They watched the mullet masses move in the creek.

Chug cast the heavy treble into the bundled mullet. They were thick from bank to bank, close enough to where the dog could bite at them. When the hook hit the top of the water Chug set the bale and jerked the

15

pole hard with both hands. He dropped his left shoulder and raised his right, his forearms were aligned, tensed. His old cowboy boots were set firmly in the muddy bank.

One or two of the barbs stabbed into a three or four pound mullet, fat with life and eggs. The fish were grabbed by the sharp hooks in the head or in the middle, even in the tail, wherever there was skin and flesh enough for the barbs to bite then work themselves more deeply into the snatched body. The fish fought better when they were hooked in the back, like shiners are baited for bass. Chug held the rod up and worked the mortally wounded fish to the bank, he horsed it in over the others. Sometimes a mullet would tear itself loose from the hooks and then swim about, wounded and dying in the school until it was bumped to the bottom of the creek. It gasped out its life in the silt. Sometimes the addled mullet would be spotted as an easy meal by a snook or a tarpon. The big fish would explode out of the water with the helpless creature in its mouth., leave pieces floating on the surface. Chug had snatched one from the thousands. He reeled it to where he was standing, tightened up the drag, lifted the mullet out of the water so it dangled from the treble hook. He reached into his belt and pulled out the leaded baton he used on niggers and Mexicans and hit the fish about the head.

After he was sure it would never move again, he carefully removed the trebles so he wouldn't get hooked himself. He let the battered mullet drop back into the brown water. He kicked at the lifeless thing to move it away, into the deeper water, into the swirl of the other fish. Then he cast again. In less than an hour the silt bottom of the narrow channel was littered with the carcasses of dead mullet. They were covered quickly, and would be devoured by blue crabs. The dog was in a frenzy to be included in the slaughter. Hitman hurled himself out to snap at the fleeing fish. He was fast and powerful, but his teeth were not barbed, they kept slipping off the scaly skin of the darting mullet. When he gave up, he sat in the water next to Chug and watched his master cast and reel and kill again. Chug had been almost an hour without a beer, he was thirsty. When he'd had enough of the sport, after he had snatched and dispatched probably thirty, prime salt-water mullet, he left the place along the bank, and climbed back through the prop roots. Hitman followed him through the old doctor's yard to where the truck was parked and they loaded up. Chug never ate a mullet, even when they were freshly smoked. He said they was too greasy for a white man an that they was bottom feeders. They was more fit, he'd said, for the coloreds to eat in a sandwich.

Chapter Four

*A*long Gladiolus Drive, vegetable, fruit, and flower farms had replaced the woods and scrub. The farms were separated by clusters of Australian pine and slash pine planted by the government. At every farm, shell driveways dropped from the asphalt road, the entrances were framed by columns or posts. The drives cut through the pines or mangos or peppers that had been left along the road, and opened up into fields. Some looked empty, some looked like smoky houses, where the gray sand was shaded by black cloth fastened on timbers. Those were the flower farms. Here and there, along the country roads and the highway, green and white metal signs were posted. They read, *Lee County Gladiolus Capital Of The World.* There were other signs next to the driveways, usually made of plywood and painted, lettered, that presented the name of the farm and the owner. The shell driveways led onto the land and to the buildings that belonged to the flower producers. They were all men who were essentially the same in their desire to grow good flowers. They knew how to go about it. The moods and rhythms and outcomes at the farms were linked to how the owners managed the people.

With the big acres of dark gray sand came a use for wells and ditches, sulfur-coated pumps and valves, posts, wires, shade cloth, dangling electric lamps, water lines, gas lines, barns, mist house, packing house, shit-house, garage and shed for tractors, sprayers, gassers, dumpsters, soil tables, eating tables. From the combinations of those things and the sunshine and rain, came plants, color. The people created movement.

Royal Glads was the last farm on the right, just before A and W Bulb Road. Its shell driveway ran through a hundred feet of mango, lychee nut, and avocado. The trees were massive for the species, dark trunks supported heavy branches that intertwined with the limbs of the others. The ground underneath the trees was deeply shaded, spare of growth, but the trees were full of birds and squirrels, flower and fruit. There were so many mangos in the summer that the colored people came out from town to pick them, there was more fruit than the people in Harlem Heights could chew down and swallow.

The shell drive at Royal Glads led to forty acres of flower farm. The whole forty acres, except for the perimeter road, was under shade cloth. The sand was a dark gray, at three feet it was almost black, that's why the first old man had bought the land. The shell drive split when it was past the mangos, it went to the right across the front of the buildings, to the left down the west side. Along the perimeter road and without interruption, there was a shallow drainage ditch that was covered, choked by enormous Brazilian pepper trees. The peppers were thick to twenty feet, covered with bright green leaves, tiny white flowers and red berries. The trees were so convoluted and enmeshed that it was impossible to pass through them. In the back, nearly aligned across the field with the entrance, there was a sand trail where a few peppers had been cleared and had been kept from growing back. A sturdy bridge had been built over the few feet of shallow ditch. The sand road stopped abruptly in the middle of a small meadow of native grasses and wildflowers, in front of a little lake.

The lake was bordered by native trees and palms. They had been planted to replicate what would have been there before. Enrique Garza had done it. He had gone to Sanibel, Pine Island, and Bonita Beach, found sea grape and myrsine and Spanish stopper and brought them back. He had planted coconut palms, cabbage palms, palmetto and royals. Wax myrtles he transplanted from pastures. The meadow was on the south side of the lake, it was speckled with beach daisy, dune sunflower and railroad vine. Garza had created a coastal hammock, a coastal glade, a coastal meadow. He brought seedlings, cuttings, and sprouts, he planted young shrubs, trees, and palms. He watered and nourished his creation. The second old man had gone to the lake, had sat and reflected, but that had been years ago. Mostly it had been the people of Harlem who went to the lake, lunched and visited and watched the little children play and feed the fish.

The lake was maybe fourteen feet deep. No one remembered who had dug it out, or even knew if it had been dug at all. It was there when the old man bought the scrubland and the groves around it to make the farm. A sulfur spring bubbled into the middle, but the aromas of the wildflowers dissipated the smell of rotten eggs. By September, summer rains had filled the little lake, it seeped into the meadow. When it was very dry, in the late winter months and spring, Enrique pumped fresh water from a deep well to his lake and saved it. He had dug the perimeter ditch when he was clearing the land. The chemicals and fertilizers that filtered through the sand leaked into the ditch. That water was pumped out front, into the swale along Gladiolus to eventually disappear in the mangrove and buttonwood flats toward the beach.

Small tarpon, fresh-water mullet, bass, bluegill, shiners, minnows and catfish swam together in the shallow lake. Turtles came and went, traveling gators visited and left. Otters came, ate their fill of fish, then they left, and the pond's population prospered. Enrique fed the creatures for many years. He kept meal and pellets in the barn. The lake water was clean, native grasses grew along the bank in the sunshine.

The trees and palms and flowers of the little lake and the tiny prairie were on the edge of the Gulf, on the edge of the Glades, on the edge of Royal Glads, but Royal Glads was fucked and Chug was the one who had done it. His management was stale, it was out-dated by a century, it was ineffective. His was an administration of the lash and the whip, it had been allowed by his father to develop. In the year he had been there the farm had gone from being one of the best in the county, because of the Garza man, to the worst. Chug was at war with the people. He hated their colors. He felt if he did not extract every nickel's worth of motion and sweat from his people then he was their fool. For Chug it was a war, and there loomed behind his daily battles the inevitability of conflict with the old man. Enrique had been the one. He had kept the farm for more than twenty years. It had been as well managed and successful as any of the others, better than most. The old man had followed his heart, now Royal Glads was Chug's, this year's flowers would be gone to shit because of it. Enrique had tried to lead the young Sinclair in a direction that would have been good for everyone, for the people, the land, the flowers. Chug wanted none of it. His time in college said he was smarter, his name said the whole fucking thing was his. His manner and villainies discouraged everyone, especially Enrique. His drunkenness diminished his intelligence but not his cunning. When he was sober he was sullen, when he was loaded he was dangerous.

Enrique gave up on the little lake first. Chug had started going there with the woman in the middle of the morning and in the afternoons. The fish began to eat each other, beer cans and rubbers littered the meadow, mice fed on catfish meal moldering in the packinghouse.

Chapter Five

*T*he four Mexican boys had arrived at Royal Glads in late June. The land was oven-hot in the daytime, uncomfortably warm through the short nights. The rain was staying east and wouldn't come over to shower the coast. They had walked the last fifty miles of a three thousand mile journey. They were looking for work. They had walked in from Immokalee, desperate to be away from a place, where in only a few days, they had seen squalor, chaos, and desolation worse then what they had known in Mexico. Although they had not known what to expect, and they were accustomed to expect very little, they were even afraid of some of the women and children that prowled the mean alleys and vacant lots. They heard from another Mexican that if they became hungry enough, they could break into a packinghouse or go through garbage cans. Men had been known, he'd said, to have walked east from Immokalee late at night and slipped into a pasture and murdered a cow for the blood and meat. They'd butchered the animal through the night and gorged on the raw muscle and fat, the man said.

"Could we carry some back with us? To the others? So all did not have to go?" asked the oldest boy.

"Someone would see you," the man said, "and you have no way to keep it from rotting. No one here," he gestured toward the poor street, "has an icebox."

"What would happen if a man was caught?" asked another of the boys.

"Someone would hang you or shoot you," answered the man, "there are many big oaks and deep swamps in Devil's Garden. Murdering cows is discouraged."

The boys decided to strike for the west, to be as close to Mexico as they could. Maybe they could go to the beach on a Sunday and look across the water, the youngest had said. Immokalee was frightening, destitute, depraved. The boys left at dark. They walked all night and all the next day.

When they inquired at the first farm on Gladiolus, they were told at the barn that the crews were kept small for the summer. Maybe at beginning of season, maybe September, they were told. The foreman pointed west, he said there were more farms to try before they would run out of land. The boys kept walking at the sun, they stopped at each place, they walked four more miles on top of the fifty. They traveled in a single file along the side of the little highway, in and out of the shade of the pines, in and out of the scorching sunshine. They finally stood in the shell parking lot of the vegetable stand beside the entrance to Royal Glads. They huddled in the front of the place. The white of the crushed shell was blinding, the boys peered into the dark of the chickee.

In a few minutes, May had them sitting on empty crates under the thatch. She gave them cold water in paper cups, grapes and strawberries that she pulled from the barrel of fruit and stale vegetables she saved for Chug's pigs. She picked up a cold watermelon and using a bread knife, she sliced great pieces and handed one to each boy. The boys looked alike, they were short and swarthy, they had coarse black hair. There was an oldest and a youngest and two in-between. They were exhausted, dirty, and bewildered, and they were a little discouraged. None of them spoke any English, but they knew that trabajo meant work. They wanted trabajo, the oldest boy told May. They had no more money, he said, they had no place they knew of to go. Probably the priest at San Jose Mission could help them, but he would have to split them up, she thought. One would be a dishwasher, one a man who cuts lawns, the other two would work in a packing house, loading bags of red potatoes into boxcars. They did not look like they would allow themselves to be separated. The priest would be annoyed at that, she thought.

May gave the oldest boy a couple of dollars. She told him there was a Spanish grocery store in Harlem Heights. Follow the road around that curve, she had said, and pointed. The groceria was on the left, about a half-mile away. Buy bread and milk and lunchmeat, she had said, then gave him another two dollars for a cooked chicken. She'd handed the boy another dollar and told him to get whatever else the grocer would give him for that. The oldest boy handed the money to one of the middle boys. That one was quickly up and walking west to Harlem, along Gladiolus.

She talked to the remaining boys in Spanish for a few more minutes, although they did not understand several of the words she used. She told them to wait in back, under the big trees. In an hour the fourth boy was back with two paper bags of groceries, they were heavy in his arms. May gave them an old bar of soap, told them to wash their faces and hands and necks. The boys took turns holding their heads under the hose. She gave the oldest boy her towel. She brought a fresh one every day to dip into the ice, to wrap around her neck and shoulders. He used the towel carefully, then the rest did the same. They were a little cleaner and felt better, when Chug pulled in to get his money.

He usually drove the farm last thing, to assess what had been done that day. He was never happy with what he saw. He was sober though, May was surprised. It was almost five and he didn't stink of beer and whiskey. She waved out the boys from under the mangos. They got up and walked slowly to the chickee. The oldest watched Chug, the others looked at their sandals. Chug at once understood this was May's doing.

"What is these?" he laughed in the faces of the four boys.

"They are looking for work, Chug. I think they'll work cheaply. Enrique needs more men," she said.

"Excuse me, May, but fuck Enrique," the man said. "I'm the one around here figures how many fuckin people I need for Royal Glads."

He looked hard at the woman, his glance at the boys was hostile. He held the oldest's eyes for an instant, turned, gestured to Hitman in the truck, then returned his attention to May.

"That's good. You say they want to work? I need men right now. Men though, not boys," he said. "They's a whole lot of shit work to do this summer. I want em cheap, they gonna understand that?" he asked her. "They gonna be low men on the totem pole around here."

She shook her head in assent. "They will work very hard," she said. "I don't think they have another choice."

"I know they gonna work, else I'll kick they little asses. These boys all look alike. Is they all gonna be little fuckers like these? Mesicans?"

May laughed a little at that.

"We all look alike some, don't we, Chug?"

"Don't fuck with me May," he shot back. "Just cause you can tell I ain't been drinkin yet today don't mean nothin. I can get real nasty without it. You want them jobs for these here, don't be sassy. Is they some Indian in em?"

"I think there is," she said, "I don't think of them that way, but probably they are Aztec or Apache, maybe with a little Spanish."

"Jesus Christ. We cain't get the niggers to work, Puerto Ricans think they white, now we got Apaches in Lee County. This country's gone to shit," he said. "Pretty soon we'll be givin them fuckin Viet Cong jobs an puttin flower knives in they hands."

"What about the white people? Where are they working?" asked May. She considered the question a good one, she knew so little about them.

"They all pussies," said Chug. "They want to be school teachers," then he added, "they soft and they weak, poor bastards."

Chug reached his hand into the cooler for a bottle of beer. He drank it down in quick swallows and tossed the empty into the trashcan.

"These don't look like much. You owe me, May," he said. "Tell em I give em two dollars and fifty cent a hour. They gonna work up to sixty hours a week, but maybe less too, dependin on the weather. I ain't gonnna pay em to sit in the barn and watch it rain."

"I'll tell them and yes," she said, "I owe you. I'll think of something special for you. What else should I tell them?" she asked.

"They start tomorra. They can work for two full days and get paid for em on Friday. Tell em I don't bring the pay, Senor Enrique does, so tell em never to ask me a fuckin question about money, ever. In fact, tell em never to ask me nothin. They get they money on Friday. Cash, no taxes, no bullshit paperwork. I don't even wanna see they fake cards. These boys is as wet as they can be, an I don't need to know a fuckin thing about em, but that they can work."

25

He looked more closely at the boys, he reached for another beer. He watched them, standing still, waiting for May to tell them more of what he'd said.

"Give em each five bucks outta the till," he said, "that'll hold em to Friday. Tell em I said they's to give it back to you then. Any of em speak English?" he asked, already knowing the answer.

"No. None."

"Stupid fuckers," he said. "They come here, an don't speak a fuckin word of the language. They probably didn't learn shit about they own lingo the three years they was in school."

"God. Go easy, Chug. They want to work, don't run them off before they've started."

Chug laughed, drained the beer. He held the bottle in his hand and began to flip it, catching it at the neck.

"What they gonna do, May? Quit? Tell em they can stay in The Quarters. It's a little shitty but it's a fuck of a lot better than the place they come from. That's why they here, May, here is better than there. Anyhow," he continued tossing the bottle, "they each can have a room, I think they's four of em. Place is a little fucked up, but they tough boys. Tell em how to get there, an tell em to be in front of the barn at six-thirty in the mornin ready to bust they ass. They gonna have to work to keep these jobs, they's more of they little cousins comin into town ever day. Tell em I get ten dollars a week, ever Friday, for lettin em stay in my apartments." He laughed. "I want ten a week from each of em, and tell em no doubt about it, I'm they big boss."

Chug tossed the bottle in the barrel and turned to leave.

"At least they ain't gooks," he said. "Leave my money under the cantaloupe. I'll get it later."

"Aren't you going to the farm?" May asked him.

Chug opened the door to the truck and swung himself in.

"No I ain't. I changed my mind," he said. "I'm goin up the road and meet Marvin, then we gonna go fuck with some hippies."

Chug started the big Ford, backed it up, drove it forward through the lot onto the narrow road. The boys watched the truck and the man and the dog go down Gladiolus. When the truck was out of sight they felt safer.

Chapter Six

Harlem Heights was like an island town of the Caribbean Sea but it was land-locked between the farm fields and the mangrove woods. The houses, shacks, cottages, small barns and garages, pig pens, goat pens and chicken coops were scattered loosely under the coconuts and flowering trees. Thin dogs lay in the sand, not far from the asphalt road. When cars with white people passed on the way to the beaches the men and women and children inside the cars assumed the dogs were dead. Dust, sand, and rain-water spatter blew over the resting dogs but did not greatly disturb them. In the September heat no one who had been left behind when the people went to work, or when the children went to school, moved across Gladiolus in any hurry. The settlement appeared empty, abandoned. The asphalt road and the tin roofs baked in the sun. From the pavement, visible bands of heat shimmered waist high. The tops of the palms were still in the motionless, heavy air, the dogs lay on the ground in stupor.

The ditch along the road was filled with stagnant water the color of dark tea, below the surface the grass and weeds were swollen, slimy. Mosquito larvae hatched by the millions, the skeeters rose from the water in the ditch like patches of swirling black dust. Lee County Mosquito Control worked Harlem Heights into its schedule after the rest of the ditches in the county had been sprayed. When the big tankers finally rolled up Gladiolus and through Harlem at five in the morning, they coated the water in the ditch with engine oil and DDT. Children too young to know better played in the water along the road, but they waited for the afternoon rains so the water would be cooler. Later, the water from the ditches seeped under the coastal trees and joined the runoff from the farms at the river.

Older kids who skipped school explored, they followed paths through the mangroves and buttonwoods between Harlem Heights and the beach. They chased fiddler crabs, hunted curlew with stones and slingshots, drank beer, smoked reefer, and carved their names in the trunks of black mangroves.

On A and W Bulb, just behind Royal Glads, there were three collapsing houses. Those shacks and a covered cistern were all that remained from the original settlement of coloreds and Spanish who had come out from the city to work at the vegetable farms. Those people had been run off by the law for squatting on land that did not belong to them, but they had successfully homesteaded a short distance away and had not been budged again. The oldest kids necked in the busted-up houses, they chased each other in and out of open doorways and empty window frames and up and down yellow-pine paneled hallways. They kicked at the sand castles built by ants and termites, brushed cobwebs from each other's hair. Dust and dirt gathered against sweaty brown skin to be kissed and licked away. Then they went to the car.

It was in an old Chrysler next to the abandoned well behind one of the forlorn shacks where the young people entertained themselves without money. They learned about human nature, lust, the thrill of the pressure, the ache of the excitement of sex. May had rolled in the water in the oily ditch, chased birds through the mangrove passages. She had kissed in the shadows of a long abandoned cottage, but it was on a blanket on the moldy seat of a forsaken car that she was changed from a girl into a woman and became enchanted with the pleasure of a naked body against her own.

Besides the predictabilities of los borachos, the drunks who were encamped behind May's cottage, there were lost people who wandered about Harlem. The demons within them were unexplainably induced. They slept on porches, under cars, against the smooth trunks of the palm trees. When they were possessed, they rolled in the dung and piss of the dogs and chickens. They seemed afterwards to be cleansed by the fit. The lost people existed from one day to the next. They were colored or spic so they were left alone in the other-worldliness, they were not attended to by the authorities. One was a short, squat stumbler who was bow-legged, close to the ground, where he often fell, foaming and retching from the poisons that he drank. He would sit upright on the footpath, his short legs out before him. His head lolled forward until it hung from his neck and shoulders, the waters in his mouth leaked out. Another was a very tall, very angular, very powerful man with a wild halo of stiff black hair and a long, untrimmed goatee. He looked like a black Rasputin. He paced purposefully up and down the road, he crowded the motorists, dared them along Gladiolus. One hand clasped a broken radio to his ear that brought forth no sound. He clutched the plastic husk as if it was a telephone. With his other hand he pointed, aimed, shook his long, bony, black fingers at the sky, at the trees, at the passing cars. He trembled with emotion and anger, he spoke very loudly to be heard over the radio. He threatened the mailboxes and the ditch and the resting dogs that jumped up and ran when they heard him coming.

A few toothless, friendless, nearly blind women also roamed the country place. They took food from porches, from the vegetable stand, they snatched young pullets that were enticed under the peppers. The hags shared itinerant campsites between Harlem and town with hobos, vagabonds, and bindle stiffs. They cooked for the groups, they mixed vegetables with bits of greens, crawdads and bits of fish and pork and goat that they begged from the people. The women's skin was supple from the humidity and oils, but they smelled of smoke and grime. They were not so badly bothered by the mosquitoes, gnats and sand fleas as were the people.

It was as if Harlem Heights had been casually placed by some giant hand, picked up from somewhere in the south salt-waters, and set down, not too carefully, in the best part of Lee County.

Chapter Seven

*T*he Mexican boys found the house. The Quarters was a concrete block building with a slanted tin roof. The tin sheets twisted and curled away from the screws that held them to the beams. Holes had been shot in the metal, dozens of holes, from twenty-two's, thirty-eight's, forty-five's. The bare, concrete walls had wide craters where they had been blasted by shotgun fire. There was no door, there were no windows. Broken glass lay inside and outside the openings where the windows had once been. There were bigger openings where the doors had hung. The floor was concrete that had been once painted a pale green, but except in a few corners, the paint was gone. The floor was covered with trash, refuse, and debris. There were filthy rotting mattresses, rags that had been clothing, moldy leather shoes, newspapers, beer cans, wine bottles, shit and scat, left by man and critter. Everywhere there was broken glass from bushwhacked beer bottles. Some people from Harlem had used it as a dump, the garbage spilled out the openings where there had been doors. The walls outside were scarred from shotguns and pistols also, one wall was blackened where there had been a fire. Outside the adobe there was more broken glass, old doors, tires, gray boards with dangerous, pro-truding nails, twisted bicycles, a rusted wheelbarrow, a child's wagon, and fifty-five gallon drums for burning and warming up on the coldest mornings. Fennel, saltbush, and sand spurs filled the yard to the pepper hedge, where there was ample sunlight. Poison ivy and wild grape crept along the walls and fastened itself to the pitted concrete. In the passing of a year The Quarters would be visited by men and women, dogs and cats, opossums, raccoons, bobcats, foxes, skunks, snakes, turtles, bats, birds, wasps, scorpions and spiders. There were saddlebacks, stinging caterpillars, and horseflies and blowflies, especially in the spring. Big piles of sand marked where the fire ants lived, in the yard and in the building. The farms pushed for two seasons, for two crops, the fields were full of rats and mice. Hawks and silent owls carried the rodents to the roof of the building to eat them without interference. There were woods nearby, there was the cover of the crops, critters were abundant. They were trapped between the highway, the city, and the Gulf. Panthers lived in Iona. Big rattlers, pygmies, and cotton-mouths crawled back and forth across the ditches and hunted from farm to farm.

The Quarters was near the front of the property, on the other side of the perimeter ditch and the pepper hedge in a small, sunlit clearing between the field and the pine woods, between the mango grove and Gladiolus Drive. May told the boys to go around the barn and to follow the narrow path through the weeds to the ditch. There was a wood plank across the water, then another path, they would see the house, she'd said. She also told them that they could come back to the barn after everyone was gone and wash themselves more thoroughly at the hose. She said that the other people would see them and know that the boys had come to work, and where they would be sleeping.

"There are few secrets here," she'd said. She gave them the soap and the old towel.

"Use the hose. There is nothing wrong with the water except for its horrible smell. It's the only water here so you must get used to it. Tomorrow we will wash your clothes and get you some more shirts and pantalones," she had said.

She told them what to expect at The Quarters.

"It will be very dirty," she'd said. "Watch out for snakes and scorpions. The ants are the worst because they are so many and so angry when they are disturbed. I will get you candles and matches and more soap tonight at the groceria, and paper for el bano. I would not want to pull my pants down out there," she said. She pointed, indicating the direction of the building they had not seen.

The boys blushed and looked down at the ground. May blushed a lit-

31

tle also, although she was just as much amused.

"I just mean it would be frightening for me," she said, "in the dark."

She gave them a bag of fruit to go with the groceries and sent them along. Each of them gave her back the five dollars to keep for them, for what she might buy for them the next day, for what they might need. It was late, they had said, they were very tired and hungry. After Immokalee, they had no inclination to go into Harlem Heights.

The bedraggled boys set off down the driveway. They had found trabajo, food, and a place to sleep all at the same farm. It was a good beginning, they said to each other. May called after them to be at the barn at six-thirty, manana en la manana, she'd said, first thing in the morning. They understood her well enough, but they were still puzzled by some of the Spanish she used.

Enrique Garza watched the four weary boys walk across the front of the barn and pass between the two buildings. He was on a small tractor, discing weed stubble where the flowers would grow. He was a hundred yards away. A few minutes later he stopped the tractor. He told another man who followed the tractor with a pitchfork that he would return in a little while. There was another hour of daylight, he would come back and they would work a little longer. He walked up the center road, crossed the yard, went between the buildings and down the narrow path through the weeds.

In front of the concrete house, the four little Mexicans sat on dry-rotted tires and cement blocks. They were silent, looking at the place where they would live, and pay ten dollars a week each for the opportunity. Having seen it, they had become too tired to eat.

"It is very bad. No one has stayed here for the whole of a year. Last season all the men found rooms in Harlem, and the alcoholics live closer to the groceria," said Enrique. He looked at each of the boys in a friendly manner. They stood up. When he spoke he used words they too would have chosen.

"One of you come back with me to the barn. Bring your food, we will place it in the icebox and it will be fresh when you eat later. I will get

32

you a broom and a rake and a shovel and some pails for carrying water. I have lotion and spray that will keep the bugs from biting you. This is the worst time of the year for mosquitoes."

The boy picked up the bags of food, they were ready to move at his direction.

"You other boys," he said, " begin by dragging everything out of your house. Start at the two doors and work into the building. Put everything that will burn beside the barrels, I will come back when I am finished with my work and show you how to burn. Clear the weeds away from the bottoms of the barrels. Pick up the glass and the cans and the pieces of metal and broken cement. Bury it next to where you make the piles. Bury it deep. I will get you two shovels. The sand is soft and it is easy to dig here, not like in Mexico. Bring out those dirty mattresses, we will burn them too." He smiled at them and continued giving commands. "Pick up all these broken, useless things," he said. "I will get you clean mattresses tomorrow. I will give you flashlights for tonight. You have many hours to go before you can bathe and eat. But tonight you will sleep in a cleaner house."

Chapter Eight

Hippies were tenting east of 41 at the end of a sand trail that simply petered out where the prairie and palmetto began. It was called Daniels Road, but it was much more of a path than a road, there were ruts in the sand where tires had passed over enough to kill the weeds and grasses. It crossed Ten Mile Canal as a paved road over a timbered bridge and then the paving stopped. The trail meandered through the biggest of the cypress sloughs in the county, named Six Mile. It passed by dark lakes covered with lily pads, lined with arrowroot. There were bursts of color from the new leaves of red maples. Large-mouth bass swam in the water in the summer and fall, cigar orchids and airplants grew on the cypress limbs and pond apple branches. Spanish moss hung as thick as the grey hair of a thousand witches and dipped into the black pond. The sand road had been built up through Six Mile but in the summer it was often under water. Even on the brightest day, the sun did not penetrate the canopy, the trail was in deep shadow as it wound through the cypress slough. It was the wettest part of the county.

Gradually the land rose a little, Daniels opened up into enormous pastures for grazing cattle and abandoned farm land. The prairie had been burned by lightning, cleared by man, farmed for vegetable crops for the cities, especially during the war. Now it was used for range cattle and horses. There was no need for ditches to run beside the road, the land flooded completely in the rainy season and ditches were useless. Barbed wire fences on weathered pine posts bordered the trail. They defined private pastures, signs warned trespassers to beware.

The land's abruptness was softened by big wax myrtles, scrub oaks, and sabals. The palms' thick trunks had black splotches from the scorch of the fires. In the spring after a rainless winter the ground in the pastures dried out, the flat land grew wildflowers, but in June the land was sodden. The sand that drained the water down to the cap rock could hold no more because the lakes and ponds and the slough itself were full. The water could not move sideways, the water had stopped moving in any direction except up. The cattle and horses were restless, they huddled together on slight rises of the low ground. They worried about food and were harassed by fire ants.

The hippies had built a sagging, half-assed platform from big maleleuca limbs, old fence posts, and pine boards they had scrounged. It was a rough, uneven platform, any carpenter's helper would have been ashamed to be on it. It was not dangerous, but nothing was fastened down very well, the platform shook with sudden movement. But they were above the water and no one was bothering them, because of where they had set up camp. They were locals, had been radicalized easily by killer joints, bongs, music, LSD and college. They were harmless, they had been caught in the groove of the moment, they hoped to experience nature. There were hubcaps braced with small rocks in which leaves and wet branches smoldered day and night. The mosquitoes circled in numbers greater than the stars. They kept themselves sprayed from top to bottom with OFF. They bathed in it. No camper went into town and came back without more.

They had erected a tepee on the platform, more of a pitched lean-to made of boat canvas, crudely stitched together. When they wanted something badly, or wanted to visit the world, they walked the long miles back to the highway, sloshed carefully through the floodwater. When they got to 41, the hippies hitch-hiked back to town, to parents' homes, to friends' homes, to bathe, get fed, get food, get more acid, get the bug spray, and got back to the platform. When they were in town, they drew the stares and comments that had been stock for queers, coloreds, and staggering drunks.

They sat on the log floor, smoked weed incessantly, swallowed strong chemicals, watched the lightning storms blow in from the east in the afternoon, and watched the moon rise through the clouds in the night. They listened to the lowing of the unhappy cattle, the frogs, the gators, and the insects. There were three boys and two girls. When they weren't tripping, all but one were thinking about doing something different very soon.

Chug had become plenty pissed when he heard that the hippies were camped out on land near to his family's own. He was especially perturbed if the stories were true that the long hairs were getting an assortment of free pussy and he wasn't getting any without having to pay for it. He had seen the platform earlier in the week. His truck's four wheels were engaged to grip and turn on sand paths, he could drive through the deepest holes that were filled with water. That had been in the daytime though, he recalled. He and Marvin were on they way to pay the hippies a visit at night, he hoped he could find them in the drizzle.

The heavy Ford moved slowly through the water, the sand trail was obscured. Chug and Marvin rolled with the motion, the headlights bounced up and down. Chug tried to skirt the deepest holes by driving half on the trail, half in the shallow ditch. He had a bottle of Bacardi between his legs, he took quick short sips from it, almost biting at the rum as it passed from the bottle to his lips. Marvin nursed his sixth beer of the early night, he farted and belched, his fat stomach shook with the movement of the truck. He was out of his deputy clothes. He was wearing a cowboy shirt, cowboy jeans, a cowboy belt, and cowboy boots. A John Deere baseball cap completed his ensemble. Underneath the hat his hair was short, bristly. The truck rode high on the oversize tires, Marvin had spilled beer on himself twice already. Hitman sniffed at the smells of the swamp, the cows and the horses. Hitman was hungry. Chug had let him gulp down a bottle of beer before they left the ABC. The beer had sharpened his appetite, he needed something filling. He smelled deeply of the air, let his tongue out to lap at the light rain. The men had the windows up against the mosquitoes and no- see -ums, the air conditioner was on. Wet heat rose from the shallow, sun warmed water, the truck caused a small wake across the flooded land.

36

In the camp the boys and girls sat on the sagging platform in front of two smoldering fires. The lean-to was behind them, the rest of the small landing was covered with wet branches of pepper and wax myrtle broken off the bushes by hand. Mostly the camp was clean. They burned trash for smoke also, what they could not burn they carried back to town and pitched in dumpsters. They were all dressed alike in dirty robes with hoods. The robes were cinched at the waist by a piece of rope. They were barefoot, they had long hair that they washed daily, standing naked together in the rain. They sat cross-legged, heads up, brains exploding with acid, chanting a mantra and calmly waving at the mosquitoes that buzzed in front of their faces. They had been there about three weeks.

Chug stopped the truck a hundred feet from the camp, he left the motor running. He shut off the tape player, put the bottle of rum on the seat, hopped out. He quickly closed the door behind him. He reached into the back and unsnapped the lock that held Hitman's collar to the chain. In a single bound the dog was over the side, standing in the water next to his master. Hitman was ready for action.

"Hitman," said Chug, "watch the niggers."

The dog bolted in the direction of the smoke.

"Go get the niggers, you crazy fucker," Chug yelled after the dog. "Don't bite em though. Goddamnit, just scare em."

Hitman heard the warning past the splash his feet made. He was running toward the platform. He was disappointed he hadn't been told the other thing, the thing he really liked, but he knew he could have some fun and maybe find something to eat. His wide paws slashed at the ground water, his huge head bounded up and down with the powerful movements of his shoulders and forelegs. He opened his mouth to bark and roar but no sound came forth. The dog remembered Chug had taken him to have his vocal cords cut, and he was disappointed again.

Chug opened the door and jumped back into the cab of the truck. He reached for the bottle, got it between his legs.

"Gimme that spray, Marvin," he said.

Chug took the can, squinted his eyes tightly shut then sprayed his face with the repellant. He sprayed his ears and hair and neck and freckled hands. He tossed the can at Marvin's lap.

37

"You better do the same, boy, then we gone open the windows. I wanna hear them pukes screamin," he said.

Hitman tore into the camp just as the hippies sensed him replace the mantra. The poor tripping freaks thought he was a panther that had come to eat them. He was out of the water and on the platform, whirling in excitement and confusion at his choices. The hippies scattered screaming, they rolled frantically in the water until they found purchase. They ran away, they held the brown robes up, they ran, calling for salvation. One boy with straight blond hair stood shock still. When the big dog jumped on his chest it was the surprise of his life. He became instantly aware of his own mortality, his hippie days were over. He was a former athlete, a basketball player and track star, young, in reasonably good shape. With a tremendous instinct to avoid a maiming, he fell with the dog, rolled on the platform, and covered up his head with his hands. Hitman opened his wide jaws and clamped down on the cowl of the boy's robe. He marveled at the smoky, sweaty, smelly mass and ripped it away, all the way down. The homemade stitches easily pulled apart. Hitman took more and more of the robe into his mouth. The boy was naked underneath. When he felt air on his skin instead of sackcloth he slithered forward on the pine, slid into the water like a snake and leaped to his feet and ran as fast as his bare legs would move him. He concentrated on his breathing to run faster and further. He did not sing out.

Chug pulled the truck up in front of the platform, the high beams of the headlights illuminated Hitman where he shook and slobbered and chewed at the robe. Chug idly thought about chasing down one of the girls. Shit, he thought, what they gone do about it? Who they gonna call that gives a shit? He decided against it because of his boots and jeans and the water moccasins that were sure to be around. He shut the motor off.

Chug and Marvin sipped at the bottle and the beer, they watched the dog rage against the coarse cotton. They could hear the hippies calling out to their brothers and sisters, they howled insults back at them. The hippies made contact across the wet pasture. They began calling the name of the boy they had left behind but there was no answer back. Chug and the deputy got out of the truck, they were fortified against the bugs by the stink of the liquor and the spray.

"That boy ain't got no clothes on, Chug," said Marvin. "I almost feel

38

sorry for his ass with all the skeeters out."

"Shit, Marvin. He's likely still runnin so fast the mosquitoes cain't land to bite em. Or else he's gone into a pond to get under the water, though I doubt it."

"They God," said Marvin, "they sure a lot worse things in the swamp water. They's cottonmouths an snappin turtles an fire ants floatin ever-where, an catfish. Whoowhee."

"That's true enough, deputy," Chug giggled, "that boy steps on a cat-fish he's in a world of hurt, an if he slows down an ain't in the water, them fuckin skeeters will bite em to death. But the worse thing out there is a old daddy moccasin huntin him a fish. That hippie boy an that snake cross paths, well shit, his life's just gone all to hell."

Chug climbed up on the rickety platform, kicked at Hitman to make him move, and unzipped his jeans. Marvin climbed up too. They pulled out their dicks and pissed in the hubcaps that burned wet leaves. Chug turned and tried to piss on Hitman and the robe but the dog had watched for him. Hitman spun away with his prize and jumped into the back of the truck. In his mouth he held the wet wad of what was left of the robe that he had not yet ripped apart and eaten. He intended to further chew on the robe, swallow it and fill his stomach. He would digest it and shit it in big pieces later in the night. He hoped they would still be out when he shit so there would be someone to watch. Chug and Marvin zipped up, kicked the fires over, climbed down from the ledge and got in the truck. Chug cranked over the engine, put the truck in gear and slowly drove it onto the sagging wood structure. He rolled over the timbers and the boards and the lean-to. Once everything was down, he rocked the truck back and forth over it a few times until it was mixed in the water and sand. He backed the Ford up, turned it around and slowly drove down the rutted lane, through the fenced range, toward the cypress slough and the highway. He turned the radio on, WQAM in Miami.

"Hitman sure likes that boy's blanket," said Marvin, " he ain't turnin queer on us, is he?"

"Fuck no, Marvin. Hitman ain't a queer but he ain't normal either," said Chug. "He ain't at all particular about what he fucks. Shit. That dog fuck a runnin horse if he could get his nails dug in deep enough to get a hold."

"Them hippies better hope they find they flashlight, so they can find they way to 41."

"They ain't even real hippies," Chug said and laughed, "they just stupid fuckers gobblin strong shit. Guess they ain't so groovy now, standin in a swamp up to they ass. Peace an love. Makes me want to puke in my hand."

"You right there, Chug. What a crock of shit."

Chug upended the Bacardi and drained it. They were in the slough. He rolled down his window just enough and pitched the empty out. He reached into the cooler on the floor, found a beer and put it between his legs where the rum had been. They crossed the wooden bridge at Ten Mile Canal and began to put on speed. He hit 41 full tilt, the tires were spinning on the wet pavement. The truck slid sideways hard to the right. He eased off the pedal until he could straighten out. The tires bit, there was another screech as he jammed down the accelerator. The men and the dog shot north, headed for Johnny Shay's.

Chapter Nine

Verdell "Chug" Sinclair was tall and lanky, the old timers called it raw boned. He had big hands and thick wrists, long fingers and knuckles the size of a watch face. His forearms and calves were corded with sufficient muscle. He had become tall as a boy, he got mean early, he threw bullfrogs at cement walls and took a hammer to box turtles when he could find them. He went to the football, basketball, and baseball games at the high school in Fort Myers, and stupidly to the smaller schools out in the swamp, looking for another boy to fight, he truly loved a bloody battle. The only time anyone could recall him losing badly was an ass-whipping he took from two basketball players in Everglades City, one boy was left-handed, one after another they beat the living shit out of Chug. The first boy had him bleeding heavily from a broken nose and busted lips and had only taken a couple of strong shots on his neck and the back of his head. He stopped fighting but Chug continued to insult him so badly, spitting blood, cursing, weaving in his cowboy boots, blowing frothy red bubbles, that the other boy was obliged to finish what his buddy had started. They left Chug laying on the crushed shell behind the school gymnasium where crab traps were piled by the hundreds.

When he was older he went away to college then returned after three drunken violent years. He gave up fighting for fun, he reserved it for profit. He brandished shooters, the lead-filled baton, a powerful truck and Hitman. Together they badgered, then, if they had to, beat anyone in Chug's circle of bars and nightclubs not clear about the way things stood. Although he had not yet shot anyone, Chug had pounded several men, set his dog on others, burned a house and rammed his antagonists' cars and trucks with his own. He let it be known around town that he absolutely didn't give a shit. He was connected in the city, in the county, in Tallahassee. Fort Myers was his town, he told his buddies, and the county was named for General Lee. He was grand fathered in, any problems short of shooting another white man with a credible white witness brought only fines and threats. The state attorney was a close friend of Chug's father, he had benefited mightily from the friendship, that was about it. Chug liked the action in the streets at night, a lot better than the days spent at the farm. He planned on being different. He acted drunk and sometimes sober, with malicious intent and immunity from penalty.

Chug was usually wasted, at least on his way, by mid-afternoon or close by. Early evening he was shit-faced until he took a cap. He started with a warm beer in the morning, had cold beers for the afternoon, drank rum and coke, or vodka or whiskey at night. It was a routine he had followed since he was twenty. He claimed that was all he had learned in Gainesville, in the agriculture school, how to hold his liquor. Now he had pills too. He had started taking speed when he began working at the farm. He liked speed. There were times when he was reeling drunk that he would pop a black beauty, a half-hour later he'd be roaring down the highway for Bonita and more beer. He had hooked up with the long distance truckers at the market who hauled vegetables and citrus north. He bought Benzedrine and black beauties a hundred at a time. He had Eddie the old colored junkie peddle the speed in Harlem Heights and back in town, on The Hill. Chug ate like a starving man between the nights when he was speeding and his binges with the booze. He stoked his furnaces for a little work, the eventuality of opportunities, and a lot of pussy.

He was hung like a Shetland pony. Everybody in town said he had the biggest dick they could recall. He was extraordinarily furnished for a white man, eight inches soft and twelve aroused. There was no explain-

42

ing the size of the boy's pecker. The family had privately speculated that some hill-billy from Bacon County, Georgia, might have assaulted a female family member, the Sinclairs had not yet come down the Florida peninsula. The old man was smaller than Chug, he was more compact, but he had a big dick too for his size. Missus Sinclair was embarrassed by it, when it reared its swollen head. Earlene at the office claimed it was delightful.

The whores on The Hill and in Harlem Heights marveled at Chug's dick and his desire, his need, to keep it frequently stroked. They had all seen a lot of dicks, but Chug's was the biggest. White girls, the ones who lived in town, who were society, had friends in Gainesville and had heard about Chug. He was repulsive to them anyway, the dick thing was the kiss of death, the girls who lived along McGregor said. Even May, although she had not seen that many, thought Chug's was impressive, fulfilling. May liked sex, she liked it energetic and conclusive. When he had started banging her, always for a twenty, always with a rubber, she liked it. She was aroused by Chug, the danger of him, his money. She squeezed every bit of him that she could get deep inside her and she came when he did, sometimes even before, from the fit, from the power of the thing.

Besides being a member of one of the richest families in the county, being a known whoreman and a speed addict and mean, everyone said he was mean, besides having that ten inches of pecker between his legs, Chug had two particular, peculiar things about him that people noticed, that were unusual for the times. The first was the way he talked. In his boyhood, he began to speak like he was an ignorant, uneducated, East Fort Myers redneck, worse even, than the poorest boy in Tice. He started it to piss off his mother, then it became an affectation. He shocked and startled other members of his family, his teachers, and boys and girls he knew. He liked it, the shortening of words, the dropping of letter sounds and confusing tenses. He liked the stark forbearance of it. He made it the drawl of disaster about to happen. He spoke that way so long and so often that it became his regular way of speech. He insisted to his asshole buddies that it scared the Mesicans and the coloreds, it reached them on they own illiterate level, he'd said. It was Klan talk, Georgia dirt-farm talk. It was dark, grammarless and beyond rustic.

His other unusual expression of personality was a penchant for wearing gold. He wore more jewelry than the Mexican bus drivers who robbed the tomato pickers in Immokalee. Chug wore gold necklaces, several at a time, gold bracelets, gold rings studded with precious stones, sometimes four on each hand, his watches were gold too. He bought from pawn shops on Palm Beach and Anderson or stole the jewelry or just took it. He wore gold every day. Sometimes he went to his duplex during his prowl, changed just the jewelry or added to what he was wearing. People wondered about how much gold and silver, how many gems the boy had, they had seen him flash plenty. Old timers at the Farmer's Market said he looked like a yankee queer, with all the shit he had on.

He was a sight, sure enough, bull-shitting in the parking lots of the bars and liquor stores. He wore high-heeled cowboy boots. His tight jeans showed the bulge of the critter between his legs. A long-sleeved cowboy shirt covered his freckled arms, aviator sunglasses hid his eyes. He had thinning red hair under a Pirates baseball hat and dripped gold adornments. Everybody said, who knew him, it was just a matter of time.

Chapter Ten

From October until Mother's Day a man could stand at the top of the drives and look down the center roads, a half- mile long at some farms, and see the flowers breaking into color. The tightly budded gladiolus were taller, less distinguishable, they all looked the same from a distance. The buds of the chrysanthemums were more recognizable as yellows and whites and pinks and purples. There were men who owned farms that were like Percy, most of them, who would walk the center road twice a day, veering off sharply between rows in the morning and again in the afternoon, when the light and humidity were changed. They held single leaves and buds close to their eyes and peered at them with magnifiers looking for mites and thrip. A man like Percy could not walk past the flowers and not touch them, he brushed and trailed his hands in the mass. When Percy was around his people moved with more purpose, with more efficiency. Percy could peer at a worker like he was using his lens, the person would feel like a flower or a leaf or a weed. He could wilt indifference. Men like him were believed to be fair, everyone knew Percy was. Things happened fast when he was cutting.

The owner was connected to his farm and the flowers and the endless days of weather by something other than power and profit. He would walk the rows, not drive them. He checked for height and weight, bud count, leaf count, tone and depth of color, thickness of stems and blemishlessness. The farmers struggled to grow perfect flowers free from disease and insects whose colors were vibrant and true to the species.

The chrysanthemum farms picked up the cuttings every week from Yoder Brothers cold storage in Page Park, the slips might come from Michigan or Ohio or Washington. They had been kept cool, not cold, and moist, not wet. They were in boxes, hundreds of cuttings to a box when they were brought to the mist houses where the women would stick them, one delicate slip at a time, one cutting to a cell of peat and perlite to be misted for four weeks, then the rooted plugs were taken out into the fields. Three hours on a hot day without mist and the cuttings were shot, there would be no planting, the season would be set back, the first holiday missed. In the fields some elements were aligned against the baby plants but they grew fast in the gray sand and the dependable sunshine, attended to and protected by the owners. Lights on for three weeks late in their lives to harden the stems, thicken the leaves, put on weight. The plants are tricked. Lights out. Percy could name the date the buds would have good color in the crowns and would open in the florist's shops. Fertilized. Sprayed. Weeded. Pinched. Cut. Attended to and protected. Percy was serious about the flowers.

Other men were connected too, and women. The hands that pinched the buds, pulled the weeds, cut the stems and carried the bundles to the waiting carts were brown, stubby, calloused and cut. Where the thumbs pressed against the forefingers to pinch and pressed against the stem to brace the cut, those thumbs and forefingers were more heavily scarred. The people did not know about lotions, their hands were like the shrimpers' hands that popped heads from pink shrimp on the decks of the boats off the beach. The headers grabbed handfuls from the pile and worked the shrimp through their fingers like a magician might move a quarter. These were browner hands, with black rings along the fingernails that were permanent.

Lights on, lights out. Fertilized, watered, sprayed again to kill the bugs the owners found. Remember to get the water on early in the day, give it time to dry. Keep it off the leaves on cool nights. Hope against too much rain and too many cold nights, hope against soaring heat when it should be temperate. The owners were concerned about bud rot, stem rot, mealy bug, rabbits, fusarium, phytophora, leaf miner, scale, mites, thrip, nematodes, clogged water lines, clogged sprinkler heads, clogged valves and pumps and neighbors with goats and cattle. They were concerned about tractors and machinery and systems and people. There were glutted markets, transportation difficulties, collection from brokers a thousand, two thousand miles away in yankee land. If a man was like Percy, he was having the time of his life. It was a perfect flower or no flower. A man like Percy would not hesitate to cut then dump, huge bundles and barrels of nearly good flowers ready for the plane ride because they were not the flowers he wanted his customers to have, because they were not perfect.

The farms were undulant. Survival depended on quality and timing, weather and people and luck. When a flower holiday approached, the fields were flush with acres of colors. At farm after farm along Gladiolus, flowers were ready to be cut and sorted and graded and boxed. The men began at seven, they were soon bending low over the stems with a curved knife. It was short bladed, honed sharp every night and again during the day. The men put themselves into the flowers and twisted their wrists. They cut the glads long, they cut the mums shorter.

The men in the fields laid the flowers on the grid, when they had a big loose bunch they carried them to carts with buckets welded onto the sides, to buckets full of cool water that smelled like rotten eggs. When the men finished cutting a row it looked like it had been mowed. They pulled the full carts up with small tractors, the drivers were careful not to drive roughly. The other men walked behind. They pushed the carts inside, used the bathrooms, drank a cup of water and then the men went back for more. The women took over. Big square fans blew air across the packing house.

One man pulled the loose bunches dripping water from the buckets, he carried them to where the women stood at the tables. The man moved from woman to woman, came with the flowers quickly when he was called. Glads were graded for the promise of colors to come, mums were graded for the size of the buds and the count. The women handled each stem, pulled them singly from the first rough bunch, tightened and ordered them into the second. The gladiolus were cut at a whirring blade for an extra clean end, tied in somber groups and laid into long boxes. The chrysanthemums were chopped with paper cutters that crunched on the stems. The flowers were weighed, bunched at thirteen ounces, rub-

47

ber banded and crossed-layered by the women, fifty each to a box, each box lined with new wax paper. The same man who carried the loose flowers to the women took them away in boxes. He put the on the cardboard tops, the owner pasted on the farm labels and the customers' names and addresses, they banded the boxes for shipping. When there was a stack of the rectangular boxes on the low cart, the man would push it over the wet floor into the refrigerated storage room that hummed with the sound of the machine making it cold.

In the afternoon the owner walked into the fields and called a halt to the cutting. He examined the rows for the next day's harvest. The men came up front, emptied and rinsed the buckets and pails, cleaned the tables and the watery floor covered with stem ends and leaves and discarded flowers. They put it all in the dumpster. The men made more boxes for the next day while the women cut wax paper from big rolls. The women watched when the men brought the boxes from the cooler. The men carefully loaded them and stacked them sometimes eighty or a hundred at a time in the truck. The loads were most often taken to the Farmer's Market, next to the Seaboard Coast Line. Weeks before a holiday, the drivers took their loads to the airport. All the owners had customers in big cities in the Northeast and the Midwest. The cut glads and mums went by train or truck or National Airline to Boston, Chicago, and St. Paul. The farms shipped flowers for seven months.

The Puerto Rican men and women were holding their own at the farms, getting along with the Mexicans that were arriving, willing to work cheap. Colored men were scarce as laborers, were more likely to be tractor drivers and mechanics and foremen. They were becoming solitary, removing themselves from the Spanish. Colored women had left behind the crushing work and the heat of the fields. They were housekeeping at the schools, where there was air-conditioning.

The Spanish men and women talked to each other while they were working. They discussed the arrival of the wind. The men talked about their trucks and chickens, the women gossiped about people they knew at the other farms. They were pleased to be working with the flowers, but from June through September, there was no respite from heat and the wet.

48

Chapter Eleven

May Valentine worked at the vegetable stand that Chug had wanted for steady cash. She had the most wonderful ass anyone had ever seen, black, white, in-between. She walked to work from her cottage in Harlem, she cut through the mangroves and across A and W. She had started out riding her bicycle but there had been an accident. A man who was driving his car locked his eyes onto May's ass moving on her bicycle seat. He ran into the back of another car which was slowing down to make a turn. The man got out of his car, told May it was worth it, he laughed, said that she had no right to have a body like that. He said he didn't care about the car, he even told the deputy about it when he arrived to write the ticket. The episode frightened May so she walked to work through the trees, avoiding Gladiolus and the cars that might honk at her. She only rode her bike when she had to. She wore loose men's shorts cinched at the waist with a belt or a sash, loose blouses and men's shirts so she would have plenty of room for movement, so people would not stare. Her ass was big, not aboriginal, not quite like the asses of the women of Africa and Australia that walked the deserts and stored fat for sustenance in their buttocks, but close. It stuck out, it was rounded and full. Her spine curved inward back to her shoulders so when she walked, it looked like she was sticking her ass out. She wasn't, it was out there on its own. The shapeliness continued down. She kept her toenails painted blue or purple. Her stomach was thick, not fat. Her breasts were like her ass, full, the glands and the dark brown nipples had not been ruined by the stretch and bites of babies. Her body was exceptional in all its proportions. When she smiled, which was often, she showed her teeth so well that people momentarily forgot about her breasts. She ate fruit and vegetables, they were free. She didn't drink beer or liquor except when a situation suggested she should. She did not often get drunk. She resisted illness, and only smoked a little reefer at night, and a cigar after. She was a colored girl, Puerto Rican, Cuban, and Haitian blood ran in her island veins and complexioned her flesh. The sunlight played tricks with the color of her hair, sometimes it was black and sometimes it was red. She was saving her money.

May was without pretension, what she did had purpose and direction. When she spoke, people generally understood that she meant what she said. She was not to be pushed around. She was one way with Chug, the play and the sex talk, fucked the boss for her job and the extra money that fucking him brought, she was another way with her friends in Harlem and the workers in the fields. She was intelligent. Her mother was long dead, her father was a withered drunk who lived under the banyan trees at the newspaper building. She had been raised by the grandmother of another girl she had gone to First Communion with.

Chug Sinclair was the only man she fucked for money. She liked sex. Once in a while she would enjoy another man, a healthy one, when the urge came upon her but no matter what, she made the man wear a rubber. When she was in junior high school at Cypress Lake she had been befriended by an enlightened school nurse. The lady urged May and the other Spanish girls to get their tubes tied at the earliest opportunity and to always insist that their men wear rubbers, at least until they were married. Even after that it would be a good idea, the nurse had said. May listened to the woman while the others did not, had the operation the summer she was eighteen, and made the men she had chosen to be her lovers keep their dicks in a rubber sheath. Unlike the rest of her girlfriends in Harlem and back in town at The Hill, she did not get pregnant and have babies. She did not catch syphilis or gonorrhea from the men she let inside her. She demanded protection.

For all that she liked her sex hard. She liked it vigorous. She didn't need false courtship, but she would have liked to have had the man be a friend. When she was growing up, sex had been the most dependable,

50

affordable opportunity for entertainment. It had improved with abandon.

She had no intention of staying in Lee County, no intention of being tied to an average man with inconsistent ways. She'd had her share of men, as good for her as for them, better, when she counted up the money from Chug. Girls grew up fast in Harlem. There was little else to do, there were the fragrances of the flowers.

May had always liked to read, she had not even seen a television set until she was fourteen. She was invited to spend the night with another girl, a white girl who lived in Pine Manor. She watched the television, fascinated, excited and happy. She had to walk ten miles to the grandmother's house, along 41 and Gladiolus in the middle of the night after she was awakened by her friend's father touching her breasts. His daughter was asleep beside her in the twin bed. She acquainted television with the incident. The grandmother's cottage was without electricity. She read herself to sleep at night, sprayed with mosquito repellant, holding a flashlight to the pages of her book.

The first time a man asked if he could fuck her there, in her ass, she was startled, she angrily told him to get off of her, he was finished without being started. Later, curious, she asked the other women about it. They told May that indeed it was done, in fact there would be more little babies to raise if it were not. Yes, they said, it hurt the first few times and then like everything else, one could become accustomed to it. Men wanted it, they told her, when they were drunk. She was willing to let a man have her there, she decided, maybe she would like it, but first there would be a lot of money. May guessed she would bargain with what she had. Whoever wanted her ass, she decided, would have to want it very badly. She wondered what it would be like, imagined it to make herself climax. Sometimes she wondered if five hundred was enough, sometimes she thought maybe it was too much.

Chapter Twelve

May had escaped for the time being, the fields where the others spent their days, one after another in a blur of sunrises, hot mornings, high noons, suffocating hours after the lunch break until the waning of the tropical sun. The work was sequenced, carrying, bending, stooping, shoveling, straightening up, walking, running, moving, pounding, pulling, cutting, stacking, weeding, wrapping, putting out and putting away without an end from Thanksgiving until after Mother's Day. That was the end of the flower season, the farms shut down for a couple of weeks. One day was mostly like another, except when it rained. The people were sent home, or cleaned the packing house and the barn and the machinery, or worked in it. The days had beginnings and middles and ends and the next was waiting, a continuation of the routine of the one before. Although the people would not have thought of it that way, because they did not perceive concepts, the overwhelming number of things to do, the burdens and demands of the flowers, what the owners wished to be accomplished, were security for them. They were assured against being on the streets without a pot to piss in.

The people moved and labored together in small groups informally arranged by themselves. They were assigned according to the needs of the crops and the instructions of the foremen. Men worked with men, women worked with women. Each day the managers went back and forth between the small groups or watched them from the tractors, to see that the people in motion were productive. For every cut flower crop, the demands on the people, the things they were set to do, were similar.

The seasons began with preparation of the land to receive the rooted cuttings. The great shade cloths had been put up again, they had been stitched and grommeted. The cloths were tightened down, wires and posts were tightened down, the over-head water pipes and sprinkler heads were cleaned. The gray sand was sprayed with a herbicide. A few days later the weeds that had grown over the summer were dead. They were chopped up and pulled out until the sand under the cloth was completely clean. From a few feet away it looked like the smooth surface of a gray lake.

The flowers were grown on raised beds, restored each year, by an expert on the tractor. He was indispensable. That man molded the sand with the blade at precise points. He maintained a grade that matched the grades of dozens of other rows, three hundred feet long, six feet across, the gray lake looked to have evenly spaced waves.

Between the beds there was a narrow space in the sand where the tractor tires rolled, where the people walked, one foot placed in front of the other, single file. If one person had to dash for the shitter or wanted a drink of water, he or she had to be careful to slip past his or her companions and not step or fall into the perfectly formed beds.

After they had been restored for the present planting, the tractor driver changed attachments. The Fords and John Deeres returned to the fields with multi-piped, multi-fitted spray injectors that dragged methylbromide into the sand. The people followed behind without masks, without gloves. They breathed in the gas and the diesel in the hot, heavy air. They rolled out long sheets of black plastic that trapped the poison in the beds. They covered the sides and the ends of the plastic with sand. In the afternoons some of them were sick, their heads pounded from the heat and the fumes. The black plastic was used only the once, only for a day and a night. There was nothing alive in the sand when the people uncovered it. They peeled the plastic away from the gassed beds. Nematodes, grubs, ants, worms, pathogens and weed seed had been

53

killed. At all the farms, great piles of the toxic plastic lay in black mountains until there was time to burn it or bury it.

The people returned to the prepared soil with metal stakes, they pounded the stakes into the ground with sledgehammers, every ten feet. The metal stakes were notched, the men and women carefully rolled out wire fashioned as a grid and fastened the wire to the stakes. Then they went for the rooted cuttings.

Timing was everything with the chrysanthemum crops. Timing was critical, more than just important, it was precise. The most perfect bunch of mums was worth little if the flowers were not budded with color at certain dates. A week late in the field, three days, five days too early, and the value of the flowers was diminished. When the owner told the foreman to plant, the people came from the mist houses with hundreds of flats filled with the tiny rooted cuttings. Thousands of the delicate baby plants were set one by one into the sand waves. The people made holes with two fingers in the soft soil, the chrysanthemums were stuck, the sand was gently patted back into place. As quickly as a bed was finished the people moved to another, in a few hours they planted many rows. They reached under the wires from both sides, moved down the narrow lanes quickly, bent over or squatted, jumped ahead so there was space for the next man or woman to have room. Just as quickly as they were planted the little flowers began to wilt unless the day was wet or cool. The foreman watched for the people to finish the first rows, he turned on the pump, opened particular valves, watched the spread, the pressure of the water as it came from the sprinkler heads. He opened more and more lines as the people moved through the field emptying the trays of baby flowers.

As the mums began to grow they thickened, they stretched, they competed for the light of the hot sun. They put on stems and leaves. When they popped up through the wire, the grid was raised on the notches. The plants were trapped into growing straight. The stems hardened, they became rigid and ridged with raised veins. They branched out symmetrically, solidly, where the tops had been pinched for the first time and the crown buds had been removed. The leaves became bigger, thicker, greener with steady fertilization. The edges of the leaves changed, became more or less serrated, sculpted according to the variety. The foremen and the owners, even some of the people, could name the flower and its color before it was evident, by examining a leaf. The flowers were called by name from the beginning, when they arrived by truck at the farm as unrooted cuttings. The foremen told the people to bring, to pinch, to weed, or to otherwise attend to the "yellow daisies," the "pom poms," or the "blue daisies," the "starbursts," and the "pinwheels."

Farmers had become very rich when a cutting they had planted did not do what it was supposed to do, what the others were doing. The farmer dug the mutation from the field, replanted it into a container, cared for it above all others, and drove it to Gainesville where it was grown on. If a patent was issued, a new variety became available to the flower market. Great monetary reward was bestowed to the farmer in whose field the evolution had taken place.

When there were problems, thrip and mites, fusarium, pythium and cigar spot, they were discovered and acted upon without postponement to arrest the problem before it was loosened upon the other flowers. The farmers dealt with too much water, not enough water, steady nutritional and chemical determinations, great weather fluctuations and fouled machinery. They were saved by the people whose hands and thumbs and careful feet were connected to the crop.

May sold vegetables and fruit to the motorists. She was called on by Chug to translate and pass along his commands when he wanted to circumvent and undermine the position of Enrique. She had a difficult job staying between the two men, she had to fuck Chug to keep it and take part in fucking over Enrique, who she knew to be fair with the people. She wondered, if she agreed to let Chug have her in that other place, what would happen then? She had read too much, she understood too well, disasters that lie in wait for the poor. She dreaded the work of the fields, whether it was potatoes or melons or flowers. May wanted money, and she wanted away.

Chapter Thirteen

Next to his family, the thing Enrique Garza enjoyed most was the time in his boat on Hendry Creek. He was very good at fishing. He had a little Boston whaler that he'd bought cheap in East Fort Myers. On some weekends, on some nights, when he could count on a breeze or the moon was full, certainly if the Poinciana trees were flowering, he drove from his house in Iona, through Harlem and past the farms, to Coca Sabal. He kept the boat tied behind the house of the old fishermen. He kept the dock and the pilings repaired for the privilege. He replaced soft planks, sealed the deck with creosote every year, and set new pilings beside the old ones. He bolted the pilings together, worked waist deep in the brackish water. The boat had a thirty horse Evinrude. He steered the whaler out the creek to Big Carlos Pass where he fished the tides and the clear water that swirled in front of the sand bars. He took his time on the way out, shut off the motor, drifted along the mangroves. He cast his plug close to the prop roots. He did the same on the way in, drifting by places he knew to be good. Many times in his fishing life a big snook had hit his plug with a great explosion. The snook took the lure into its wide mouth and then swam, twisted, splashed in the shallow water until it was exhausted and brought to the boat. On the sand bars and with the tides he caught trout and redfish but it was along the mangroves when the Poinciana's bloomed that he caught the big snook. When his children were younger they went with him in the boat to fish and to see the birds. They trailed their fingers in the water and licked off the salt, but they lost interest in fishing so he went alone. He enjoyed it. Fishing was his recreation, he derived pleasure from it.

He worked sixty to seventy hours a week, depending on the flowers. When he was on vacation, after the last big flower day and the farm was shut down, he cleaned and painted his house, or made improvements to it. He repaired the lawn and the driveway. He owned a 1963 Rambler station wagon. He had bought the car new, eight years before, it looked like it had the day he bought it. He drove his wife in his Rambler down McGregor to St. Francis for Confession and Mass, to the new Publix grocery on Cleveland Avenue and to the American Department Store. They made trips in the car to Naples, Sarasota, and Ybor City.

Enrique listened to the radio at night after supper, he liked the baseball games. The Pittsburgh Pirates came to Fort Myers in the spring for camp and training, the players and coaches stayed at The Dean Hotel or The Edisonian. They played home games at Terry Park, he managed to get there at least once a season for a night game. He liked the Pirates most but he would listen to other teams play if that was what was on the radio. He liked to hear the excitement in the announcers' voices, the names of the players called out as they pitched, hit, and grounded out. He did not watch television. The things he saw that Anita and the children watched as he passed from the porch to the bathroom or the bedroom made no sense to him, although he knew that his wife and the boy and girl enjoyed the silly faces and animated gestures of the actors. His wife told him the news. He had bought Anita her first television set in 1956, he remembered seeing the conventions for the Republicans and Eisenhower, but couldn't remember watching another since. He bought her another new one in 1964 when they were said to be much improved, but he didn't know about that. He would buy Anita anything she wanted. The television did not bother him, he just ignored it.

Everything he bought for himself had to have a purpose, a usefulness. Enrique Garza did not spend his money on frivolous things. He had wanted to have a farm for his retirement and raise goats and chickens because that was what he remembered was there, but his plans had changed. He would always want to work, but not, he decided, with dirty animals and birds.

He bought new tools, nice clothes and good furniture. Anita drove a car that was paid for, he had money for groceries and gave cash to the church. His boat and the little bit of tackle he did not consider to be unnecessary.

Inside the closet of his carport, he kept his things arranged. There were tools for cleaning and repairing and maintaining the house and the grounds and the cars. He had a bench and necessary things that hung from pegboard. In front of the shovel and rake he kept his two Hurricane rods with black Mitchell reels and his tackle box. His fishing gear was a great comfort to him. He was afraid someone would take something from his boat so he carried the rods and the tackle box home when he was finished fishing. He rinsed the rods and reels with fresh water from the hose and put them in the closet in front of where the Rambler was parked. He bought his tackle new when he wanted, he gave the old rods and reels to the firemen for the Christmas round-up of toys for poor children. He bought his tackle at American Department Store like everyone else. He enjoyed going there with Anita and the children, they had shopped together. American Department Store had everything, he thought, but especially they had fishing tackle. The place was known for it, no one else was even close.

Enrique was careful about fishing, regarding laws, licenses, regulations, limits, and registrations. He followed closely in the sports section of the *News Press* for information that applied to conditions and catches, but he did not ever keep a fish, he released everything that he brought to the boat. Anita didn't like to cook fish and the children didn't like to eat them. Enrique was not comfortable with the idea of killing a fish to which he had been mysteriously attached, which had given him great pleasure. If the fish was hooked solidly he would take his time with it so it would live to swim again. With the plugs there was seldom a danger of a snook or a redfish swallowing the body of the lure and its hooks but sometimes in their great frenzy to be at the plug they would catch their bodies and eye sockets with the small trebles. Enrique would hold the fish in the water, cut the barb with pliers and withdraw what was left of the steel hook. He moved the fish back and forth until it was breathing water smoothly then pushed it back into the creek. He liked to think that he had caught the same fish more than once or that he would, over the years. Maybe they returned to places after long absences, he didn't know. He wondered how far away they might have gone, how they could find their way back to such a small creek?

It was on Hendry Creek that Saturday morning that he decided he would not go back to Royal Glads. He hadn't missed a Saturday morning of work in over twenty years. Even during his vacations he went to the farm to make sure that all was as it should be. That morning he woke early as he did every morning, and he thought suddenly that it would be very nice to go fishing sooner in the day rather than later. Chug would be glad that he did not have to see him. He would fish the creek under a different light that way, enjoy it in the sunshine like he had years earlier with the children. He could not bear the presence of the young patrón. The thought of the barn, the packing house, the field, even the thought of being with the people who worked the flowers was rejected by him that morning. He had soured on the farm because of Chug, on the water he decided he would not go back at all. Just like that, he thought, and snapped his fingers. He did not want to be in the same town or county or state as that man. I will take my wife and my money and go now to Mexico, he thought. His ideas mushroomed in scale and determination. It would not surprise Anita, her mother was alive in Mexico, Mexico was where they had said they would go. The children were grown, they would not want to go, that would be difficult. The old man would be very angry, Chug would be angry too, but the father and son would have different reasons to be disappointed. What does that matter, he thought, they will be here and I will be there. The people at the farm would be disappointed also, for a different reason. They would be afraid, they would be unable to endure the epithets of the patrón. They would leave, no one would want to work there, the flowers would wither and die, then the farm would follow. No matter, it is not my farm, he said to himself. He had grown vegetables, glads and chrysanthemums for the Sinclairs for all those years, the old man had not once had them at his house. The old man was an adding machine, nothing would happen with Chug until his dealings added up to beyond what the old man would pay for. Chug would get worse, meaner, before the old man noticed, he thought, Enrique did not want to be burdened with it. The children were young adults, they had left the house and taken apartments, one on Sanibel, the other close to town. They could live together in the house and save money. He would pay the taxes. They would be very happy to have their own house, he thought. He would give it to them. They had jobs and friends and other interests and they would never go fishing with him again. Why should he and Anita stay any longer?

He decided he would tell the old man at his office on Monday morning then go to the farm to get a few things, his rubber boots and rain suit and some tools. No. He would leave everything at the farm and not go back, not tomorrow, not Monday, not ever. The people would understand. Enrique and Anita would leave Wednesday. His mind was awhirl with plans and schedules. They would take the Rambler, they could come back for the other car in a few months, fly back, he thought, that would be an adventure. They would take only clothes and personal, sacred things, pictures, gifts, Anita's little bit of jewelry. He would get his savings from the bank on Monday and take it with him. He did not trust the bank to move his money smoothly from Florida to Mexico, he imagined there would be difficulty, delay. He would carry the money, it would be safe, he would put it in a bank when they got to Brownsville. There would be Mexican banks, they could deposit the money in one of them. The children could have the house and all that was in it. What the boy and girl did not want they could give to the Witnesses or the Catholics in Harlem Heights. They could be in San Miguel de Allende by Sunday next, a week from tomorrow, perhaps a week from Monday. They would miss Mass in the cathedral on Sunday but they could be walking in the great plaza by evening. Monday at the latest. No matter, he thought. The imperatives of time in his life were changed. They could leave Wednesday and be there when they got there.

He cast his plug for another hour, no longer in a hurry. He was more relaxed then he thought he would be. More boats were coming out of Hendry and Mullock Creek, someday it would be crowded, he guessed, the fishing would be ruined. It was very hot on the still water, no breeze blew, the sun stayed put, directly it seemed, over his head. He put his rod

60

down, next to the spare. He would take his best one with him, he decided, in case there were fish in Mexico, but he could not remember ever seeing any. He pulled up the anchor, the outboard caught with an easy tug on the knotted cord. He steered the whaler back up Hendry Creek, not stopping to cast again. He passed schools of mullet swimming to the bay and the Gulf, he saw a bald eagle perched in the top of a dead pine, staring out across the marsh. He went beyond the dock where he kept his boat tied, then another quarter of a mile or so where the creek became very narrow and twisted and the water was very dark. He brought the whaler alongside a rough seawall where another, older boat was hitched by a rope to a post. Big buttonwoods and sea grape leaned out over the water from both sides putting him in shadow. He was in a green tunnel, leaves and pine needles moved past him, following the mullet to the opening of the creek into the pass.

He reached up and pulled a ship's bell that hung beside the seawall. In a few moments a white haired little man and a big black Labrador came out from the screen porch. Enrique had met the man out on the water, he admired the way the old man fished. One time the man had pulled Enrique in with his own boat, stopping his fishing to help when Enrique's propeller pin had sheared, just worn out, they had guessed. The white haired man was very old. He was a retired army captain, regular army, he had explained, not reserve. He had been stationed all over the world. He had left the army right after Korea, he had been in the artillery, fired cannons and howitzers at Remagen Bridge, at The Bulge, and Pusan. He had come to Fort Myers, bought the house on the creek, built the seawall and learned how to putter, he already knew how to fish. Up and down both creeks he was the man year after year against whom the other fishermen measured their skills and luck. He had caught more snook then anyone else. The old man ate the fish he caught. He told Enrique how after a lifetime of casserole, grilled cheese, and pancakes on Fridays, he was eating fried snook fillets, and sliced tomatoes from his garden instead. The old man kept by the rules too.

He fished with plugs and trailers, never used big shrimp or pinfish or cut ladyfish. He didn't want to wait for the snook to bump into the bait, he cast his lures repeatedly into the lairs of the big ones lurking under the mangroves. Because he was retired, and because he had favorite television shows he liked to watch at night, the old man fished the daytimes. He took his desire and luck onto the water while the sun was up, the fish could see, and the tides were moving, bringing sustenance up and down the creek. He made his own plugs and trailers. The salesmen in the tackle department at American wanted him to make dozens so they could sell them, but he only made a few to use himself or to give away. When he saw Enrique on the creek, when the boats crossed wakes at dawn or dusk, he would motor over to where the Mexican man fished. He waited until Enrique was finished with that spot, then got beside him and gave him a new lure to try. He made the plugs from old broom handles and mop handles that he found in trash cans, driving through The Villas. He cut the wood into five inch pieces, whittled and sanded down the ends, and painted on eyes, stripes, and chevrons in a multitude of colors using model airplane paint and nail polish. The man inserted pieces of old spoons for action, and screwed in two small treble hooks and an eye for a trailer. He experimented with feathers and broken pieces of costume jewelry, incorporated the bits into his designs. He hoped to outsmart the smartest, the biggest snook of all, the one that had not yet been caught.

"How is Molly the dog?" asked Enrique.

"This dog, you wouldn't believe how smart she is," the man answered.

"She looks very healthy, well fed," Enrique laughed.

"She costs us a fortune at the vet," said the man. " I give her fish for her coat. My wife bakes her the back strips, she loves it, but look how fat she is. She eats anything we put down for her and biscuits besides and she's still hungry. How was the fishing?"

"I am skunked," said Enrique. It was a phrase he did not understand completely but he had heard the captain use it. He believed it meant the fish had won that day.

"I was thinking of other things," he added.

The captain pulled a cigar from his shirt pocket and lit it.

"I don't smoke in the house," he said, " my wife doesn't like the smell."

"My wife would not like it either," said Enrique. "I don't smoke anyway. I tried it once but it made me very sick."

"Do you need some new plugs? I've got some I just finished, they're going to drive the fish crazy."

"No. No thank you, captain. I want you to have my boat. I want you to take my boat and the tackle, I am going to keep one rod and reel and the box with lures, but I want you to have the rest. You need another small boat, forgive me, yours is very old. I want you to have mine, I don't need it any longer."

"You are not sick, are you Enrique?" asked the old man.

"No, I am not sick, I am retired."

The old man took the cigar from his mouth and looked closely at his friend down in the boat. One side of the old man's mouth was wet from where the face muscles had loosened, where he held the cigar between his teeth. He wiped the spittle off with the back of his hand, he didn't understand what the man in the boat had said, he didn't know what he meant.

"I am going to be retired like you," Enrique told him. "My wife and I are returning to Mexico, very soon. I set my mind this morning, on the water. I will not be able to fish here again. I wanted to say goodbye to you. I want you to take my boat, so I know it will be cared for."

The old man put the cigar back in his mouth and leaned forward on the piling.

"Awful sudden... sudden, isn't it?"

Enrique began straightening things in the boat, stowing away the spare rod and the anchor and the vests, dropping leaves and bits of branches back into the whiskey colored water.

"Sometimes that is the very best way to do things, before others can interfere or move you in a direction that they want you to go, but you do not. This little boat is for you. I hope you catch many snook from it. Do not eat too much fried fish, eat some broiled and baked, it is better for you. I know you will take good care of this little whaler, take good care of yourself also."

The man told Enrique to wait on the dock a moment, he said he had something to show him. He went into the house. Enrique climbed out

63

of the boat, boosted himself over the seawall rather than using the steps. He stood on the concrete deck. The dog had stayed, she put her big head against the man's leg so he would rub her ears. Enrique looked down at the boat in the water, his gear, the captain's gear now, arranged neatly under the seat. The old man came out a few minutes later. He handed Enrique several new wood plugs he had just made, they were arranged in an empty cigar box like soldiers at parade.

"These are for when you decide to go fishing in Mexico," he said. "They're there, you know, same waters, same fish, same cover as here, all along the Gulf coast. Take this too," he said. He reached for Enrique's hand and put a check in it.

Enrique looked at the check. It was made out to cash for five hundred dollars. He looked at the old captain.

"I was going to buy myself one and give it to me for Christmas," he laughed. "Honest to God I was. Your boat is worth twice what that check says and a new one is a lot more, plus the rod and the new Mitchell. I'll take your boat, if you'll take that check for it. You'll need that money when you get to Mexico, so you can fish."

"Thank you," Enrique laughed too. "This is very, very generous. I had meant to give you the whaler, not trick you into buying it."

"Oh, I want the boat all right," said the man, "but not for nothing. That just isn't right. Deal ?"

"It is a deal," said Enrique. He carefully folded the check and put it into his shirt pocket. "And now I must go. I cannot give away or sell my wife so she will go with me. We have a lot to do to get ready."

"Can't you fish in wherever it is you're going in Mexico?" The captain could not imagine a place where people could not get in a boat and go out a creek and cast.

"I don't know," said Enrique, "I have not been in Guanajuato for many years. I think there are trout there, in the mountains, but I am not so excited about fishing in narrow rivers."

"Where?" asked the old man.

"Guanajuato," answered Enrique.

"I knew that," said the captain, laughing at himself.

They shook hands. Enrique asked the captain to say goodbye to the old brothers for him, he was afraid he would cry when he saw them. The retired captain and the retired flower grower walked around the yellow house, down the sand driveway. The old man patted the younger man on the shoulder goodbye and watched as he walked down the lane carrying the fishing rod and the cigar box. He was under the canopy of the Australian pines, then out of sight.

"Come on, Molly," the captain said to the dog. "Let's go back and look at that boat."

The Rambler was parked in the shade, under a big avocado tree. When he pulled it onto Gladiolus Drive from Coca Sabal he got it going good, checked, for firing and pickup and balance. He let the tiny pieces of paper of the shredded check slip through his fingers, out the open window and into the wind as the car began to put on speed.

Chapter Fourteen

The Sinclairs had been as good as the others until Chug took over Royal Glads. They had hired good men like Garza, given them a reasonable hand to run the farms, but the old man had been feckless, he had not honored his responsibility to be responsible for the behaviors of his son. Separately they had arrived at the same sorry place. The old man had believed that there was an entitlement, Chug should have a position in the great plan of the family, the holdings, the industries, the power. Now he was not so sure. The Sinclairs had been Florida farmers, cattlemen, landowners, for many years. They bought the property on Gladiolus, chased off the coloreds who were squatting there, grew red potatoes, then glads and chrysanthemums. The place had always been called Royal Glads, that was the name the first old man had chosen for it. Glads were what he had wanted grown there, but a blight mutated and destroyed the bulbs in the middle-Sixties. The second old man decided to grow mums. Now it was Chug's domain, because Chug had a legacy, he was grand fathered in.

The old man didn't come around much, he knew very little about farming. His father, the first old man, from whom he had inherited the ranges and groves and fields, had been connected to the land by something more substantial than paper. He had an interest in the gray sand, what would come up from it, produced in combinations with rain, sun, and warmth. He had, however, been made dead before his natural time, killed on a Sunday morning when his car stalled on the railroad tracks crossing Fowler Street. The refrigerated freight cars were on their way to the last terminal in Bonita Springs, twenty miles further south, for vegetables.

The new old man, Chug's father, took over Royal Farms and Royal Cattle Company. He should have let his second son be a cowboy, assigned him to some remote place where he would have been less involved with the people. The family had its hands in everything that was Florida except for amusements. They had ranches in LaBelle and Arcadia, oil wells in Felda, sugar cane in Clewiston, vegetable farms in Fort Myers, and citrus in Winter Haven. They had owned phosphate mines near Orlando, which the old man was happy to dump. He made a killing, he sold the land to developers who wanted to build theme parks, shopping centers, and residential communities where there would be gates with guards to keep unsavory types from mixing with the homeowners.

The old man ran his companies without shareholders, without opinions, without interference. He ran his businesses the way he wanted. He was an office manager, a lawyer, a numbers man who had been raised in Miami, gone to private schools and a private college. He had belonged to elite, exclusive groups all his life. He was careful, meticulous, reviewing paperwork, contracts, sales figures, payables, receivables, production, operation, transportation and collection costs. He was a bottom-line man, if something wasn't paying its way, it was shit-canned. He believed that people were the most casual component of profit making. No one was indispensable.

The first old man bought the land on Gladiolus the year Chug was born, the same year he had been killed by the train. He had been alive, however, long enough to tell the young Mexican he had hired what he wanted. The next old man honored his father's wishes that a flower farm be prepared. Enrique Garza worked skin-blistering days, dripping wet salt, covered from head to foot with fine particles of gray sand. He cleared with bulldozers and managed fires, he stripped the land where the field would be, of palmetto, pines and myrtles. He rode a backhoe for three weeks to dig the perimeter ditch. He ordered crushed shell, he spread it out with a tractor to make the roads and driveway. He punched

67

the wells himself, installed the pumps, valves, and main irrigation lines. He furrowed and plowed. He smoothed the cleared land time after time until it became a sand lake without a ripple to its surface. He built the barn, built the packing house. He built a place for the seasonal workers to stay, he called it The Quarters, he had learned the word in the army. He left the big avocados, mangos, and lychee trees by the main road for screen, from the wind and the noise from cars. There were more of them passing. The land up front was not needed. The old man had told him he wanted forty acres made ready, there was plenty left over. Enrique knew the people in Harlem Heights and the people in the city would be glad for the free fruit. The pond, the little lake was there in the back, perhaps that was why the coloreds had tried to settle that piece in the first place. He asked the old man if they could leave the houses. The next old man said the houses could stay, but he didn't want anybody living in them. Enrique asked if he could plant some trees and things around the houses and the lake. The old man approved.

Royal Glads took two years to build, to prepare for the first planting of gladiolus. Enrique had built it for Chug. The old man planned on his boy growing flowers, that was what his father wanted Chug to do. His other son, the older one, would eventually manage everything else. He would be the next old man, that was the way the Sinclairs carried forth. Chug had seethed with fury and resentment since he had been a boy, over what he considered a particularly shitty arrangement.

The old man knew his second son was a thief, as a boy he had taken silver dollars and jewelry from his mother's bureau. He found out he was a drunk, that he ran with colored whores. Those were bad things, the old man decided, that couldn't go on. Times were changed, the boy's lawlessness could not continue. The old man was in a quandary, his son was reckless and careless but he was a Sinclair. He was not to be trusted, but he was part of the great scheme of the family. The old man had not been a responsible father, he'd other things to worry about, big numbers, contracts for cattle, grapefruit, squash, beans and chrysanthemums, investments. He had heard the situation at the flower farm was uneasy but he had not acted. He found out that Chug was shaking down people on The Hill, that he was screwing the girl who ran the vegetable stand. It was finally too much bullshit, he was sick of it. He worried about losing the Garza man, the Mexican had been with him for nearly twenty five years, since after the war. The old man had let him get away. There was another war going on now, he didn't pay it much attention. Contracts, holdings, gold and silver, fuel, cattle, groves, vegetables, development, those were the things that held his interest. The nature of the county was changing. There was big money to be made in the next ten, twenty years, all they had to do was sit tight on the land along Gladiolus and grow flowers. Chug couldn't, wouldn't, sit there by himself. The Mexican had left him to deal with Chug. The farm was in danger.

The old man figured he would talk to Earlene, let her suggest what to do. She was his secretary for everything, he wanted another opinion. Earlene knew the bottom-line, knew Chug. The boy's reputation, his carryings-on were getting worse, the old man wasn't stupid. Men like Percy, the people in town who mattered, were talking about the irresponsible scoundrel the young Sinclair had become. The old man was annoyed, he was worried about Royal Glads. Without Garza the farm would cost him money. Let Earlene come up with something, he decided, she knew the score. Jesus Christ, he thought, he should have talked to Enrique sooner. He and Chug were going to have a meeting, and there was not going to be any bullshit to it. The boy's proclivities could not continue.

Chug didn't give a fat fuck, for Earlene or the old man. Earlene didn't scare him, he was a Sinclair, same as the others, what the fuck was they gonna do? The Mesican was gone, so what, he'd find him a new one. Someday him and the old man was gonna have a talk, an it wasn't gonna be about no bullshit.

Chapter Fifteen

*E*nrique drove his car past the vegetable stand and the entrance to Royal Glads, he didn't slow down as he went by, he didn't look over. He passed the shacks and cottages, the sand trails and flowering trees that were Harlem Heights. He turned right at McGregor, made a quick left onto Iona Road. The Garza family had lived in the quiet neighborhood near the Caloosahatchee for many years. Iona was mostly farms too, and small houses and duplexes. Along McGregor in both directions there was change, farms were shutting down, developments were filling the open spaces where crops had been grown. Iona continued to Shell Point, where the river joined San Carlos Bay and the blue-green waters behind Sanibel.

The Garzas had lived in two houses since they had been married. The first was in Page Park. After the war, barracks and Quonset huts had been released from the service and put up for sale. Enrique had an honorable discharge, a good reputation, references, and he had a considerable amount of money saved to bind an agreement. He was the first Mexican to own property in Lee County. Ten years later they sold the place in Page Park and bought a new house on Chatham Circle in Iona. Again he emptied his savings. They made a good profit on the barracks turned into a home, they bought the second house outright. He started saving to retire, to return to Guanajuato. By that time there were at least twenty other Mexican families, who along with the banks, owned the houses they lived in. Enrique's was paid for, and it was in Iona, not Harlem Heights or Tice or North Fort Myers. He didn't like Harlem, he was insulted at how the Spanish and colored people lived on Anderson Avenue. He did not approve of the way the people behaved. He wanted more for his wife and children than he saw, than he heard, that other fathers were providing. At the farm he was courteous, friendly and helpful. He was fair to all the workers and the laborers, but he left work at work. He tried not worry about the people when he went home to his family or out in his little skiff.

The house was well-kept. It was air-conditioned, which was considered luxurious for the times. Each little bedroom and the living room had its own window unit that he had installed himself, each family member shut his or her air-conditioner down when he or she were not using that room specifically. When they were gone, they shut the doors behind them. For most of the year the family ate its suppers on the screened-in porch. Enrique liked it, there was space, it was shaded, and cooled with the breezes that blew from the river. The kitchen was small but it was not cluttered, when the family ate inside they were comfortable there also. The house was as clean as a whistle, it was as neat as a pin. No paper or scrap fell to the floor that the nearest hand did not reach for and pick up. The terrazzo was swept and mopped every other day by any one of the four Garzas until the children had finished school, gotten good jobs, grown up, moved out. When he came home from work Enrique took off his boots and socks in the carport, shook out the cuffs of his pants, and walked barefooted on the cool terrazzo floor.

He kept his yard, like Anita kept the house. It was neatest, the greenest on the street. The lawn was coarse St. Augustine, the flat blades were thick, dark with fertilizer. He mowed it with the third old Sarlo that he had found abandoned and rusting, and that he had restored and repaired. He edged the grass with machete strokes, he watered it in the evenings. He stood in the cool grass in his bare feet, held his thumb over the end of the hose, and soaked his lawn. Pink ixora lined the front of the house, under the windows and along the wall. Anita's roses grew on trellises on the sunny side of the screen porch in back. A Royal Poinciana tree towered over the little house and yard, the biggest one south and west of downtown, forty feet across, magnificent in its bloom. In the

71

islands it was called the Flamboyant. The tree spread high over the top of the house, it had a massive gray trunk, spreading branches. When it bloomed in June and July, the roof and the grass of the Garza's neat house were carpeted with the orange red flowers.

Enrique Garza had gone to work for Royal Farms right after the war. He was born in Mexico, in the state of Guanajuato. He lived there until he was a young man, moved to Texas where he got his green card and then his citizenship papers. He worked as a mechanic's helper and as a carpenter's helper. He learned about electricity, plumbing, and concrete, along with the other things. When the war started he enlisted right away. He volunteered to fight for his new country and was accepted into the army. That was 1941. He was bounced from post to post like nearly everyone else who was stateside. He was finally assigned for the duration to the aerial gunners instructors' school in Buckingham, a cattle and scrub range east of Fort Myers. Enrique was smart, he looked smart. He learned to speak English correctly, the army made him a sergeant. He worked on engines and machine guns, and supervised the privates and the corporals in the motor pool. He taught them how to drive and maintain the big trucks that brought food and supplies and more men down the Tamiami Trail. When World War II was ended he was almost thirty years old. He mustered out, married Anita, whom he had met through a friend. He took the first job he could find. He liked the rural nature of Fort Myers, the sunshine, and the people, and he wanted to learn about fishing. The town was very small, reputations traveled fast. The first old man heard about the former sergeant and mechanic and master of several trades. He found out that Enrique was working at a half-assed citrus grove near Alva. The next old man, Chug's father, was making his way into managing the operations of the businesses. The two Sinclairs went to talk to Enrique. They hired him away from the grove owner after an hour of discussion, hired him on the spot, agreed to pay him well. The first old man was glad to have a Mexican. The next old man didn't see that it made any difference, but the coloreds had been leaving the farms for years, especially with the war, they were moving in big groups to the cities. The old man thought Mexican Spanish was about the same as Puerto Rican Spanish, and he believed more Mexicans would be coming to the states, especially the warm states, looking for work at the farms. It would be good, he reasoned, to have a man like Garza there to pick the workers and keep them at their tasks. The old man wanted to grow flowers. He was tired of red potatoes, squash, okra, and cucumbers. The war was over, people were going to want flowers, color, he was sure of it. He wanted to get producing them, gladiolus, chrysanthemums, stattice and gyp. People were going to celebrate, he had said, at Thanksgiving, Christmas, Easter and Mother's Day, at birthdays, weddings and funerals in between. The old man had heard that Mexicans were good with flowers, that they were a peaceable people. He was very happy to have the Garza man.

Enrique started out at the big vegetable farm in East Fort Myers and learned the routine of the sand and the sun. Because the old man was smart, he had the Mexican begin by experimenting, by growing a few rows of flowers, so he would understand what they would do, what he would be responsible for. Royal Glads would be the first time the Sinclairs had invested in a farm that was devoted to a crop that was not meant to be eaten, but simply looked at for its colors and sentiments. The place on Gladiolus was started, the old man was excited about growing cut flowers, then he was killed by the train. The next old man went ahead, Garza was prepared, it was what his father wanted.

The composition of the population did change. More Mexicans came, the coloreds continued to leave, the Puerto Rican population did not grow. The Mexicans had been migrators, followed apples, peaches, lettuce, and beets all over the country. In the winter they came to Florida to pick citrus, strawberries and tomatoes. In the Fifties the flower farms took hold like the old man had predicted. All over the state, vegetable farmers became nurserymen and growers. They produced caladiums, day lilies and palms, they grew hibiscus, gardenia, bougainvillea, ixoras, azaleas and poinsettias. The plants were for the yards of the homes that had sprouted up as thick as blades of grass. The Mexicans began to want to stay year after year at the good farms and nurseries, end their traveling ways, join in the expansion of the economy.

Enrique could have stayed longer, as long as he could work, he guessed, but he detested Chug. He had been revolted by him since Chug had been a teenager. Enrique watched him grow mean, shit on the farm, steal and piss away the old man's money and name, although he would not have used those words. He watched Chug commit outrage against the men and women who worked there, who were a humble and peaceable people. Chug was an embarrassment to his family and to the farm because of his behaviors and his manner. Other foremen spoke to Enrique about it when they saw him at the Farmer's Market. They were interested in what Enrique would do, they were concerned for him and how the flowers would be affected. Men like Percy and the owners of the other farms were angry about the boy's treatment of Enrique and the people. They were readying themselves to speak to the old man about his son. The chrysanthemums at Royal Glads would not be good if it was left to Chug. Brokers and wholesalers in the north and in the Midwest who bought the Sinclair's flowers would think that all of the farmers in Lee County might be indolent, careless, unskilled. The mismanagement of one farm could affect the reputations of others, that was what they feared. In one year, Chug had turned the clock back ten. He wanted to make Royal Glads his plantation first, a place where he was a ruler, then he wanted to sell it, or turn it into a shopping center. Although Enrique Garza did not hate the young patrón with the bad manners and evil dog, he was close to it. He wanted to be away from him.

Chapter Sixteen

He walked into his house, he stood in the middle of the little kitchen where Anita was ironing his work shirts on the counter.

"I gave my boat to my friend the captain," he said, "but I kept a rod to take with me to Mexico."

Anita stopped the iron and smiled broadly at her husband.

"When are we going to leave?" she asked.

"We could go," he said, "right away, in a few days. We can leave everything here for the children and it will be very easy for them, they will not have to buy anything. It will be very easy for me because I will not have to move it all, everything would stay the same for now. We can come back for Christmas. Those places they share with their friends are not as nice as here."

"I am very glad, and very sad at the same time," she said. "I have been ready to leave since that man came to the farm, but I know you will miss the season and the people."

"His family name makes him the boss. The farm is their business."

"I am also sad that our children are grown. They will not want to go," said Anita.

"I am not going to go there and sit on my hands and watch the pigeons in the square. I was thinking, coming up Gladiolus. I am not so excited about goats and chickens. I don't like them. I am accustomed to

75

the flowers," he said.

"I know that, Enrique, and I have an idea for you, for us. I have had it for several months but I wanted to wait until you said we were leaving before I said it out loud."

Enrique looked out the window at the screen porch and the yellow roses that were blooming along the back of it.

"And," he said, "I am concerned about the cold temperatures in the mountains and the absence of fishing. I want to be able to fish, that is why I kept my rod."

"Enrique, I do not want you to do something, anything, that you do not like. I want a happy husband. I think we should go to Tampico or Vera Cruz. I know what I want us to do there. Those places in Mexico are straight across the water from here, it has to be almost the same. Is that not so?"

"That is what the captain said."

"We have not been in the mountains for many years. My mother can visit us in Vera Cruz, then she can go back to San Miguel. I am afraid of the cold now. My blood is thin and Latino, not Indio," she laughed.

"Perfecto," said Enrique, "that is where we will look for a place to live. But what about money and work?" he asked. "What is your plan to keep me busy ?"

"It is a plan for both of us," she answered. "We can grow plants and flowers that we can sell for ourselves. I want us to have a business together. I am not going to stay in the house while you go out. We are going to work together and grow lovely plants that we will sell to the hotels and restaurants, and at the markets and paseos on Saturdays."

"No chebas?" he laughed, "no pollo?"

"No, no goats and no chickens, except when we are served them in the restaurants. You have raised pretty flowers and gone for the fish for many years, it would not do to put you in a desert cleaning up after dirty animals and birds. I want to have a plant place, a nursery that is our own."

"It could be done," he said. "I could do it cheaply, we I mean. We could do it as well as anyone. I could mix my own soil. We can get empty metal cans from the schools and hospitals and restaurants, that is what they are doing here now, that's why the farmers call them egg cans, because they held powdered eggs. That's what they use for growing orange trees and hibiscus and all the rest."

"What about the babies? Do you know where we would get the baby plants to grow big ones?"

"I will buy a book and read about it, English or Spanish, either one will do. I am sure most of the plants are started as we do the chrysanthemums, from cuttings under a fine mist of water. Seed can be gathered from palms and trees, no one minds a man gathering seed, they usually think he is loco for doing it, not smart. There is another way too," he said, "Louis Romaine has talked to me about something he calls air-layering, mossing-off, he said. We can start with bigger plants that way. We will need a flat place and good water. But I do not know about the selling, there have been many good farmers who were poor because they could not sell the things they grew."

"We will not be farmers," she said, "there is another name for what we will be doing. We will have to find out how it is called in Spanish. I have been reading too," she said. "The newspaper calls people who grow plants nurserymen, but it should be nurserymen and nurserywomen or the nursery people because women do as much as men."

"When have they not?" he asked. "But what about the selling?"

"Our flowers will sell themselves," she answered. "We will grow the most beautiful flowers along the Gulf, lilies and ferns and roses. When they are blooming and green we will put them in the courtyards of the best hotels. We will have signs that say the name of our business. I will sell them, I will go to every door in the city if I must."

"Every door in Vera Cruz? I do not think so."

"You grow them, my friend, and I will sell them. Agreed?"

"This is the second agreement I have been asked to make today," he laughed. "Yes, I agree in every way. It is a wonderful Saturday. Let us not speak of that man again, but only of what we will do in Mexico. I will see Mr. Sinclair Monday morning and tell him I am gone from the farm forever. We will leave for Mexico on Wednesday if we are ready. Can you call the boy and the girl to come tomorrow so we can speak with them about this?"

"I will call them as soon as I am finished with my ironing," she said, "whether they are at work or not. They will come here tonight, there are many things to talk with them about. I am going to tell them the things to pay attention to, to write down on paper so they don't forget. This is still our house and the rules that we make for them are going to be very strict and they are going to agree to them."

"Do you want to come back at Christmas for the Mass or to check on the house?" he laughed.

"Both," she said. "I want to come back every year unless something unforeseeable keeps us away, but I don't know what that would be. We will stay here with them so they will have to clean it at least once a year." Anita laughed too. "Are you going to write down things you want them to do?"

"No," he said, "I am going to think of things, that will be hard enough. Someone else can do the writing. I want the son to keep up the yard and the daughter to keep up the house. We will let them write down what that means."

"They will take good care of everything, Enrique, they love this house, it is their home and they miss it, both of them have told me so. They left to give us more room for just each other and so we would not have to provide for them any longer. They are very good young people, not like that pig man at the farm."

"Anita," he frowned for the first time since leaving the creek.

"Well he is," she said. "They will be very happy to be here. They will be very happy for us, but they must pay us a fair rent every month."

"We can save that money for them," Enrique said.

"No, Enrique, they will save their own money, like we have. What they pay for the rent is ours, but it does not have to be so much that it is a hardship for them. We will have expenses also. We are going to spend what we have saved for land and a plant nursery and a truck and workers, and a house," she smiled at him. "There will be new boat with enough room for two so we can fish together. That will cost money, will it not?"

"Now you want to fish?" he exclaimed. "Now that we are leaving the best place for it in the world?"

"Yes. I want to do a lot of things I have not done before," she said, "but answer my question. Does fishing cost money?"

"A little," he said.

"I think more than a little."

"It will not cost nearly as much in Tampico as Tampa, nothing will. American money will go very, very far in Mexico. But what about the plants?" he asked, "does that not mean that they will be cheap also?"

"That part will be different, I think. We will be wealthy in Mexico. Rich nursery people can make better flowers than poor ones. Our plants and palms and orchids will be the finest, because of what you know and what I am willing to learn, and do. I think the hotels and banks and markets will want to pay well for the things we bring them."

"Anita, it is as though you know more about this than I do, which is very good."

"If we leave Wednesday," she asked, "what time would we go?"

"We will start very late at night. I like the highways when there are not many cars, I like the space when I drive. We will start at midnight. We always have when we have made long trips. We will drive the next day until we are tired of it. We will stop and sleep and then drive again the next night. I think we will be in Tampico by Saturday. But we will need to stop in Brownsville for a time to do our banking business."

"Isn't the driving, aren't the roads more dangerous at night?" she asked.

"No. Fewer cars is better. It will be all right. I am young enough, my eyes are still good," he laughed, "even if there are other parts of me that are worn down."

"You are only fifty six," she said.

"And you are only fifty five but you look to me like a young woman, twenty five, I think. Get me the bank book. I want to look at it, please," he said. "I will leave a little in the savings, that way the boy can deposit the money there."

"What about our daughter? She can do the same things as our son that have to do with responsibility."

"Of course she can, let them share or do it together, that is the best way. Do we have any obligations?" he asked.

"Only the taxes that are due in three months, and the insurance in January. Why are you going to take the money from the bank?" she asked. " The bank will send it to Mexico."

"They will not know where."

"They will know when we get there and tell them, Enrique."

"It will be nearly all our money. I do not trust the banks to move it quickly or safely. I do not want to go to Mexico and worry about it or worse, have a problem with a bank two thousand miles away. I want my money with me."

"We can have them make us a check and take that," she said.

"No, no check. Banks in Mexico are even worse than here. There could be difficulties with a check."

"I don't think that is true, people do it that way, I am sure. I don't want to travel with all that money. I will be afraid the whole time we are in the car that something will happen to us."

"It will be safer with me than with anyone else," Enrique said. "I will go to the bank on Monday after I have said goodbye to Mister Sinclair. I will go to American and get a new tool box for the money. We will hide it deep in the car."

"What about the border?" she asked. "What about when we are in Mexico? The guards are known for their dishonesty and los federales are even worse."

"That is why we will stop in Brownsville," he said. "We will put the money in one of the Mexican banks there, there are many Mexicans and it is close to Tampico. The banks there will be connected. I have never enjoyed the poor service from the Barnett here, they would probably lose our money if we allowed them the chance. In the army..."

"I am not happy with this at all," she said. "I think there are better ways to get our money to Mexico than carrying it in a tool box."

"No, Anita, there will be no opportunities for the banks to cheat us. The temptation to the people there is very great."

"You are a suspicious man. I did not know that."

"No, I am a cautious man. That is our money for our nursery and a house and a boat. The money will be safer with me than with anyone else. You may depend on that. Besides," he laughed, "I will buy a very strong tool box."

"Oh, Enrique," she said, "this is not the way."

"Call the children please," he said. "I am excited to talk to them. Tonight they can stay in their own bedrooms. We will leave Wednesday night, that will give us time to say goodbye to our friends and to pack our things. I want the boy and the girl here so they can have a good understanding of what is expected of them before we leave."

Anita put down the iron and went to get the bank book while Enrique stood looking out the kitchen window.

"How much do we have saved in that account?" he called out after her.

"You know as well as I do," she said, "more than forty thousand dollars."

"We will grow chrysanthemums," he said. "We are going to have a farm."

Chapter Seventeen

Chug was plenty pissed when he heard from the old man that Garza wasn't coming back at all, that he had the balls to quit them, on the spot, no notice, no advance warning, no discussion, just like a fuckin Mexican, he had said to the old man. It seriously fucked up his Monday. Garza's leaving was going to cause him a whole lot more work, a whole lot more involvement with the farm and the workers, which Chug wanted less to do with, not more. He figured he should have let the Mex slide, now he would have to find a competent mechanic, who was a good tractor driver, who could measure chemicals. Who could read, for Christ's sake, the directions for the powders and liquids, who wasn't a drunk, and could work the eleven month season, seven days a week, ten hours a day, all night maybe fifteen times, depending on winter frosts and cold winds. He would probably have to find another man too who could speak English and greaser, could get it straight to the workers what he was going to want them to do. Chug would be Goddamned if he was going fuck with them any more than he had to. He needed May up at the vegetable stand, that's where his cash came from. Besides, he didn't want her in the fields, mixing it up with the beaners.

Them fucking chemicals, he thought, they is a pain in the ass. The farm used Timek, Chlordane, Methyl-Bromide, and Diazanon. Every one was poisonous, toxic to humans, every one was spread or sprayed onto the flowers, the weeds, the ditches, every one beginning to be scrutinized for use by agricultural men, government men who came around checking labels and records and rates and applications. It was enough, Chug thought, to make him want to fuck somebody up. He would have to watch it personally for a few days or a few weeks, until he could find a nigger who could drive a tractor, he figured. The old man would fucking go insane if they didn't have clean flowers to ship for Thanksgiving. If the flowers were thin because they were choked with weeds, or there were holes in the buds because they had been eaten by thrip, or the leaves were spotted and blanched because of the mites.

"Managing the farm is what I sent you to college for," the old man had said. "It's what you've been prepared to do. There is nothing else you can do for the company until that farm is running smoothly," he had said.

What a fucking bunch of bullshit, thought Chug. What I'm prepared to do is shut that motherfucker down and build me a nightclub.

He had seen Enrique move the greasers around the farm like they were a herd of goats, now they was his goats. Fuck. Most of the beaners was new, the experienced ones, the ones that knew the drill, was working at other farms along Gladiolus and toward the beach. He'd had the problem start the year before. The little bastards just wouldn't stick. He figured they was lazy, he hoped the other farmers was gettin less than they money's worth. But now the ones that was here was his. Chug had not figured on the Mexican leaving, he thought the man would stay until he was old, and take the shit he threw at him, then he would dump him on his ass. Now he thought about the year ahead, his being responsible for the beaners. He inventoried the work ahead. There would be sticking, pinching, weeding and cutting, driving in the iron stakes, raising the wires that held the flowers upright, checking and changing five hundred light bulbs, cleaning the sprinkler heads, repairing overhead lines that had leaked or burst, checking the propane emitters, mending the shade cloth, digging trenches to get the rainwater off the field, servicing, fixing, maintaining, pumps and valves, the banding machine, the conveyor belt, the steam table, the delivery truck, the generators, the tractors and the spray rigs, the barn and the packing house, the mist house and the cold storage room. There would be problems with weeds, bugs, heat, cold, rain, Mesicans and his old man. Jesus Christ, Chug thought to himself, it just ain't gonna happen.

Chug tooled around town in the big Ford, thinking. Hitman stood in the back, gulping at the air as it went by. For the year he'd been there, since he had left school, Chug had mostly driven around in circles. Every day was nearly the same, he cruised the farm in the morning, asked Enrique how it was hanging, argued with him if he could start something and then took off. He would make his way to town, to the family offices on Palm Beach at the river, ogle Earlene's tits, get purchase orders for chemicals, tools, and fertilizers. He went nearly every day to Marine Hardware, to get something for the farm or some bullshit thing he wanted for his duplex, his truck, or his and Marvin's hunting camp. When it was close to noon he stopped at The Chicken Coop next to the bus station, drank his first cold beers, and sorted through the paperwork Earlene allowed him to have. He lived in a kind of a haze but he was used to it. He claimed to his drinking buddies that he had to be stupefied just so he could meet the greasers on they own illiterate level. Even next summer, he thought, he was going to have to be at the farm because the old man would want to grow his own okra, green beans, and sweet corn after the stems and roots of the last batch of flowers had been disced and buried into the sand. He recalled that last September he'd come to the field in the late afternoon, he'd drive real quiet, stop, shut down the diesel. He'd pull his twenty-two off the rack and shoot the quail that nibbled at the weed seed in the rows. The bob-whites just stayed and looked back at him while he picked them off one by one. He'd toss the little bodies to Hitman, the dog crushed them in a single bite and swallowed them whole. He felt like shooting something now and it wasn't no fucking bird. It seemed to him that the place was already out of control and the Mexican had only been gone two days. Everything the greasers did seemed slow and sloppy. They was problems, May had told him, with the rooted cuttings. They were wet but they were wilted, wouldn't stand up, and they was problems, the fucking bitch had told him, with the beds, there weren't enough ready for all the flowers they had to stick. Chug laughed at that. If the fucking cuttings died, he figured, they

84

wouldn't be no problem with space. What the fuck, he wasn't gonna drive no tractor. He was Goddamned if he was going to have to work twice, three times as hard as he had for the same amount of money. The old man hadn't said a fucking thing this mornin about more money, he remembered. Even if they sold a shitload of vegetables in the season and he made plenty, he figured he wouldn't have the time or the energy to spend it, he'd be so fuckin tired and pissed off at the beaners. He would go to The Hill he decided, and find a nigger that could at least drive the John Deere and maybe know something about pipes and valves and all that shit. That would be a start. When he went back to the farm he would have a look at the cuttings. He was going to get on with it, he figured, but he might have to kill him a couple of Mesicans along the way, maybe before Christmas.

Chug had known the Garza man and his wife, since the years when he was supposed to be growing up. They bought gifts for him when he was a little boy, for Chug and his brother too, who had been appreciative and respectful, but aloof also in his own Sinclair way. At Christmas, birthdays, graduations, the boys got pointed boots and cowboy hats and hand-tooled leather belts with big buckles, from Texas. One year, Enrique gave each of them a new rod and reel. Then the Garzas had quit giving, just like that. Chug had never thanked them once for anything, ever. He never showed them a gesture of anything warmer than toleration, controlled impatience. What he got, he figured, was owed him for being a Sinclair. Fuck. He was part of the package that let Enrique and his Mesican wife and they kids have food on the table and a roof over they heads, thanks to Royal Farms, when they could have been shittin beans and cornmeal in the desert in Mexico. Just like a Mesican, he thought, to pick up and leave at the beginning of the season instead of the end. I get a chance, he said to himself, I'm going to kick that old boy's ass. They should have give me a lot more, he thought to himself, instead of they fucking kids. Maybe I wouldn't be so inclined to violence right now.

He knew about the Garza children, the old man had told him that morning that just Enrique and his old lady were leaving, the young Garza's were staying. The old man told him he thought the girl worked at South Seas on Captiva and the boy worked at the new grocery store on Cleveland Avenue.

"I don't give a shit where they work," Chug had told him, "unless they want to come out to the farm and pick up the slack for they daddy."

Chug figured the boy was a pussy, couldn't take the heat and the sun. They was selfish too, he figured, else they would have gone to Mesico with the others. He'd see that Mesican boy around sometime, he guessed, that little fucker would need a doctor.

He found out about the money from May, late Monday. He would have found out about it eventually, but the timing was good for him, bad for the Garzas, they were not leaving town for another two days. Chug had stopped at the vegetable stand to pick up his dough and a barrel of unsellable, spoiled things for his pigs. Hitman stood shock still and glared at May, followed her movements with his yellow eyes. Whenever she could, as she moved around the stalls, she tried to put something between her and the dog. Kids on Honda motorcycles went by, on the way from The Villas to Fort Myers Beach. Old vans with colored maids went by on the way back to town, the women were sleeping, daydreaming, or planning supper for their families. A tractor went by, its wide load of gassing pipes swayed back and forth across the single center line of the road. A red Corvair passed the stand, a blonde haired girl, very, very lovely and friendly, waved at May and the dog and Chug but did not slow down.

"You all been busy today?" Chug asked.

"Yessir, jéfe, two hundred dollars so far. I'll stay open another hour," said May.

"That's good, that's about how much money I need to get myself feelin good, less you pay of course."

"You feel bad, Chug? We thought you'd be real happy today," she said.

"Well I ain't yet," Chug answered, "but I'm fixin to be."

The vegetable stand had been Chug's idea. He had told the old man

86

that the land out front was wasted, it wouldn't cost the old man anything much. Chug was sure to not tell him it would make him anything either. Chug said he needed extra income for investments, the old man let the bullshit slide. Chug had a nose for cash, though. He set up a network with his asshole farmer buddies, and drivers and foremen at the loading docks at the market. He gave them a little cash or pills or an hour with the colored whores, in return for big sacks and bags and boxes of fresh vegetables and fruit. He picked the goods out himself, that was his thing, and carried them in his truck out to the stand. Just in case someone became interested in something that didn't concern them, one look from Chug and Hitman was enough to caused the people at the market to not be interested in anything the boss from Royal Glads did. His reputation and bearing pronounced him dangerous.

He had Enrique build the thing, the first summer he came to the farm as the patrón. He laid it out for the Mexican on paper and asked him what was he waitin for? Enrique augured the holes, went to Florida Power and Light for rock hard telephone poles, cut them for length, concreted them into the sand and the rock underneath. He used the farm tractor and the farm men. They framed in a roof and fastened down tin sheets. Chug called Cement Industries, they delivered several loads of drain field rock that the men spread with shovels and then raked smooth for a floor. He had the Mexican build shelves and stalls. They brought out the oldest of the flower carts and painted them green. Fine sand blew from the top of forty acres, stuck to the wet paint, so the surfaces of the buckets and carts were rough, before more sand began to smooth them. Royal Glads paid for the stand, the profits went to Chug. He cleaned up during the flower season. He had the women bring fresh cut mums out front, and set them in the buckets filled with water. The flowers were cut as "shorts" in the field according to his instructions, not grown long enough for regular customers, Chug told the old man, culls, miscounted, or ripped off, he said as often as he wanted, by some dock hand in Atlanta or Jacksonville, and the old man had let it by.

Women bought the flowers, especially yankee women down for the winter. Almost everyone who passed by stopped at the stand sooner or later. They came back after that because of the freshness of the vegetables, the sharp bite of the fruit that Chug had stolen at the market. Chug made lots of money there, more than he made as general manager of Royal Glads. It was cash money, no bullshit with taxes, twenties, tens, and silver dollars every day. In season with the yankees and the flowers he made three hundred, four hundred a week. May got two hundred for her trouble and all the peaches she could eat.

"We about through here," he said, after studying what he needed to get for the morning. "I'm gone up the road an have a drink, be back in about a hour, then we gonna go to the lake."

"Not today, Chug, it's too damn hot for that. Besides, you've got that damn dog with you. How can I enjoy myself with him there?"

"May, Goddamnit, we gone go to the lake. I'm fuckin up to here with people tellin me what I'm gone do and not gone do. I tell you what though, I'll take Hitman on home an leave his sorry ass there. How'd that be? Then you an me can get to it."

"Chug, it's hot. I've been here all day, while you've been driving around in your truck. Can't we get together tomorrow?"

"No, we can get together today, like I want, or you can try to get you job back peelin shrimp up at the restaurant. Maybe you make sixty, seventy dollars a week choppin lettuce and washin dishes. How you like that?"

"Okay, okay, we'll go. But you be back in an hour. I'm tired and I want to go to my shitty little shack and lay down. Will you bring me back a bottle of wine? Cold. I need to taste something different, all I've had all day is that smelly water. God, I'm sick of that smell."

"Shit, May," Chug said, "that's Florida, that's what Florida smells like."

"Well whatever it is, I've smelled it and tasted all of it I can stand for one day. It reminds me of something rotting," she said.

"I'll bring you wine, baby, an I'm comin back with a stiff dick too."

"I want the air-conditioning on."

"I want you ass, May," he laughed.

"The price for me there is the same, boss, five hundred dollars, and it might go up. I was thinking of letting you watch me. We'll talk about it when you get back. Go. Get rid of Hitman. I'm ready for today to be over."

Chug looked at the girl and smiled.

"Do I need a rubber?" he asked.

"You won't get near me without one," she said."

An hour and a half later they were at the lake behind the farm. The truck was parked facing the water, the late afternoon September sun was behind them. May was naked, Chug had his shirt open, his pants slid down around his boots. The truck was running, Chug had the air- conditioner on high, it was cold inside the cab. He was drunk. He had stopped at the groceria in Harlem Heights on his way to get rid of Hitman, bought a bottle of rum that he mixed half and half with coke and ice. He took big swallows from a mason jar. In an hour he had drunk most of the bottle. He stopped at the same store on his way back for the girl. He bought her a bottle of wine and a six pack of beer for himself. He glared at the beaner behind the counter through bloodshot eyes behind dark glasses. Chug was ready to slap the fucker because he wouldn't speak English.

He was slouched in the truck with a beer. He was too drunk, he figured, the son of a bitch wouldn't get hard. May leaned back against the passenger door, her legs were spread to the cool air and to Chug, but only one was touching her today, she decided. She put one long brown leg up over the seat and rubbed Chug's head with her toes, put her other foot on the steering wheel. It was very late in the afternoon, but the low sun was still scorching, gnats and mosquitoes were still hiding in the shade.

"Everybody is going to miss Enrique," she said.

"Fuck if I am."

"They have saved their money forever, and now they can retire. That's what I'm going to do," she said."

"You drunk May, what money you talkin about? What you got to save with?" he snorted.

"Like the Garzas, I'm saving everything I can so I can leave this place."

"Well you ain't leavin with you ass, that's mine first. After you let me fuck you there I don't much give a shit what you do."

May kicked at Chug's head with her foot and he laughed.

"No," he said, "I'm just foolin, I believe once I get some of that, it'll be a thing I'll want regular."

"Everyone says they have a lot of money that they are taking to Mexico. If they can do it so can I." She didn't want to talk about her ass.

"Yeah," he said, "I know the motherfucker is goin to Mesico an I'm sick of hearin about it. Who the fuck you think is gonna have to pick up his slack? Me, that's who, I'm gone have to work twice as hard around this fuckin place, just to keep up."

"Your time will come to retire, if you live long enough."

"I ain't so much interested in then, I'm interested in now, an I'm real pissed off about that old boy quittin me and the old man at the beginning of season."

"But now it's all yours to run the way you want it."

"I run it the way I wanted before. Havin the Mesican just give me extra time for more important things."

"They are going to live well in Mexico, Enrique is going to grow flowers," she said.

"What?" Chug exploded, choked on his beer. "What's he gone do?"

"They're going to grow plants and flowers, wherever they decide is the best for it. It was Anita's idea. They have enough money to start a farm, more money then anybody has ever left this shitty place with," she said.

"Well I'll be Goddamned," said Chug. "Growin his own flowers after learnin all our secrets. Probably try to steal Royal Glads customers up north from fuckin Mesico too. Nothin costs nothin in Mesico, they can raise flowers cheaper then shit, cheaper then anybody here. I'll be Goddamned," he said.

"I wish I was going away," said May. She looked out at the lake.

"Well fuck," he said, "how much money has they got?"

"Who?"

"Who the fuck you think, May? Them Garzas, how much they saved up for they farm?"

"I don't know. Thousands. They would have to have thousands I'll

90

bet. Enrique is so tight with his money people say he squeaks when he walks," she giggled.

Chug spit out the beer he was holding in his mouth and laughed too.

"I wish I was going away," May said again, mostly to herself. "Somewhere. California, maybe. Even Mexico would be okay as long as I was by the ocean."

"You got more Puerto Rican in you than anythin else. Why don't you want to go to fuckin Puerto Rico?"

"Because it's hot, like here. I want to live where it's cool."

"Well fuck," he said, "California and Mesico is mostly deserts. You gone live in the desert?"

"Not everywhere there is desert," she said, "you're too drunk to think straight. California is right beside the biggest ocean in the world."

"Jesus Christ, they's a ocean offa Fort Myers Beach."

"It's not an ocean, Chug. The Gulf is a big green puddle of salt-water mixed with run-off from the river, and water from the ground that smells like rotten eggs and turns everything brown. I'm talking about a blue ocean, not a shitty green one."

"Speakin of water," he said, "I gotta piss."

Chug swung himself out of the truck and stood, swayed, beside it, facing away so he wouldn't be tempted to piss on his tire but he was sloppy in the shaking, dribbled piss down his leg and onto his jeans bundled at his cowboy boots. May had hopped out the other side and squatted, holding onto the door for balance. She was a little drunk. She brushed the droplets of her water from her dark pussy and got back in the truck quickly, before the bugs could find her. She spread her legs out like she had before. She reached out and turned the air-conditioner down so it was not so cold. Chug got back in, slapped at mosquitoes around his head. He sat behind the steering wheel and looked at his dick. He was having difficulty with his head bent down like that, he couldn't seem to focus. He slapped himself lightly in the face a couple of times and looked over at May.

"Whoowhee, I'm drunk, I got me a whiskey dick, darlin. It just won't stand up. That don't happen very much. Maybe I'll get a boner, maybe

91

not. You said you was gonna do somethin special for me, what was you was talkin about? Was you gonna blow me?"

May laughed at Chug, it was good that she was a little drunk or she would leave the twenty behind and head for the restaurant. She was amused that even now, Chug could surprise her with his pig ways.

"I'll make myself come for you, Chug," she said. "It'll be crazy. You'll have something to tell your friend Marvin about. But it'll be forty. We had a good day, you can afford it. You just save yourself there for next time, or for one of your other girlfriends. Right now," she licked her lips, "you just watch. Can you do that, baby, would you like that? For forty?"

"It's fine by me Goddamnit, let's see the show. My pecker's gone to sleep but my eyes is startin to get hard just lookin at you pussy. Forty? Fuck, forty ain't no problem." He reached out, squeezed her breasts then put a hand between her legs. " One day real soon I'm gone buy what I ain't had. Consider the extra as a binder on our agreement," he said.

May pushed his hand away, spread her legs as wide as she could get them. The horsehair was scratching her on her ass, she reached down for the wad of clothes that was her blouse and shorts and put them under her. She began to rub her pussy. She swallowed down the last of the wine and placed the bottle between her legs. She looked at Chug then down at her breasts. She began to tease the nipples, which were already hard with the air-conditioning. She squeezed a breast with both hands, slid her hands down to the tip and pinched it. She kept it up, going from one breast to the other, pulled on the nipples to make them longer and stiffer. Chug took a long pull from his beer, belched loudly, set the beer beside him on the seat. He put both hands around his limp dick and squeezed but nothing was happening. He let his dick go, put both hands on the steering wheel. He looked at May sideways, trying to take it all in.

She left her breasts, she rubbed the heel of one hand just above the swollen, dark gash of her pussy. She dropped the wine bottle to the floor. Her other hand trailed up and down the length of her leg that rested on the back of the seat. Her hips began to move up and down. She returned to her breasts and began teasing the nipples again, first one then the other. She looked at Chug. Her eyes were as heavy-lidded and swollen as his, she licked her lips and moaned.

"Watch this, baby," she said.

She began trailing circles over her clit, big, loose, soft circles, then she got serious, she tightened the circles down to where she was drumming, bouncing, scratching the ends of her fingers against the nub at the top of her pussy. She looked down at herself.

Chug's mouth was very dry. He sucked at the empty beer can but didn't want to reach for another. She looked for his eyes, grit her teeth when she found them, her thighs were beginning to tremble too, she began to rub herself even harder.

"They God," said Chug. He had forgotten about his own body, he was intent on what May was showing him.

Finally, gasping and laughing, she came hard for several seconds, came again after the first rush, slowed down, stopped. She was breathing through her mouth and flared nostrils, her eyes were wide in surprise and arousal. Her shoulders sagged, then her arms, at last she let go of herself. She drew her legs up under her and put her blouse over her shoulders. She held her shorts in her lap. She looked out at the water, it was closer to dark. Entertainment is cheap at the lake, she thought. She looked at Chug, smiled and laughed.

"I'm embarrassed," she said. "I think I got too excited."

Chug was almost sober. His hands had clenched the steering wheel so hard he thought he might have bent it, he had to make himself think to let it go. He rubbed his palms on the seat cover and reached for a beer from the cooler. He took a long drink from the can, set it down, shook his head slowly back and forth. He looked down at his dick, it was thicker he believed, but he still couldn't cut butter with it, let alone get it into May. Just as well, he thought, that there was something else all by itself.

"Goddamn, May, that's the wildest thing I ever seen."

May giggled again. She was glad he wasn't going to want to fuck her.

"Ain't this a great country, May? I feel like I'm king of the hill now, although they ain't a hill around, except if you count where the niggers live in town. Before I was so pissed off I couldn't see straight. Now I'm thinkin again."

He put his dark sunglasses back on and looked out the back window of the truck at where the sun had finally set. He drained the beer, tossed it out the window and opened another, but he let it sit in his hand, he didn't drink from it. May put on her blouse, wriggled into her shorts, while Chug just sat there with his jeans around his cowboy boots. She began to laugh softly and when he turned to look at her, she pointed at his useless dick. His eyes slitted down. He pulled his jeans up, fastened the steel button and buckled his belt. He reached into his back pocket, pulled out his wallet and fumbled for two twenties.

"Damndest thing I ever saw, here May," he said, "worth ever fuckin penny."

She laughed out loud at herself and the man in the truck who had just paid her to play with her own body. He's right, she thought, sometimes it was a great country.

"Just a question, though," he said. "How much has they got? The Garzas, how much money they got to start they flower farm?"

"Forty more than you, daddy, but you'll never miss it. Enrique would shoot himself before he would spend any money on a girl show."

"Do people say they got a lot of money?"

"Wait, Chug. I don't know anything more than what I said. People say they have a lot of money. They are going to Mexico to start a farm or a nursery, that's all I know."

"But old Enrique, he don't like to be away from his money, does he?"

May opened the door and got out.

"I'm going to walk home from here," she said, "I need to stretch my legs back out. It was good for me Chug, in the air-conditioning. I guess if I was cool all the time I wouldn't think so much about leaving," she stuck out her tongue at him and laughed. "See you tomorrow boss man."

Chug rolled down the tinted window and called after her.

"I'm gone ask you one more time, darlin. Is they a lot of money?"

She shrugged her shoulders, then disappeared behind the peppers. Chug sat for a long time at the pond behind the field, drinking beer, tossing the cans out for the Mesicans to pick up. Finally he put the truck in gear, he turned it around, and drove along the perimeter road. When he left Royal Glads, he didn't bother to put the chain back up. He drove slowly back to his duplex, drunk, wondering how he would spend the money.

94

Chapter Eighteen

Marvin Johnson believed he was Chug's friend, although Chug did not think of Marvin or anyone else with that much sentimentality. They had met in Gainesville, trying to pledge the Kappa Alphas, but even that group of southern traditionalists found the two young men from way down in Florida too overly steeped in racism, bigotry, and hatred to fit in. They were discouraged, rejected, shitcanned from joining the fraternity. They had, however, found each other, they remained drinking and whoring and burglary buddies until Marvin flunked out of everything he was enrolled in and returned to Punta Gorda. Marvin was short, overweight, ineffective, he was easily led by the more hardened, more dangerous Chug. Marvin's daddy was the sheriff of Charlotte County, had been for many years. It was a sparsely populated, spread-out jurisdiction whose center of government was Punta Gorda, a quiet, nothing-bad-happening little town at the mouth of the Peace River. Sheriff Johnson was as careless about his responsibility for Marvin as the old man was for Chug, but he was trying to work with the boy. He made him a deputy, and had him almost permanently assigned to the graveyard shift five nights a week, nearly always on Fridays and Saturdays. If Marvin was not working, those were the nights he was most prone to be stumbling, puking drunk, or brought to his house by the city police for disorderly conduct. He could be killed, the sheriff believed, his death less likely to be from confrontation with dangerous criminals, than from an oak tree in his way. Marvin was a besotted, fat

95

little fuck with small brains. His flaws were appreciated by Chug, who included Marvin in his routine when it was convenient. When he was with Chug, Marvin believed himself to be inspired, protected, and there was the badge, which, although it had not been previously used by the two for any significant personal gain, was in his pocket. They had discussed many drunken times, the opportunities that having the badge presented.

Marvin drove his big Ford with the lights and the siren around the town a couple of times each night he was on duty. He crossed the river to Port Charlotte, drove north and west almost to Englewood and Lemon Bay, or he would go north and east, take 74 past the Babcock Ranch, and cruise up and down 31, looking for yankee speeders to fleece. He usually finished his shift in the sheriff's office, sleeping or with his eyes glazed over, flipping through the pages of the hunting magazines to which his daddy subscribed and had mailed directly to the jail. Marvin liked to look at the hunting magazines and he liked to be in the woods, doing some hunting himself. He was not bad in the pine scrub and palmetto. He kept a kennel of dogs. He ran the string whenever he had a chance and had not gotten himself too drunk to drive and walk and shoot. Usually he followed the dogs as long as he could in his jeep. They chased and then cornered the wild pigs that were as thick as range cattle in the palmetto and the underbrush. He would get out of the jeep, follow the sounds of the snarling dogs and the screaming hog. When the dogs had the pig on the ground, teeth sunk into its ears, throat, tail and balls, Marvin or Chug or another cowboy would step down hard on its face while the dogs held it still. The partner tied the snout first then lashed its feet together. The bound, muzzled hog was turned over, nutted without ceremony, and hoisted up on a pine pole and carried to the jeep for the ride back to town. The castrated hogs were softened up, fattened on sweet corn and vegetables and fruit from Chug's stand on Gladiolus. Marvin and Chug shared the enterprise and shared the driving back and forth to feed the pigs. They rented a pen from a junkyard dealer behind Suncoast Estates, the shittiest part of North Fort Myers. After a few months, the wild hogs were domesticated and healthy, their

96

coats sleek and their bodies heavy with meat from good eating. Marvin and Chug got to shoot them then, right through the hogs' thick skulls, using Chug's big forty-five. The boys enjoyed the killing. They laughed at the variety of ways the hogs reacted to a bullet in the brain. They bled them there, gutted them, buried the offal, and drove the carcass to a good butcher in East Fort Myers whose customers were enthusiastic about the flavor of the meat of Marvin's and Chug's hogs. They were encouraged by the butcher to bring more. It was the fruit, he said, that gave the meat its taste and composition. Chug and Marvin took the money for the butchered pigs and spent it on beer, whores, and bolito, and hamburgers from McDonald's.

Other times, without the dogs, they hunted from the jeep. They shot at more pigs, blasted turkey and skinny deer. When they took these to the butcher, he told them the turkeys they brought were shot to pieces and worthless, and that he didn't want any does. They laughed. Chug told the man they were lesbian deer and deserved killing. After that they just let the deer lay where they had been killed. Sometimes Chug would come up late at night while Marvin was working, to ride with him in the patrol car. They cruised fast, over the lonesome county roads. They would finish the deputy's shift just before dawn, barreling across 74, and up and down 31, swerving in the powerful Ford to hit raccoons and opossum and foxes that were trying to cross the asphalt just to get to the other side. When the water table was high in the late summer and the ditches along the roads were flooded, turtles and otters were on the move. They ran them over too. The turtles were crushed by the big tires with a loud pop. The otters stopped, turned to look at the lights, were startled, scared, then broken into bloody pieces by the sheriff's car, traveling at seventy, eighty miles an hour. Marvin would be at the wheel, whooping and hollering, Chug beside him with his bottle, pointing out the next critter to kill. Hitman would be locked in the back seat with the heavy steel mesh between him and Marvin or the deputy would not let him in the car. The dog's ugly face pressed against the screen. He would try to bark, and bite at the metal grid.

Marvin didn't have the kind of money Chug did, but he was anxious to get some. He wanted new tires for his hunting jeep, big fat ones so he

97

would be up over the palmetto. He wanted a new rifle, a thirty-aught Marlin with a scope, and he wanted a new shooter, a forty-five with a clip like the one Chug had. He wanted new furniture, eight-tracks, and some jewelry like Chug wore. He wanted to go to Disneyworld and to Daytona for the races and to Fort Lauderdale in the spring to look at young pussy, and he wanted to go out to Colorado and kill a mule deer like he had seen in the hunting magazines. Chug had been telling him for a long time that a good score would come along, they would make some real fucking money. It was only a matter of time, Chug had told him. What good was the badge, Chug asked, if he never got to use it?

Chapter Nineteen

C hug called Tuesday morning for a boy who worked at Barnett Bank. He told the boy he wanted to know if the Garza man had withdrawn his money. When the boy balked about giving up the information, Chug told him he had about three minutes to get it, or his next call would be for the manager of the bank or the boy's father, to tell them that the boy went to The Hill looking for queer niggers. He would spread it around to his buddies that there was an authentic black dick sucking faggot at Barnett on Cypress Lake, and leave them to figure out what to do with they money, and what to do about him.

"But that's not true," the frail boy stammered into the phone.

"Listen, Goddamnit," said Chug, "git me that information or I'll make it true."

The teller told Chug he had been there when the Mexican man had come in. Yes, he had said, most of the savings had been withdrawn. There had been some confusion with the head teller, who didn't want the man to take the money. The Mexican walked right into the manager's office, they shook hands, they spoke together for a few minutes. The teller brought Mister Garza bundled cash, the boy said. He added that three thousand was left in the account. Chug told him he really didn't give a fuck about how much was left in the bank. He wanted to know, right now, he said, how much was out of the bank. Forty thousand, the boy told him quickly.

"Certificate, bond, check, money order, what?" said Chug.

Cash, the boy had told him, new hundred dollar bills, the boy said.

"When?" Chug asked, his mouth was suddenly dry.

Yesterday, the boy had said, late morning.

Chug told the nervous boy to forget about the conversation, that he'd just been curious because of the farm and all.

"Doesn't sound like he needs unemployment, or a retirement bonus," the boy snickered into the phone. He was relieved that Verdell Sinclair was finished with him.

No, Chug told the boy, he ain't gettin no bonus.

He went to the vegetable stand, he told May to have the beaners start pulling the rest of the shade cloth out of the barn. They was ten acres of it, he figured, it should keep them busy for a couple of days, he told her. He wanted the cloth spread out, piece by piece in the turn-around, swept off, mended where it was torn, grommets sewn in where they was missing, carried out to the field and hung up. Every piece is the same size, he told her, so they is no way they can fuck it up. Chug told May he had business for Royal Farms in LaBelle, that he would come back late that night, get his money from her in the morning and then he would have to go back to LaBelle, maybe even have to stay over. He went to his duplex, washed down a Quaalude with a beer, called Marvin and told him to meet him at eight at the Snack House for some meatloaf, then they was going out. Chug had a new girl that Marvin would want to fuck. They were going to raise hell, get drunk, and talk a little about a thing that was happening. When he was finished with Marvin, he threw everything that was on his bed to the floor and fell forward with his face sideways on the rumpled sheet. He blinked his eyes for a while, thinking, then he went to sleep.

Chug and Marvin had a good start on a long night by ten. They had each swallowed a black beauty after the meatloaf and were drinking fast.

"I'm gone fix that motherfucker," Chug told Marvin. "I'm gone fix him good. He's done about three things to piss me off, any one of em is enough by itself to earn him a whippin, but he's done three, an now I'm

100

gone fuck that boy up," he said.

"What we gonna do?" asked Marvin. "I mean about the details."

"We talk about that tomorra. We gonna meet at the marina out on Burnt Store in the afternoon, an you gone make sure you workin tomorra night," said Chug, "that's the big thing. I tole you enough for now."

"Fuck," said Marvin, "I work nearly every night."

"We gone need the sheriff's car an you in uniform and that silver badge to get us where we want. Can you deal with that, Marvin? You understan what we gone do?"

"Hell yes. You ain't talkin to a school boy," he snorted. "But why cain't we discuss it more now?"

"I ain't ready to discuss it now, that's why. I want you to have a good time tonight, boy, we ain't gonna talk any more business."

"We gettin some pussy?" asked Marvin.

"We on our way," said Chug.

They were in the old man's car, a light blue Pontiac four-door, a Bonneville as long as an outboard. The old man liked big cars, he especially liked the Bonneville. He had a license plate made for the front that read Royal Farms, and was bordered by painted gladiolus flowers. He was gone out of town, Earlene had driven him to Page Field for the plane ride to Tallahassee. Chug and Marvin went by the office after eating at the Snack House. Chug knew the old man was traveling, he had a set of keys for the Bonneville. Chug figured he could tool around with Marvin and the girls without being crowded in the front seat of his truck. Fuck the old man.

They drove slowly out to The Hill to pick up Chug's colored whores. He pulled into the parking lot of a little grocery store and blew the horn. Two girls came from around the side, out from the high weeds and the dark of the cover of the mangos. They walked in front of the lights of the car. One leaned down to look in the driver's window. Chug pointed with his thumb over his shoulder to the back seat, the girls got in. Chug headed the Bonneville back toward the town and the river.

They were Chug's girls sometimes, they also belonged to a colored pimp. Chug fronted him cash for dope deals. Chug shilled the girls to the high school boys in North Fort Myers. He buddied up to the dumbest football players and the rednecks, did public relations on the idea of genuine nigger poontang. Shit, he'd told them, he'd even deliver so they didn't need to go out to Anderson Avenue an be worryin an gittin in trouble. He got some of the action from the girls, who did not object to pulling trains for the white boys, and Chug found an opportunity to wander the family's house where the boys were having their fun. Quickly, expertly, he went through drawers, cabinets, and closets, looking for something to steal that would not soon be missed, most often a piece of jewelry from the bottom of the pile, that he would have melted down with a handful of others and fashioned into a new bracelet or ring. He stole silver dollars and rare coins, just to keep his hand in, he was always on the look out for cash.

"You folks gone," he would tell the boys gathered to make the deal, "you all want to have a party? Shit boys, I'll bring em to ya and carry em away when you all fucked out or ashamed of youselves, whichever come first," he'd laugh. "Anythin missin though, that ain't my problem. Maybe you friends playin jokes on you." He narrowed his eyes, and the boys understood that part of the price of the girls was Chug on the loose in their parents' houses.

Usually the boys were so drunk and horny when he found them in their cars parked across from the Exhibition Hall, or under the dark canopy of the mahogany trees along the river, that they were talking about each other's sisters, if they could get one of them to come across. The whores were easy to line up, but if the boys didn't have a place that they could use because no one was home, Chug told them no dice, to go home and jack-off. Chug made a lot of money putting the boys together with the colored whores and some decent loot besides.

"Where they got bolito on Friday?" Chug asked the girls in back.

"It's at Twenty One," said Precious. "You all want me to put sumpin down for you, Chug?"

"Hell yes, I'm gone have a shitload of money for the numbers on Friday. Meet Marvin, girls. Me an him are bettin on ourselves."

Marvin turned around in his seat and took in the girls. He reached out and stroked their legs where he could find them. He ran his hands all the way up to the wire.

"Whoowhee," he said, as he turned around and laughed, "poontang."

Chug looked at Marvin and grinned with him. "An," he said, "I got a little somethin for you to do tomorra night, Precious. It's a easy job, don't even have to fuck nobody, you just got to watch somethin for me. I tell you more about it later," he laughed, "towards mornin."

"You all do what he says," Marvin said to the girls, "an you have money for bolito too."

The sheriff of Lee County was rumored to make a good income for himself and several of his high ranking deputies from bolito. It was a Cuban numbers game that attracted crowds of colored men and Puerto Ricans who wanted to gamble, but were not welcome at the dog track or by the bookies at the Elk's Club. The games began after dark and lasted long into the night, at different bars in the shadow of Anderson Avenue on Fridays and Saturdays. Men came, some with their women, to gamble and drink from as far away as Moore Haven and Pahokee. Once in a while the sheriff would have a game busted up, for the newspaper, but it was back in business at another club in a week, and the sheriff got another sack of money from Chug, who handled his pickups. The money had been horribly earned, clutched for a moment, then permanently lost, by cane cutters, field hands, and construction laborers. Marvin's father told him he didn't want a game in Punta Gorda. Just because the money was good, he'd said, it wasn't reason enough to have a bunch of coloreds and Spanish all in one bar. There were too many problems when you had em holed up in one place, gambling, drinking, shooting-up, fighting and cutting each other over anything, especially pussy. He liked it better when the coloreds were spread out, and so should his deputies, he'd said.

Chug wanted to drink, drive and make a big loop. The Pontiac was powerful, big inside, there was lots of room for them to stretch. City police, deputies, and highway patrol knew the old man's car and his fancy license plate. Chug guessed that nobody would fuck with them short of a head-on. He was a ace, he thought to himself, he could do what he fucking pleased. Right now what he wanted was to hit several bars between downtown and Bonita Springs, blast up the new causeway from Bonita Beach to Fort Myers Beach, and close down the Surf Club.

103

They would call a cab for the girls from the beach, he told Marvin. The Surf Club didn't cotton to many, he'd said, especially a couple of town boys with colored whores.

Chug and Marvin and the girls stopped at The Chicken Coop, next to Trailways, had a few drinks, then tooled down Cleveland to Johnny Shay's where the women were allowed inside again and could drink. It had nothing to do with the fact that they were whores, there were plenty in there besides Precious and Baby, but these were colored girls, not every bar along 41 was as cordial. The girls were not extremely dark skinned, but they smelled very strongly from the perfume they wore and the musk. They wore cotton dresses and pumps rather than the tiny leather skirts and the stiletto heels that the high school boys preferred. Chug had told them not to dress like they was from a Miami slum, if they wanted to drink inside the clubs where they could all get in.

. They drove south, after Johnny Shay's, down the highway, stopped at The Oasis and then the Spanish Main. They listened to a band called The Tropics. The bar was dark, people shouted to be heard over the music. They drove further south, to the outskirt of town, stopped at the L and N. Marvin and Chug went in alone, the girls waited in the car. Drunk, listing when they came out, Chug and Marvin hopped into the front seat of the Bonneville and leered at the girls in the back. Chug opened it up on the straightaway from Estero to Bonita Springs, they did not see another car until the north end of the little town. He parked the car under a big banyan tree and went into The Dome by himself. A few minutes later he came out with a bottle of whiskey and four quarts of beer in a big paper sack. He drove the car south a few more blocks, passed the Wonder Gardens and Shangri La, turned west onto Bonita Beach Road. After a few miles, the road curved north at the Gulf of Mexico.

They passed the beach cottages, seagrape covered lots, and coconut palms that lined Hickory Boulevard. He let it all out on the new causeway, the heavy body of the Pontiac bounced up and down with the rises and dips in the road and coming on and off the bridges. Chug slowed down on Black Island, just before the big bridge that spanned Big Carlos Pass and led onto Fort Myers Beach. The car fishtailed on a sand trail that led deep into a coastal jungle of Spanish stopper and joewood, cat'sclaw, yucca, and mangrove. He stopped the car inches away from the trunk of a big cabbage palm, turned the radio up and the air-conditioner down. He looked over at Marvin, slumped, stoned, slouched against the passenger door.

"Marvin," he said, "get the fuck back there with that skinny girl. She's waitin on you. Precious, you all shuck out of that dress there and git up here with me. You all climb over the seat," he said, "an don't nobody open that fucking door."

"What's wrong wif de door, Chug?" asked Precious, already wriggling out of her cotton, naked underneath, moist between her legs.

"Mosquitoes," he said. "They so bad down here a man could die. Be a good place to bring that motherfucker, Marvin. Bring im down here, strip off his clothes, tie im up and leave his ass for the skeeters and the ants to eat. Jesus Christ, eat alive by skeeters and ants, what a fuckin way to go."

"That's right," said Marvin. "Here they about as bad as in the woods in Charlotte, damn near as bad in the daytime as at night. Mosquitoes can fuckin kill ya. They ever figure how to get rid of them bastards, this part of the state gone bust wide open with yankees."

Marvin let Precious come over the seat first so he could take a long lick at her ass as she straddled it, then he tried to bite a nipple, kiss her, get a finger in her bristly cunt and his tongue in her ear until Chug told to him to quit fuckin around and get in back. He finally settled in next to Baby, the skinny one, who had also pulled her dress over her head. The air-conditioner blew cool over the four, but the car stunk of spilled beer, cigars, cigarettes, whiskey breath, and cheap perfume. Then a new smell mingled with the others. It was pungent, acrid, like stale piss in a toilet.

"What you want me to do, Chug?" Precious asked, undoing his jeans and reaching for his long white dick. She wrapped both hands around it, and only covered half.

"Blow me," he said.

Marvin had the skinny girl climb on top and ride him, the fat one slobbered over Chug's pecker like it was candy. Try as she could, she wasn't able to get much of it in her mouth, so she used drool and her tongue and her hands and faked it. They needed to give the white boys a good time. Shitpeel, Precious thought, Chug was her pimp, he made her a lot of money setting her up with horny rednecks and high school boys. He had to be able to brag about how good she was, how she could suck the milk through a coconut husk.

Chug had paid them as soon as they had gotten in the car, both girls folded the money and put it in their shoes. They were carrying nothing when he picked them up, except a For Sale sign, an orange and black thing that Baby thought was funny. She flashed the sign at cars with white people in them on their way to Lehigh Acres, not exactly strategically placed, not far enough away from The Hill. Sometimes she showed them some pussy. The sign was on the floor now, along with the empty beer bottles, empty peanut bags and cigar wrappers. Precious was thinking about a tip, maybe a little extra for the extra.

Marvin hadn't thought to put on a rubber, he was worried for a moment about getting the clap. The skinny girl humped him, ground her pelvic bone hard onto his, raised herself up and slid herself down on the sorry excuse of the thing he called his dick. She'd seen plenty bigger and felt she'd been cheated. She started working to get herself off, the deputy from Punta Gorda could take care of himself, she figured. She moved her hips around and around, forward and backward, put her hands down there to rub herself and felt it. Marvin's pecker was softened. She looked closely at his face in the dim light. His jaw hung open, his eyes were closed, his head lay slack against the back rest. Marvin had passed out, but in Precious hands and mouth, Chug's dick was just getting bigger and bigger.

"You frens gone to sleep, Chug," said Baby. She climbed off of Marvin and leaned forward into the front, she rubbed Chug's bare chest with her hands, pinched his nipples, licked his neck and stuck her wet fingers in his ear.

"Git up here then," he said, "they's room enough for three."

Baby climbed over the seat. Precious scooted herself around so there was room for both of them on the leather cushions with their asses stuck up in the air. They took turns burying their faces in Chug's lap. Finally Precious raised her head and pushed Baby's away.

"Don't waste this big hard on comin in her mouf, Chug. Let me get on my knees wif my face in Baby's pussy an you can fuck me from behind. Deep as you can go, hard as you can fuck, I can take it," she said, and she meant it, she was blurry with desire for Chug to be inside her.

"Whoowhee," laughed Chug, "girls fightin over my dick, everman's dream come true. Git in a stance," he said.

"What you mean?" asked Precious.

"Git like you said, turn around and stick you ass up in the air where I can get to it. I'm gone turn on the light too. I wanta see you face down there in Baby's cunt." He laughed, "drive the fucking mosquitoes crazy, they see the light on an all this skin."

The girls swiveled and swung, arranged themselves to suit the man. Chug got up on his knees behind Precious, he shoved and squeezed his blood-swollen dick into the girl. She grunted when he did, she felt him all the way up. He began hammering away at her, he pushed at the back of her head, he pressed it into the other girl's crotch. He took it all in, he was the main man. In spite of the booze and the pills, the tight fit of his bare cock in Precious' little pussy caused him to come, it seemed, a bucketful.

When he was finished he pulled himself out of the girl and slid back around, got his legs under the steering wheel. Precious had climaxed too, had been spasmodic, shaken. In her reverie she lapped at Baby's pussy until Baby came also. Baby held onto her friend's head and ground her pussy against the fat girl's chin. When they were finished, they sat up too, Chug turned out the overhead light. Precious found a napkin in the bag with the beer. She wiped herself then threw the wet napkin on the floor. Chug didn't notice, he was fumbling in the pockets of his jeans. He dug out a small handful of tiny white pills, popped one in his mouth and washed it down with a long gulp from a new beer.

"You all want a hit of speed?" he said.

"Is we through fo the night? " asked Baby.

"Fuck no," he said, "we gone up the beach an drink a little more, then we gone go to my house an start fuckin all over again. I ain't fucked you yet, Baby, an Marvin there, why he ain't even come once. You all don't wanna have to give me back his money, do you?"

107

He turned on the interior light again and showed them another little white pill he held between his forefinger and thumb.

"Watch this, you all," he said. "I'm gone fix that boy right up. Then you can have some."

He turned around in the seat and dropped the speed into Marvin's slack mouth, poured in a slug of beer from his bottle, and covered the deputy's mouth and nose with his hand. Marvin sputtered and choked, blew snot through his nose, then swallowed. Chug wiped the snot on Marvin's shirt, turned back around and finished the beer. He dropped the empty bottle on the floor.

"He be wide awake in about fifteen minutes," he said. "Here, you all take one of these, they black too. They called black beauties, ain't that a coincidence? You all be wantin to fuck my dog by the time we in Iona."

After twenty minutes and another beer, they were dressed, and coming out from the sand road. They crossed the high bridge and were on Estero Boulevard at the south end of Fort Myers Beach. Chug stopped in the parking lot of the Holiday Inn and gave Precious ten dollars.

"Call you a cab," he said. "You know where my place is, Precious, tell im leave you off there. You all wait on the porch in back, out of the skeeters. They's bug spray just in case they inside with you, but don't turn the light on any longer than you have to, you'll just git bit more. We be there in about a hour."

"You shitten me, Chug," said Precious, "why ain't we gone stay wif you?"

"Cause me an Marvin goin to The Surf Club, Precious, that's all the reason I got to give you. We ain't through partyin yet. Ain't nothin better then closin up a bar an comin home to some pussy, even if you gotta pay for it. They's an extra fifty for you in my jeans, it'll be worth you while. An later, after you cooked my breakfast, you an me got somethin to talk about, worth a lot more than fifty dollars. Shit, Marvin here ain't even got his rocks off. Them all good enough reasons?"

"That's right," said Marvin. "We be there directly."

"You all got change for the phone, Chug?" asked Precious.

"Jesus H. Christ," said Chug, "don't you all carry no money with you?"

"We got bills folded up in our shoes, daddy, an ain't nobody been payin us quarters to fuck. An they damn sure ain't gone let us in the lobby of this hotel to borrow a telephone."

"Not the way we look now," Baby said, starting to pout.

"It's a motel, not a hotel," said Marvin, who had come around quickly, "they's a big difference."

"Whatever it is, they ain't gonna want two black girls like us walkin in after midnight. We look like we been gang-banged out on the beach somewhere," Precious said, shitty-like.

"You ain't black, Goddamnit. Why you barely brown," said Marvin.

Chug reached into his jeans and pulled out his roll, peeled off another ten and gave it to Baby.

"Here," he said, "you all figure it out an don't fuckin argue with me no more, I'm thirsty. Just make sure you at my house when we get there. An Precious, you better lose that snotnose."

"We be there, bossman," said Baby. She reached over and massaged him between his legs. "We ain't finished wif you an Marvin, that's fo sure. Don't be mad. Whoowhee, it's early again, thanks to you medicine. We can sleep all day tommora, ain't that right, Precious?"

"Where's you dog gonna be, Chug?" asked Precious. "You dint say nothin about him. I be scared to go in you house wif Hitman there."

"He's inside the house, locked in. Just stay on the porch an don't make no noise. He's inside, you all be outside. He won't come out after you. It's when you inside you got to worry."

"Well, what the fuck do that mean?" she asked. "What we gonna do when we go inside you house?"

"You know, Precious, I tole you I didn't want to hear no more shit outta you. I'm gettin tired of this fifty questions. You wanna lot of answers, go back to school."

"Well, what are we gonna do when we go inside?" asked Marvin. "I don't like Hitman sniffin around me neither."

"Then I put him outside, Marvin. Jesus Christ, are you really that fuckin dumb?"

"Oh," said Marvin, "yeah. I see."

"He's got a chain to worry with in the back yard, just like in my truck. It's hooked to a fucking tree about three feet around."

"Don't he bark?" asked Baby, as she and Precious were finally getting out of the car.

"No, he don't fuckin bark. I had to get him a little operation when he was younger on account he was barkin a little too much. Now he just looks at people an they shit. Go on, call you cab," he said. "We see you all in about a hour."

Chug and Marvin took off in the Bonneville, tires screeching, burning rubber at one in the morning, hauling ass up Estero. They rounded the curve by the Catholic church at sixty then settled down to a fast forty, cruising the beach road. Marvin was wide awake and thirsty as hell. He was puzzled, he wondered to himself how it worked, that first you got real drunk, then you took some speed that got you back to where you wasn't drunk no more, so you could get drunk again. Shit, he thought, maybe he could not drink, then he wouldn't have to take no speed, an he could be right where he was now an save a lot of money. It was too confusing, he decided, all that shit in you head.

"How come you made them girls get out back at the motel?" he asked Chug. "Why ain't we take em with us the rest of the way?" he asked. He looked at the spare lights of the scattered white cottages as they tooled up the boulevard.

"Boy, you don't know nothin about Fort Myers Beach, bein from Punta Gorda an all. We goin to The Surf Club, they all shrimpers an stone crabbers an diesel mechanics in there. They even git a whiff of pussy they kick the shit out of us an take them whores to they boats. Shit," he said, "they like I used to be. They fight an cut us for fun, for somethin to say tomorra about what they done tonight. Just cause we ain't commercial fishermen. Shit, I've fucked up as many fish as most of em, mullet anyway."

"Shit youself," snorted Marvin, "we got commercial fishermen in Punta Gorda too."

"Not like these you ain't," said Chug. "Don't say nothin about them

110

girls to anybody an don't say nothin about farms and flowers or any of that shit when we in there either. Shrimpers is unpredictable. I hate to have to come back here tomorra an kill one or two for fuckin with me."

"I thought we got important shit for tomorra and tomorra night?" Marvin said, concerned. "Why we goin in The Surf Club if it's a chance we gone git beat by some fishermen?"

"No worries, Marvin, I ain't gonna give no reason to fuck with me. I just wanna have a drink with them peckerheads. You know? They lower on the food chain than the Mesicans," he laughed.

Chug parked the Pontiac in the sand parking lot next to the blue building. They got out, walked up the four cement steps in front, in the center. There was a man in white rubber boots passed out on the corner steps that led to the package store. Chug opened the heavy glass door below a green neon sign of waves and letters that blinked on and off. The square bar was right in front of them, just a few feet from the door. It was one o clock in the morning and the place was slap full of men and women. The Surf Club sat right at the edge of the beach. Water lapped at the lower blocks of the back wall, but the windows were closed, so the Gulf breeze and the scent of the ocean did not penetrate and freshen or carry away the aromas of stale beer, cigarette smoke, unwashed bodies, and fish. Everyone at the bar turned to look at them as Chug and Marvin came in, gave them a slow going over, looked at their eyes for challenge. The shrimpers figured they were not yankees or college boys, saw that they were as fucked-up as themselves. They turned their backs, picked up a beer, a hard drink, or a smoke, and resumed talking. If it had been niggers or Spanish who unknowingly stumbled into the bar, the group would have risen as one and stomped them to death.

Chug and Marvin each ordered a shot of Jim Beam, sipped the whiskey down, then asked for beers.

"My last one," said Marvin, "I cain't drink no more."

"You mean forever?" laughed Chug.

"Hell no, I mean tonight. I aim to hurry to you house an fuck one of them gals," he said.

Chug laughed and sprayed his beer. He wiped his mouth off with the back of his hand.

"Well, Marvin," he said, "why don't we take our time goin home and fuck em both?"

Chug was getting hungry though. He looked at the big jars of pickled pig's feet and deviled eggs floating in red brine, on the back side of the wooden bar. He didn't want any of that shit. He figured they oughta get goin while the goin was good, he'd done what he set out to. Chug knew about fishermen, he remembered the boys from Everglades City that had kicked his ass. Shit, he thought, they was boys, these here is a lot worse. He had wanted to sit beside danger, he figured, an have a drink. He knew about shrimpers, even shrimpers from the docks downtown were careful in The Surf Club. An they all carried knives. They was armed, he told Marvin, every fuckin one of em. He had brought his Smith and Wesson with him but it was in the glove box. He'd never get to it, he guessed, these boys decided to go crazy.

He nudged Marvin with his elbow and they left. An extra twenty on the counter for the bartender made Chug feel important. He had got his drink in the roughest white bar in the county and was going home to his whores an have breakfast. Meanwhile he figured, most of them dumb bastards in the bar would be jackin-off in they shrimp boats.

He drove the car slowly across the old swing bridge that joined the little island to the big one. It was a flat bridge with narrow steel sidewalks that had been made by Champion Bridge Works in Wilmington, Ohio, back in the Twenties. It had had been used for many years somewhere else before it had been brought by barge to Fort Myers Beach. During the day it opened every half hour or so to let the commercial fishing boats, cabin cruisers and sailboats move in and out of the shallow bay. On Sundays, when all the teenagers from town came to the beach, they crowded the bridge with cars, weekend fishermen crowded the bridge with boats. Traffic on the road and on the water would be backed up the whole day. At night the bridge stayed open to cars and closed to boats.

Maybe that's why they so pissed off, Chug said to Marvin, the shrimpers, stuck out in the boat an extra night an couldn't get to a bar. That'd piss me off too, he'd said. Course I'd swim in, he told Marvin, tell the captain to get fucked.

Chug slowed the car when they were across the bridge, pulled into a shell driveway that led to the docks. They got out to piss. Marvin had wanted to piss when they were back in the bar but Chug had told him it was better to wait.

"What you gone do, Marvin?" he'd said, "some horny shrimpers come in there with they knives an tell you to git on you knees?"

"Jesus Christ," Marvin had asked wonderingly, stunned, "people do that?"

"Happens all the time," Chug said.

They crossed the road and stood in the dark in the shadow of a shell and concrete archway that covered a sliver of San Carlos Boulevard. A curved wooden sign announced to the traveler that he was coming onto Fort Myers Beach. *The Safest Beach In The World*, the sign read.

Chug pointed at the sign. "That don't include the bars, do it, deputy?"

The arches were very old, they had been there before the swing bridge had been brought. They were Spanish looking, the rock and the shell and the cement that bound them had darkened. At the base of the arches there were abandoned ixoras, agaves, sand spurs and torpedo grass.

"I like to piss on this thing ever chance I git," said Chug. "It's half the fun comin to the beach. All the water around makes you wanna piss more. You know that, Marvin?"

"I gotta piss because I got a bellyful of beer an whiskey," tittered Marvin, "not because the ocean is out there. Lordy, lordy, what a night," he sighed. "I think I got to be at work tomorra at three. I switched with Deputy Bledsoe I believe. But I still gotta work Friday an Saturday. My daddy, he insists on it," he giggled again.

"That's a pair, sure enough," said Chug, "you daddy the sheriff an my old man the big boss. I think they time has come to step aside. Now you listen, boy, we got lots of night an dope left to fuck one of them gals or both, and then git some sleep. I got medicine for that too. You just make absolutely fucking certain you workin tomorra night without no help or I swear I'll fuck you up good, friends or no." He looked over at Marvin as he was zipping up. "You got that, deputy?"

Some cars passed, drunks from the beach coming back from town, drunks from town leaving the beach.

"I'm you man, Chug, ain't no reason to get so scary," Marvin said.

113

"Shit, Marvin," Chug said, "you don't even know what scary is."

When they were back in the car, Chug fiddled with the radio until he got some country music, they settled in for the last little haul down San Carlos. He swerved to hit a raccoon but missed, then they were past the red potato farms that the Kelly's owned and into Iona. When he spoke again to Marvin, he cut his eyes back and forth between Marvin and the road.

"We gone meet tomorra at Burnt Store Marina," he said. "I ain't fuckin with the farm or anythin else for a couple of days until this thing is over. We gone move fast an catch that old boy with his dick in his hand. You be sober tomorra an I won't drink as much as I usually do. I won't be drunk, just loose. I got a shitload of plannin to do tomorra, we gone knock off that Mesican an git his money. That girl Precious, she gone help, she just don't know it yet."

"What you gotta plan? Exactly?" asked Marvin.

Chug laughed out loud and pounded on the steering wheel.

"How to spend they money," he said.

"How much you really think they is?" asked Marvin.

"Lots," said Chug. "Ten, maybe twenty thousand dollars. Five, maybe ten apiece."

"That's a lot more'n I make drivin that fuckin deputy car up an down the road," said Marvin. " Like I told you, I'm you man."

"I know you are Marvin, an that's good, that's real good. You know what I'm gone do when we get to my place?" he said. "I'm gonna get them nigger girls to cook me a couple of hamburgers, then I'm gonna make one of em bark. I sure do miss hearin Hitman bark."

Chapter Twenty

At six in the morning, without an hour's sleep, Chug and Precious and Baby got dressed, got in the front seat of the Bonneville. He drove them past the Garza house, just a mile from the duplex, pointed to the Rambler in the carport. Hard to miss, he'd said, they ain't many of em around no more. Be like having a Cadillac in Mesico, he'd laughed. He drove them to where Iona Road joined McGregor, pulled into the puddled parking lot of Miners Grocery, he told Precious what he wanted.

"I done found out what time these folks is leavin," he said. "You all borrow or rent you a car from one of you brothers an be out here tonight, ten o clock on. When you see that fat little car come past this corner, you haul you ass to that telephone box next to the shrimp tanks an you call me here." He gave them a piece of paper with Marvin's telephone number at his trailer in Suncoast. "I'll be waitin," he said. " I need to have a visit with these folks, you all understand?"

"We understan," said Precious. "But we need money to pay somebody for a car, Chug. Nobody loans nothin out on Anderson. They ain't stupid."

"You right, Precious, I know what you mean. Here's another fifty dollars, but don't come here in no pimpmobile that's gone attract attention. Come in a plain lookin car an don't be drinkin or dopin. I'm tellin you all right now, you all fuck this up an I'm comin after you, you all better understan that too. Make sure you memorize that fuckin telephone number." Chug looked hard at the women in the early light. He found the eyes of each and waited until they both nodded that they understood before he let them go.

"We do right by you, daddy," said Baby. "We won't miss that ugly car."

"You all check that phone when you get here, make sure it's workin. Call somebody, anybody back in town, see it rings through an you talk. If it don't work you git youselves to Deep Lagoon. They's another phone there. They be by here about five after midnight, I expect," he said, "knowin that man like I do. His people done let it out of the bag they goin on they great journey at midnight."

"We see em we call you." Precious stated clearly what was expected.

"Let me know. I'm gonna be waitin. I hear that phone ring an it's you I'm gone bring you each two hundred dollars for you good work."

"What these folks do, Chug, got you so anxious to see em?" asked the fat girl.

"I'm gone fuck em up, Precious," he told her, "cause they asked me too many questions."

Chug drove down McGregor to town. He went by the office first and left the old man's trashed Bonneville. He took the girls back to the grocery store where he had picked them up the night before.

"You all can walk from here," he said, "I gotta get back an git some sleep my own self. You all plumb wore me out." He swallowed another pill he'd held in his fingers for several minutes.

"This here will put me out by the time you all done checked on you kids," he called out after them, shaking his head at the girls. They were high stepping barefoot through the wet weeds.

He moved quickly with the morning traffic. He was leaving town, not going in, and was back at his duplex by seven thirty. He fed Hitman in the carport and went inside. He looked around, not surprised by the mess. Marvin was asleep, the fat deputy was curled up on his side under a blanket against the chill of the air-conditioning. Chug went into one of the bedrooms, swept everything from the bed, set the alarm for one, lay down and closed his eyes. He had decided to take the Garza money the first instant he had heard about it from May. Everbody knows about it, he thought to himself, could be anybody took it.

Just past one he slapped Marvin awake and told him to hit the road. Marvin staggered out to his Jeep, parked in the weeds in Chug's yard. Chug walked with him, waited for him while he puked, handed him a towel to wipe off the cold sweat that dripped from Marvin's face. He told Marvin to be very careful and to meet him at the marina on Burnt Store Road at seven o clock. After the deputy left, Chug went back inside. He didn't notice the dog shit on the concrete as he passed it or the stinking sour smell of the duplex once he was inside it.

He kicked things out of the way, walked to the bedroom where he stripped out of his soiled clothes. He showered, shaved, put on clean jeans and a cowboy shirt and lots of jewelry. He put Hitman in the truck and drove to the vegetable stand. He told May they was still a lot going on in LaBelle, took all the money she had rolled up for him, and grabbed a big bottle of cold orange juice to mix with his vodka. In the back of the truck, Hitman had tired of May. He was watching the cars going by, figured maybe he was going somewhere too. Chug didn't ask about the Mexicans, she noticed, just said he had a lot of ground to cover.

Chug wanted to drive, to let the afternoon roll by with the miles and the plan. He went over the Cape Coral bridge, up Del Prado to Pine Island Road. He stopped at Matlacha for a bottle of vodka, Pall Malls, and beef jerky for him and Hitman. When he paused at the four corners at Stringfellow he looked back and forth, then turned right. He had decided to see Bokeelia first. He drove past fields with dark soil, not sand, and acres of mango, banana, and tapioca.

Bokeelia was deserted, nothing moved in the red-hot afternoon sun, the fronds of the coconuts along the edge of the water were still. He parked the truck under a very old mastic tree. He told Hitman to stay, and walked with his drink out onto the dock.

He watched a small man, barefooted, in overalls, wearing a sweat stained baseball cap, emerge from behind an old whitewashed house with a newly shingled roof. The man walked quickly across the sand

117

spurs and the sharp shells and in a moment was on the sun scalded dock. He carried a wriggling pinfish in one hand and a stout bamboo pole in the other. His skin was leathery, the color of mahogany. The tide was about to go out. The man walked past Chug, hooked the pinfish behind the dorsal with a single barb, a big one. The line was all leader. He dropped the bait over the edge, laid flat on the boards, got his toes dug in and held the pole down, pointed at the water. He began to move it in a slow figure eight, dragging the pinfish through the water in front of a dozen big snook that were motionless under the pier. In less than a minute there was a great pull downward on the pole. The little man grabbed it tighter. In a few seconds he muscled a snook up and onto the sun bleached, weathered wood dock. The snook was thirty six inches long, about twenty five pounds. Before it could jump and spatter itself on the deck the little man reached into his pocket, pulled out a long, thin bladed knife, cut the fish across the throat, opened up the stomach and spilled the guts back into the green water.

"Makes it less to carry," he said. "An I don't like to see them beat themselves up."

He squinted up at Chug who stood between him and the sun.

Chug laughed at the little man in his overalls and bare feet and old baseball hat.

"I like you style," he said.

The man stood up with his snook. He held it under the red gills, its tail dragged on the wood. He put his pole on his other shoulder.

"I get one evertime I want," he said.

"Me too," Chug told him.

He got back in the truck and went south. He turned off Stringfellow to go to Pineland. Chug didn't notice the Indian mounds and the gumbo limbo trees and the water, but he laughed when he saw The Cloisters. Rich men who were drunks in town went there to dry out, but the mullet fishermen that lived in shacks up the beach were paid well to stash bottles of vodka and gin in the mangroves nearby. Nobody was gettin cured of what ailed em, he figured, except him. He did a loop at the marina that handled the boats for Useppa. He drove slowly back out the

118

twisting narrow road past horses in pasture and avocado groves.

Chug figured to drive on down to St. James City. He took short swallows from his drink. All he saw in St. James was trailer parks, they wasn't nothin fancy. Airstreams and campers and Volkswagen buses were parked crookedly on shell lots. There were a few people moving around before the rain came. They were wearing sandals and short pants. He looked out at the low beach. He knew it was Captiva and Sanibel across the pass but he couldn't quite figure out the curve. He tilted his head up at the Australian pines that lined the beach and heard the whistle as the wind blew through the long needles. Then he tilted up the orange juice and vodka.

Chug turned in the truck, slid open the rear window and spoke to Hitman.

"That's the beach, an those," he pointed at the trailers, "is poor yankees or Germans or some shit." He pushed Hitman back and then tossed another strip of jerky out the rear window. Hitman was on it in an instant.

"They gone be everwhere," he said. "Shit. They already is, only they gone be even more. These here ain't the rich ones, they the ones I want to come on down, so I can take some of they money. Mostly legal, though, not like tonight." He reached out and slapped at the dog.

"I'm gone take that old boy's cash, Hitman, an then I'm gonna get the old man to let me sell that fuckin flower farm. We be set up, go into some shady business. We gonna trim yankees. Shit. They must be all kind of ways," he said to his dog, "stupid as these ones look."

Chapter Twenty One

Chug was waiting for Marvin at Burnt Store Marina. He sat on a warped wood bench next to a weathered wood picnic table under a stand of old yellow pines. Hitman lay at his boots on a carpet of pine needles. Chug picked at grit on the table. The marina was very quiet, it was the middle of the week. Rain was expected, everyone was gone. Chug watched the driveway with the setting sun to his back.

The marina had started out as a fishing camp. Gulf menhaden had been caught in great nets let out from big boats in the deeper water, brought to the fish camp, and sucked out of the holds of the boats through enormous hoses. The fish had spilled like silver, sheeted rain into tanker trucks. In Tampa the loads were changed into meal for cheap fertilizer. Several years before, two fishermen had been killed there. They had gone into the hold of a boat that was filled with menhaden. When the generator outside kicked on, there was a release of hydrogen disulfide that had been trapped in the coils and ribs of the rubber hose. The men were poisoned in an instant. The fish camp closed after that. Several years later Punta Gorda Isles bought all the land around the old camp for development and it became a marina. There was a big metal building under construction. The building was still a skeleton of steel beams that layered and crossed. A hundred boats would be stored there. Chug turned away from the building and the driveway when he saw Marvin's deputy car. He looked at the dock. There were Daniels, Aquasports and

Bayliners tied at the davits. When the tires of the big Fairlane stopped crunching the shell and the motor was shut off, he turned back around. Deputy Johnson got out.

"I'm gone get me a boat, Marvin, gonna keep it right here too. I like this place," he said, "ain't so many fuckin people."

"You gonna go out to Boca Grande and fish for tarpon? They's big ones out there, big as them hogs we chase down."

"Fuck no, Marvin. I'm gone fish for pussy. Think about it," he said. "You drive a fancy Daniels with a cabin right up on the beach where they's some girl from Ohio in a bikini an she's had about three beers an you invite her for a boat ride." He laughed and nudged Hitman with the toe of his boot.

"What you think happen I take her outside about ten miles. The water ain't green no more, it's real dark blue cause it's so fuckin deep, an I tell her to strip down or start swimmin?"

"I believe she drop her bikini suit in a hurry, if you tell her about sharks an barracuda, specially. We get two of em together. I believe them girls on vacation from the north travels in pairs," he said. "That's funny," he added, "I was thinkin about gettin a boat too."

Chug snorted. He took off his sunglasses, shook his head at his partner. He set the sunglasses on the table, reached into the cooler under the bench and dug out two cans of beer from the ice. He tossed one to Marvin.

"How you feelin this evenin, sheriff?" he asked.

"I ain't the sheriff, Chug, but I'm a deputy sure enough, see my badge?" He pointed at his chest and giggled. "I'm feelin pretty good. That was a wild time last night with them girls, but I liked to puke all the way to Punta Gorda. Took me a nap like you said to, then got up an ate half a dozen bacon sandwiches."

"If you get sleepy, Marvin, we can take care of it real quick."

"I ain't sleepy, see, I switched with Leonard, I'm doin a double, I had to get fired up. I been on the clock since three, I be workin till three tomorra, course I had to give Leonard twenty dollars to let me do his shift. An I got to work two nights for him over the next two weeks. No, I ain't figurin to get sleepy."

"You sly fucker," said Chug, "you already gobbled you a little speed. I'm real proud of you, Marvin, figurin it out how it works. We gonna be tight when it comes time to snatch them people's money."

"It's almost eight," said Marvin. "What we gonna do now?"

"I'm gone follow you back to the jail. Is all the cells empty?"

"Ever damn one. We ain't had no one in em for three weeks."

"That's good. An you the only deputy on duty?"

"Yeah," said Marvin. "Anything happen the phone'll ring in the office an I'll take the call, unless I'm gone of course, an then they call the fire station or highway patrol, or the hospital," he added.

"Well it's Wednesday, an it's gonna be late, ain't likely anythin will happen," Chug said. "We ain't gonna be on the road very long. Now we goin back to the jail an I'm gone put Hitman in one of you cells. You gone stay there an wait for me to call you. You have you fuckin keys in you hand, you got that? I'm goin to that fancy trailer of yours an be there when Precious calls. Should be right at midnight. You come to The Shell Factory. I'll be waitin."

"I can be there in twenty minutes, provided I don't have no accident," said Marvin.

"Marvin," Chug laughed, "you have a accident I guarantee you never recover. You be there in ten minutes an pull alongside my truck. We gone nab em just north of The Shell Factory, about three miles up. They ain't a fuckin thing there except woods. Good thing there ain't but one way north to Mesico."

"They ain't shit for traffic on 41 that late at night, except in January when the yankees is comin down. Those people gone be scared outta they minds," he snickered. "We gonna get em for speedin?"

"We gone get em for they money, Marvin, that's what we gonna call our primary purpose. Think about the money an you new Bayliner and pussy on the beach, just waitin for somebody to take it for a boat ride. Then you be rememberin why we takin em."

Chug slipped his sunglasses back over his eyes, he looked into the last moments of the sun. It was setting out over the mangroves and the shallow water for the other side of the world. Behind them, to the east, the sky was already dark.

122

"You think it'll rain, Chug?" Marvin asked.

"Marvin," Chug laughed, "you sound like a fuckin farmer, always wantin somebody to give em a answer whether it's gonna rain or not. That ain't the question, boy, it's when it's gonna rain, not if it will. Ground's so fuckin wet now they be catfish swimmin in the drainage ditches, we get any more, an it looks like we fixin to."

"Okay, Mister Goldtrap," Marvin giggled, "when we gonna git it?"

"You mean Goldtrap the weatherman? Skinny dude drops his chalk in his coat pocket after he done drawin clouds an shit on his blackboard? You funny, Marvin, but since you ask I say it's gonna rain in about a hour an keep up till ten, ten thirty. Road's gonna be slick, ditches gonna be full."

Chug crumpled his beer can and dropped it in the trash can.

"You know Marvin?" he said. "The worst thing that can happen tonight is I might have to kill them people. They give me the feelin they gonna talk or make trouble, I'll kill em like they was mullet an leave em for the crabs. What you think about that? You worried bout after, bout goin to Starke, you bein the law an all? They fuckin eat you for breakfast in there, Marvin, or you eat them. What you think about these people bein around to make trouble?"

Marvin cleared his throat and spat a thick white gob. "I ain't personally plannin on killin nobody," he said, "but I'm you man for everthin else. I sure don't want my daddy to be the one send me to prison though, it'd break his heart. I don't figure I know what I think."

Chug pointed to the water. "Think about the cash, Marvin. That's a big old Gulf of Mesico out there, they's lots of deep holes in it. The world ain't gonna weep hot tears for a couple of missin Mesicans. I ain't takin no chances on goin to prison, not for one fuckin hour."

"You gonna convince em we ain't fuckin around, Chug?"

"It'll come to me, Marvin, when they shiverin and shakin in front of you an me an Hitman. Takin they money is gonna be easy, makin em decide we better off with it than them is gonna be harder. I think of somethin," he said, "they gonna know."

"Well, I'm the law," Marvin said. He spoke a little louder over the wind that kicked up. "I know they ain't stupid enough to carry on about me. They don't know me at all. I just say they dreamed it up, or they blamin us for somethin some other Mesican or nigger did to em. You different though, you connected to em."

"I ain't connected to nothin, Marvin, except Hitman here, an I ain't at all sure about him. Lots of people know about they money, it's just a accident we the ones gonna git it. We gonna save em from gettin robbed, killed on the spot maybe, down in Mesico. We gone take they money, almost all of it. I'm gone leave em enough to get wherever the fuck it is they goin an I'm gonna explain to em real good what happens I ever even hear they fuckin name again."

Chug took a long pull from a new beer.

"You ain't gonna git drunk? I cain't handle this by myself, you too drunk or wobbly."

"Shit, Marvin, don't make me laugh. You the only one here passes out an wakes up pukin in his fingers. I'm fixin to start callin you Puker for a nickname."

"Well I ain't gettin drunk tonight," Marvin said.

"Well I ain't neither," said Chug. "I had me a nap before you got here. I feel myself gettin sloppy I have me a snort of coke. I got it sittin in the cooler."

"Jesus Christ," said Marvin, "you got coke? Can I have some?"

"Later, deputy. I have a line ready for you when you get to that parking lot, figure you make it in about eight minutes," he laughed. "We be toasted when we nab em. I'm gone keep my temperament just right an get them folks on they way, but I tell you damn dead certain, Marvin, I kill em if I think I have to. Come to that," he said, "you best be standin over on my side of the boat."

"I be right there, Chug, but I surely hope it don't come to that. Killin makes everbody nervous."

"It's up to the Mesicans," said Chug. "It's dark. Me an Hitman will follow you back to the jail. We visit some, I wanna look at all them shotguns and rifles you lawmen have. Then I'm goin down to Suncoast."

Chug stood up and stretched, then stomped his boot next to the dog's head. Hitman came up fast and looked at his master.

"Load up, Hitman," he said. "You been a bad dog, now you goin to jail."

124

Chapter Twenty Two

Chug had bought Hitman from an old boy in Belle Glade who raised pit bulls to sell for fighters and who was a Klansman. Belle Glade had no Mexicans or Puerto Ricans or Cubans or any other kind of Spanish. What was there besides a few whites were black people, not colored, black. The Negroes had come to work the vegetable farms there forty years before and had stayed. They had been there when big sugar started. The population was kept dark by cane cutters from Haiti and the Dominican Republic. The whites and the blacks in Belle Glade did not mix, except for one to give orders and the other to follow.

When Chug bought the dog it was still young, however the breeder had started its training, it was responsive to the boot and the fist. The Klansman showed Chug how to whisper the word nigger into the dog's ear and then slap it hard across the face or kick it in the ribs so it would associate the word with anger. As he grew older, Hitman redefined the response that was expected from him. The dog threw himself into a frenzy of barking and snapping, he threw out streams of saliva, he hurled himself against his restraints to get at the nearest body, when Chug said the word. On the nights Chug drove with the dog into the shell parking lots in front of the bars on Palm Beach or Bayshore, the other cowboys made sure Hitman was fastened before they came over. They could laugh then as Chug said the word over and over to the dog on the chain, bringing it near to madness and then finally telling it to stop and lay down.

He'd fucked up, he told Hitman, they wasn't any around.

Chug liked the name, Hitman, he longed for a chance to have the dog put a big hurtin on some skinny colored dude or fat little Mesican, something more involved than just a bite. Hitman often lunged at passers-by, but the chain was always there to restrain him. When Chug told him to sit or to stay, he did, but his eyes followed human motion. His great round head cocked slightly on his massive shoulders, his long tongue hung clean pink and obscene over his big white teeth.

Hitman depended on Chug for the things he needed, he had been trained through a series of beatings to accept nothing from anyone else. The dog ate all he could hold, whenever he wanted, Chug wanted Hitman to get bigger and bigger. They were not friends but they had an understanding. Even a group of men would have a hard time getting past Hitman before they could lay hands on Chug. And there was always the forty-five, Chug let it be known, in case some lucky fucker avoided his pit bull. Chug still hit the dog hard once in a while. He aimed his closed fist at the dog's jaw, he would kick him if Hitman didn't move fast enough. He was reminding Hitman, he'd say, that he was a fuckin dog. But Hitman had his own moves, to remind Chug that he was the one with hands. Once his food made the floor of the house or the bed of the truck it belonged to the dog. Bowls of dry food, bones, whole cooked chickens, smoked jack and when Chug was drunk, hamburgers and French fries, were tossed or set out for the dog. A deep, dangerous noise came from Hitman if there was any movement by Chug towards his meal. Hitman walked deliberately to his food, he seemed to invite inter-ference. He ate faster than most dogs. He crunched pellets, flesh, veg-etables, and bones between his teeth. Hitman gulped it all down, then stared hard at Chug, figuring there was more. Even at his most drunk-en, most reckless self, Chug had never but once held out food in his hand for Hitman. That time brought a bad bite across the top of his thumb, and stitches and shots. The dog had lunged for a pork chop Chug dangled in front of him. His great mouth opened wide and when his jaws closed, Chug's hand was punctured. Chug had a quart bottle of beer in his other hand at the time, he deftly flipped it, caught the bottle by its neck, and smashed it over the dog's head. He knew it didn't faze Hitman but it gave Chug a lot of satisfaction. He thought for a minute

126

about shooting the fucker but decided it wasn't Hitman's fault, that he ought not put food in front of him in such a way. Where there was food concerned, he guessed, Hitman wasn't gonna be no gentleman.

The dog got in the truck by himself. He pushed off the ground with his powerful hind legs, up onto the closed tailgate, then jumped down into the bed. Once he was in, Chug had him sit or at least stand still. He reached over the side to fasten Hitman's heavy leather collar to a stout chain. The chain was only three feet long, it was bolted to a steel plate that had been welded to the truck, so Hitman couldn't reach over the side and bite someone. A greaser or colored would have to be extra stupid to get any closer, Chug figured, and Hitman couldn't hang himself jumping out of the truck to get at another dog.

Hitman hated everybody but Chug, some he hated more than others. Chug had explained to him which ones to hate the most. Hitman had come to recognize them by color and scent, he eyed them for carelessness and insolence, anxious for challenge and confrontation, anxious for one to come closer. He stood in the back of the truck or beside Chug on the ground, malicious, malevolent. His muscles shook with desire for action. He wanted to bite faces, shoulders, legs and necks. Hands were common things, he'd learned, or Chug would have killed him. Nobody reached out to touch Hitman, nobody went near that fucker. They were warned by intuition, and the dog's yellow eyes.

Hitman had liked to bark when he was young, he liked the effect it had on people. The bark stopped them from what they were doing, attention was focused on him. Then he began to bark incessantly, all day, at night if he was disturbed. The old man told Chug he couldn't bring the dog to the office or the big house, the people at Marine Hardware complained, the greasers threatened to quit. Enrique Garza told the old man the people couldn't work with the dog barking at them. Chug's cowboy partners wouldn't stay with him and drink in the parking lots, and Chug wasn't gettin no sleep. He took Hitman to a vet. He told the man to cut the dog's vocal cords. The vet agreed to do it but only on the condition that Chug never bring the dog back. The vet was worried that Hitman would remember him, what he had done to diminish his aura. Hitman still opened his great mouth, his head inclined backward on his shoulders, he took big gulps of air, but he barked to himself. When the silence was too much, he started a deep growling and rumbling. When he was upset, Hitman breathed hard through his flattened nostrils, he ground his strong teeth together, he paced and panted on the short chain, wanting to be over the side. He was pissed off he couldn't make no noise.

Chapter Twenty Three

U.S. 41 was a simple two-lane highway that ran straight north once it was over the Edison Bridge and beyond the sprawl of North Fort Myers. The last lights along the highway ended at the parking lot of The Shell Factory. Beyond that, until the driver was upon Punta Gorda, the land was empty and flat. The yankees had not come down yet and there was no reason for people to travel back and forth between the towns. Many minutes could go by without a car moving on the highway, especially late at night. The sides of the road sloped down to shallow ditches, then back up to the edge of forests of pine, myrtle, and palmetto. Where the land was lower, near the creeks, there were thick stands of scrub oak, maple, and holly trees. In the daytime a motorist could see that the woods were very deep. The forests and scrub were not frequently interrupted by side roads and parking lots. At night, with a moon covered in clouds, the edge of the woods was black and appeared to be impenetrable. The shallow ditches and most of the sloping sides were filled with water from July to October. The water looked like dark tea or whiskey, from the tannins that seeped out of the woods. It was stagnant, hot and thick except for a few moments after a heavy rain.

The Fairlane came up fast on the Rambler. When he was right on Enrique's ass, Chug popped the light and the siren. Enrique and Anita jumped in their seats, their shoulders hunched up around their necks, their lungs expanded with violent pulls at air. Anita bit her lip very badly, she put her hand to her mouth to cover the hurt. Before they could even turn around or look in the mirror, nerves screaming from the noise of the siren and the demon of the flashing light, the Fairlane was beside them. The angle and the size of the bigger car forced Enrique to turn his wheels to the right and then he was off the road, sliding dangerously on the wet grass, finally stopped in the water-filled ditch. The Rambler was off the highway maybe twenty feet, up to the top of the tires in water. Enrique put the car in park. He started to get out, the noise of the siren had stopped, the red light was not flashing. A truck, he could tell because of the high headlights, came up quickly and stopped behind his car. The sounds of the ditch and the woods replaced the siren. Water hissed where it touched the engine. Crickets, frogs, birds, and gators made noise from the blackness.

There was not another light showing at any distance from either direction, there were no other cars about to come by. A man in a deputy shirt and cowboy hat jumped from the sheriff's cruiser and was around the front of it, suddenly next to where Enrique was opening the door. The window was down. The deputy pushed the door closed and stuck a forty-five under the Mexican man's chin. He pushed hard, upward, so Enrique's head was forced way back, he could only see the cloth cover of the ceiling of the car. With his other hand the man threw in a sour, stinking mix of beer and whiskey. He flung the stuff from an open jar. Garza's shirt and pants were soaked with it, the man dropped the empty glass on the floor of the car.

"You all git out. The woman first," Chug told them. He kept the pistol under Enrique's chin, his first finger was coiled around the trigger.

Anita quickly came from around the passenger side, doing what the man said. The water was up to her knees. It was thick and warm, she thought, like walking through syrup. Another man jumped from the truck, he grabbed Anita by the arm and pulled her, then pushed her, into the back of the sheriff's car. Chug opened the door and put his hand around the Mexican's arm, he put the pistol to his temple, and brought him from the car. Marvin came back, got behind them and handcuffed Enrique. They shoved him into the seat next to his wife. Marvin got in the police car and Chug made for his truck. There was a car coming from the south, maybe two or three miles away. Two minutes, Chug figured. He ran back and jerked open the door. He put the forty-five against Anita's head. There was a sharp click when he cocked the hammer. Anita was shaking, like she was cold to death. Her teeth chattered uncontrollably, her mouth bled through her cupped hand.

"Where's you money, motherfucker? You tell me right this fuckin instant or I'm gone shoot her brains and face all over you."

Enrique looked at Chug. He was surprised. My brain is slow, he thought. He blinked at Chug without understanding.

"Where's the money, Enrique? Tell me or I shoot you wife," Chug said.

"In the back, in a toolbox. It is pushed up against the back of the seat."

Enrique became enlightened, this was about his money.

Chug thought about kicking the window in but there wasn't time enough for that, or to find the right fucking key in the dark. Mosquitoes were stinging his face and hands, they were swarming over the people in the car.

"Put you red lights back on an pull up off the road in front of they car," he shouted to Marvin. "I'm gonna git in."

The two people in the back sat without moving, the men in front were breathing heavily. They slapped and cursed at the mosquitoes that filled the car. The other late night traveler passed by without slowing down, the red tail lights were soon gone in the mist that rose from the ditches and floated over the highway. Chug got out just after the car passed. He found the Rambler key in the lights of the Fairlane. He told Marvin to shut off the bubble again, splashed through the water in his cowboy boots, and opened the back door to the Garza's car. He reached over cardboard boxes and suitcases, found the handle to the metal tool box and pulled it out. He closed the door, went to the front and tossed the keys on the floor, next to the empty mason jar. He left the window down.

"Follow me," Chug told Marvin, "an stay close. Flick you lights these dead people give you any cause for worry."

Chug spun out on the slick pavement. He went a hundred feet before the truck's tires bit and he had traction. Marvin was right behind him. They drove fast for three miles then slowed down and turned into an abandoned tourist stop that had sold sand dollars, tanned baby Caimans and salt water taffy and gasoline. It had been the only place like it along the road between the towns on the two rivers. Chug pulled around back, Marvin did too. They cut the lights. Chug jumped in beside Marvin again.

"Here, boy," he said. He pulled out a small mirror. He sprinkled a nice pile of coke onto it, smoothed the powder with his knife into two fat lines. "Have you another hit," he told Marvin.

Marvin pulled a straw from his shirt pocket and noisily snorted up his line. He swallowed at what had run into his throat. He handed the straw to Chug, who brought the mirror close to his face and sucked up the powder into his nose, there was the slightest sound of a sniffle. Marvin liked the coke, but it made his teeth grind and his heart beat faster. It took away his being scared, as long as they had it to do, but it was heavy comin off of, he thought. He hoped Chug had plenty for the rest of the night.

Chug turned in the seat, and spoke to the man and woman in back. "Don't you Mesicans know you cain't drive aroun an drink. You cain't hold you liquor worth a shit, everbody knows, an here you is drinkin on the highway. You smell like a fuckin wino, Enrique, serves you right."

"We got big penalties, big fines in Charlotte County for drunk people who is operatin cars," Marvin pitched in. "You all in a shitload of trouble but don't start cryin yet, they's more."

The Garzas sat in the seat like stones, not moving, not speaking, concentrating. They were trying to guess what the men were saying.

"Call for the wrecker, Marvin," Chug said.

Marvin reached for the car radio and pressed down the speaker button.

"Terry you there?" he said. "Terry, you hear me boy?"

"This Terry, Marvin. What you want?" A man's voice crackled through the radio.

"Terry, this is Deputy Johnson. I'm callin you from a fuckin patrol

132

car. You call me Marvin again except when we huntin you never git any more police business, ever," he said. Marvin looked at Chug for approval.

Chug winked. "That's tellin em, Marvin," he said. "You gettin tough in you old age."

"I'm sorry, deputy," the voice said, "I surely am. What can I do for you?"

"That's better," said Marvin. "I got me a couple drunk Spanish, Cubans or Puerto Ricans or some damn thing. I'm gone take em up to the jail, make sure they ain't wanted for nothin. I'm probably gone lock em up a few hours, fine em," he winked back at Chug, "an let em go."

"You want me to git they car?" asked Terry.

"That's why I'm callin you, Terry, stead of some outfit from in Fort Myers. You git on down The Trail an pick up they car. It's about ten miles south of town sittin in the water pointed north. The keys is in the front somewhere. You copy that, Terry?"

Chug nodded his head at Marvin's words, he looked at the big pistol he held in his lap.

"Yessir, deputy, I copy. But Marvin, I mean, I'm sorry Deputy Johnson, I didn't mean to call you Marvin again. It's late," he said. "Who's gone pay me?"

"I git you money from the fine these people gonna pay, you dumb ass. Who you think's gone pay you, me?"

"Okay, okay, deputy, I'll get right on down there. What kind of car is it, in case they's more than one in the ditch along 41. It happens, you know," Terry said.

Marvin looked at Chug and released the speaker button.

"It's a Rambler, Marvin. Tell you cousin it's a Rambler. He cain't miss it," he said, "it's the only fuckin Rambler in the ditch."

Chug shook his head and poured out another pile of powder.

Marvin eyed the coke, he spoke quickly into the radio. "It's a Rambler, Terry, you cain't miss it. Bring these Spanish car up an put it in the alley behind my jail. Leave the keys on the seat an go on. I bring you money tomorra, you understan? I don't need to see you till tomorra, just leave the car where I said an go on."

"Yessir, Deputy Marvin," Terry said, "you got a man on it. Ten miles down The Trail, Rambler. Leave it in the alley, see you tomorra."

"10-4, Terry," said Marvin, "an make it quick."

Chug bent down over the coke, he snorted a lot more than half of it up. He held the rest out for Marvin, who had not noticed the split. Chug shook his head, he watched the rain run down the window. Goddamn, he thought, what a fuckin group.

Chapter Twenty Four

The Charlotte County Sheriff's office and jail was in a two-story brick building almost fifty years old. Sheriff Johnson kept his own office things, desk and files on the second floor, drooping flags of the states of Florida and Georgia filled the corners, big windows opened on the brick street below. On the ground floor, where the deputies stayed, there were several plain cells, a great mahogany desk, a back door and a case for rifles and shotguns that ran half the length of one brick wall, but was mostly empty of firepower. The sheriff's building was across the street from the Seaboard Coast Line Railroad station. The track ran through the town and further south where freight cars were loaded with flowers, citrus, vegetables, and cattle, to carry north. The railroad station was made of brick also but was distinguishable from the sheriff's building because of the wide metal-roofed porch that extended from the freight office over the tracks. The Punta Gorda ice house was next to the train station. It was a low, creaking, wooden structure with a sagging porch. There were rusted pipes with sprinklers to wet the building down, keep it cool inside. The pipes extended above the roof and could be seen from the street in the daytime.

Inside the jail, none of the walls of either floor had ever been covered up with boards or drywall or stucco or paint. The bricks were still red, the concrete between them was gray. Black and white pictures of former sheriffs and deputies who had distinguished themselves hung in frames against one wall. The portraits were lined up in rows. They had been carefully hung and were dusted often along with the glass and wood of the gun case. The men in the old photographs looked like Texas Rangers. Their faces were thin, very dark from the sun except for lily white foreheads and the tops of their ears. Broad brimmed cowboy hats had kept the skin from being burned brown and made cancerous by the relentless Florida sunshine.

Enrique and Anita trembled on the wood floor. The boards were solid oak cut from big trees milled near Arcadia. The floor had been cared for over the years, it was polished to a shine and glowed softly under the bright overhead lights. Anita had lost the water in her bladder in the deputy's car. The loose skirt that she had bought new for the trip was wet. Drops of urine trickled down her legs onto her bare feet, then onto the polished oak. She looked very small, suddenly older. She held both of her hands to her mouth, her teeth had gone through her bottom lip. She was trying to keep it from bleeding and pinched her lips together with her fingers. Her face was swollen from her wounded mouth and tears and the terror. Enrique was barefoot also, the men had pulled the shoes from the Garzas when they roughed them out of the patrol car. He was still handcuffed. He stood very quietly, very close to his wife, he tried to move his spirit into hers. He wanted to cut himself in half, give the best part to Anita. His eyes were focused on a spot on the floor, they had turned down at the spectacle of the dog.

Chug and Marvin had pushed them in the front door. Chug yelled nigger and flipped the lights on, he and Marvin stepped to the side. Ten feet away, in one of the empty cells, Hitman heard the word and smelled the sheep. He sprang up and down, up and down, against the iron bars. He coiled, collided, and jumped almost to the ceiling. When he fell back down to the wood floor, he gouged the polished wood with his nails, scrambling to lunge again. He drooled and threw slobber, his whole body shook with an effort to bark but no sound came forth. He bit at the bars, stuck his ugly dog face through them and ground his teeth at the people. When he stood against the bars, scratching for purchase on the wood, his pink tongue and obscene penis lolled from his front and shook with the rest of him. In the bright lights, under the blank stares of

136

the dead lawmen, the Garzas were exposed to the vile nature of the dog. They believed it to be demonic, evil, not of their world. They averted their eyes, they stared at a spot on the floor.

Chug walked to the cell and swatted at Hitman's face with his hat. "Sit the fuck down," he yelled. "Sit, fucker, an quit showin us you dick. I need you," he said, "I let you out."

Hitman stayed at the bars for another moment. Chug slapped at him twice more with the deputy hat and threatened to come in. Finally the dog lowered himself and stood on all fours, watching the Garzas.

Marvin stayed to the side of the Mexicans. Chug leaned on the side of the big desk, folded his arms, and began to run his fingers under his gold necklaces.

"Look here, Enrique," he said, "you fucked. You know about baseball, boy? Well here you go. You done struck out an I tell you where you misses come from. First, you Mesican. Goddamnit," Chug said, "I'm sick of niggers and greasers. You all is everwhere, I'm so sick of it I could puke in my hand. Second, you left me holdin the bag at Royal Glads. You quit right at beginnin of season. You just up an fuckin leave, no notice, no warnin, no chance for me to git somebody else, though I don't doubt it'd be another colored or a Puerto Rican, just as much of a pain in the ass as you. An, I hear you gonna grow flowers in Mesico. Huh. That's three. Right off when I heard that one I figured I was gonna have to fuck you up."

"You gone have to pay a big fine, bein drunk and drivin," Marvin said. He was looking at the Garzas as hard as he could. "This here is my county."

"That's right," Chug said, "you gone be penalized big time for strikin out an drivin drunk. You been lucky most of you life, workin for my old man, gettin good pay, even had you own house on a white man's street. But you luck's gone down ahead to Mesico without you. You all hear what I'm sayin?"

"You got nothin now," Marvin added, "except to worry."

Enrique looked up, Anita stayed focused on the spot she had chosen in the floor. He moved his eyes to the dog, at attention behind the bars. He turned his head imperceptibly to take in Marvin, then landed his

137

eyes on Chug. Enrique's face was blank. He looked like he had been abandoned of will.

"The sheriff can jail you right now, you stinkin drunk. We can smell it, so can a judge. Celebratin on you way to Mesico, that's how it'll look. You could lose you car and whatever else shit you got, maybe you lose a hand or a arm, I throw you ass in there with Hitman. He's just waitin, ain't you dog? What's that word? Oh yeah," he laughed, "nigger. Hitman, watch the nigger." He suddenly grabbed Enrique by his shirt front, spun him around and pushed him hard toward the dog. Enrique stumbled then tripped. He was unable to break his fall with his hands cuffed behind him, his head cracked loudly on the oak. Blood spurted for an instant, then his thick hair slowed the bleeding to a red leak. He lay where he fell and looked up sideways at Hitman.

The dog had again thrown himself violently against the iron bars. He jumped on the cot and tore at the pillow and blanket, he bit out big mouthfuls of the thin mattress. He snapped at the chains that held the cot off the wall, he pissed in his excitement. A terrible rumble and growl came from his chest and throat. He shook his massive head back and forth and side to side, his frustration maddened him.

"That's enough! Sit!" Chug yelled again. "Sit. Goddamnit," he roared, charging at Hitman, slipping a little in his boots. Hitman dropped and backed up. He stood, panting loudly, glaring at his master.

Anita was sobbing, the three men could hear her. Her shoulders shook and her chest heaved. Chug worried she was about to begin screaming, he moved quickly to where she stood. He started to slap her, remembered she had busted her mouth or some damn thing so he grabbed her upper arms, pulled her hands from her face and shook her twice, very hard.

"Shut the fuck up, lady," he said, "or I give you somethin to cry about."

Enrique looked up from where he lay on the floor. He twisted himself around so he could see Anita. He listened for what Chug wanted to tell them.

Chug thrust Anita away from him and turned to face Enrique.

"Maybe," Chug said, "you all got that money stealin, smugglin wet-

138

backs. Maybe you the one been pilferin flowers and supplies from the farm. Maybe you gettin a kickback from you Mesicans to not work em so hard. Farmin for you self in Mesico? That take a lot of money."

"You can have the money," Enrique said.

"That's good, boy, that's real good." Marvin moved to where Enrique lay and stood over him. Hitman's ears stayed up. "That's what we was countin on," Marvin said.

"Maybe," said Chug, "you go to another police, the fuckin FBI, I don't know. Maybe you make a lot of trouble for me an Marvin here. Git our asses thrown in prison or somethin."

"I think we can cut this old boy a deal, Chug, I think we can give im a chance to get gone to Mesico," Marvin said. He was nervous and shaky. "Let's wind this thing up," he said, swallowing hard at the sour, bitter taste in his throat. He looked at Chug, then down at Chug's pants pocket. "You gone put down another line pretty soon?"

Chug reached into his jeans, pulled out a vial and dumped the powder on the top of the mahogany desk. He drew a hunting knife from his boot and began to dice the coke.

"Maybe somebody will kick up a big fuss on you behalf, maybe not. I got the old man by the balls, he's been fuckin his secretary. Missus Sinclair can clean him out for somethin like that. Marvin here, his daddy is the he-coon of this whole county, police ways anyhow. As much as he probably don't give a shit about Marvin, he ain't likely to help send him to Raiford. Not over you. Here, Marvin," he said, moving out of the way of the lines, "help you self."

Enrique looked up at Chug while he talked, again at Anita when Chug bent over the desk and snorted his share, then he forced his eyes to the floor. He was surprised again, like he had been when Chug had screamed at him about the money, but now he was not so slow, the pain from his head wound had wakened him. He hoped that Chug and the deputy man were as careless, as lazy and stupid as he thought they might be.

"Jesus Christ, Chug," Marvin said, his voice had changed, the pitch had become higher. "I ain't leavin it to my daddy to help me out. He ain't

139

even gonna know about this, ever. I cain't fuckin worry about these folks even accidentally tellin im. We got to do somethin, we gotta have insurance or somethin about this thing."

Chug looked at Marvin closely. Chug's eyes were red, his pupils were dilated, dark. He ground his teeth and fought back the bile that was rising in his throat. Marvin was doin all right, he thought, he could do it. But Chug decided he wasn't gonna kill the greasers, something way back in his dope-addled, whiskey-soaked brain remembered the electric chair for him, remembered all the big niggers that would love to beat someone like him almost to death, let the guards save they lives, an beat em again. But Marvin was makin the Garzas wonder.

"I just as soon kill these folks too, Marvin," he said, "like I told you I would, that way there ain't ever any more problems. Maybe though," he said, "we can convince em to beg for they lives an promise never to come back here, maybe, but it's gonna take a lot of persuadin. What you think?"

"Well, shit, I really don't wanna kill em but savin they lives ain't worth no time in Starke either, me bein law an all. I guess I just don't know."

"Goddamnit," Chug said, "then let's just play this thing out now."

He stepped back close to Anita, very close. His face was only inches from hers, he towered over her like a giant to a dwarf. Anita started to gag and choke from the smell of his insides, his mouth and his teeth.

"Lemme explain this to you Anita, we gone take you money," he laughed ugly and then his face got ugly. "Shit on that, we already got you money. You an you old man think you can live without it, nod you head. Good," he said, "that'll work. See I need that money. I got a lot of shit I want to waste it on, course you wouldn't know about none of that. Marvin here, well he's sick of his shitty job, an he wants to buy a boat. Ain't that right, Marvin?"

"Here's what we gone do," he said, turning back to Anita. "We gone leave you three thousand dollars an you car an you things. I doubt you got any jewelry that's worth a shit. You all goin on to Mesico. You better convince you old man here that that's the way to go. Git you selves into the Panhandle an on to Brownsville without stoppin."

Chug reached down and grabbed Anita around her throat with one of his powerful, ring studded hands. He squeezed, her eyes popped and new water spilled from between her legs. Enrique struggled to come off the floor but the side of Marvin's boot caught him in the back of the head, where it had split on the oak. His teeth were violently jarred from the blow, his wound began to bleed badly.

"You tell you man there on the floor right now, he fucks with me, I'm gone git you kids. I know where you house is. Shit. It's too easy. I know where they work too. Me an Hitman an Smith an Wesson tear them little gooks to pieces, I ever even hear you names mentioned alongside of mine. Then I come git you. Then I come git him. Even accidentally, the law comes down on me, I got lots of friends owe me favors. I git em to rape the girl, cut you boy's nuts off an feed em to my dog. They be happy to do it, or else they be sorry too."

He let her throat go. Anita was in misery but outraged by the evil man. She gasped for new air. Her teeth had bit into her broken lip and it was bleeding again.

"Tell im what I said, tell im in English. I wanna hear it. I can tell from lookin at his face how it's gonna come out."

Chug and Marvin listened to Anita tell Enrique that it was not up to him, she would never risk the bodies and spirits of the children, she said, for money. In her anguish she switched to Spanish, Chug didn't interfere, he guessed what the old lady was saying. Between sobs and stinging tears she implored Enrique to promise the men that they would go and never, never make trouble. The men would be safe from them. They were welcome to the money. Enrique nodded his head dumbly. He nodded and nodded and mouthed the words yes and yes, si and si. He spoke from where his head lay pressed against the floor by Marvin's boot. There would be no trouble, he said, there would be no trouble from the Garzas.

"We will do whatever you want, I swear it. We only want to go to Mexico. We will have others there send for our children so they do not bother you. The money you want is yours, it is not important to me, but please," he said, "do not hurt my wife again. I am sorry," he said, "that I offended you. I am sorry that I did not obey you at the farm."

Chug barked at Marvin to get Enrique up and stand him beside Anita. "I'm gettin the toolbox," he said, "outta my truck. Put you deputy skills on em till I get back."

Enrique remembered what the soldiers had talked about at Buckingham, the ones that had been overseas, about capture. If they could get past these moments they would probably live, he thought, this was the most dangerous time. He believed that they were going to be allowed to go on to Mexico, that the men would let them leave. Pendejos. If he could get Anita out, if he could just get her out the door.

Chug stepped back inside, set the toolbox on the desk. He held a pair of bolt cutters. He cut the lock on the toolbox, then he whirled on Enrique. He swung the bolt cutters down, he smashed the Mexican's knee. The blow crushed Enrique's kneecap. It tore through the muscle and cartilage, ripped the flesh and splintered the bones that met there. The bolt cutters opened a deep, instantly bloody gash that spurted through the tear in his trousers and onto the polished floor. Enrique screamed. Chug reached down, pushed Marvin's boot away, grabbed Enrique by his shirt front and hammered two punches at his mouth and nose, splitting the Mexican's lips, cutting the skin on his cheekbone with the stones in his rings. He had missed on the second punch and had not broken Enrique's nose, but wasn't bothered enough to hit him again. Enrique lay flat on the floor. Anita ran forward and crouched over her husband, and covered his face with her hands.

"Jesus Christ, Chug," said Marvin, "you liked to kill him already. Looks like you cut his fuckin leg off."

"Insurance," said Chug, "or somethin. Git em up," he said. He was breathing heavily, sweating worse, stinking sour water seeped from his hair and face and arms.

Marvin reached down and pulled Anita from Enrique, not as roughly as Chug had handled her. He got her to her feet and then they worked together for a moment to get Enrique standing, leaning against her. His face was swollen, bruising already, and his eyes did not focus.

"Goddamn, Chug," said Marvin, "he's bleedin bad an the woman's pissed all over herself an the floor too. These people is makin a mess of my office."

"Don't you worry none, Marvin, soon as these is gone, we git Hitman to clean this shit up."

Anita struggled to hold Enrique. His head was numb from the boot and the fists, his tongue was lacerated and several of his teeth had been

142

knocked loose, but the pain in his leg was the worst of it. He was afraid he would faint, and that they would decide then to kill them.

"How much money you all got in you wallet an you purse?" Chug asked.

"Five hundred in each," Anita answered.

Chug opened the lid of the toolbox, he and Marvin saw the money for the first time.

"You know, deputy, I got two more grams of coke for us to celebrate with, an I ain't sure that's enough. Goddamn," he said, "lookit all that cash."

Chug took out three bundles of crisp bills and handed them to Anita. There were thirty seven more still in the box.

"You all need to use this here and what you got in you pockets an haul you sorry selves to the desert. You gonna need food an gas an probably a doctor, but I wouldn't stop for one till you in Texas, in case we change our minds an decide to come after you. See?"

"Besides," Marvin giggled. He was relieved there was more coke to snort. "You all gonna need that little bit of money to bribe the law down there to let you back in, on account you all so fucked up. Up here, over here," he said, trying to get his geography right, "it's a lot more expensive for police."

"You all listen to Marvin," said Chug, "an git goin."

"You want me to help em out, Chug? Git em out the door?" Marvin asked.

"Naw. They got each other, Marvin, they used to this shit. Anita," he said, "you gone have to do the drivin looks like. I seen to that. You git you man out that back door, you car's outside. You put him in that station wagon of yours an git you selves north in a hurry. Nod you head if you understand. Good," he said. "Enrique, you shoulda stayed on Gladiolus Drive, you still have you job, you bed tonight, you still have you money too, at least for a little while longer. An you leg wouldn't be all fucked up."

Anita looked up at Chug and then at Marvin. Enrique kept his eyes on the floor. He was wondering if he would ever leave it.

"Marvin take them cuffs offa im, he ain't lookin so good."

Marvin unlocked the cuffs. Enrique held onto his wife's arm with both hands. It was very difficult for him to stand up, his head pounded with pain but not as badly as his leg. He felt that there was a saw cutting across his knee. His pants were wet with blood, it had pooled on the floor below him.

"Go on," said Chug, "git. Remember I give you lives an some money to go wherever the fuck it is you people come from, when I coulda just killed ya. Still might, for that matter. I don't care how you git to Mesico so long as it's fast. I cain't keep the deputy from comin after you if he changes his mind, an he's got all them rifles," Chug snorted. The gun case was nearly empty.

Anita looked at the door. Her own legs felt detached, worthless, not part of her, unwilling to help. She struggled to send them a message to move. She leaned the upper half of her body forward, toward the door, she hoped her legs would follow to keep her from falling on her face. Her feet moved a little, she shuffled, and put her arm around her husband's waist. They moved that way toward the back of the jail. Enrique's ruined leg dragged behind the rest of him. He had never encountered such pain and relief at the same time.

Marvin came around them and opened the door.

"You car's there," he said and pointed where the Rambler was parked in the narrow alley. "You all don't never come back to Charlotte County. Anybody you know up this way dies, have the fuckin funeral in Mesico. Don't come back to my county. I'm law here," he said. "Don't come back for anything, ever, cause I know Chug'll kill you for certain."

They passed through the door slowly, then it was closed behind them. It was raining again. The world around them was black, with the night, with the indifference of the sleeping town.

144

Chapter Twenty Five

Anita and Enrique moved toward the Rambler. It was parked against the brick wall of the jail. She helped him get in the car, got his bad leg in, managed to make herself walk around the car alone to the other side, open the door, and sit behind the steering wheel. The keys were in the ignition. The empty mason jar rolled under her bare feet. Anita reached down for it, she gagged at the smell and the remembrance of danger. She picked up the jar and dropped it behind the front seat. She believed she could smell her own fear in the salt rivulets that seeped from her body. Enrique sat upright, his ruined leg held out before him, he grasped a place above his knee. He did not pay attention to his head wounds, he knew they were not serious, only bloody, but he was worried about his leg. Anita started the car, left the alley and was in the center of Punta Gorda in a minute. He told her to turn left. In a moment they were on the flat bridge across the Peace River. He saw that there were men fishing, they were hunched over the cement rail of the bridge staring down into the black water. When they were across the river, heading north on 41, he turned his head toward Anita.

"When I tell you to turn, do it without hesitation. I do not want to be followed. Go right at the next road."

She turned northeast on 769 toward Arcadia. When they were out of the scrub and the range and in the old cow town, they passed under massive oaks with great gray trunks. The rain had stopped but water still

145

dripped from the big trees and the Spanish moss that trailed almost to the ground. He told Anita to take State Road 70 to U.S. 27. They went due east, at 27 they turned south. Anita asked him once what they were doing, going east and south instead of north and west. He told her he was making a plan, she should drive the car. They crossed the bridges at the lettuce ponds and the cypress museum and passed the turnoff to LaBelle. There had been no lights behind them since they had left Charlotte Harbor, but Enrique continued to adjust his mirror, he checked it every few minutes. He told her to go through Moore Haven, a small hunting and trapping and fishing town on the west side of the lake. They went further south, then west through Big Sugar. Although dawn was an hour away, they saw tall black men walking along the road carrying machetes and lunch pails. Enrique had taken off his belt, wrapped it around his leg above his shattered knee. There was a little ice left in the cooler. He twisted around and grabbed it. He held handfuls of the ice on his knee, he gave Anita small pieces to put in her mouth.

Incredible relief, immeasurable pain, he thought. He was surprised that he could split what had happened into two values and study them, first the one, then the other. He became in his delirium, enthusiastic. As pain like stormy waves rolled over him, so did a great need for revenge, retribution, restoration. Joy would replace despair. He believed despair was surmountable, provided there was opportunity and resolve.

He had lost control of his bladder. His pants were very wet. The urine cooled with the wind passing through the car, he began to be cold and feverish at the same time.

It was dawn when they drove into Immokalee. The town was stirring to its work and its poverty.

Immokalee sat in the center of twenty five hundred square miles of prairie, range land, unruly forests, and farms. It was perched on the edge of the Everglades, on the edge of modern times. The cattle business had taken off in 1900. Drovers and cowboys pushed lean scrub cattle west to Punta Rassa, the steers were loaded onto barges and shipped to Cuba. After the cattle boom, because the land had already been cleared by fires and grazing, because the year-round weather was good, farmers began working the soil. They planted tremendous parcels of tomatoes, squash, cucumber, eggplant, melons, and green beans. In Devil's Garden, because the weather near Orlando became very cold in the winter, they planted citrus. Mile-long rows of oranges and grapefruit grew without interference except on the coldest nights, but mostly the town existed because of vegetables. Tomatoes, squash and the rest were picked as precise crops, all at once ripped from vines and stalks, much less than ripe, hard yellow and hard green, never red or purple or the color they were supposed to be. They were brought in wooden crates to the packing houses, huge buildings that covered several acres of land. The vegetables were graded, cleaned, put in bags and boxes, loaded in railroad cars and refrigerated trucks, gassed, and rushed north. When it reached its destination, the produce was still hard, but had more color.

Immokalee remembered it had been a cow town. Everybody who could afford to dressed like a cowboy. It was a small place. The flat range and the farms surrounded and dwarfed the packing houses and the cattle pens and downtown. The workers stayed there to avoid the even worse poverty and deprivation of the farm camps and migrant villages.

Cypress stands and clusters of sabal palms could be seen in the distance. The prairie petered out just south, the land sloped imperceptibly down, and became the Everglades. In Felda, between Immokalee and LaBelle, small derricks sucked crude-oil from under the lime rock below the sand. In Naples, just twenty five miles to the west, people played golf, sunned on the beaches, and ate dinner in expensive restaurants.

To the east is Devil's Garden. Except for the citrus groves, it is a vast tangle of woods and swamp. Men come from both coasts to run down wild pigs and shoot turkey and deer. Great flocks of buzzards nested in Devil's Garden. They perched in the cypress trees when they were tired of hunting or full from eating. When they circled over the land on high currents they blended together in dozens and hundreds and appeared to be a single giant shadow that floated over the scrub. The vultures had no natural enemies, they reproduced with impunity. They floated over the land in squadrons, vision and scent and instinct on alert, hundreds of the big black birds at once above the range. When nothing would die, because they were not content to wait, they flew down in groups to peck the eyes out of newborn calves. When the calves died soon after, because they couldn't find the teat, the buzzards ate again. Cattlemen, ranchers, cowboys, and farmers carried high velocity rifles with powerful scopes. When they could, they stopped their trucks in Devil's Garden and shot at the buzzards circling overhead. The men felt hatred for the birds in their hearts and revulsion for them in their sensibilities.

The packing houses in Immokalee ran all day and all night when the farmers were harvesting. In late summer and fall they planted, in the winter and spring they picked. The town was swelled then with migrants, wetbacks, and transient human wreckage. Twenty four hours a day in season, seven days a week for months on end the packing houses were full of vegetables, people, and roaring machinery. The farmers squeezed in another crop after the first one. They planted in December and January if the weather was mild, harvested again in late March and April. By May it was over, and the people had no work until August. The farmers gambled every year on the weather, the people gambled on the farmers' luck. Sometimes there was a shortage of warm days or a surplus of nights of bitter cold. The farmers lost everything, they had to go to the banks and the government to borrow money. The people lost everything too, including what it had cost them to come, and opportunity. For them, however, there were no banks or government offices to lend money. They simply became more poor than they had been. They relied on the churches to keep them from starving.

It was a town overflowing with Mexicans. The colored people had been there for many years. They owned the small grocery stores and bars and kitchens but it was the Mexicans that filled them. They were everywhere. The squat, black haired little men walked in pairs on the cracked sidewalks, peddled beat-up bicycles, or paid to ride in the back of dirty truck, a filthy van, or an old school bus. They were in the fields and the packing houses and slept ten men to a room in ramshackle wooden shelters that the landlords called houses. They played soccer in parking lots, they killed time in the laudromats and grocery stores. A Mexican could lose himself for an hour in a small grocery store, just looking, and leave with a grape soda. He'd walk back a half a mile two hours later for the nickel deposit on the bottle. That was entertainment.

If a Mexican was in trouble in Naples or Fort Myers or Sarasota, he ran to Immokalee because it was a good place to hide from the law, to get lost in the numbers. The deputies left Immokalee alone unless there was a killing in the streets. They didn't go to Devil's Garden at all, there was the swamp and the prairie and all those buzzards. A corpse didn't last long with the heat, the water, and the birds. The deputies figured there were too many wetbacks to sort through anyway, they didn't speak a fucking word of English and the cards they carried were just so much bullshit. The law left the Mexicans to fend for themselves.

There were churches in Immokalee, Catholic and Baptist and Jehovah Witness. The churches looked out for the people. There were voodoo shrines for Haitians and Jamaicans. The deputies figured the sugar cane cutters ate the Mexicans alive. They came to Immokalee for the gambling, the dope, and the alley whores, they all carried knives and pistols. So what, the deputies figured, there'd just be less beaners. If they couldn't handle it, they should have stayed in Mexico.

The cow town had become a farm town, there were more greasers every year. White people who lived in Fort Myers and Naples never went to Immokalee, but winos and vags came out of the weather from the Northeast and the Midwest at the onset of winter. They wanted to be warm. They collected disabilities and pensions and stay-away money, they picked vegetables or worked in the packing houses when they were up to it. They slept in flop houses, in alleys, in old cars and hidden places under the old wooden buildings where rats ran over them to get at rotting fruit and squished tomatoes. Startled Mexicans stepped around the vags where they lay diminished or dying on the sidewalks.

It was a town filled with drunks, dope fiends, robbers, murderers, feudal laborers, serfs, indentured servants and plantation hands. If a man was in Immokalee, he was sucking hind tit, without much chance at better.

Chapter Twenty Six

Anita stopped the Rambler in front of the Catholic church, Our Lady of Guadalupe Mission. The night was ended. To the east, the sun was already a half-circle of orange and yellow fire. Anita and Enrique were chafed between their legs. Anita's lip had stopped bleeding but had swelled up so badly she would have difficulty speaking. The blow to Enrique's knee had left his flesh torn and his kneecap divided. Chug had missed the artery. He was slumped against the passenger door, his hands tired, fallen in his lap. Anita forced herself to loosen her fingers from the steering wheel, she opened the door and got out. She walked to the small house that was behind the church building and tapped softly at the door. The priest who lived there was accustomed to late night and early morning and afternoon and evening entreaties. There were emergencies, accidents, desperations and eventualities every day. He answered the door quickly.

Anita and the priest Hidalgo dragged and carried Enrique into the clean little house and into the small extra bedroom for guests. They laid him down on the single bed. Anita sank exhausted into the only chair in the room. Hidalgo went to the front of the house, to a desk in the corner that was his office. He used the telephone to call the two sisters. The nuns lived nearby in an old wooden house with a small sitting room, a kitchen, a bathroom, and a bedroom that had space for two cots and a dresser. The rooms for the nuns were attached to another room with beds that served as the midwifery. Haitian and Mexican and mixed babies were delivered and saved along with their mothers. Enrique was on his back when the sisters came in, his face was very white except for the welts and bruises Chug's fists and Marvin's boot had made. He stared at the fan that turned overhead. The sisters and Anita cut off the pants leg that was wet with water, blood and urine. They shook their heads and were very solicitous when they saw the injury to his knee, although they had seen wounds that had been worse. They repaired stabbings, shootings and maimings as nearly often as they delivered babies. When they were not ministering to the mothers and babies, and the sick and the abused, they walked without fear to the houses in the very poorest part of town. They encouraged the people they met there to eat better, to wash themselves, and to brush their teeth as best they could.

One sister gave Enrique a shot with morphine and he instantly slept. Together they bathed his leg and very thoroughly examined his wound. They cleaned the torn flesh and covered it with gauze. They left the room when Anita asked them. While her husband dreamed with the morphine she removed his shirt, his fouled pants and underpants. She bathed him with a hand cloth she dipped in a porcelain dish of warm soapy water that the priest had brought into the room. She washed his face and cleaned the cuts, she soaped and bathed his shoulders and arms, his stomach and back, his testicles and penis, his legs and feet. She emptied the bowl in the bathroom and filled it again with water. She squeezed the hand cloth clean and returned to her husband to rinse and caress his battered body. She left him for a moment, she went to the Rambler for his suitcase. She brought it back to the room and dressed Enrique in clean underpants and undershirt.

When the nuns came back in, they discussed her husband's badly damaged knee. They could drive him to a doctor in Fort Myers, they said. Anita told them they would have to wait until he was awake, that he would decide about a doctor. She asked the sisters what they could do. The nuns squeezed the split flesh together with their fingers. They put in several perfect stitches and wrapped the wound with layers and layers of clean white cotton. His kneecap would be protected, they said.

Hidalgo insisted to Anita that she rest in his room. He would be at the church or visiting people who needed to see him. She lay down on the priest's bed in her dirty clothes. She clasped her hands in front of her, on top of the center of her body, and closed her eyes. Later, she thought, she would wash.

The priest often spoke with his God about his gratitude that the sisters were there to do things, real things to help the people that he could not. He trusted the sisters instinctively, besides oaths and vows of holy orders and obedience. They had saved babies all over the world when no one else would, they mended the wounds of the little men that came with lacerated thumbs and missing fingers from the machinery in the packing houses, cuts across their faces from the knives of the angry black men, and broken teeth and noses when they had turned against each other as do animals in cages. The sisters were hard not to like, he thought, and they did not speak out of turn.

Father Hidalgo had a one year old, dark blue, four-door Dodge with air-conditioning that he bought from Bob Corner's dealership on Cleveland Avenue. He used it when he and the sisters went to Fort Myers for High Mass or groceries and supplies, or to Miami to visit with representatives of the bishop. The Dodge was fast, it ran like a horse. It was kept immaculately clean and the gas tank was always full.

The priest and Enrique and Anita were sitting at the table in the kitchen. Enrique was looking through the window at the car. It was late afternoon, almost dark. They had been refreshed by sleep, Anita had bathed and been ministered to by the sisters, her lip had stitches also. The Garzas were dressed in fresh clothes, Hidalgo had removed his coat and collar.

Hidalgo's housekeeper and cook was a colored lady who had worked for the mission for many years. She had not liked any of the priests better than she liked Hidalgo. She understood that they were strange, devoted men that she was responsible for feeding and straightening up after, their lives were not their own. The priests, and the sisters who were the midwives, she believed, belonged to someone else.

The lady's name was Miss Irene, she was the finest cook in Immokalee. While the three people spoke politely together in Spanish, she placed full plates in front of them, of sliced red tomatoes picked ripe from her own garden, of sweet white corn, of cucumbers and sweet onions in mild vinegar. Miss Irene served them crisp fried chicken breasts and golden waffles with butter and honey. They drank iced tea from sweating metal glasses. The tea was sweetened with cane sugar from Belle Glade, it was tart with juice squeezed from a sour orange. Father Hidalgo apologized for the food.

"Irene is from Immokalee," he said. "She feeds me as she feeds her other family. This food may not be what you like."

The Garzas continued to eat, they said everything was very good, especially the chicken and the waffles. They complimented Miss Irene, thanked her over and over. They ate well. She was still putting more food out when the people declared they could eat no more. Enrique's appetite had been very sharp. He wanted food for fuel, to repair his wounded body, to have energy for the events that were ahead of him. While he'd slept, there had been confusion, images and anticipations had crowded into blurs and shadows. Now there was clarity. A man runs on fuel, he stared at Hidalgo's car, just like a boat, a farm, an automobile.

After the meal, Miss Irene removed the dishes and packed the food that was left. The nuns would eat and give the rest away. She reminded the priest of an errand and said goodbye to the Garzas. Father Hidalgo walked her to the door.

Outside, the heat still raged against the land, but a breeze had kicked up, storm clouds were approaching from the direction of the big lake, thunder could be heard in the distance. Inside, they were comfortable. The priest's house was air-conditioned, like the big Dodge. Hidalgo could have gotten along without the air-conditioning. He was from the desert and was accustomed to a fierce sun and stifling heat, although he would not have liked to wear suits that contained wool. He had the air-conditioning for the people. They would not have to sweat when they were in front of him, when they were forced to sweat in front of so many others, in so many other places. He wanted the people to be at ease when they were with their priest, when they were petitioning, entreating, confessing, seeking divine intervention and relief.

Enrique told Hidalgo what had happened to them. He omitted nothing except the names of the men who had beaten them and taken the money, and the foul words they had used when they did it. He had been very foolish to take his money with him. Anita had warned him, pleaded with him, he said, but he had not listened and had been careless. It was his fault that he had placed such a temptation in front of men who were so greedy. He was very sorry for that, he said, now there were other things to consider. He told Hidalgo that the men who had robbed them, ruined his leg and threatened the lives of his children were sons of powerful families. The fathers would not do enough, he said, to correct what had been done. Enrique told the priest that he wanted his money back, before it was wasted, spoiled, spent on evil things. They had saved since they had first been married, he would not go to Mexico without what was his. He would be certain, he told the priest, that no one would harm his wife or his children. There would be confrontation and reparation. He opened Anita's purse and removed a bundle of bills. That was a thousand dollars.

"For the mission," he said to Hidalgo.

He reached in again and brought out another bundle. Another thousand.

"For the hospital and the mothers and babies," he said.

He placed the money in front of the priest.

"I will need to use your car. We cannot be recognized. No one can know that we have not gone to Vera Cruz. I must have an opportunity to surprise those men, I will not get close if we are discovered. I will return your car when I am finished," he said.

The rain had arrived, it was heavy on the roof. Hidalgo looked at the Garzas.

"There are wicked men who cause the people to suffer, whether it is in Immokalee or somewhere else," he said. "There are women, girls, who come to the sisters who are victims of outrage. There are men, and boys too, who are abused because they are simple, or don't know to fight back."

Hidalgo looked at the money.

"I cannot endorse violence," he said. "I do not know if I can forgive it."

"You misunderstand me, Father. I want to explain to those men,

154

make them understand that it is better for them to surrender the money to me, and surrender themselves to the authorities."

"You should not lie to a priest, senor, that is bad business. There will be no killing?"

"There will be no killing. I do not want to go to prison."

"What we pray for," said Hidalgo, "is that wicked men can be redeemed."

"Keep my car in the back of your house until we come for it," Enrique told him. "Give the clothes and things in it to the sisters for the poor. My wife will remove her pictures and treasures. We will buy new clothes in Fort Myers."

"Guadalupe watches out for los pobrecitos as best as she can. They will have a better life because of her intercessions. Like the other saints, she is very uncomfortable when the people are abused and children are threatened."

"So are their fathers," Enrique said.

"I would have loaned you the car without asking for money," said Hidalgo.

"It is advisable to keep the Rambler hidden," said Enrique. "Anita will get you the key."

"I will listen to your confession when you have returned with my car," said the priest, "if there is time for it."

155

Chapter Twenty Seven

The Garzas left Immokalee at ten. Steam still rose from the wet asphalt and from the ditches alongside where the cool rain had mixed with the hot, stagnant water. Anita drove west on 82. She was dressed as a Catholic nun, she was in religious habit with regalia. A stiff rectangular linen blinder pinched her brown face. Her hair and neck and shoulders were covered with a headdress and a cape. Beneath the cape she wore a pleated blouse that buttoned close at her throat and wrists. Her skirt was pleated also, and was made of light wool, like the headdress and cape. She could feel the wool through her stockings. High-laced black shoes completed the disguise. A large set of rosary beads with a crucifix rested in her lap, a Red Cross insignia was pinned at her breast. Her wedding ring was on her finger. She had been dressed by the midwives.

The night sky was angry. Heat lightning flashed behind them, it illuminated the cabbage palms and palmetto that crowded the sides of the road.

Enrique sat next to her as he had in the Rambler. He was restored, rested, resolved. He wore black shoes, black socks, black pants, and a black shirt with a stiff white collar. The black shirt was short sleeved. Hidalgo's second best black coat was on the back seat.

"May will bring Chug to me," he said. "She can get him alone. She will be a part of it."

"What has May to do with him other than to sell his vegetables?" Anita asked. "How can she make him alone?"

"They are intimate with each other," he said. "It is not a secret at the farm, or anywhere Chug has been to boast. May is May. She is unusual. She has many fine qualities but she allows herself to be one of his women. I think she is his favorite."

"Does she let him take her that freely?" Anita asked.

"She is intimate with the man for money. He pays her to do things with him, sex things and she gets money. Tonight he will be very drunk or crazy with dope, or sleeping, that is what we must hope for. I do not want him to have an opportunity with our money. He will have it another day, perhaps two, then he will want to put it somewhere, maybe a bank. May must have him for me tomorrow," he said.

"He will come. He has the gypsy's curse," she said. " I am embarrassed to say it in English, 'Que encuentras un cono que tu medida.' I had heard about May," she said. "The women say that the man is insane, that he is relentless in his lust for her."

"I know they do," he said. "I hope that it is true."

They were on Anderson Avenue. The Hill was frantic at eleven o clock, filled with sound and movement. Black people roamed the streets, celebrating Thursday because Friday was only a few hours away. They crossed the railroad tracks, passed the water tower and the sewage plant and turned south on Fowler. They stayed on the ugly street until it ended at the fence at the airport. Anita turned left on a sand road then drove south along Ten Mile Canal. The ditch was filled with rainwater and runoff. They went through Page Park, through Beacon Manor, into The Villas and out Sunrise to 41. It was almost midnight. Anita stopped the car and looked both ways. There were no lights. She turned left onto the highway, drove carefully four more miles and turned right where Australian pines crowded the corner. They were back on Gladiolus.

She stopped the Dodge in the palm and mango coppice of Coca Sabal Lane. It had rained late, recently ended, the ground was wet and very soft. Enrique opened his door, swiveled himself carefully around. Anita came from the other side, held his hands, together they pulled him erect. She reached into the back seat and gave him the crutch Hidalgo had borrowed from a man who had several, and the black coat. There was a plastic jug filled with water, there was fried chicken and ice and morphine in a cooler. She held those things in her hands. In his wallet Enrique had his five hundred dollars, in his pocket he had the last thousand. He had a jackknife, a strong flashlight, and a Saint Christopher medal that the priest had insisted he take.

"It is only fair," Hidalgo had said, "your wife has so much protection and you have so little."

"I will wait for you in there," he pointed, "where Mister Congdon keeps his orchids. No one will come to this place before morning. I am going to rest inside. Think and wait. Set those things down, I will take them in."

Anita set the water and the cooler on the ground. She waved her hands in front of her face.

"The mosquitoes are terrible. Can we sit in the car?"

Enrique reached into a pocket of the black wool coat and pulled out a can of spray.

"Close your eyes," he said. He misted her face, then held each of her hands and sprayed them also. He set the can down and reached into his pocket. He held the bills up to the light of the moon.

."Go to May. Give her this," he said. He handed Anita five hundred. "Tell her we will give her five thousand more when we are finished and we will pay for her to go anywhere. She must get Chug alone for me, then do what I tell her."

"What is that?" asked Anita. "She cannot help you subdue Chug. What else can she do?"

"I will tell her when I see her," he said. " Get in the car, the mosquitoes are very bad."

"I will ask May to help us. I hope she is not indifferent."

"That is what the money is for. To overcome her indifference."

He kissed Anita on both cheeks and waved her to go. She drove slowly around the cypress building. The car brushed against wet palm fronds and mango leaves. In a moment she was on a road named for a flower, three miles from Harlem Heights.

Enrique used the crutch and moved his supplies to the front of the orchid house. He opened the unlocked door and stepped inside. The house was made entirely of glass panes held in place with strips of wood and lead solder. The panels on the top were louvered open during the day to let the heat and extra humidity escape, they were always closed at night. Overhead, metal pipes for irrigation ran the length of the glass house. At one end, big fans drew cool air from condensers at the other. Everywhere there were orchids and miniature ferns, epiphytes and bromeliads. They were suspended from wire holders, crowded, set pot to pot on the wire tables, gathered and clustered underneath, spilling out onto the narrow gravel walkway. Many of the orchids were flowering. Enrique marveled at the strange convolutions and heads of the blooms, he inhaled deeply at the scents. They reminded him of the florist's refrigerator at the Farmer's Market. The plants were thick-leaved and heavy. The terra cotta and wood pots that held the orchids tipped and leaned with the weight, they were attached to wires hung on the metal pipes. Long aerial roots traipsed down like tendrils, the roots were white in the illumination from his flashlight. He turned off the fans and the condensers so he could hear the noises outside. He prepared to sit down at the far end, facing the door. He lowered himself to the gravel, careful not to knock any plants to the ground and careful not to break open the stitches in his knee. He leaned his back against the damp glass and listened for the sound of cars passing on Gladiolus Drive. He heard none, so he listened to the crickets. He guessed at the colors of the flowers of the orchids. He began to refine and put detail to his plan.

159

Chapter Twenty Eight

*I*t was dark. The Mexican boys were sitting at the campfire. They used a metal shelf ripped from an old refrigerator, they placed the shelf on concrete blocks over the fire. That was the stove. They cooked coffee in the morning, at night they warmed cans of beans, chili, and hash, and roasted fish, meat, and vegetables. The smoke from the campfire kept the mosquitoes and gnats from biting them to distraction but the boys always smelled of it. They also smelled of bug spray.

Friday was the only day they did not cook for themselves. Women at the farm brought tacos and tamales, sold them to the men who worked there. Everyone liked Fridays, for the good food and it was payday. The boys lit the fire every night, whether there was cooking or not. It was an only light against the darkness. The fire was a comfort to them, they talked of Mexico and other things until they were sleepy. The boys crushed the cans they used, and picked up trash and scraps of paper that had blown over the pepper bushes from Gladiolus. They pulled weeds around the camp. They placed the things that would burn under the ledge or in one of the big barrels as Enrique had shown them to do.

Inside the concrete building, each boy had a room for sleeping, a place, a cell, where he had a mattress on the floor and nails hammered into the crumbling cement where he could hang his clothes. Each room had an opening in the wall where a door had been and an opening in the opposite wall where there had been a window. The boys covered the mattresses with old pillows, sheets, and blankets and quilts that May found for them at thrift stores and church sales. They gave May money. She bought groceries for them, and a few shirts, pants, socks and undershorts so the boys could have a change of clothes, for Friday, or when they had become especially dirty or when they had been soaked by rain. The boys each had a single pair of dirty canvas tennis shoes. Enrique would not let them work in the huaraches they had worn when they walked in from Immokalee three months before. They wore the sandals at The Quarters.

There was a great room that was entered by the front opening, near the campfire. That room could also be entered through another opening that led into the back yard and into the mango woods. The hallway cut away from the great room at a right angle, it ended in a pockmarked wall. There was no kitchen or closets or bathroom.

The rooms where they slept, the hallway, and the great room were brushed clean every day. The place was free of cobwebs and spiders, ant mounds and litter, but they could not control what climbed or flew through the openings. They covered themselves at night with repellant, slept under sheets that became wet with humidity, and checked their shoes in the morning for scorpions.

They had a pantry made of fruit crates where they kept canned food, soap, toothpaste and brushes, toilet paper, plastic water glasses and spoons. They used the flower knives Enrique had given them for can openers and to cut apart flesh and fish they cooked. They ate mostly with their fingers. The boys plucked at cooked food from a newspaper or spooned it out of cans into their mouths. They had ragged, thin towels and washcloths too, they kept the extras folded. Everything was arranged neatly and in order of its use inside the wood boxes that they placed against the wall.

The boys bathed under the hose in front of the barn after everyone else had gone for the day. One boy held the hose for the others while they lathered with soap and rinsed, then it was his turn. The next day they smelled of smoke and sweat again. Once a week, while they were washing themselves, they washed the dirty clothes. The boys hosed down what they had worn, on a rough concrete pad in front of the barn. They washed the clothes as they had seen mothers and sisters do. They rubbed soap into the wet clothing, worked the soap into the fabric. They pound-

161

ed the clothes hard against the concrete to shake loose the sand then they rinsed them again and again. When they were finished they carried the wet bundles back to camp, they draped the things on bushes in the clearing, the clothes would be dried by the sun the next day.

When the boys had to piss, they turned away from the others. When they had to shit, they ran up the center road or down the path between the buildings to get to the bathroom in the packing house, or they went the other way, into the woods, dropped their pants and squatted and wiped themselves from the roll of paper that they shared. They were afraid to shit in the woods after dark, so two went back to the barn together, they each took a turn in the filthy bathroom that they shared with the other people of the farm. No one cleaned the shitter.

May gave the boys an old transistor radio and some extra batteries. They propped the radio on a window ledge and listened to whatever station came in the most clearly that night. The radio brought music and talk from Cuba and Texas and Miami. Although much of the commentary was gibberish, indistinguishable to the boys, they liked the noise. The radio dispelled the solitude, it diminished loneliness, it battled with them against the night.

They had been in the country almost three months but had not learned any English words beyond here, there, shovel, git, and fuckhead. They tried to listen for words that they might recognize when the patrón spoke at them, but Chug's drawl, inflections, and half-sentences loaded with curses and threats threw them off. They just stared at the ground or nodded dumbly when he talked in their direction.

They had worked every day since they had started at Royal Glads. Most days they worked ten hours, a few days they had only worked six, when the rains had refused to move on west. They had worked at least some, every day, for almost ninety days in a row. They were very happy with that, that they had not once lost a whole day's pay for their savings. Chug told Enrique when he had decided the rain was not going to stop. He'd drive out from whatever bar he had holed-up in just to get to send the people home, so they could not gather in the barn and get paid to watch it rain. He wanted the people off the clock the moment they were not likely to be able to work, not likely to make him money. There had been lots of rain but if it had not been sustained, Enrique ignored Chug, and the people worked through it and finished what had been important enough to start. The people worked in the rain on behalf of the farm and the flowers and themselves.

Chug took ten dollars from each of the boys on Friday for renting them The Quarters. They had earned about twenty dollars a day for the ninety days they had worked, less the ten a week for the patrón. They spent money for food and things to keep themselves clean, and bug spray, and sodas and fireballs on Friday. Other than those things, they did not spend. Each boy had saved about eleven hundred dollars. They kept the money inside fruit jars. Enrique had labeled each jar with the name of the boy who owned it. The jars were kept stashed together, hidden under a neat pile of concrete blocks in the oldest boy's little room. On Fridays the boys made deposits.

They had killed a big rattlesnake that morning. One of them had seen it crossing the center road in the shade house. The boys had circled the snake. The oldest boy hit it hard with a shovel. He cut off the snake's head with his flower knife and carried the five foot long carcass back to the camp. He gutted the snake, put it in a bucket of ice, and set it in a corner of the great room. When work was finished he skinned the rattler, cleaned and rinsed out its insides with cold water, and cut the pink flesh into pieces. He put the meat into a cleaned pail with lightly salted water and more ice, he tacked down the skin, inside out, on an old wood board. He salted it too, the rattlers hung at the bottom.

Enrique had told them to stay away from the big black racers and indigo snakes that lived at the farms, those snakes killed mice and rats and rabbits. Nearly anything else that moved, the boys hunted with the intention of killing and eating. Since they had come to the farm they had slain possum, armadillo, rabbits, and turtles with machetes and knocked down doves and swamp ducks with stones hurled from sling shots. Enrique had not discouraged them from it, except for the black snakes and the few little quail. Those he forbid them to molest. He told them to kill any water moccasins and rattlesnakes they saw, the little ones were the angriest, he had told them, he worried about the women working in

163

the flowers. This rattlesnake was the biggest one they had killed. The youngest boy had rattlers in another fruit jar. He liked to take them out and shake them next to his ear. These rattlers were much bigger than the rest, he'd told the other boys.

It was dark. They were roasting chunks of the snake meat, tomatoes, onions, and peppers, retrieved from the barrels for the pigs. The meal was skewered on wire coathangers.

The happiest time for the boys was fishing in the little lake behind the farm. They were not distracted by electricity. They had no television or games and sports or books to read, they could not read ten words together even in Spanish. They did not drink or smoke, two things they regarded as incredibly, unbelievably, expensive and wasteful. They were unsure of women and could not afford them.

Enrique rigged monofilament, leaders and bobbers and tiny single-barbed hooks to long bamboo poles, like the colored people used along the bank of Ten Mile Canal. He cut the bamboo from the big stand at Coca Sabal, he bought the tackle for them at American. While they were in the fields, the boys watched for grasshoppers and crickets and flower worms, caught the insects, dropped them into jars they carried with the lids punched for air. When the chain was up across the drive-way, when Chug was certain to have gone, they went as a troop to the lake and fished. Because they smelled so strongly of smoke, because they used the spray, the bugs were not so bad. They fished until dark. The boys were very careful, very cautious approaching the lake. They spread themselves out around it until they were all the same distance apart and the water and the fish in it were quartered. They did not make unnecessary noises. The boys caught fat bluegill, careless little bass, and catfish. They pulled the fish from the water, lifted them over the tall grass that grew along the bank, removed the hooks from the mouths of the catch and placed the living, swimming creatures in buckets half-filled with water. The size of the fish did not matter, so long as it could be picked up, held between a boy's fingers while he nibbled at the delicate white flesh and could spit out the tiny bones. When they had caught enough for a supper, they sat or squatted together in the early dark and gutted and scaled the catch. One boy took the pail back to the barn and rinsed the fish with water from the hose. Another boy started the fire, another gathered more fuel. They baked the fish in aluminum foil on the refrigerator ledge over the fire that was their stove and oven.

In the ninety days they had been at Royal Glads, Chug had never spoken to any of the boys directly, not once, other than to curse at them as a group. He communicated his wishes, his orders for the day to Enrique or May. The boys did not understand why a woman so wonderful as May was not the director of a bank or the principal of a school. The boys learned about the flowers from Enrique. They had only known about desert corn, addled chickens and mangy goats. He showed them how to work smart, how to work together, what could be accomplished by the cooperation of men and machine and will. The boys imagined the flowers, where they would color in the rows. Enrique caused them to anticipate the beauty, to understand the logic of the work that would produce it. He taught them to grasp why things were done for the flowers, how, and he taught them about fishing. They learned nothing from the patrón except bad words, that he wished to be feared, and paid his ten dollars every Friday.

They did, however, understand the tone, the intention of his voice. No matter who he spoke to, it was insulting. He ridiculed and demeaned, he threatened, promised retribution. They had heard stories how the Spanish soldiers had been. They had killed Indians with impunity. They believed Chug was the same as the Spanish. He cursed at them, threw half-filled cans of beer at them, even tried to kick at them in the fields when Enrique was not present. Always with the patrón was the dog. Hitman growled, he snapped at the boys. He tried to get loose, he wanted to be at them where they stood. The boys had been afraid, the fear had changed to hatred. The oldest boy hardened first, he passed his steel to the others. They believed that the dog had set his yellow eyes upon their throats. They wished for the opportunity to be at the dog, with shovels and hoes and machetes.

The boys understood the timbre of the patrón's voice when he spoke to May also, they were aware of the sad nature of that arrangement, but what had caused them to become truly dangerous was the way Chug had caused Enrique to leave. Enrique had explained the nature of flowers to them and taught them how to fish. Now he was gone.

"I wish it were that dog's balls we were cooking," said one.

"Would you eat them?" asked another.

"No,' said the first one, "but I would like to cut them off and cook them and leave them for the foxes that come at night."

"That dog is very bad," said the youngest, "I would like to cut it to pieces with my machete, but I would want it to be chained or I would not attempt it."

"Would you get in the truck with it?" asked the oldest, "if it were chained?"

The youngest boy thought a moment before he answered. "No," he said, "I would bring up a chair or a ladder and swing at it from there."

The rest of the boys nodded their heads, they turned the snake over the fire.

"That dog is a reflection of the man who owns it," said the oldest. "He has made it into the devil it is."

"That is true," said one of the others. "I wish it was his balls we were cooking for the fox."

"Bastante," said the oldest.

"Maybe we could feed the patrón's balls to the dog, then we could kill the dog with machetes. That is what I would like to do," said another.

"That is enough," said the oldest. "You should not talk of such things."

"He is an evil man. I did not think I would ever meet one. I did not know men could be so mean." said the youngest.

"Are there more gringos who are equally as bad as this man? Or have we found the worst one?" asked another. "It is said in the barn that he is not happy anywhere. He despises the flowers and the people. When he drinks cerveza and tequila he becomes even more hateful."

"The people in the barn say he is very angry Enrique has left for Mexico," said the other middle brother.

"He will be worse, now that Enrique has gone," said the oldest. "He

166

will be more vile and more dangerous, because there is no one who will challenge him."

"He is cruel and a drunkard," said the youngest.

"Why doesn't the real patrón, that bad man's father, why doesn't he... why did he allow Enrique to leave? Enrique is a good man. He is good for the people."

"That man Chug is a pig," said one.

"He is a sodomite," said the youngest.

"Where do you hear such things?" asked the oldest, "Why do you repeat them? What about the woman who is his victim?"

"I am sorry," said the boy, "I do not mean to be coarse. I think I have been here too long."

The boys reached for the snake and tomatoes and began to eat.

"Why did Enrique leave us?" asked a middle boy, chewing at his food.

"Enrique has worked long enough. He and Senora Garza are very wealthy, and he could not tolerate the foul nature of the patrón. Those are the reasons he is gone to Mexico," said the oldest. "It has nothing to do with us."

"In Mexico, the people do not ever stop working, unless they are maimed or become borachos," said another.

"He is not stopping work, he is changing the place where he works. The people in the barn say he and Senora Garza will grow flowers in Vera Cruz," said another.

"Someday we will have worked long enough in Florida," said the oldest. "We will leave here, never to return. We will have our goats and chickens and corn for flour. Enrique saved his money for the things he wanted. That is what we must do, work and save, and go back to Mexico together."

"I don't dream of going to Mexico any longer," said the youngest. "I don't like the desert. I am attracted to the ocean, but I have not seen it yet," he laughed.

"And I don't like chickens and goats," said another, "I want to drive a truck."

"I want to drive a tractor," said the third brother.

The three younger boys looked at the oldest and waited for him to speak.

"We are changed, that is true."

He looked at his brothers, each in the face, told them what he wanted.

"I want a house that is our own," he said. "I want a house with windows and doors. I want electricity inside. I want a bathroom," he said, " where I can sit when I shit."

The boys laughed together out loud. They chewed the meat, and swallowed sulfur water that had aired out in pails and lost much of its stink.

"The gringo is not the worst one, but he is the one that is here. We have no protection from him now that Enrique has left us," said a middle one.

"He has not yet come to this place," said the oldest. "That is what concerns me, that he will come here drunk, with his dog and his pistols, with his friends. He will want to harm us."

"He will come someday," said the other. "He is the son of the owner, he can do with this place as he pleases."

"We can leave," said the youngest, "we can go home."

"We are not leaving yet," said the oldest. "We must have more money. We will stay here and work as long as it is bearable, until that man forces us to go. I only want to be in this country once, I do not want to come back. I also wish Enrique had not left us here with that man. Think about the women, how they will be afraid. He is a sodomite," he told the youngest boy, "you were right."

"This would be a good place for work if it were not for that man and his dog," said one of the middle boys.

"It is a puzzle to me," said the other middle one. "We are to grow flowers that must be perfect for the rich people's tables, or else we will throw them away. Enrique told us they will be beautiful in the fields, but the mood of the farm is ugly, where the negritos and Puerto Ricans live it is poor. The patrón curses at us, pays us a little, takes some of the money back, and he hates the flowers. We work like burros. Do you think the people who will buy the flowers know?" he asked of the others.

"Of course not," said the oldest, "they think the flowers grow themselves."

"I would like to fix that dog," said the youngest. "I would like to fix him so he doesn't frighten other boys like he has frightened me."

"The dog and the man are inseparable," said the oldest. " You could not fix one without fixing the other."

Chapter Twenty Nine

*A*nita Garza drove Hidalgo's Dodge up Gladiolus. She passed the driveways to Tamiami, Burdette's, and T & K Farms. She went by Moroni's place, Joe Povia's place and Weissmeyer's. She passed the vegetable stand and the entryway to Royal Glads. The lights from the car shined for just an instant on the tin roof of the little market. The chain hung across the driveway, fastened at the ends to white-washed pillars of concrete block. The white was reflected back at her, she remembered that Enrique had painted the columns just a few weeks before. After A and W Bulb, the road curved left then right. She was in Harlem. She turned off Gladiolus at the second sand lane and slowly, quietly, stopped. A shell path led through a hanging gate into a dense coppice of guava, poinsettia, cherry, copper leaf and ginger. An enormous night-blooming jasmine had established itself against the small blue and yellow house. It grew over the frail tin roof, cascaded and spilled into the yard, its fragrance was powerful. There was a narrow front porch with a tattered screen. The door to the porch was flimsy, it shook a little when Anita touched it.

A short distance away, maybe thirty or forty feet, she guessed, she heard the murmur of low voices. She went to the side of the cottage, peered through the plants and trees, and saw the light from a small fire. It was the alcoholics, los borachos, whispering over the last of the wine for the night. She knew a few of the thin vagabonds from when they had worked for her husband and had lived with the other people of Harlem.

170

Now they were in el campo, they drank under old Poinciana's, jacarandas, and tamarind trees. The men lived in shacks and old cars behind May's cottage. They would have died to defend her, if it had ever been necessary, but it was not, May was her own protector.

Anita stepped back up to the wooden porch and knocked softly at the screen door. Inside the frame cottage, candles burned and flickered. Spanish music played from a radio on a wood packing crate next to the open inner door. A white cat came from under the sagging porch and stood next to Anita, anticipating an opportunity to dash inside. May appeared in the doorway, she was in a bright red cotton shift that hung loose from her shoulders to her feet. Her dark hair was wet and very long. She smelled like apples and lavender.

"Quien es? Who's there?" she said.

"May, it is Anita Garza, Enrique's wife. Will you let me come in?"

"You don't look like Anita Garza, Enrique's wife. You don't look like anyone's wife, of this place. You look like una hermana de la iglesia, a sister of the church. Have you come to save me?" she asked.

Anita removed the wool headdress and the stiff linen blinder that had been cutting into her face since Immokalee. She held the habit at her side and looked up at the younger woman who stood with her hands on her hips. Recognition came to May, she moved toward the door.

"There has been trouble," said Anita. "Can I come in? Can I speak of it with you?"

May crossed across the porch and undid the hook that latched the fragile door in place. She held it open for Anita and the cat to enter her cottage. The wood floor was gray, like the sand outside. It was very smooth, the wood had been polished by the sliding steps of calloused feet. The windows were open, multi-colored cotton cloths were bunched at the sides of them. A slight movement of air caused the dozen candles that burned to flicker, bend, and change direction. Old fruit crates covered with cotton tapestries were tables, more crates were composed into a large bookcase that covered the only whole interior wall. The shelves were filled with books. Most of the books were thirty and forty years old, many of them in delicate paper jackets. On the other side of the small room was a glass-topped wicker desk and two wicker chairs. There was a thick oriental rug. Anita could see into a tiny bedroom where more candles burned, the bed nearly filled it. In the passageway to the back door that was the kitchen she saw an old fashioned icebox and a porcelain sink with a hand pump attached to the side. There was no electricity or running water in May's house.

May read by candlelight or by the yellow glow of a kerosene lantern. She swept her floor, rolled up her rugs and shook them outside. She did not cook at a stove, and bathed herself in rainwater or water pumped by hand from a shallow well. The rainwater stayed fresh in the summer months, it was held in a cistern.

Everything that furnished her house, adorned her body, was used, second-hand, bought right. She knew the ladies at the thrift stores, Saint Vincent's, The Salvation Army and Goodwill. She brought the ladies vegetables when she hitched a ride with a neighbor going into town, or a bag of fruit and managed it on the handlebars of her bicycle. She hoped there would be no more accidents. The old ladies liked May, they saved things for her to consider. They paid no attention to May's breasts and bottom. She was a favorite because she was friendly to them and polite, she brought them ripe tomatoes, avocados, and sweet corn. May learned from the old ladies what rarity to buy, what drivel to reject. What she had bought to keep was flawless, of exceptional quality and condition. Expensive clothing in her tiny closet had never been worn. She had a cigarette lighter and a pen and pencil set that were Tiffany, a Faberge broach, a Patek Phillipe watch. She had sterling ashtrays and coasters, a leather coat and a mink one, exquisite underpants, sheer nightgowns, silk sheets and pillowcases. She bartered for things that others had discarded. The old ladies had nice things to show her when she came to visit them. She bought men's' shirts, pants, caps, socks, and gave them to the alcoholics, she had bought a few things on behalf of the boys at The Quarters. She bought very seldom for herself, just the very best. She kept her smallest treasures in an old leather physician's bag under her bed.

May took two velvet covered pillows from where they nestled together in a packing crate, she dropped them on the rug.

172

"What's the trouble? Why are you here?""

"I am very thirsty, May," said Anita. "My lips are very sore."

"We can sit there," she said. "Give me a minute to get us something to drink."

Anita sat down on a cushion and turned her body sideways. Everywhere she looked in the little house, wherever there might have been a bit of space, that place had been filled with house plants in small clay pots or antique ceramic and brass ones. There were philodendron, dieffenbachia, pothos, spathyphyllum, and moon dust aspidistra. The plants lined the walls, filled the corners. They were placed on the wicker desk, the kitchen counter, and cascaded from the top of the bookcase. In the blue, brown, and frosted bottles, between the clay pots and the others, cuttings grew as if from good soil. Delicate white roots of avocado, Swedish ivy and crotons were suspended in water.

The fragrance of the jasmine outside was very strong, it mixed with the scents of the candles. Anita breathed deeply through her nose. She untied the laces of the stiff leather shoes and slipped them off. She wanted to rub her feet, they had been too long in the tight shoes, but she wouldn't do that in front of May. She raked and scratched at her scalp, she ran her fingers through her hair instead.

"I am not used to a hat," she said. "Do you know, this headdress is made of wool?"

"Of course it is," May answered from the kitchen. "Who else but a nun would wear wool in Florida?"

"I do not think the sister who lent me this wears it very often. I think she dresses in her habit for funerals and special Masses," said Anita. "She and the other sister are nurses."

"Being a nurse is good, but I don't have anything in common with nuns. There is a girl in Harlem who dresses in potato bags during Lent," May said. "She is a prostitute, she does it for repentance. She looks like a poor nun for forty days then she goes back to la vida."

May opened the oak and enamel icebox, she brought out a bowl of chipped ice, two chilled tea glasses, and a jar of dark brown tea steeped in the sun on the front porch while she was at the vegetable stand. She poured the tea over the ice, squeezed in a cut key lime. She handed one of the glasses to Anita, and sat down with a grunt on the other big cushion. In the kitchen and in her bedroom she had lit incense, it burned in small brass bowls, that aroma blended with the others. May's body was in repose under her shift. She dragged her fingers through her own hair once, then put the pillow under her ribs and lay on her hip, her legs crossed at her ankles. She looked at Anita looking up into the rafters. Anita would talk when she was ready, May guessed.

"Where you live is very lovely, May. It is not like a house at all."

The beams of the cottage had been painted white. Coils, twists, knots of braided rope, sisal, and flax made from agaves hung down. Entwined in the ropes were pieces of cypress bark, seashells and spoonbill feathers, Spanish moss, air plants, and orchids. The orchid pots were dark brown. The tin roof above the plants and the rafters was rusting, the candle smoke escaped through small holes and separations.

Anita bent her head forward and rubbed her neck. She looked at May. "Tell me please," she said, "where do you cook and eat?"

"I don't cook," said May, "but as you can see I like to eat. I like to eat too much. When I am hungry at the farm I make a salad or I have fruit. Sometimes at night I have melon or grapes or just bread and butter. If I want chicken I invite myself to a grandmothers' house for supper. I bring the vegetables. If I want rice and beans, Wito will have them cooked for me. I get enough for a few days and I give Wito a plant or some flowers to give to his wife. And, " she paused, drew a breath, and smiled, "I get smoked fish from the beach and when los borachos are roasting a small pig or a goat or the church is having a fiesta," she patted her stomach, "I always get my share."

"You really don't cook then, at all. What a pleasure that would be."

"I would rather read than cook but I would rather eat than read."

May laughed at herself and all the talk about food.

"Do you drink? I mean do you drink alcohol?" asked Anita.

"Why?" said May, "Do you want something else? You being a nun you should be careful."

"That was impolite of me to ask," said Anita. "I was thinking of the men in the back."

"I don't drink much," said May. "I don't want to become una com-

174

paniera to los alcoholicos back there. They are addicted, it can do that. I drink sometimes. I have used it to make things easier for me when I am alone with Chug, but I don't like it." She looked at Anita closely. "Do you know about that?" she asked.

"I don't drink either," said Anita. "It costs too much money."

Enrique had told Anita not to rush at May, to wait until they were comfortable in each other's presence before she related what had happened, and what they would pay for.

"Those men in the back," said May, "it is a terrible waste. They were boys once, like the ones in The Quarters."

"You live simply. I know you have always worked and that you have done things that are difficult, for money. Are you wealthy? Have you saved a great deal? If you have no electricity, no vices, no one to cook for? Are there other things you want to have?"

May reached across the short space between where she rested against the pillow and the lowest shelf of books. She pulled out a few books, then a small ceramic jar hidden behind them. She placed the jar on the floor in front of her. She took out a reefer. She lit the joint with a wood match and inhaled deeply. She held the smoke in her lungs for a long moment.

"It stinks," said Anita, "and that is a vice."

May laughed, choked, then showed her pretty teeth. "Bullshit," she said. "I grew this plant from a seed. I smoke the flower of my own plant and it helps me to concentrate or to relax, whichever one I want. There is no sin in that. I don't buy the plant and I don't sell it. I am not part of what can make it a vice."

Anita laughed too. "No," she said, "there would be no sin in smoking your own plants."

May looked at the joint, flicked a little ash, then toked deeply on it again. She blew the smoke at the ceiling.

"The smell will be gone in a minute," she said, "it will mingle with the others."

She reached out and rubbed the head and ears of the cat laying on its side on the wood floor. She sat up, took a last hit at the reefer and put it out in a heavy, cut-glass ashtray.

"I have saved a little," she said. " I am not wealthy but I am not poor either."

She frowned, she had reminded herself of her in between-ness.

"I do not smoke around the men I know, I don't like them enough. I have nothing to say to them when my head is like this. I have some money. I have taken money from Chug for having sex with him, but I like sex anyway," she giggled a little and coughed. "Can I say this to a nun?"

"Why are you saving your money?" Anita asked.

"I want to go away, but I don't want to wait as long as you have. Yes, I have money, but I cannot lend it," she said, "even to you. Is that why you are here?"

May was a little stoned. She took a long drink of the chilled tea, melted ice and lime. She put the roach into the jar, put the lid back on and hid the jar again behind the books. She reached for her cigarette case, tortoise shell and gold. She took out a thin, dark cigar, lit it, she puffed smoke rings at the orchids.

"My real vice," she said. She squinted at the smoke, she looked more closely at Anita. "But it annoys the bugs."

Anita put her fingers to her wounded lip.

"Your lips are very swollen. I'll get you something to put on them. I have leaves that will take away the pain and help you heal more quickly. What happened to your mouth? Why are you here at one o clock, two o clock in the morning, when you have never been here before?"

"We want you to help us," said Anita. "My husband wants to be alone with Chug."

Chapter Thirty

"Where do you want to go, May? How soon? How badly do you want to be there?"

"I want to go to Monterey. I want to live in California and I don't want to wait until I am an old woman to get there. Since you asked I've told you."

"You can be in California by Sunday," said Anita. "This can be your last night in this house, you will be wealthy besides. This will be a long night, maybe you will sleep, maybe not, tomorrow night will be a long night also, and more difficult, dangerous." Anita drew in a deep breath and asked the girl, "Do you want to hear what Enrique wants to say?"

The women were through it in an hour. Anita's account of the robbery was accurate, her proposal to May was clipped, to the point. May knew Chug had big balls that went with his dick, but she had not realized that he was so stupid, greedy, and cruel. Anita recounted the scene at the ambush and in the sheriff's office. She told May how badly Enrique had been battered. She told May about the sisters and Hidalgo in Immokalee. She said that her husband was very angry, that the two men had beaten and robbed him and threatened his children. He said he was going to get his money back, she told May. His children would not be in danger, ever, he'd said. May asked Anita right out if there would be killing. Life was cheap in Harlem Heights. Enrique had told the priest

177

that there would not be any killing, Anita said. He had told Hidalgo he would recover his money and see justice done. He would see to it that the children were not in danger. Anita told May that Enrique wanted to be alone with Chug. What he did then was not up to them. They needed May, she'd said, to arrange for that encounter. There was another thing Enrique required of May but she did not know what it was. Enrique would tell May when he saw her. They would leave Fort Myers as soon as the second thing was finished. They would meet Enrique in Tampa, one day after the day that was only hours away, she'd said. They would leave Harlem Heights in the priest's car, never to return. For getting Chug alone, and for the second thing Enrique wanted her to do, the Garza's would pay May five thousand dollars, and they would buy her an airline ticket to fly to anywhere she wanted.

"Anywhere," said Anita, "from the airport in Tampa."

"Enrique does not like planes, he gets airsick," she'd said. "The things we will do are decided by Enrique. He is angry, he will punish those men. If you agree to any of this you must agree to all of it," she'd said, "that is what Enrique told me to tell you."

May held the cold cigar in her fingers. She sat up and curled her arms around her legs. She looked directly at Anita.

"Nuns can't lie," she said.

She dropped the cigar in the ashtray and got up from the cushion. She picked up the empty glasses and went into the kitchen again. In a moment she was back with more steeped tea and sugar.

"The smoke makes my mouth dry," she said.

May lay back down, she put her head on the pillow, she looked up at the things hanging from the rafters.

"What does Enrique want me to do?" she asked, "for the first thing?"

"Enrique said by the lake, after the farm is closed. Today. Enrique said that except for the boys at The Quarters, everyone will be gone. Today is Friday. Payday. The people will want to be home."

May reached for another cigar. She heard rats running on the tin roof. They were returning from eating the mangos on the ground, she thought, or were going to the campfire of los borachos.

178

"Enrique said Chug should be drunk but he does not want him to be so drunk that he does not come to you. You must make sure he will be at the lake," said Anita.

May rolled over, she drank deeply at her tea, then burned a match to the end of her cigar. She put her head back down on the pillow and puffed.

"What else?" she asked after a moment.

"Out of the truck, that is what he said, and the dog, chained in the back of it."

"Those are not unusual things for us when we are together, except for the dog."

"Enrique said the dog must be with the patrón."

"What else does he say?" asked May.

"Enrique said that nothing bad will happen to you. He said not to be afraid, he does not think you will be."

"Even with his pistols," she said, "Chug won't have a chance with Enrique and those boys. What about you, Anita," she asked, "are you afraid of Chug?"

"Yes. I have seen the bastard and his dog and his friend the deputy from close by. It would not take much for them to murder," she said. "I believe they want to kill someone. I am afraid for my children and for Enrique and for you just as much. Why do you speak of boys? Which boys?"

May put the thin cigar between her lips. She smiled around it for an instant, she inhaled and then blew a light gray smoke at the roof.

"I am known here as a whore," said May, "although that is an exaggeration. Enrique will want help. Enrique is wounded, he is old. He will get his help from the boys at The Quarters."

She trailed her free hand behind her and touched the books.

"I don't like the sound of the cars going by the stand, everyone is going somewhere but me. I don't like the heat or the flat of it any longer. There will be another patrón. Who knows? Maybe he will be a good one like Enrique, maybe he will be worse than Chug. Maybe the farm will close. I don't like working in kitchens," she said. "I'll die insane if this is the only place I've known."

"Why do you want to go to Monterey? Do you have family there?"

May twisted on the pillow and pointed her finger at an upper shelf of books.

"Because of those," she said. "Those books are about California and Monterey and paisanos."

"Italians?" asked Anita.

"Mexicans," said May.

"Why haven't you gone before?"

May waved her hand, her palm up and her fingers spread. She moved her hand in slow circles and patterns, playing with the shadows from the candles.

"I had my plants and my house and the alcoholics under the coconut palms. We have been together a long time. It would have been difficult to say adios."

She looked sharply at Anita.

"And I have been waiting for an opportunity," she said.

"Can you get Chug alone? Out of the truck? At the lake in the afternoon?"

"Oh yes," said May, "I have something he wants. Enrique will not be offended? Because of how he will see me?"

"Enrique will not be watching you," said Anita.

May sat up, she brought her face closer to Anita's. She picked up the nun's wool habit and handed it to her.

"I have much to do if I am leaving," she said. "Tell Enrique we will be there. The dog will be on his chain. Tell Enrique to take Chug when he is with me on the blanket."

Chapter Thirty One

Anita left May's cottage to return to Enrique. She left the head-dress off, she placed it on the seat next to a bundle of wet leaves. May had sent the leaves to wrap against Enrique's leg. Anita told May she should pack her things and be ready to leave after dark, after the time at the lake with Chug was over.

She wandered through her house, moving from the kitchen to the front room to her bedroom, back to the front room and the kitchen. She was looking, thinking, letting her fingertips touch and trail over the tips and ends of the flowers and the plants. She found an aluminum pot and went out the back door. She dipped in some rainwater and carried the pot to the camp of los borachos, the coals of the fire still glowed. May put the water on the grill to heat for coffee and sat down in a chair to wait.

The encampment of the alcoholics was small. It was composed of rusted cars, tin and sheet metal lean-tos, huts and sloppy chickees thatched on the top and sides with palmetto. The camp was only thirty feet from May's but it was well hidden. It was screened, rendered invisible from Gladiolus by dense black mangrove. A wall of sorts circled the settlement of winos, made of old washing machines, tires, refrigerators, engine blocks, stove-in wooden boats and broken bicycles. Wild grape, honeysuckle and passion flower had been planted by the first of the hobo

181

settlers when they made camp. The vines had grown over the abandoned things, obscured them from view, the alcoholics lived within that green stockade. A single footpath led from the sand road, around May's cottage to the back, into the circle of los borachos. On the other side the path continued east into the mangroves and buttonwood. The path stopped at A and W.

The fire was edged with rocks. It was surrounded by cast off chairs and couches. Things to sit in were arranged around the fire like furniture in front of an idiot box.

There were a few fifty-five gallon drums with the tops removed where the drunks burned trash and threw bottles when they were empty. Once a month they loaded the rusted Red Flyer wagon and took crushed cans to Hipolito. They gathered cans from the ditches and dumpsters. Dogs lay in the weeds during the day. At night, when the fire had burned down and the men had gone to sleep, the dogs took the chairs and couches. The dogs watched the men carefully when they were around to make sure they did not get too close. The pack explored Harlem Heights for something to eat. The mongrel dogs were often seen clobbered by cars and in pieces, alongside Gladiolus.

Some of the people in Harlem and some back on The Hill knew the men, remembered them when they had walked in the world. They had been friends or cousins who had plummeted from the ledge of life. They could have been alive a hundred years before, they would not have recognized that there was a difference. The men did not stand as much as teeter and shake. They did not walk as much as shuffle and drag. They did not speak as much as mumble and drool. They ate infrequently. They were not beyond roasting a dog when they were starved for meat, but they kept that a secret. They stole chickens and found fresh dead possums and raccoons along the roads to put in a stew. They ate fish when one or two worked at the beach for money, sheephead, and jack-cravalle. Mostly they drank beer and wine. They wandered, they worked at nothing hard but securing the kick for the night. Later, after they had been by the fire and had passed the bottles and talked, they stumbled away alone to sleep. Sometimes they fell sideways off the paths to the cars or the lean-tos, they slept where they lay in the weeds. In the places they used for shelter they dreamed on filthy mattresses inside plywood houses on sagging plywood floors. In the winter they covered themselves with the blankets that May found for them, in the summer they sank to the mattresses and slept in the things they wore as clothes. The mosquitoes were not attracted to the men. They went past the camp of the borachos and on to Harlem for softer, cleaner flesh. Each man looked twenty to thirty years older than he was. Most were toothless, all were scabrous and thin, they shook until the medicine coursed through their blood. They preferred beer and wine and vodka but would drink shaving lotion, Lysol, or vanilla extract. Because they were weak and without equities, they were harmless. They were frightened creatures who were startled by loud noises. They could not look the people in the eye, they looked instead at the tops of their ragged shoes. Each had been defeated by work, poverty, disappointment, and hopelessness, by some of the powerful forces of life. Each found oblivion and relief in big bottles of cheap wine.

The men's lives leaked out like drops of water wrung from a wet cloth. May tried to dress them in decent clothes but they didn't like to wash, wounds were current, continuous. The new clothes she brought them became stained and dirty like the mattresses until she insisted the men let her replace them again, she made the men burn the old ones. Some seldom wandered far from the circle. The others cashed pension checks for them and brought them the wine they needed. If they had last names they were not remembered or used. If they had mothers or daughters or sisters or wives, thoughts of them had been pushed in too deep, and could not be brought forth again. But where they had worked the vegetable farms in Georgia, Alabama, Florida, and the fruit orchards in Connecticut, New York, and North Carolina, they could remember exactly. They named the small towns and the routes to get to them, they recalled the natures of the managers and the foremen, and discussed crops and weather they had seen.

Sometimes a man or two would work. The day might be pleasant, the opportunities for money from other places might have been diminished. The priest let them pull weeds, cut the grass, clean the bathrooms and empty the trash at the church and the little house next to it where the Catholic people had suppers together and parties for the little children. The colored lady who ran the fish house on San Carlos Island gave them rubber boots to wear and put hoses and brooms and scrub brushes in their hands. They washed the tables and floors where mullet had been headed, gutted, and split for smoking. Men who built houses passed through Harlem in the early mornings looking for helpers to carry block, to mix sand, cement, and water into concrete. That work was very hard and could only be done one day out of very many. Mostly it was Wito who gave the men something to do for money. He took the money back when he sold them wine.

Wito owned the only grocery store in Harlem. Miners was another half-mile up Gladiolus and there was no shade along the way or any near the old wooden building. Wito's store was screened from the sun by fat coconuts and tropical almond trees, the big green leaves turned burgundy in the winter. He owned a junkyard behind the grocery and did mechanic work at night, after he had closed his store. He planted palms for people who lived in Iona. He started the palms from seed, they were thick about his property. Wito was severe with the alcoholics, he made them pay for the wine. If they borrowed against the contract he would make them work off the balance before he gave them more to drink. Los alcoholicos raked the junk yard and shoveled up the dogshit. They cut the weeds and sand spurs with a push mower, they cleaned the palms with machetes. If one was not too drunk, if one's hands were not terribly unsteady, Wito would have the man hold a wrench to a bolt. They emptied pans of old motor oil into one of the drums or pounded nails to repair the shithouse, the garage, and the pig pen. The men liked Wito, better than they did the priest, but not as much as they liked May.

May scolded them like they were chicks, like she was the mother hen. She cajoled, begged promises, petitioned the men to take care of themselves, to keep themselves alive. She found them food, she found them clothing, blankets and medicine. She did not buy them wine and she did not give them money. May was saving her money. Los borachos would only drink it down and piss, shit, and vomit it out.

She walked to the grocery and used the telephone to call the hospital when one of the men was gravely ill or had died during the night. She bandaged the wounds from a fall or a cut or an accident. She grew herbs in the rafters of her cottage, she made the men tea and poultices when they were sick, feverish, lacerated. She did not allow them in her house, however, they stopped at the porch doors. It was not because she was afraid of them, she could have broken a man in two if he had assaulted her. It was because of the way they smelled. The smells from the men's' mouths and bodies and clothes were overpowering.

May had not tried to convert the men. She remembered, looking into the orange coals of the campfire, she had not tried to make them responsible, or chastised them because of the wine. It was too late for that when a man arrived in el campo. She argued with them, however, about how they treated their bodies. She tried to get them to eat, to wash, to brush their teeth, even if only once in a while. She made them throw away the filthy shirts and pants that stuck to their bodies. She made them put on clean clothes. She talked to them, she treated them as if they were still part of the world of the people. Each would have suffered for May, none were called to do so.

Chapter Thirty Two

May fixed strong coffee. The boys would be leaving also, she guessed. The men in back she would tell to sleep in the house until the landlord discovered she was gone and threw them out. The women from the churches could have her plants and the things she was leaving behind. She began to move with purpose. She swallowed big gulps of the coffee. She was in her bedroom. She reached under the brass bed and pulled out an alligator suitcase. It was a beautiful piece, tanned, sewn together with great care and expertness, probably in the Thirties. May had traded for it. The funeral home at the downtown end of McGregor was rummaging off the remaining possessions of the last of two old men. They had lived together for years in a Spanish style house along the river in East Fort Myers. She lit the kerosene lantern, it brightened the room with yellow light. She pulled open the cotton curtain and peered into her closet. She reached for her best things, clothes she would wear on her trip, what she could fit in the suitcase. She folded silk blouses and linen slacks, a Cashmere sweater, a velvet coat. She was finished with loose men's' shorts, stained shirts, tennis shoes. In Monterey she would find work in a real store and dress like a lady. In the evening, when she was walking along the edge of the Pacific, she would wear blue jeans, leather boots, and a jacket. At night in her bed, she would sleep in flannel pajamas. She was finished with looking like a fruit picker, she decided, and being half a whore.

186

She picked out a bright white, long sleeve cotton blouse, a pleated indigo skirt that came down over her knees, a belt made of silver conchos, blue and white pumps that she had owned for three years and never worn, and a navy blazer. Those things she would travel in.

When the suitcase was nearly full, May brought out the physician's bag. She used fine linens to wrap the Tiffany things and the others, a crucifix of silver inlaid with tiny pieces of tile, a strand of pink pearls arranged in a clamshell case and a pair of silver candlesticks. She pinned her Faberge piece, a palm tree of diamonds and gold, to the front of the blazer, she laid the coat at the end of the bed. She reached down low into the closet. She put her hands on a small thing and drew it out. It was a wooden cigar box. The top layer was composed of dark Cuban cigars in wrappers, the lower layer was money, four thousand dollars cash. She added the five hundred Anita had given her. May wrapped the box in newspaper, taped it tightly, and placed it in the suitcase. She would travel on her pay, she decided. She closed the luggage and locked it, she set the suitcase beside her bed and went to the front room.

She looked for a moment at her books. She went out the front door, down the sand road, walking quickly to the grocery. Under the overhang she found two dry boxes. May grabbed them and an armful of newspapers. She hurried back to her cottage.

She set the boxes down. She placed a wicker chair in front of her bookcase. She sat in the chair, she looked at the books, she looked at the boxes. She decided she could take twenty of the hundred, ten to a box. No more than that, she thought, or the boxes would be too heavy to carry. Then she decided she would fill the boxes and she would manage. If there was room in the physician's bag she would take a few more. She wrapped each book neatly in newspaper to protect it. There were eleven Steinbecks.

The steadfast old queers had lived openly together before it was generally acceptable. They had been book men. One worked in the downstairs store at Viking in New York, his compadre worked in the downstairs store at Scribner. That was how they had met, over books. Each man had a favorite writer in the publishers' stables of the Thirties, Forties, and Fifties. The Viking man's favorite was Steinbeck, the Scribner man collected Hemingway. May had five of those. The man at the funeral home had taken the men's possessions in payment for services. Distant relatives of the last one dead wanted nothing to do with the effects, nor would they be responsible for paying for a funeral. The undertaker cleaned up on the furniture, art, carpets, and silver, all the good things the men had gathered with money to spend, and cultivation. There were a hundred or so books, roughly stacked against a wall. He had not seen the Steinbecks and the Hemingways, no one else had bothered to look. The books were in unmolested condition. They were in dust jackets, the paper covers were clean and bright, they had been kept from the light of the sun. May sat beside the books on the carpet of the funeral home, she pulled them one at a time from the stacks while other people milled and moved around her. Many of the books were signed, the Steinbecks and the Hemingways, a Thomas Wolfe and a Marjorie Rawlings. Inside *Sweet Thursday* there was a long, handwritten letter from John Steinbeck thanking the man for selling his books. Inside *Death In The Afternoon* there was a short note from Ernest Hemingway, thanking the other man for selling his. The books were the most beautiful things May had ever seen. She delighted in the pictures on the covers, she wondered what the titles meant. Her inclination to own the books was very strong. Later, through Steinbeck, she found Monterey.

May stood in front of the books and waited for the funeral man. When he came by she leaned very close. She told him that if she could have the books and the suitcase and a ride back to her cottage in Harlem Heights and if he was not afraid to come in, she would make love to him like he had never been loved before, or was likely to be again. She smiled at him and asked where his car was. The man thought about the old dead body waiting for him in the embalming room, then he looked closely at May's live one. He decided he would end early, the sale had gone on long enough. The body on the table would be there tomorrow, but probably the girl would not. He adjusted himself in his trousers and looked at May.

"It's eleven thirty," he said. "We could go at twelve. Would that be all right?"

"I hope you can stay after the first time we make love. So many men want to leave right away. I'll take every one," she said. "Can you help me get them to the car?"

May went home with a hundred good books and the alligator suitcase. Under a divan she found a hand-tooled leather Bible with a clasp. The paper inside was brown, pitted with minerals. It was three hundred years old, it had been printed in Scotland. She didn't even bother to ask, she figured the man would not object. Maybe, she thought, he would want her to have it. May loved the Bible. She loved to stick her face into it, she smelled the age and paper and ink. She held it in her lap and stroked the pages, but she didn't want to read it. The funeral man left right after, May laughed at the bargain. The man's face had flushed when she handed him a rubber. She kept the most delicate books wrapped in wax paper, she put a tiny bit of baking soda inside so the paper would not mold or sour.

May had read the Steinbecks, she believed she knew California. She was going anyway, she thought, to Monterey and the Salinas Valley. Reading about those places had made her want to be there, and she wanted away from the Gulf. She filled the two boxes, became angry, went to Wito's for a third. She pushed in crumpled newspaper so the books would not shift. She wrapped the boxes in tape and tied them with string for carrying, by then it was almost sunrise.

May Valentine blew out all the candles and the lantern. She went into the tiny bedroom, lay on her bed and wrapped herself in her quilt. She began to count money. Four thousand in the suitcase. Five hundred more in her suitcase, the money from Enrique. Two hundred from Royal Glads for pay. Five thousand more, five thousand dollars from Enrique. Five hundred more, she counted, from Chug. Ten thousand dollars, she figured, maybe a little more. She could start new in California. May rolled to her side, she put her hands between her legs. She wondered what the second thing was.

Chapter Thirty Three

Anita turned the car from Gladiolus onto Coca Sabal. She parked behind the old cypress building, in front of the orchid house. She shut off the lights and the motor, got out, she closed the door softly behind her. She quickly reached back in the car for the repellant, she sprayed her face and hands. She looked around the yard, let her eyes become accustomed to the dark. There were heavy clouds blowing high overhead, between where she stood and the moon. She walked through the wet grass to the orchid house and opened the door.

"Enrique," she said, "are you here?"

"In the back. Ahead of you," he answered.

Anita followed the sound of his voice inside. Although the air was fragrant with orchid flowers, the scents were not as strong as the jasmine and gardenia at May's, she thought. Enrique was stretched out at the end of the concrete walk. His hands were crossed under his head.

"Are you alone, Anita?" he asked.

"Yes," she said. "Is your leg very bad?"

"It will see me through today."

"Have you used the medicine the sisters gave you?" she asked. "The morphine?"

"Once," he said. "It stopped the pain but I was sick at my stomach and my mind was confused. I don't like it."

"There are two needles left," she said.

"Yes. I will use them when the pain is not bearable. I cannot take morphine any more tonight. After tomorrow we will go to a doctor."

"May gave me leaves to wrap around your leg. They will ease the pain. Can I pull up your pants leg?"

"Cut it off," Enrique said, "that will be easier. Father Hidalgo will not mind, he will not want these pants back."

Anita took her man's knife, she sawed the pants leg free. She cut the knot that held the gauze, held the dressing in place, and unwrapped the bandage. The dressing was wet with blood and water. In the glare of the flashlight, she saw that Enrique's knee was grotesque, suppurated, angry blue and gray. Quick tears came to her eyes. She brushed hard at them, blinked rapidly, drew in a deep breath. She reached into a dripping paper sack and pulled out loose handfuls of wet leaves and herbs. She placed them carefully on the worsening wound. She held the mass in place and reached with her other hand for the new gauze. She wrapped the wet green against her husband's battered knee.

Anita tied off the new bandage. She fashioned the rest of the gauze into a tight bundle and pushed it into Enrique's shirt pocket.

"What the sisters have done is not enough, we must go to a doctor. I do not want you to lose your leg. I do not want to lose you," she said.

"My leg is bad, but it will stay where it is. We will go to a doctor in Tampa when this is finished," he said. "The sisters did well, the leaves will help and your bandage will hold. It is only the pain that is difficult to manage. It is not so bad that I would lose it," he said gently, "and you are not going to lose me."

Anita went to the other end of the walk. She washed her hands and splashed water in her face. When she was sitting beside Enrique she reached into the cooler and brought out two pieces of the cold chicken.

"Eat," she said, "then I will give you aspirin."

He sat up for the chicken. He ate very slowly, he chewed each mouthful very carefully, he swallowed every one with a sip of cold water. He felt better right away. He could feel the bit of food and the water moving into his body. He chewed everything from the piece, to the very bone, then he ate the other one. When he was finished Anita held three aspirin to his lips, he washed them down with a final drink of water. He laid his head back down. His legs, one good, straight, and the other not good, crooked, were splayed out. The pain in his head and his knee began to recede. He kept himself very still, he spoke softly to Anita.

"Are we agreed with May Valentine?"

"All this time, and with her tonight, and I did not know her last name," she said. "She has a nice name. May will help us, she said she will do as you have asked, she wants to go to California. I told her what you said, that we would pay her and help her get away. I gave her the five hundred dollars and promised her the rest. I told her there was another thing for her to do, after she gave you the patrón."

"If we fail he will kill her also."

"I told her what you told the priest, that there would be no killing. I told her you would protect her. You do not intend to kill Chug or the sheriff?" she whispered the last words. She was afraid to say them aloud, even in the place where they were hidden.

"The other man is not the sheriff, he is only the worthless son of the sheriff of Charlotte. No one will be surprised they are gone."

"That does not answer my question, Enrique," she said.

"They are dead men. I will confess my sins when we are in Mexico, at the first church we see." He closed his eyes and breathed deeply through his nose. He smelled the wet, the bark, the soil and the orchids.

"We will have our money back and raise the flowers you wanted, and orchids," he said, "in memory of tonight. They will be surprised, they will never know what hits them. The patrón would kill his own family if he believed he could get the money and go unpunished. He would shit on the farm, the people, and live his life in a bar and a whorehouse, and that foolish deputy helped him."

"Please, Enrique, please do not be killed," she whispered.

"What time is it?" he asked.

"Four o clock."

"In one hour we will leave here. Let me sleep for one hour then wake me. You can rest for an hour also, then more later. The leaves and the aspirin have helped. You are going to take me to the front of the farm. The young boys will help me."

"How much are they to be included in this ugliness?" she asked.

"This ugliness has not been of our making," he said. "Touch your hand to my knee, feel the heat through the bandage. There is shattered bone, and gristle underneath. I cannot walk without the crutch, when I stand the pain will be worse because the blood runs to my leg. I may be able to throw myself forward on the crutch and drag my leg behind me. Do you think I can battle with Chug and the dog and the deputy and the guns by myself?"

"I did not know what you would do," she said, "but I think May did. She spoke of los muchachos. They will be in great danger because of us."

"They are in great danger because of Chug," he said. "They are kicked at by Chug and menaced by the dog. They will be safer when they are gone from there. They have much to fear from him, with me retired and moved away." He smiled a little at the irony. "One day the dog will bite a boy, badly, Chug will blame the incident on the boy. They have no future at Royal Farms," he said, "one way or another. Now let me rest."

Enrique stopped talking, Anita laid herself out beside him. She closed her eyes, she breathed in the air of the orchid house, she began to say the "Hail Mary."

She shook Enrique's shoulder at five. He raised his mouth to hers to kiss her on the lips. Her breath was very sweet, he thought, while his own mouth tasted sour, bitter. He took a long drink of water from the jug then stood up, balancing himself on the crutch. He asked Anita to splash water on his hands and his face. She patted him with wet hands as he had asked, she lifted the hem of her wool skirt to dab at the water. He bent to pick up the paper bag with the wet leaves and the cooler with the ice and morphine. In his own wallet he had money for the boys, enough to get them away. There would be more cash, he guessed, in Chug's.

"What did May tell you?"

"She said she would be alone with the patrón at the little lake. She said the chain would be up. She said the dog would be in the truck. She will be naked with him on a blanket."

"Here is what you must do. You have your money? How much is left?"

"All of it," she said, "except what I made the sister take for her habit. Four hundred dollars."

"Take me to the front of the farm. I can make my way through the mangos to The Quarters. Give me more aspirin," he said, "put it in my pocket. Drive the priest's car downtown, all the way to Saint Francis. Sleep if you want, there in the car, or go inside the church and refresh yourself in the air-conditioning. Listen to Mass. Rest," he said, "and compose yourself. At nine o clock go to American, do your shopping quickly. Buy four baseball bats. On the top of the handle is a number, buy twenty-eight or twenty-nine, they are smaller and lighter. Buy four of them. Look for a name where the bat is wide. Get the ones that say Duke Snider, they are the best ones. I want five white shirts and five black pants and five pairs of black shoes. Buy white socks, undershirts and underpants, buy five of everything in my size or a size smaller. I want a fillet knife and another flashlight, handkerchiefs and a roll of strong rope. You should buy the shoes a little wider," he said, "I think the boys' feet are broad. If anyone asks," he said, "tell him the clothes are for priests at the missions. Can you remember all of that?"

"Yes."

"Go to Thad Wilson's. It is on the corner across from the Coca Cola building. Buy six of the biggest hamburgers he makes. Eat one. Stay in the shade at Saint Francis until the afternoon, then drive back to May's. Leave everything there. I do not know her house," he said. "Is there a back porch?"

"She has steps in the back but no porch."

"Leave the things in her kitchen. A boy will come for the bats first, he or another will come for the clothes and the food later. Eat one of the sandwiches, Anita, even if you are not hungry. When you are in the church pray for us. Maybe the saints will pay attention."

"What am I to do when I am finished at May's?"

"Return here. Enjoy the peace. Sleep. I will turn the fans on, the air will be cool inside. If Mister Congdon comes, tell him you would like to buy an orchid. Wait here until the sun has set, then go back to May's. She will be there. I will tell her when I see her what else she must do. Drive her where she says, stay with her. When she is finished at Chug's house, go to Tampa. Sleep in a hotel. I will meet you at The Columbia in Ybor City at twelve o clock tomorrow. Anita," he said.

"Yes, Enrique?"

"When you are at American, buy yourself a dress and shoes, and sun glasses for driving. Leave the nun's wool in the hotel."

Chapter Thirty Four

*A*nita stopped the Dodge just a few feet from the vegetable stand, in the sand spurs at the side of the road. Enrique left the back seat with the cooler, the herbs, and the crutch. He shut the door quickly and hobbled into the inky dark under the mango trees. Anita turned at A and W Bulb. The car was gone from sight, it could not be heard through the woods. The ground was sodden. Mosquitoes rose as an invisible storm to meet him. The insects stung him, dipped into his flesh. They buzzed his ears, tried to get to his eyes. He had not encountered them in the orchid house and had neglected to spray himself in the car. He wanted to slap at the mosquitoes about his face but could not let go of the crutch, he was afraid to drop the cooler with the morphine. He hurried through the trees, splashed in the shallow water, and found the clearing behind the barn. He moved sideways, he dragged his bad leg behind him, followed the sand path into the cavern of the pepper hedge, crossed the wood plank. He was in the yard in front of The Quarters. The fire was out, but with the very early light of the dawn he could see the camp clearly, saw it was clean, saw the snakeskin curing on a board. He moved slowly through the opening that had been a doorway and hissed. He made the sound again, louder. The boy in the first room woke up.

"Who is it?" Who is there?" he whispered.

"Enrique esta aqui. Soy Enrique. Ve para los otros. Get the others," he said. "Where is the spray for the mosquitoes?"

The boy dashed to the packing crates, brought the can to Enrique. He handed it to him, then ran into the hall to wake the other boys. Enrique closed his eyes, he held the can close to his face. He felt the cool of the aerosol on his skin, then felt the juice sting where it touched the cuts on his face from Chug's fists and rings. He sprayed his uncovered leg and the bandage and his hands and forearms, his shirt, front and back, the rest of his pants, then he sprayed his face again. Instantly, he was relieved of the bugs except for the fearful stings where they had already found him. He felt one eye closing with the swelling from the bites.

In another moment the four boys stood together in the doorway. They looked at Enrique, at his bloody bandaged leg, the slashes on his face, his one hand that held a small cooler, the other that held him to a crutch. They looked only at him and not to each other.

"Something very bad has happened," he said. "The patrón has robbed me and outraged my wife and ruined this leg," he pointed to his knee but watched the boys' faces. "I cannot protect my family. He has the money I was taking to Mexico. He is beyond the law, the sheriff would not be interested. Anyway," he asked them, "do you think there are laws that can fix my leg, or keep him and his friends away from my children? I don't trust the law. The man has promised to kill us if we speak of it. I am in pain," he said, "and very, very tired."

Enrique's shoulders slumped, his head fell forward. He had slept an hour in the orchid house. The journey through the trees, the mosquitoes, had worn him down. The boys moved as one, barefooted across the threshold. They helped Enrique to sit in a wide chair they had made of lashed pieces of straight pine. One of the boys hurried for a concrete block. Enrique boosted his leg up, he closed his eyes. One boy started the fire, another went inside. He returned in an instant with an old coffeepot without a lid, filled it with water from a plastic jug, set it on the ledge over the flames. The oldest boy came out fully dressed for work, then the others went inside and dressed also. In a few moments the four were seated around Enrique, sipping at strong black coffee from old fruit jars.

Enrique was very glad the mosquitoes were finished with him. He touched his pocket to make sure the can was there. He opened his eyes and looked from boy to boy, he thought he was seeing the same one over and over.

The boys' faces were dark brown, their bodies were muscular, hard and lean from much work, frugality, the absence of vice. They had left Mexico together, he knew, crossed from Matamoras to Brownsville, adventured, starved their way on foot, in rickety buses and in the backs of pick-up trucks that bounced them on their spines from Texas to Immokalee. They were of one will, inseparable. The oldest boy was the leader, but the others were encouraged to speak for persuasion.

"What can we do, Don Enrique?" asked the oldest.

"Only call me Enrique," he said, "I am not your patrón."

"Enrique," he said, "you are more to us than a patrón. It is a title of respect."

"Thank you, then, my friend," he said, and nodded to each of the boys in turn. "I need your help to bring two men to justice, one after another, the worst one first. There is the patrón, and a man who is a rurale, a deputy in a small town a little to the north. They are the sons of decent men, but they are worthless. I am a citizen here. I was a soldier. But I do not want to burden the law with what has happened. The law has much to do without my problems." Enrique paused for a moment while he studied his next words. He spoke as formally with the boys as he could, they understood him. His idioms, pronunciations, and patterns of speech were the same as theirs. "I want you to help me bring them to a place, a condition, where I may recover my money. Then we will help them move into another place. It will be dangerous. Do you understand?"

"How will they be subdued?" asked the oldest, "we have no weapons."

"We will use baseballs bats. Bats are very reliable as weapons," said Enrique, "especially if there are several. You will each have one and you will strike at the men together. Five of us," he said, "for each of them."

"Why do we not use machetes?" asked one boy.

"Machetes may kill the man before I have spoken with him, and they make very ugly wounds. There would be much blood. Blood is difficult to ignore. We must batter the men unconscious but not kill them. The dog we murder without hesitation."

198

"Baseball bats are very hard," said the youngest.

"Los Zapatistas used rocks and clubs and shovels against los federales," said another.

"Zapata did not have baseball bats or he would have used them," said the oldest boy, "they make fine weapons."

"Pancho Villa hung bad soldiers and roberos from telephone lines," said the other boy.

"Think of yourselves as good soldiers," said Enrique, "and listen to what I tell you. We will swing those bats at the heads and the hands and the ankles of the patrón and his friend the deputy. You must not miss the first swing, there may not be another chance. Connect with the heads of the men the first time. If the police catch us, if we are interrupted, if we are arrested, I do not think it will go as bad for us with the bats, as it would if we held machetes or a pistol or a strangling rope, but I don't know. Maybe it will make no difference."

The oldest boy watched the eyes of the others, then looked directly at Enrique.

"We have not been happy here," he said, "but we stayed. We are afraid, not when we are together, but when one of us is alone. We are especially afraid for the young one. What could have been worse for us? You have gone, we are left with the patrón and his dog. There is a chance he will hurt one of us badly, then we would have to kill him anyway. Why not do it now," he said, "and get it finished?"

Enrique listened to the boy, then turned to the youngest one.

"What do you fear the most about this?" he asked him.

"The dog," the boy answered, "and the man, he has a pistol."

"Would you be afraid to hit at him with a bat if he does not have a pistol and the dog is chained?"

"Not if that is what the others do," he answered.

"We will swing the bats together," said the oldest.

"Where do you want to go when we are finished?" asked the man. "This farm will close, I think all of them will close soon, the land has become too precious for farming."

"We will make up our minds later," said the oldest, "we will discuss

199

it today while we are in the field."

"When will we attack the patrón?" asked one of the others.

"It will happen tonight, early tonight and late tonight, all of it, both men. It will be over this time tomorrow. You must move quickly, do what I tell you. If I say to do something, you must not delay, you must not think about it. Do you agree? All of you?" He looked at each of the faces again. He saw that they were distinguishable, especially the face of the oldest. He is already a man, Enrique thought.

The boys nodded gravely.

"You will not be paid for your work today. It is good today is payday, but your wages for this one are lost. Mister Sinclair will bring the envelopes for you and the others to the afternoon break. Do you have savings? I guessed you would. We will leave Fort Myers tonight," he said, "we will finish with the patrón then go for the other one. You will have more money. I know that you do not do this for reward, for money, but that you do it for me. I am honored," he said, "and I will honor you back."

The boys stood up, it was time to go to the barn.

"I will stay inside your house this morning, and in the woods this afternoon, when the house has become too hot. One of you go to May's. Slip away after twelve, through the peppers and the mangrove. Make sure you are not seen by a motorist. The one who goes will find the baseball bats. Bring them here. Whatever happens today," he said, "do not provoke the patrón. Stay away from him and his dog. Do not even look at them. We must get through this day without incident, I do not want that man's plans interrupted. Except for the one who brings the bats, do not come here until after the farm is closed. I will wait by the adobe. I will be thinking about Zapata and Villa," he told them, "and what they could have done with men like you as soldiers."

The boys stood, each came to Enrique and shook his hand. They went inside, they came out with jugs for water, a bundle of soft tortillas, a small plastic tub half-filled with snake meat and cooked onions. They carried flower knives in their pockets. They left the yard single file and entered the hole in the pepper hedge. It was sunup. The boys had gone to the field, Enrique was alone in The Quarters.

200

He sat in the chair for almost an hour, then hobbled into the early morning cool of the scarred building. The boys had arranged a mattress with blankets and pillows for him against a wall where he could see into the clearing. There was another jug of water and an unopened bottle of apple juice and a small box of animal crackers beside the mattress. Enrique arranged himself against the pockmarked cement, he stretched his legs before him. He reached into the cooler, moved the capped needles aside and grabbed handfuls of wet chips of ice. He held the ice with both hands to his knee. When the ice was melted he did it again and again, until his hands were numb with cold, until the pain in his leg was receded. He pulled small clusters of wet leaves from a paper bag. He squeezed the moisture from the leaves on top of the bandage, then carefully laid them on, layering the leaves as much as he could. He wrapped the new mass around the old one with the roll of gauze Anita had put in his shirt pocket.

Enrique unwrapped the box of sweet cookies. He began eating them one at a time, he held the little biscuit close to his face to determine what the animal was. He washed down the crumbs with apple juice, he stared through the doorway at the greens and the blue outside.

Chapter Thirty Five

Chug had been asleep in his duplex late Thursday morning when his telephone rang.

"What the fuck?" he said when he answered.

It was Earlene, calling from the old man's office.

"Chug," she said, "Mister Sinclair wants to speak with you this afternoon. He said it's important."

"I got me a headache, damnit, an I'm tryin to sleep it off." He cracked open an eye, spotted the toolbox next to the door into the bedroom.

"Your father said no matter what, he wants you here after lunch."

"Well, shit. What time is his lunch finished today?"

"Be here at one o clock, Chug."

"You know, Earlene," he'd said, getting pissed, feeling shitty from the long night behind him, the booze, the coke, mildly concerned about the Garzas, "you know how good old boys rank women, you know, one to ten?" he asked. "You ever heard of it?"

"Yes," she'd said, "I have, but I wouldn't give it any mind."

"Well you, Earlene, bein from Tice an all, you what we call a East Fort Myers ten, you all know what that is?"

Earlene was silent on the line, ready to hang up.

"You don't know, I guess. Well I'll tell ya. She's a blonde four with a six-pack." He jammed the receiver onto the cradle. He propped his aching head in a cupped hand. He stared at the toolbox for a moment, then rolled over and went back to sleep.

At two o'clock he pushed open the door to the business office of Royal Farms, flipped Earlene a middle finger, and walked into the old man's space. Mister Sinclair's private office was Spartan, no pictures or plaques or paintings hung on the oak paneled walls except for a 1971/1972 trade calendar that highlighted shipping dates for flower holidays. The old man had an enormous wooden desk that had been his father's, he was sitting behind it when Chug came in. The desk was in the middle of the office, a neat pile of paperwork was centered on it. A flag of the state of Florida hung next to the window.

The old man was angry, underneath the freckles that mottled his thin face his flesh was red, it pulsed with emotion. His hands trembled, not from fear, but with barely controlled rage. The old man hadn't ever been this mad, never even close. Enrique Garza had told him Monday morning that he was leaving the farm, in fact he'd already left, he would not go back. He was going to Mexico to work for himself. The Mexican had told the old man that he no longer wanted to work in Florida. He'd been with the Sinclairs twenty six years, he'd said, that was long enough. When the old man had pressed him more for a reason, Enrique had maintained only that it was time for him to go, that there was not a need for two managers at one flower farm.

The old man suspected that Enrique's hand had been forced by Chug's play. He began to make phone calls. He called Percy. He inquired of other responsible men who owned and managed flower farms what they knew, what had they heard? When farmers he had known and respected for forty years began to tell him about his son, about how he treated his people, about the thefts from the market, about beatings and robberies out on The Hill, about Chug being a whoreman, Mister Sinclair's scalp began to itch, his ears began to burn, his face became that fiery red. Paying for a whore once in a while was one thing, they'd said, owning some and renting them out to boys at the high school was different. The farm was going to fail, the men had told him, they said it would happen fast. The old man began over the next few days to review shortage reports, tickets from Marine Hardware, fuel expenses, bills for vegetables and fruit. The Garza man had been pushed aside by Chug. He was worried, angry with himself as well, for letting things at the farm get to such a low place. He hadn't paid attention, he thought, now with Garza gone, the season would be a wash at best, maybe a disaster. He was not accustomed to hard hits at his bottom line.

The old man looked at Chug through his thick glasses. He put his hands flat on the wooden desk in order to control the trembling.

"Verdell," he said, "the fact that Enrique's gone is going to cause a whole lot of extra work for those of us left at Royal Glads, especially you. Now that you've run the man off, you are the manager. By God, you've got to act like it. You've got to straighten yourself out, take hold, run the farm right. Goddamnit, the whole county's talking about us. They say you can't cut it. They say you're more interested in being a whoreman than a farmer."

"Yeah?" said Chug. "First of all, that Mesican was just another mouth suckin money outta my pocket, an yours too. Anything that old boy could do, I'm gonna do better, for this season anyway. As for the other," he said, looking hard at the old man, "where I get my pussy ain't nobody's business, includin you."

"You wouldn't know a good flower if I slapped you with it," the old man said. "You won't ever be the farmer that Garza is, or was. I thought you'd come back from Gainesville with some brains and some feel for the industry, instead you got a pocketful of DWI's and a bad attitude. You didn't learn anything about farming and that place," he said, "is an agricultural school. You didn't learn anything about being a manager, and they have a school of business. Royal Farms is not going to pay for ignorance and carelessness. I won't have it."

"Fuck that," said Chug. "They ain't nothin to pushin some shitass flowers three feet outta the ground an cuttin em off at the balls. Anybody can do it."

The old man bit his lower lip and shook his head, he felt that the trembling in his hands had stopped. The boy was making it easy.

"You are a disgrace to us, to your mother and your brother and to me. You don't even talk like a Sinclair, let alone act like one. You sound like a field hand or a mullet fisherman from Tice, and you behave as if you haven't a clue how you are supposed to. I won't allow that farm to fail because my own son is too lazy and drunk and mean to run it properly. The business with the colored girls, maybe the sheriff will want to do something about it after he hears from me."

Chug laughed at that, but recalled that lately the sheriff had not been so happy to see him, even when he was delivering the old boy his bolito money.

"What about the white ones, what you gonna do about them?"

"What white? What do you mean?" the old man asked.

"White whores, daddy, what you want me to do about them?"

The old man ripped off his glasses and made as if to slam them down on his desk.

"You're even worse than I was told," he said. "God only knows what you've done that we don't know about. You and I need to reach an understanding. We don't have to like each other, but we have to agree to something that will guarantee that the farm will get through this and go on."

Chug looked the old man squarely in the face, his own skin was beginning to flush and pulse, first pale, then white, then red and hot looking. Here we go, he thought, and about fucking time too. He leaned in real close over the broad desk, he rested his thick forearms and braceleted wrists on the wood. He laced his fingers together, nearly every one sported a gold ring.

"You know?" he said. "That Mesican leavin is a good thing for me an you. It's like a sign, him an his old lady cuttin out like that, headin for they home, I bet they in a hurry to git there too." He continued, watched his father's eyes. "We need to quit this farmin shit an move on. Start sellin off some pieces of property or build us some houses and stores for the yankees that's comin. Fuck em over an take they money. Shit, we can call ourselves developers, that's what everybody else is doin. We can put us up some strip centers, big groceries an shitty apartments an make a killin. That's where the money is now," he said, "not waitin around for posies to grow. Jesus Christ, this whole farmin routine is so lame I cain't believe you still a part of it. You ain't so fuckin smart either, old man. You should be sittin under a palm tree somewhere lookin at young pussy, or at least playin golf. What's you point, workin like a nigger seven days a week? You the big man, but you divide the hours you work into what you takin for a salary, it ain't shit. I ain't fixin to end up like you, a man who's a slave to his own company. Let's quit this dickin around," he said, "an have some fun."

"Enrique Garza leaving us is a disaster, especially because of the timing, don't forget that. We're farmers, not clerks and real estate salesmen. And those words you use for colored people, they offend me, they are not the words an educated man would choose. You and your redneck friends are behind the times, boy. Don't you know work for its own sake is good, that it always has been?"

"Listen pal," said Chug, "don't give me that times are a changin shit. You ain't exactly ever mixed it up with Africans or coloreds or niggers or blacks, whatever it is we supposed to call em today, tomorra it'll be somethin different. You ain't mixed with the Mexes neither. You sit here in you big office with Earlene, thinkin of things for me an the boys at the other farms and the ranch to do. You here in you office, so you ain't exactly had to deal with em like I have, else you woulda knowed a lot sooner about me an you favorite Mesican not bein fast friends."

The old man came up out of his chair, he glared at the thing across from him. Chug didn't even blink.

"First of all, and don't you ever forget it, you miserable bastard, I'm not your pal. I'm the one who says it's okay for you to get paid every week and has gotten you out of trouble more times than I can count, and I hire and fire. You get that, boy? I hire and fire from the dumbest field hand right up to you. I say who stays and who goes. I'm the boss here, not you. Secondly that old name for colored people was never a good one, it's got nothing to do with the times. The only men who use that word are ignorant hillbillies and rednecks like you who don't have the brains to do otherwise. I don't want to ever hear that word again, coming from your mouth. You have the disposition of a water moccasin and the morals of a goat."

Chug unfolded his arms from the desk and stood up. He hitched his levis higher on his hips, nodded at his father.

"Yeah, you right about one thing, old man, you ain't my pal. I don't need none. You just another chickenshit farmer who don't know nothin different. You hangin on to somethin out there on Gladiolus that shoulda been bulldozed years ago, somethin that ain't no good no more. I'm gonna work there," he said. "We got the season started, though I could give a shit about that, except I'm plannin on makin a lot of money peddlin them stolen vegetables and flowers you probably know all about. An I'm bangin the hottest piece of ass in town ever afternoon out by that little scum pond you Mesican made, so I'm gonna run that shithole one more year. By then I'll be finished with that gal too, then I'm gonna turn her out for my buddies. I'm gone run that place like I want," he said, "an have some fun chasin greasers an what coloreds is still around. An you know what? You gone start payin me more money, right now. Whatever that Mesican was gettin you gonna pay me on top of what I'm makin. Works out right, his twenty six years is about worth the same as my one. I'm doin his job an my own, I want his pay. An then, after Mother's Day, I'm gone shut that fucker done an take that land off you hands. I got my own money, lots of it, an I got people want to buy up all them shitty farms along Gladiolus. We gone develop the son of a bitch. Shit. I'm gonna have my own McDonald's up where Miners is."

"Verdell, we aren't ready for that yet. Your grandfather wanted you to have Royal Glads, that's true, but not to sell at the first opportunity. He wanted it to be something you could make a career of. You wanting Enrique's pay in addition to your own is too ridiculous for comment, you don't earn what you make now."

"A career?" Chug laughed. "That figures. You an my fuckin brother sit on you asses in a air-condition office while I ride around in circles in my truck keepin herd on a bunch of Mesicans or whatever comes along next. I ain't workin that farm but one more season, an the clock, she's a tickin. I'm gonna bulldoze them shade houses, them barns an buildings is comin down. I got me a lawyer, we lookin at papers that say that land's already mine. A career? Shit on that. I got other plans an they don't include gettin up ever mornin at six thirty an babysittin beaners all day. Flowers? I could give a fuck."

The old man sat back down in his chair. He dismissed Chug from the company with a wave of his hand.

"Well, boy," he said, "I think the whiskey and the dope have addled your brain, though you didn't have much to work with. You're probably syphilitic too. This conversation is over. Anything, everything, that any Sinclair owns, is mine to keep, give away, or sell as I see fit. Your lawyer is feeding you a crock of bullshit. He probably went to school in Gainesville too."

Chug put his ringed knuckles on the old man's desk.

"Remember you said it, about not being my pal. I ain't yours neither. I mean it about the pay, too, or I'm gonna tell the old lady about you an Miss Tice out there. Shit. Everbody but her knows you been fuckin Earlene for years. That'll start some shit. Then I'll jump in an sue you for what's mine, you bein negligent and immoral an all. An then," Chug said, "I'm gonna half kill that piss ant I got for a brother, just cause I want to."

Chug stood up straight, dropped one hand to his crotch, squeezed his nuts and dick. He smiled at his father, pointed where Earlene would be and drew a finger across his throat. The door had just closed behind him when the old man reached into his desk for the telephone numbers of judges, lawyers, bankers and accountants, men that he could rely on.

Chapter Thirty Six

Enrique set the empty box of crackers and the water down, he lay back on the blankets. He looked at the sky through the bullet holes in the tin roof. He had been in The Quarters many, many times, he had known and worked dozens of men and a few women who had lived there across the flower seasons. Few had left with more than they had when they arrived, most had left with less, he thought, if he counted ruined backs, missing fingers, eyes damaged and filmy from the glare of the sun, the burn of chemicals, the sting of the gray sand. The names and faces of those people were indistinguishable to him.

He had been in a building like this in Buckingham, when he had been in the army. He closed his eyes, he let his mind go to that place.

The buildings were new, the soldiers kept them clean. There were comfortable beds, hot showers, screens on the doors and windows, big fans that blew the air across the rooms. The soldiers came from all over the country to be trained as instructors. They in turn would train the aerial gunners that would fire heavy caliber machine guns from the bodies and bubbles of the big planes, B-17's and B-24's. It had been a long time ago, everything was changed.

Enrique had driven big trucks with wooden benches, the cadets had sat in the back with loaded shotguns. As he moved them along at a good clip on a soft sand trail through the palmetto and scrub, the men would learn to lead the targets. They stayed seated, and shot at clay pigeons launched from behind the palm clusters. Later in the training the men climbed into little Venturas with a single pilot in the back. The cadets ran off thousands of rounds of machine gun ammunition out over the Gulf, they fired at dummy planes and skeletal gliders towed behind Mustangs. The pilots asked Enrique if he wanted to see the land and the water from the plane. He went only once, he was so sick that he didn't see anything while they were up but the tops of his boots and the bile that covered them. He vowed he would never ride in a plane again.

He liked to march, he recalled, he liked to march in formation on the parade grounds on Saturday mornings. He began counting the old cadence to himself, one, two, three, four, hup, two, three, four, something about a woman, something about the army. It had been an exciting time because of the war. He had not gone overseas, but he had found Florida. He recalled with great clarity the sand trails through the pine woods and driving his car along the beach. He thought about the quiet town and the river when he first saw it, the big farms, the sense of space and future.

He had gone into Fort Myers on weekend passes. He and the other sergeants and corporals drank sodas at the drug store at the corner of Main Street and Jackson. They walked down toward the Caloosahatchee to the USO Club. The soldiers talked and smoked, a few danced with the local girls in the flat-roofed building across the street from the yacht basin. It was the library now, he knew, there were shuffleboard courts behind it. He had been introduced to Anita at the USO. They met on weekends after that, they walked up and down the brick streets and through the little downtown where Sears and Roebuck and the J. C. Penney's stores were. They sat in the lobby of the Dean Hotel or the Bradford and sipped at coffee or iced tea. He remembered leaning on the carved concrete railing of the old bridge, fascinated at the splash in the water when big snook and tarpon hit at pinfish and mullet. He remembered he and Anita looking up at the moon high overhead, then at the water and the moon's reflection. The surface of the river had been as smooth as glass. They had been startled the first time they heard the whistle of the train, they watched it cross the water on its own bridge just three hundred feet upriver.

Anita was the only woman Enrique had ever known and he was the only man she had ever known. They came to love quickly during the last year of the war. He gave her a ring, they were married right after he mustered out. He had met local men, mechanics, electricians, and farmers, who came to him in Buckingham for surplus parts and help with engines that didn't run like his did. He found work quickly as a civilian, even though he was Mexican, even though others were looking. Word got around about Enrique, that he was a good one. The first old man and his son found him and persuaded him to come to work for them and learn to grow gladiolus. He had been married to the same woman and the same job for twenty six years. He thought the time with Anita was better. He hoped they would be together another twenty six at least. They did not think about a time when one might be gone and the other left behind. It was not possible, he believed, that he could be without her. He began, again, to count cadence.

The sun was high when he awoke, the building was like an oven. He was wet with sweat, Hidalgo's clothing stuck to his skin. As his children had gotten older he had reported to them his recollections of the war. They were interested the first several times, his duties at different posts, who was a good captain and who was not, maneuvers in north Georgia, when he fired artillery in Tennessee where it was cold and rained every day, close calls at the airstrip with the little planes and gliders, what the land was like. The children lost interest in the stories, like they had about going with him in the creek. He remembered alone, he fished alone, maybe that was better, he thought. That was how it would end with Chug, they would be alone.

He got up from the pallet, his leg was inflamed with pain and infection. He picked up the cooler and another jug of water. He leaned on the crutch to make his way out the back opening and into the yard. He limped a few feet to the shade of a sour orange tree that had grown from a seed some long departed, nameless man had spit on the ground many years before. He sat down under the green canopy and leaned his back against the smooth, mottled trunk. There was a mild breeze and he was in deep shade. He opened the cooler, scooped out a handful of wet ice and put it in his mouth. He picked out one of the syringes. He pulled

211

the cap from it, shook the needle like the sisters had shown him, and injected himself with the morphine into the thigh of his bad leg. When he was finished he pushed the needle into the sand.

He floated between where he was and where he had been, between under the tree and dream and nightmare. He had never stopped marveling at the flowers, the colors, the scents, the excitement. Year after year he had made them grow, then cut them down. They depended on the gladiolus to grow back. The bulbs were stored away from the hot, wet summers. The people dug them out by hand, never with a machine, cleaned them, graded them, took the best ones to cold storage behind the airport. In the fall they brought the bulbs back to the fields. The people planted them in the gray sand, very carefully patted them in, he turned on the water, the hard bulbs began to sprout again. Until the blight, he remembered. The chrysanthemums were more difficult. The roots were as delicate as hair when they developed under the mist. When they were planted in the shade houses, they wilted at first, they would be sensitive until they were cut, sensitive to drying winds, soaking rains, disease and pestilence and carelessness. The mums were tentative until they were vigorous. Plant them right. The sand gassed to make it sterile. Water them in. Spray the leaves for mites, fertilize, spray them again for thrip, water, pinch the crown buds, turn on the lights, trick the plants, fertilize again, turn the lights off, perfect timing. Ten days before Thanksgiving they would harvest the first crop. No blemishes, no light counts, no spots, no thrip, no nothing or he'd tell the old man and he would say to throw the flowers away. The good ones cut, graded, boxed and gone. Over and over the rhythm of the flowers like the cadence of the march. Cut, graded, boxed and gone, hup, two, three, four. The flowers had been his working life. He swooned with the morphine. His head drooped, the pain in his leg was forgotten.

He dreamed he was marching with other soldiers through the flowers. The soldiers were trampling the chrysanthemums but were staying in formation. All the marchers were in uniform but their faces were different. They were bright, like the flowers, he thought. His marching companions' faces and hands were blue, gold, pink, and scarlet. When as a young man he had found himself to be guilty of suspicion, hatred, bigotry, he had been ashamed. He learned to respect every man, no matter. In the army, he remembered, there had been a little of it, anger, resentment, the men had learned to live and work together. Maybe they were more tolerant because of the uniforms, maybe it was because they had the Germans and Japanese to hate, he didn't know. The first time they sent flowers to Germany he was stunned. He had never bought anything that had been made in Japan. He preferred to pay a little more for his Hurricane rods and Mitchell reels because they had been made in America. He had been an American soldier.

After a time he wakened from the spell of the morphine. He was groggy, his head felt thick but the pain in his leg had diminished. He pulled his wallet from his pocket, he pulled the rest of his cash from his pants. The money would be enough for diesel for the truck, for things he might have to buy, for the boys to escape. They would have to have money for where they wanted to go, they would have more after that. The boys would help him, he would help them in return. He wanted the boys to have new lives, not as pobrecitos, not as poor ones, but as men with means, men with a future.

He dozed again. He was not disturbed by the whoosh of the cars and trucks and tractors that passed in front of the vegetable stand and the entrance to the farm. No sound reached him but the drone and buzz of insects and the far off rumble of thunder. When he woke he looked at his watch. Three o clock. He swallowed a big drink of warm water. There would be a great deal of money, he thought, more than his own, more than a man would need to start a farm in Mexico, more than May would need to start a new life in California, more than the boys would need for reparation and reward. The patrón would keep his riches in his house. Enrique would tell the woman to find it, all of it, and take it from there. Chug would have no use for money and gold after tonight. It would be a shame about the flowers, he thought, it would be a very bad season for the old man, perhaps the last one. Maybe he would sell the place to one of the other farmers, maybe he would build houses around the little lake. Imagine, Enrique thought, houses along Gladiolus that were not part of Harlem. The old man should have anticipated these troubles with his son, he should have known there would be problems. He would not have allowed his son to turn bad, Enrique thought, even if he had to beat him. He had not thought that his son could help him. He wondered at the differences between his boy and the four brothers, which was more fit to survive in a world where gentleness and a delicate nature would not do, where every time a man like Chug was dealt with, there was another to take his place.

No one knew he was there that was not leaving with him. That was the most important thing. Everyone, including his children, believed they were gone to Mexico. They will never know, he thought, the old man will never know. The priest in Immokalee expects me back, Enrique smiled a little to himself, he will be disappointed that his car is gone. He will have money to buy another, there would be one for the sisters as well. They would keep the Dodge, send Hidalgo cash instead, there would not be time to go there again. The Rambler would dissolve into parts in Immokalee and when it had no tires and no engine and was sitting on concrete blocks it would become someone's home. That was a good priest, thought Enrique, he had known others who were humorless and dry, rigid with power, who would have called the police and the bishop. He would ease the burdens of the priest and the sisters, he decided, that was what money was for. No one would miss the boys. Mexicans were like that. May? May was no different from the rest of them, he guessed, she would never be found. Chug and deputy? He narrowed down, he focused on images of the men as he had seen them last. They were leaving too.

There would be a lot of money, Enrique was certain of that. The patrón had bragged of the women he owned, what they did for him. Money without work, he had said, easy, easy money. There would be jewelry from robberies and beatings, cash from bolito, money stolen from the farm accounts and the vegetable stand. Enrique knew all about it. Money without the fuckin flowers, and the fuckin farm, and the fuckin old man treating him like he was hired help, Chug had said it often enough. Lots and lots of money, Enrique had heard him brag. He believed it to be true. Even if he was wrong, there was his own thirty seven thousand dollars, he hoped, unless Chug and the deputy had already divided it. He doubted that had happened and it did not matter, Enrique would see the deputy also. He loathed Chug and the foul words he used, he had never spoken

214

them himself, but he understood that they were essential to the language of the man, that he could not form sentences without them. He thought Chug was stupid and lazy for that as well.

He poured the last of the water over his head, rubbed his eyes and face, then sat very still. Three thirty. The boys would be back in half an hour, the people would be gone. The chain would be across the driveway until Chug came back for the girl. He would have met with May by now, he guessed, and be gone again. Enrique hoped he would be drunk, that would make it easier. It was unfortunate, he thought, that the dog was not a drunkard too, the dog was going to more difficult to subdue. He smiled a little again at the idea, the dog staggering and sloppy under the influence of drink, trying to bark, forgetting he could not, puzzled that his efforts would not produce sound. The destruction of the dog, the deputy, and the patrón, would be penalty. Enrique could not be lawfully compensated for his ruined knee, the interruption of his just retirement, the outrage against his wife, the ugly threats regarding his children, for having his money taken from him. Killing the man would be easy. He sat up straight against the trunk of the sour orange, against the gray bark. He heard voices in The Quarters, softly calling his name. The boys were back, the farm was closed for the day.

Chapter Thirty Seven

Chug had kept it in a frenzy, it was the only way he knew. He liked to make people jump, liked watching them, the higher they jumped the better. The slow motions of the women pissed him off plenty, and he ranted at May because of it. He couldn't get used to the idea that no matter how loudly he yelled, no matter how vile and abusive were the words he chose to use, red in the face, sputtering invective and epithet, sinful in his desire to make them afraid, he couldn't get the women to move any faster. He couldn't get at them, couldn't get face to face with one or two and scare them to death. The women avoided Chug as if he were a leper. Enrique came when he saw the women cornered by the patrón. He interfered, suggested that the women did not understand English, that the old man would not want them abused. Chug couldn't fuck with the women because he needed them to cut, grade, and box the flowers, to do the other things at the farm that they were especially good for. Other women were not exactly lining up for jobs at Royal Glads. Enrique was known to be a good foreman, but Chug was the boss. He was known for his behaviors. The women mortally offended him, but the men and the boys took the brunt of his anger, dumber than the women even, because they didn't know how to stay out his way. The men too, were defended by Enrique.

Every day Chug was at the farm he drove the big Ford around the perimeter road, or up the center drive, looking for someone's shit to step

216

in. He berated, derided the men he encountered for not being fast enough to shift to his will or his whim. Hitman stretched himself to the side of the truck where a man or a boy or a group was gathered. He agreed with the harangue of his master. He glared at the men, he panted with heat, with anticipation. He drooled from his rubbery gummed, tooth-lined mouth. The men were foolish if they were caught more than once walking in the roadways or standing at the end of a row of flowers. They were less likely to be accosted if they stayed in the middle. He was nearly content when he saw them with shovels and rakes and hoes, digging, chopping, shoveling at the thick patches of weeds that had popped up from invisible seeds, blown in moment after moment with the mildest of breezes. Chug had a thing for weeds, an obsession, not for clean fields, but for the work he believed his Mesicans should be doing.

He had taken a dislike for the four boys, he set for them more than for the others. He would watch the boys for some minutes, then descend on them like a carrion bird. He thought May was probably right, they was Indians. He remembered how he had read about the Spanish in school, that they had dropped the fuckers in deep holes, told them to dig silver, how they never got out. Chug thought that was the way to go. Whatever the boys were doing, however they were doing it, he intoned first sarcastic, then caustic, then angry at the boys' ignorance of what he'd been saying. He spewed at them, words that the boys understood, not by meaning, but by inflection and tone. They were lazy, they were dumb, they were worthless Mesicans, he'd say, too fucked up in the head to get the job done like he wanted. The boys had trembled, barely stood in place so anxious were they to run, to bolt, to scatter and escape the words of the patrón, the glare of the dog. The fear that Chug instilled in the boys had become steady in its escalation, but they had jobs to keep, they were making money.

He was worse in the mornings, hung over, poisoned by drink, dope, and dark desires. If the boys had eaten lunch and the day passed into the afternoon and Chug had come and gone or had not come at all, they felt a little less afraid.

Enrique had to stand for the people when Chug came to the farm. It was less necessary for the women than the men because the women were capable of avoiding Chug, they pretended not to hear him, they let May know they would quit, they would find other work if he bothered them. The men needed more protection, they were not as assured as the women.

Since Chug had arrived, he and Enrique had gone boot to boot, it had caused Chug to hate him, it had caused Enrique to leave. When he saw the Ford rumble into the driveway of the farm, Enrique looked next to where the people were working, he began to move towards them. His scalp itched, his fingers tingled with dread at another confrontation with Chug, the ugliness it would bring. He went forward anyway, directly, without hesitation, to where Chug had stopped the truck, where he scolded the boys and the men. He would listen for a moment, then step between Chug and Hitman and the prey they had cornered. Since the beginning of the last season, it had gone the same way, to a Friday in September.

"Enrique," Chug had said, "you need to get the fuck out of my line of vision, I'm talkin to these boys. I ain't gonna eat em. I'm explainin what I want em to do. But I tell you truly, I'm Goddamn sick of seein you face evertime I come out in the field. You got you own work."

"Watch how you speak to them, Chug. They will do anything that needs to be done, but I tell them. That is what my work is."

"Listen here, pal. For the last time, this is my farm. You hired help, just like the rest of em. I'm gonna talk to them an you however fuckin way I want. These boys is doggin it. I'm so sick of it I could puke in my hand. They slow and stupid, that's a shitty combination at a farm. I ain't got no idea at all how you managed to get along before, how you grew any flowers an made a profit for the Sinclairs. We ain't in business, though I could give a shit about it, to give these Mesicans money for standin around with they dicks in they hands. These beaners, especially these ones here, they move quicker when they see me comin. That's the way it oughta be."

"These boys work hard, ten hours, every day you let them," Enrique said. "They work steady. They cannot run from one thing to the next, nothing will be done as it should be. We have boys and old men here, we should treat them less harshly."

"That's bullshit," Chug said. "They gettin paid to work like they was prime labor an now you pullin this boy an old man shit. You Mesicans is thicker than mosquitoes when it comes to coverin up for each other. They probably payin you somethin on the side just to stand up for they sorry asses."

"We had no problems until you came here, Chug. We paid attention to the flowers, not to senseless instructions from a man who should know better. These boys are no different than the boys that were here last year, the ones you scared so badly they left before Easter and the cut was interrupted."

"That's tough," said Chug. "These boys ain't workin like I want em too, that's the bottom line. Evertime I come around, everday, I see em bullshittin, wastin Sinclair money, tellin lies about how good they had it in Mesico."

"That is not what I see, that is not what I hear them talk about whenever they take a minute to speak to each other. Most of the time," he said, "they just work."

Chug slapped his hand hard against the side of the truck. Hitman lunged at his chain.

"Are you sayin I'm a liar, you mother..."

Enrique suddenly stepped in close to the truck. He was mindful that the dog was close, but was secured on its chain.

"Get out," he had said.

"...fucker." Chug spit at the man, gunned the truck, the tires sprayed sand down the center road.

Enrique had looked at the boys looking after the truck. They did not appear to be afraid any longer. The boys' faces had hardened, their eyes had become black slits, their lips were pressed closely together. They clenched the handles of the shovels and rakes and hoes very tightly. He had told them to go back to what they were doing, he had walked slowly to his tractor.

Back and forth it had gone, day after day, bile and venom rose in the stomachs and the mouths of the two men when they saw each other, words and postures became tense, there was no suggestion of patience or compromise. Chug had been persistent in his bigotry, his perception of his power, Enrique had been just as consistent in refuting him. One of the men had to go, the Mexican man had decided which in his boat on Hendry Creek.

Chapter Thirty Eight

May Valentine foundered, she was nervous when Chug came to the chickee and she had customers there. Usually he was drunk, at least had been drinking, she could smell the alcohol fumes in his mouth, smell them seeping from his body. He would be by every day to pick up his money, to see what she needed for fruit and vegetables so he could steal it or trade for it later at the big market. He would pat her ass or squeeze her titties, tell her what he wanted to do to her later in the day, whether there were other people around or not. If there were, May was embarrassed that they would guess she was his whore.

Chug had seen May around, driving through Harlem and at Miners. When Enrique finished building the chickee, the young patrón wanted the girl with the perfect ass to run it. She working at the Holmes House at the beach, washing dishes and making salads. He sauntered right into the kitchen where she was peeling shrimp, the smells of grease, cooked fish and roasts were strong. He persuaded her to come outside and talk. He looked her over closely, stared at her breasts and lower unit. He told May he needed a good woman to work his new fruit stand on Gladiolus. May didn't know Chug, he was recently returned from the university, his reputation had not preceded him into Harlem Heights. He told May he was the boss, that the pay would be good, that she would be close to home, and she could eat all the strawberries she wanted. The next morning, after she had quit the restaurant and come to the fresh chickee to start her new job, Chug told her the rest of the deal. She could have the stand, run it the way she wanted. She would need to help him get across to the beaners once in a while and she would have to fuck him pretty regular. May was not surprised, she had figured that would be in the contract anyway, sooner or later. She didn't want to be miserable fighting him off. She liked the way the stand looked, the openness of it compared to working in a kitchen. She looked him in the eye and said that was cool, but it would cost him twenty dollars every time. He could have her mouth, her pussy or her hand, but her ass was not part of the bargain and he always had to wear a rubber. May told the man she wasn't going to his house very often, that he was never coming to hers. They could go to a motel or have the privacy of the little lake in back or the air-conditioned cab of his truck. That was how it had started and stayed.

May had no despair over the arrangement, there was a steady accumulation of twenties. Still, she did not like the way Chug acted in front of the people who came into the stand. She was especially concerned about the older people, what they must have thought. Chug would be drinking, shooting off his mouth about niggers and spics, greasers and Indians, while Hitman stared at her from his post in the truck. Hitman stared at her like he wanted to eat her. Chug often told her that was what he wanted to do, later, by the lake. Twenty dollars for her, same as always, he'd say, and he'd make her come so hard she'd forget she was a Puerto Rican. May was used to his shit, but it bothered her when she had to share it with her customers.

He would drop by late morning, early afternoon, drink a beer, sit on an upturned packing crate while he waited for her to rustle up his cash and the groceries list. He snickered when an old man stopped at the stand for oranges or cukes, sweet corn and cut flowers. May liked the old men who came to the chickee. They were decent and polite to her, probably widowers or men taking care of the wives who still lived with them, she often guessed. The old men liked to touch the vegetables and fruit, they liked the shade under the thatch and the breeze that blew through it. When an older man came in who Chug had not seen before, who likewise didn't know the lanky cowboy with the gold necklaces, Chug would approach the man, next to the grapefruit or the bananas. He'd ask him if he was from out of town. If the man said that he was, that he was from Ohio or Michigan or New York, and he looked at Chug expectantly, like maybe he was a nice young man trying to be friendly, Chug would smile. He'd ask the man if he knew what young folks did in south Florida for kicks, for fun, for entertainment? The man would usually take the bait and smile back.

"What?" the man would ask. "What do you do?"

"Well," Chug would say, real slow at first, "we hunt... an we fuck."

"What?" the startled man would say. "What?"

"An guess," and Chug would reach out with ring studded fingers and pinch the old man's shirt, "what we hunt?"

The old man would lower his eyes, look at the gravel on the ground, no longer interested in grapefruit, ears burning, knowing that the tall man in the checked shirt and blue jeans was about to answer his own question.

"Somethin to fuck!" Chug would say loudly, regardless of whether there were old ladies there too, clap his hands together and laugh. May would pretend to be busier than she was, her ears burned too, for what the old people had heard.

The old man would look at Chug, then at the woman, astounded at the younger man's coarseness, ashamed for the girl. He would move away from Chug, pay no more attention to the oranges and corn, get in his car and leave. Very seldom did a man who had met Chug depart the vegetable stand happy to have been there.

Chug came in at noon. He was hung over. He had been sick from booze and coke three mornings running. He could not remember a night he hadn't been wasted. He popped two Benzedrine as soon as he rolled out of bed, he washed them down with a warm beer, which would get into his system faster than a cold one. In a few minutes he had his buzz right back. But even at that he felt sick. He got out of the pick-up with a beer in his hand. He squinted in the glare of the sun and its reflection on the white shell of the parking lot. He had not bathed or shaved since he had gone to see the old man the afternoon before. He smelled very strongly of himself, liquor and dog. Hitman stood in the back of the truck, he shivered with his desire to be on the ground and torment May.

222

The man and the dog were at that moment, unfulfilled. Chug's insides were empty, hollow except for the poisons he had burned, snorted, and swallowed down. He had not eaten since the morning before. His hands trembled.

He had money though, he reminded himself, more fuckin money than he knew what to do with. He was going to buy May's ass, not rent it, however much it cost, no matter. Five hundred, a thousand, fuck. What was that to him with the Garza money in the tool box sittin in his bedroom? He could buy her ass fifty times, still have money left over. Cash was rolling in. Despite feeling like shit he had smiled as he recalled what he was taking in from bolito. Truck drivers were crazy to get their shaky hands on the speed he was dealing. Precious and Baby were sucking the high school boys dry every weekend. There would be more stupid Mesicans and niggers to rob, a little further down the line on that one he figured, and there was the good, every day money from peddling potatoes and carrots and flowers to dumb yankees. But for all of that, he felt at loose ends. Somethin wasn't right. Maybe it was the old man. Maybe, he suspected, that old fucker was fixin to cause him some trouble. Having May's ass in front of him after all the time he had spent waitin for it was what he needed, he figured. It would turn him around, make him feel really good to know he'd got there first, powerful even. He didn't give a shit how she felt about it. She'd said when he coughed up the five hundred he could have it, and by God, he said to himself, they was no fuckin confusion about it. A deal, he'd laughed out loud when it came to him, was a deal. Chug wanted the afternoon done with, he wanted to be alone with May. Jesus H. Christ, he thought, he could feel his dick gittin hard in his jeans. He went into the shade of the chickee, took a long pull from the beer, and there she was.

Chug walked along the bins and barrels and boxes filled with the fruit and produce that were displayed for sale. The stuff was colorful, good looking. May kept it that way but that afternoon he didn't notice, he didn't care. There were two old ladies going over the tomatoes like they were the last things they would ever buy. It drove Chug crazy when he watched old people do that, spendin all that time over a fucking tomato, he wanted to kick em in the ass and tell em to go to Miners. Time, he figured, was a wastin. Finally the old women left. Each had bought a bag of mixed vegetables and some bananas and a hanging basket. Chug went to where May was sorting red potatoes, dropping blemished ones and others that had started to turn into a big barrel for his pigs. Her books and her small treasures were packed, her money was in her suitcase, her traveling clothes were laid out on her bed. She was ready to go to California. She had everything a woman could want. Almost, she thought. What she wanted next was a big bundle of cash. Chug got closer.

"You smell Chug," said May, "you smell like a bar."

"It'll wash off, I had me a couple of rough nights. I got finished with what I had to do in LaBelle," he lied then continued lying. "Look here baby, I won big at the dog track last night, had to get drunk to have any luck but Goddamn, I got me a lotta money to spend."

"You smell like a dog too," she said. "Did you go into the cages with the greyhounds and have a beer?"

"I fuckin said it'll wash off. Don't be loadin me up with a lot of shit right now, May, I ain't feelin so good."

"Well go do it, Chug, go wash, because standing here next to you is making me feel not so good either. What if more customers come in and they see you like this?"

"I don't give a shit whether they's customers or not, you should know that. Look here," he said, his voice dropped a pitch, he looked at her body, he tried to smile, "I want to buy you ass today."

May looked at him, made a face, and laughed out loud.

"You must still be drunk, or drunk again," she said. "I wouldn't let you near me today, the way you look, the way you smell, the whores you've been with, I can smell them too."

"Goddamnit I'll get clean an that's perfume you smell. I'll get so clean my own asshole squeaks, but it's yours gonna get fucked. We got us a deal, May, so how much, how much was we talkin about for me to buy you ass?"

Chug had quit smiling, he leaned in close to the woman. May backed up a step.

"What do you mean buy my ass? It's attached to me and I'm not for sale."

224

"What I mean, Goddamnit, is how much money I gotta give you to have you ass today, an you like it, at least you act like you do. This time, ever time. I pay you a whole shitload of money but it's gonna be today an you ain't gonna be so stingy with it no more. I pay you course, ever time, you regular cost. I know you got some special feelin about it so I'm gone be generous today. You understan all that?"

"Chug," she said, "you are really turning crazy. I'm not going to let you near me back there for twenty dollars anytime you want. If Mister Sinclair knew you were like this he would be disgusted, and you're dirty, I don't let dirty men touch me."

"Fuck him," Chug said angrily. "An I'm a farmer, Goddamnit, I'm supposed to be dirty. Now you startin to piss me off real bad, May. You tole me when I was willin to pay that I could have you ass. Now one last time, fore I let Hitman out and just throw you down on the sand out back there, how much you want, just so you happy with the whole idea?"

May smiled at Chug with as much lechery as she could command.

"Okay baby, you got me. You've finally worn me down. You pay me one thousand dollars for today, and I'll be happy. You pay me a thousand dollars, Chug, and it's free after that, whenever you want."

"Sold," Chug exclaimed, "an worth ever penny."

He reached into his wallet with shaky hands. He pulled out ten new hundred dollar bills and thrust them at May.

"I figure you want this right away," he said, "most do."

"I'm not most, baby. That's why you're paying me so much. The perfect ass, that's what they say. It's never been touched by anyone but me. Thank you for the money. I'm going to save it," she said.

"I don't give a shit what you do with it," said Chug. "Let's go, out back. You can drop them shorts. I want you ass so bad I cain't stand up."

"Chug, baby. Baby you can have me. I'll make it real nice for you and I'll like it, I know I will, but not here," she said. "It's the first time for me. We don't want to be disturbed. And you are very dirty. You must be clean for me. I need to wash myself too, I'm sweaty. I want to wash there, and everywhere else."

"Jesus H. Christ, May, it ain't a weddin," he said.

"I'll bring oil. I'll prepare myself for you, baby. You'll like that. I have

225

to, to make it easier. Bring two rubbers, we'll do it twice back there. All this money makes me want it, Chug," she said. "I can't wait much longer either."

He reached down in front of her and squeezed himself. May covered his hand with her own. She found the head and rubbed it with her palm.

"God," she said, "it's big."

The blood in his head was making a sound as it pulsed, he thought. His ears were ringing, his face was flushed. His legs felt like rubber, he believed they would drop him any minute.

"When?" he croaked.

A car pulled onto the shell. Its tires crunched, another came in behind it.

"You promise me you will be clean? And maybe a little drunk? But not too drunk. You need to eat. Do you want some watermelon or an apple?"

"I don't eat that shit. When?" he croaked a second time.

"I want you to be like this when we are together. I want to feel it all," May said. She patted his dick a last time and moved away. "There is only one ass like mine, Chug, and it's never been let out. God, now I'm as hot as you are. I wish those people weren't coming in."

"Fuck," said Chug. He had started to pant. "You want me to let Hitman out?"

"We'll meet later, baby, at the lake. I'll get home and bathe after I close the chickee. There'll be more time for everything later. I think you should do me just as the sun is setting. We can watch it go over the water while you're behind me."

Chug had to sit down, the beer and the speed and May were mixing in his systems. He wiped his wet palms on his jeans. Truly, he thought, I feel like shit.

The customers bought big bags of oranges and grapefruit, sweet corn and tomatoes, then left. May walked to where Chug sat next to the melons. He was holding ice shavings against his face. She handed him the twenty dollars the people had spent.

"See, baby, you'll always have more money."

226

"I pay you somethin ever time, May. It ain't just satisfyin my pecker, they must be more to it. Right now, though, I gotta go lay down. Like I said, I ain't feelin too sporty. It'll still be hot when the sun's dyin, don't you wanna go to a motel?"

"By the lake, Chug, our place. I'll bring a big quilt and a bottle of oil. After dark we'll go to a motel. You can play your music at the lake. Bring that tape you like."

"Jimi Hendrix," said Chug, drifting a little with the heat and the poisons. "He's a wild fucker. Course I'm partial to Steppenwolf, I always liked the name."

"I'll be ready for you, Chug. You can wet me with your tongue and mouth before we fuck. If you're a little drunk I think you'll like that, and I want to hold as much of you as I can in my mouth. You'll last longer inside me the second time. Don't forget rubbers," she said.

"What about the skeeters after dark?" Chug had gone way off with May, but was interrupted by a sudden bad vision of clouds of black mosquitoes and him naked.

May turned pale. Chug's dread of mosquitoes was not unknown.

"I want to see that sunset, Chug, on my hands and knees. That's the way I want to let it go. After that," she said, "we can get in the truck and go to a motel at the beach."

"Fuckin A right," said Chug. "They ain't nothin I cain't handle till after dark. You ever been to the Surf Club, May?"

"Go on now," she said. "Go get a sandwich or bacon and eggs. Put something in your stomach so you don't get sick. You said today, Chug. You miss today because you're drunk and don't show up, when you've got me so hot, you bastard," she said, "you're going to have to start asking all over."

"You shittin me, May. You think I'm gonna miss this? I done paid for it already."

"You'll feel better after you've eaten and rested, Chug, and you'll smell better after you've washed. I want you to make love to me all night."

"Makin love's for schoolteachers, we gonna fuck our brains out. I'm gonna bring Hitman, me an him has talked about this several times."

"Not unless he's chained in the truck." May hissed in the direction of

227

the dog. "I'm not even taking off my sandals if that damned dog is running around and scaring me. No...fucking... way. You got that, Chug?"

"Don't get all pissed off. He's gonna be in the truck, just like always. We gone be in front. He won't be able to see us over the cab, he ain't tall enough. Hitman won't care anyway, he'll be lookin to spot a Mesican comin down to fish. He cain't bark, you know, he ain't gonna make no noise."

"Go on now, Chug. I'll meet you at the lake at seven."

"You damn sure straight about that, May. You got you money, an you got you head on right. Ain't nothin between us now but a couple of hours."

Chapter Thirty Nine

Chug went to his duplex. He let Hitman inside. He filled an aluminum bowl with dry food from a big bag, pushed the bowl with the toe of his boot in the direction of the dog. The air-conditioner was running, the apartment was cold. He filled another big bowl with water from the sink and set it down. Chug watched Hitman crunch and gulp.

"Damn you sumbitch," he said, "you eat like a fuckin wolf."

Chug looked at the kitchen and the front room. The place was a wreck, his shit and Marvin's stuff from when he'd stayed were flung over chairs or lay in heaps on the dingy carpet. They had been with Precious and Baby two nights before...three nights before, he remembered, he could smell the shit they used for perfume. They must have rolled in it, he figured. The place looked so bad he would need to get someone over to clean it up. He wondered if he could get a stray. They was poor white women who cleaned houses, maybe he could get one to come across for a twenty.

"Money," he said out loud. "It'd buy anything, it'd buy anybody."

He walked down the hallway to the bedrooms, kicked aside bottles, cans, and trash. He turned on a light. A drape hung slack on a bent rod, the sheets and pillows were on the floor, the stained mattress had new stains. He looked more closely, broken glass littered the window sill, it sparkled in the carpet. The bedroom smelled like spilled whisky and stale smoke. He went to the bureau and checked a drawer. He stuck his head in the closet for a moment. Everything was where it was supposed to be. Them whores knew he'd kill em if they fucked with his stash, and Marvin? Shit. Marvin was just too lame to think about it. He was gonna have to give old Marvin a few thousand of the beaner money, he figured. Marvin probably whine and mention some bullshit thing about a half or a third, them bein partners. Tough shit, Chug figured, he'd buy a boat an let Marvin use it. Marvin wouldn't steal from him, Marvin was his friend. Chug thought about that for a minute. He decided he didn't need no friends, and Marvin wasn't gettin no half.

When the telephone rang it startled him, he was jittery. He'd figured if he dropped a Quaalude or a couple of Valium he could sleep for a few hours then be ready to drink a little and have at May. Right now, he knew, he needed some shut-eye. He guessed that it was Precious on the phone to see if he had anything lined up for her with the high school boys. He remembered it was Friday. She was outta luck, Chug decided, they was no time for huntin them fellers down. He had more important things to do instead of helpin her earn a livin. He picked up the phone.

"Yeah. What you want?"

It was Earlene on the other end.

"Chug, I need you to come by and get payroll. It's all ready. Your father likes for the employees to have it early enough so they can leave and pay their bills before the offices close," she said.

"You shittin me, Earlene. You expect me to ride clear across town for that? Why don't you bring it out, you so anxious for the beaners to get paid?"

"Because it's your job to do it."

Earlene's tone was pure bitch who knew the lay of the land.

"Since when?"

"Since you ran Enrique Garza off. You come get the payroll. I don't think you'll have to do it again, but this week you do."

"Whoowhee, Earlene, you talkin tough. You got my check ready?"

"Of course."

"Is it a lot bigger than it was last week?"

"Of course, not," she said, "why should it be?"

"Well, fuck. Is my old man there?"

"No he's not. He's gone to the attorney's office."

"Well I'm gone talk to the sumbitch," he said. "When's he comin back?"

"It won't be today," Earlene said. "Your brother is coming down from Tallahassee. He and Mister Sinclair are meeting to discuss business and have an early supper."

"Well ain't that cute, them boys thicker than thieves an old Verdell ain't included. Just as well to know which side of the road everybody's standin on."

"Will you please come get the payroll? I can't leave. The people need their money."

"Yeah, fuck, I'll come down there for my check and the beaners' money. Hitman be happy goin downtown, he git to see lots of people he'd like to bite. Maybe I bring him in to say hello to you Earlene? You all like that?"

"That's okay with me, Chug, just so you don't mind me shooting him when he comes through the door."

"Jesus, Earlene, you turned into a regular Viet Cong. But that little pistol you keep in you desk ain't enough to slow Hitman down, them little bullets'll just bounce off his head."

"I got a bigger one since you've been in my desk," she said.

"All right. Goddamnit. I'm comin down an you can show me you big pistol. First I gotta shower up an scrub my balls. I'm dirty, I heard."

"How did you get dirty, Chug? Were you working at the farm?"

"That's funny, Earlene," he said. "Everbody's funny, now you funny too."

Chug hung up the telephone and undressed where he stood. He let the clothes he dropped make a new pile. He showered in the filthy bathroom. The tub wouldn't drain, it was clogged with hair and soap. He stood and washed with scum water up his ankles, then got outside the shower and stuck his ankles and feet back in under the running water to

231

rinse them. He sat down on the toilet and shit a runny mess, fouling the air so badly that he had to open the window. He walked to the kitchen, found a can of Lysol, walked back to the bathroom. He saturated the air with the disinfectant, he dropped the empty can on the bathroom floor. He showered again, dried and shaved and dressed. He stood in his boots for a minute and rolled his ankles on the high heels. He bent down in front of his dresser, he drew open the bottom drawer and lifted out a wooden box. He concentrated on the jewelry. He picked three gold chains for around his neck, a gold bracelet, and two rings for each of his hands. Two of the rings were clusters of diamonds and two were mounted with gold doubloons. When he was finished adorning himself he put the box back and closed the drawer.

He went into the bathroom again, half-assed brushed at his teeth, then dumped a cupful of English Leather into his hands. He splashed the cologne over his face and neck, he ran his wet fingers through his thinning hair. In the kitchen, Hitman was laying on his side on the dirty linoleum. Chug stepped over him carefully, looked in the freezer, opened the bottom door and took out a beer. He picked up his fat wallet. He sipped at the beer while he counted the money, three thousand in new bills in the wallet. His usual roll was already in his pocket, a couple dozen twenties and some fives for singles. Chug looked closely at the new money.

"Don't look like greaser money, do it?" he asked Hitman. "Looks like my money to me."

He went back into the bedroom and grabbed a small handful of pills from the top of the dresser, he slipped them into a shirt pocket. He picked up his gold Gruen and snapped it at his wrist. Back in the kitchen he found his keys, told the dog to get the fuck up, he took a final look around his apartment. Shitfire, he thought, he would have to move next door, that'd be the easiest. He got Hitman in the truck and fastened to his chain. When he was behind the wheel he leaned this way and that to see that all his weapons were accounted for. He turned the key, fired the truck up.

Chug drove the big Ford fast, the dog gulped at hot air as it blew by. He took McGregor, past the Schultz's red potato farm, over Whiskey Creek, he turned right at Colonial. He shot past the cemetery, laughed at the drive-in church, bounced across The Tamiami Trail. He took Fowler

232

north, to the foot of the Edison Bridge, and parked in front of the office on First Street. He sat in the truck for a few minutes, letting the air-conditioning blow at him, listening to John Kay sing about *The Pusher*.

"I said Goddamn. God, Goddamn the pusher man."

Chug sang along with Steppenwolf. He believed he was every bit as bad.

Earlene handed him the pay envelopes for the thirty people who worked at the chrysanthemum farm. Each person's name was written clearly across the top. Inside was cash, calculated to the penny for the time that man or that woman had worked the week just ended. There were no checks for any of the people costed to the farm but Chug, now that Enrique was gone. Those other people, the old man's accountants had told him, most of them weren't even officially alive, anywhere probably. They didn't need to be on the books. Royal Glads paid no Social Security, no payroll taxes, no unemployment and no insurance. Cash for payroll was loose change for the operation, his accountants found him the money, he was saving a bundle, it helped the bottom line. The people in the fields didn't complain. They were paid cash with no taxes held back and lots of hours to work, the old man figured. If some of them needed shelter they could stay in The Quarters.

Chug looked at his check and snorted. He dropped the pay envelopes for the people into his satchel. He reached in and stirred the envelopes by hand. He watched Earlene, then he picked the satchel up and gave it a hard shake.

"I'll let them beaners sort this here out," he said. "I'll just dump em on they lunch table in a pile. They cain't read for shit. We'll see how many of em even recognize they own name, whatever name it is they usin this season."

Earlene looked hard at Chug and shook her head.

"That was shitty the way you left your father's car. It was filthy, he showed me."

"Yeah, well, tough, he can get it cleaned."

"It's been cleaned. If there is a next time, he's going to report it stolen," she said.

"That fuckin car cain't be stole by me, Earlene, my name's all over this place."

"You need to see that lawyer friend of yours about that, Chug," she said, "but I doubt he'll want to help."

Chug bit at his lip and fingered the pills in his pocket. He was going to have to go out on The Hill, get some coke before he went back to Gladiolus. What Earlene had to say didn't mean shit.

"Well that's interestin, Earlene, you all figurin out how to make somebody want to leave someplace. I always thought of that as one of my special qualities."

"Why did you leave the salt on the car, Chug? Nobody leaves salt spray on a car if they care about it. Salt ruins paint. Where were you?"

"I was at the Surf Club, Earlene. It's next to the ocean. You get it?"

Chug picked up his valise, opened the front door. He stepped into a blast of heat and the blinding light of the afternoon sun. He put his aviators on. He looked up and down First Street. No cars were moving, no breeze drifted from the Caloosahatchee.

He dumped the pay envelopes on the lunch table, just as he'd planned. The people were assembled for the afternoon break. He'd only snorted a single line on the way out. He thought watching the beaners try to find they pay would be funny, then he'd snort another line, a little bit bigger one, he figured.

Earlene always liked Enrique. They had started at Royal Farms within a year of each other. He had always been respectful, he had made the old man a lot of money. Enrique had been picking up the pay envelopes and passing them out every Friday for as long as she had been adding up the hours and counting out the money. Mister Sinclair was busy with other powerful men. They had been in communication with his oldest son, they were seeing to it that Chug was removed from the family business. She believed they would finish the papers today. The old man had told her to stay in the office in case he needed something and to get on the phone with their customers. Tell them a new manager would be starting soon at Royal Glads, the old man had said, or she would have taken the money to the people.

The men and women looked at the pile of white envelopes on the table. After a few minutes of whispering, a thin, stooped man in sun bleached khakis came forward. He picked up the top envelope and read a name. Each time he spoke, a person slipped up quickly, nodded a thank you at the man or said gracias, compadre, took the money and backed away from the table. The stooped man read all the names until the last person had been paid. One of the women had taken May's envelope and gone to carry it to her. Chug leaned against the barn door. He was disappointed that there hadn't been any confusion. He could give a fuck, he figured, this would be the last time he'd do this shit.

The oldest of the Indian brothers reached into his pants pocket. He removed four, wet, ten dollar bills. He walked to where Chug stood. He held out the limp money.

"Thank you, patrón," he said. He gave Chug a stiff bow.

Chug looked at the people gathered in the barn, several of them were smiling. He looked at the pitiful bills in the boy's hand. He wanted to beat the shit out of him.

"Keep it, fucker," he said. "You gonna need it for you medical bills."

He looked at the people again.

"You all ain't worth a kiss my ass," he said. "Break's over, now git back to work."

Chug turned on his heels, he walked quickly back to the truck. He pulled a cold beer from his cooler, popped the top, drank it down. He dropped the empty can out the window in front of the people, gunned the truck and made it spin on the packed sand. Hitman skidded in the back until he was yanked up short by his chain.

235

Chapter Forty

*T*hunder rumbled across the prairie and woods and sounded at the
coast. Over Okeechobee the sky was black but to the west the sun
was burning bright. The air at the little lake was laden with humidity.
The people at the farm had worn it all day, shirts, pants and canvas shoes
were soaked with sweat. On the shirts especially, the salt had spread further and further down the cloth. It left staggered white ridges where it
dried.

May and Chug and the dog were at the lake. Chug had parked the
truck so the sand trail was blocked and Hitman was in the shade of the
pepper hedge. Chug had gone right to the Spanish Main after he had left
the farm. He'd had a half dozen rum and cokes, bought a bottle, ice and
soda, and headed back for May. He was leaning against the front of the
truck, watching her.

The woman stood in the center of a big quilt, she could see herself in
the reflection of his sunglasses. *Electric Ladyland* spilled out the open
windows of the truck, May moved with the music as if she too were a
voodoo child. Chug could see May but there was two of her sometimes,
he kept blinking his eyes to get back to where there was just one. He
couldn't remember the drive from the Spanish Main to Royal Glads, did-
n't have no idea how he'd got here. The sun was cookin his brain, he figured, the powder hadn't helped worth a shit. He vaguely wished May
could drive, she could get them to a motel and he could get out of the

236

fuckin heat. He even thought about telling her he was too drunk, that he wouldn't be able to get it up, maybe they could wait until tomorra. Shit, he thought, she got the money, what difference would it make? He decided a moment later he was fine. All he needed was to see her shucked down, his limp dick would turn to wood. But his hands trembled badly and he could taste the rum backing up in his stomach. Chug's head ached and his mouth was dry, no matter how much he kept pouring into it.

May slipped off her shorts, she was wearing the tiniest panties Chug had ever seen. He laughed at how small they were, then tried to focus on the thick patch of hair that framed the piece of silk. She unbuttoned her shirt, dropped it next to the shorts, she kicked off her sandals. She came to edge of the quilt and peeled down the panties.

"They God," said Chug, "you a hot property."

"Get undressed, Chug," she said. "Do you want me to help you?"

"Yeah, baby. I believe I can manage my shirt but I'm so fuckin drunk you gone have to relieve me of my jeans and boots."

May came to where he was braced crookedly against the truck. She undid the buttons of his cowboy shirt, unfastened his belt and the steel button and zipper to his levi's. She knelt down in front of him, and as he raised a leg, pulled off his high heeled boots. In a moment all his clothes lay in a heap at his feet. He was naked too, except for the jewelry. Chug's face and hands and neck were mottled and red, everywhere else he was very white.

"Do you have protection for me?" May asked.

"Jesus Christ, I got to cover my helmet, ain't I," he giggled.

Using the hood of the truck to steady himself, he moved around the truck and opened the glove box. He pushed his pistol aside, found the package of rubbers and pulled one out. He fumbled with it, dropped it to the ground, cursed, picked it up, ripped the foil with his teeth and managed to roll it on. He stepped on sand spurs making his way back to the edge of the blanket. Chug stood while May helped, he balanced on one foot and then the other, so she could pull the stickers out. He took a long drink from his rum. He tossed the glass on the ground and began pulling at his dick.

237

"Let's git to it," he said.

May was sweating heavily, her skin glistened with beads of wet salt, it ran in rivulets to the folds of her skin. She was hot from the sun, flushed with the anticipation of sex, and very nervous.

"Watch me, baby, keep your eyes on me," she said.

May bent over, she picked up a bottle of baby oil. She unscrewed the cap and held the opening over her shoulders. The contents ran out over her back and her breasts, down the length of her body, the oil pushed the sweat ahead of it. She dropped the nearly empty bottle, she used her hands to smooth the lotion onto her skin, she combed her greased fingers through her long black hair. She cupped her heavy breasts, squeezed her nipples, pinched them to make them stiff. Abruptly she spread her legs, rubbed the oil into her thighs, bent over, worked it into her calves, her ankles, the tops and bottoms of her feet. She reached for the bottle again, she shook a few more drops of the baby oil into her hands. May turned away from Chug. She massaged her fabulous ass, she pulled the cheeks apart so he could see what he was getting, so he could see what he was paying for.

May was on fire. She had made herself incredibly excited. She imagined how it would feel, to have Chug inside her, to be filled at last by the naked man with her on the blanket. She looked over her shoulder at him. His dick was as stiff as a piece of iron.

"Take off your sunglasses, baby, you'll see it better," she said.

Chug threw the sunglasses to the ground and stepped forward. May let herself down to her knees, her hands, she lowered her face to the quilt. She smelled the oil where it had dripped on the cloth. She put her face sideways, her breasts were flattened. She reached back with both hands to hold herself open. She had forgotten about her other bargain, she had forgotten about everything.

"Kiss it," she said. "Lick it all over, then I want you in me."

Chug dropped to his knees behind her. The Hendrix tape had finished. Hitman was resting in the back of the truck. There were no sounds by the little lake but the drone of insects, the rumble of thunder closer in, and the uneven breathing of the two people on the big blanket.

238

Chapter Forty One

Enrique and the boys rolled out from under the pepper hedge where they had concealed themselves. They were within a few feet of where Chug knelt behind May before the dog sensed the movement and sprang to his feet. Enrique hobbled as fast as he could on the crutch, the boys were way ahead of him. They moved through the sand and the weeds without shoes, toes dug in for traction. The boys were on Chug in a flash, just after Hitman saw them. The dog tried to bark, he threw himself violently at the chain in hope of being loose and at them. They swung the bats in sequence, the oldest boy struck first, then each of the others, then they all hit at Chug together.

The first strike connected with the front of the patrón's head, it bounced from the impact of that bat into the oncoming impact of another. The third swing was wide but moved through the air with such velocity that where it caught Chug along the side of his face, it took that ear off. The youngest boy dashed in between his brothers. Chug had turned, raised his arm against the blinding light of the late sun. The boy swung his bat at the upraised arm and broke it so badly that the arm and hand were useless. Chug fell forward on his crushed face, his body doubled up over his knees, his broken arm was cradled in the embrace of the other. The bats descended again. Two boys hit him with sideways swings that broke his ribs, punctured his lungs, another boy swung his bat down, very hard, across Chug's ankle. The oldest boy looked first at

Enrique, then hit Chug one more time in the head, solidly, but not enough to split the skin again. Chug toppled over sideways, unconscious, he gulped for air through his smashed mouth, blood flowed from his nose.

The boys with the bats turned and ran for the dog in the truck. Hitman was insane with rage, he hurled himself desperately against the short chain. He had stopped trying to bark, but he could growl, and from deep inside him there came devilish noises. The boys surrounded the truck, they tested the reach. The dog was too high for them and could not be cornered. Two boys climbed on the back bumper. They stretched to swing the bats, to keep the dog to the front, but they did not connect or inflict any harm. The oldest boy slipped back to the front of the truck, climbed up on it then onto the cab. From where he knelt he took powerful swings at the head of the dog and hit him repeatedly. The boys on the bumper stepped over the tailgate, they began to shorten the distance between themselves and Hitman. The blows rained down, the hammering at Hitman began to take its toll. They hit him on his spine and on his wide head. Bits of teeth, blood spatter, smashed toenails and pieces of hide were slung around the truck with gobs of white spittle and bright yellow piss. There was little noise, only the breathing of the combatants, the sound of the bats when they landed, and the sound of Hitman's nails scratching at the plywood.

Hitman began to cower. He looked frantically for an opening, to get away from the clubs that were killing him. A sharp, square blow on his forehead caused the dog to bleed very badly. The blood ran into his eyes, his nostrils, his mouth, it slickened the dog's hair. Hitman backed himself away from the chain, despite the agony of the bats. He dug in against the plywood, shook his massive neck and pulled his bloody head through the collar. He turned on a dime and sprang for the back. He was out of the reach of the oldest boy, the other two jumped to the side. He scrambled up onto the tailgate and launched himself into the air.

Hitman would have disappeared in seconds in the thick pepper but the youngest boy was waiting. As the pit bull landed, that boy swung his bat as hard as he possibly could. He kept his eyes on his targets, didn't blink or falter. He broke both of the dog's front legs as they touched the ground. Hitman lay motionless in the sand after that. His long pink tongue hung slack from his black gums, the blood from his head wound filled his eyes. The other boys circled, then the four struck at the dog with a vengeance. They broke its jaws and ribs and the legs in back. One after another, a dozen more blows pounded the brown body. In a moment it was finished.

The boys were breathing heavily. They were spattered with blood from Chug and the dog. They prodded Hitman with the ends of the bats, they touched his lifeless body with their toes. They returned to where Enrique was motionless, staring at Chug on the blanket.

"Enrique?" said the oldest.

Enrique looked up, he shook his head to clear his thoughts. The youngest boy slapped Chug on the face and let out a little high-pitched yelp. Another boy reached down, before Enrique could stop him. He used his flower knife, he cut a lock of hair. He put the bit of hair in his pocket.

"No more," Enrique said. "All of you go to the other side of the ditch and wait. When you hear me call, three of you come back, the other stays to watch. Go."

May was crying, shaken and scared. She had been as surprised as Chug. She had scooted forward when she heard the first blows to the head of the patrón and the grunts of the boys with the effort. She had rolled free of the quilt into the sand and the sand spurs. Every place on her naked body where there had been oil was covered with gray sand and weed seed. She reached up, shivering, she tried to pull clusters of stickers from her tangled hair. She turned her nakedness away from Enrique. She sobbed, she wiped at her face but her tears had already turned the sand to black water. Her face and neck and breasts were streaked, her lover's blood mingled with sweat and oil. She bent down for her clothes, she thought she might fall over. She dressed quickly, just her shorts and shirt, slipped her feet into her sandals, put the tiny panties into one of her pockets as the boy had done with the lock of hair. She rubbed her arms and hands, trying to brush away the sand. She looked at Chug on the quilt and then at Enrique. The sun was going down fast.

"Is he dead? Anita said you wouldn't kill him."

"No, he is not dead. Look," Enrique said, "he is breathing. Look."

From Chug's broken mouth and smashed nose came bloody, frothy bubbles of air. When he inhaled, he made a sucking sound that came from deep within his chest. When he exhaled it sounded like a wheeze or a whistle.

"He is alive, although those men could have easily killed him. Remember that, that when you saw him last he was alive."

"What else do you want me to do?"

Enrique moved to the driver's door, he reached in, pulled out Chug's keys. He removed the ignition key. He handed her the others then leaned to look in the bed of the truck. What he wanted he did not see.

"Go to your house," he said. "The boys will come by, then Anita. There is clothing and food at your house that she left there. Give it to the boys," he said.

The sky was darkening quickly, the clouds that had been in the east were almost overhead. The coming rain was pushing cool air ahead of it, the wild, salt-water grasses were bent in the direction of the Gulf.

"Get yourself ready. Have your things by the door when Anita gets there. Load them into the trunk of the car. Do you understand?" he asked.

"Yes. But I am very dirty."

"You have time to clean yourself. Bathe. Wash your hair. You will feel better. Wait until the storm has ended before you leave your house. Take these keys. Go to this man's duplex, you know where it is. You and Anita go together. This one was lazy and very careless."

He touched Chug's broken ankle with the tip of his crutch.

"My money will be there, in a new toolbox. It will be easy for you to find. Give it to Anita. Put it into the trunk."

May looked at Enrique closely in the dusk. She could see his leg was bleeding through the bandage. He looked much older than when she had seen him a week before. He seemed to sag on the crutch.

"Go through the patrón's house very carefully. Look for money and jewelry. He is rich with gold. You know good things, Anita told me you do. Find the gold that he dresses himself with, watches, rings, bracelets. Whatever you see that you know to be valuable, take it. Find his money. Find it all. Put it in the trunk with the toolbox. Do you understand? That is what I want you to do."

"I'll find whatever is there," she said.

May turned and ran from the clearing.

Chapter Forty Two

*J*ust east of 41, lightning was striking the flooded land. At the little lake, the temperature suddenly dropped. It would be raining in a few minutes. The mosquitoes were gone. Enrique could not bear to look at Chug's nakedness. He bent over and rolled the man to his side. Chug's breathing became easier, less labored. Enrique looked closely at the blood matted in the man's copper hair, the odd angle of his forearm. When he leaned over, he saw that Chug's lips were pulled back. His teeth clicked when he breathed through his nose, the sound stopped when he opened his mouth to gulp at the wet air. Even in the dusk, Enrique could see that a lot of blood had leaked from the head of the man. Enrique called for three of the boys to come to him.

"You left the youngest to watch? Good. Help me carry the patrón to where the dog lies," he said.

The boys and Enrique reached down, each grabbed a handful of the quilt. They carried Chug, dragged him, dropped him next to Hitman. Enrique told one of the boys to run for the cooler he had left in the pepper hedge. When he had the cooler, he opened it, removed the morphine, and injected the works into Chug's hip. He had thought about saving the last needle for himself, in case the pain in his knee became unbearable, but he didn't like the sick feeling it gave to his stomach, or the confusion he'd had with it. He wanted to be alert, awake for what was ahead. He would manage the pain, he told himself. He decided

244

Chug needed it now, to keep him asleep, to keep him from calling out, to let him dream one more time. He used the heel of his shoe to gouge a hole in the sand and dropped the needle in it.

"Put the man in the back of the truck," he said, "and put the dog beside him."

The boys lifted Chug's heavy body into the bed of the truck, they arranged the blanket so he was in the middle of it. They picked up Hitman by his broken legs and swung the dead dog up.

"Place them side by side," said Enrique. "We will wrap them together in the blanket. Who has the rope?"

One of the boys dashed to where it was hidden in the peppers.

"Bind them up tightly inside the blanket."

The boys set Hitman alongside his master. They stretched out the dog's mangled forelegs and hind legs, they wedged him against Chug's naked body. Fire ants had already found Hitman, they bit the boys' hands. In a few moments the dog and the man were covered by the quilt, they were tied together beneath it.

Enrique heard the sound of rain slapping the lake, in another instant it fell on them. The rain came down in sheets that announced the end of that day, it plunged them into darkness. The rain soaked them, it caused the boys to tremble.

"Get in the truck," he told them. "One of you go for the youngest. We will sit inside until the worst of it is over."

The five squeezed into the cab. Enrique sat behind the wheel. He used his good leg to depress the clutch, he put the gears in neutral. He started the truck, turned on the heater, the air inside became warm, the boys stopped shaking. The noise from the rain on the roof and the noise of the heater were very loud. They sat without speaking for several minutes. When Enrique felt he could wait no longer, he shut the heater off.

"There is much to do," he said, "whether it is raining or not. We will warm ourselves here for a moment longer then all of you but the oldest must go. You," he said, pointing to that one, "you will be our driver, my leg is useless for it. While the others are gone I will show you how to shift the gears and use the clutch."

It was a great responsibility for the oldest boy. Enrique had singled him out for it. He knew how to drive already, his father owned a taxi in Jalisco. On some occasions, when he was boracho, he let his oldest son drive the fares. But the boy did not volunteer that he knew. He guessed that Enrique would want him to learn his way, the way he would show him.

"It is good that it is raining," the man continued, "it will wash away the gore from the truck and the ground. You," he said to the youngest, "when I tell you, get out and bring me all of the patrón's clothing, every-thing, his pants, his shirt, his boots, his socks. Make sure there is noth-ing on the ground where he was with the lady."

The downpour had eased slightly. The air in the cab became too hot, Enrique became nauseous from the smells of the boys. He turned the truck off and opened his window. He breathed deeply through his mouth at the fresh air.

"Go now," he said, and that boy was out of the truck and in the rain.

In another minute he stood next to the driver's door. Enrique opened it, the boy dropped all of Chug's things inside, sunglasses, the rum glass, the empty bottle of oil.

"Come close, compadre," Enrique said. "I want you to go to the barn. Be very cautious. I want you to come back with a bag that we use for garbage. This truck is filthy inside. I want you to pick up all the trash that is on the floor, and the patrón's clothes and boots. I will be finished with those things. We want nothing in this truck that speaks for him. Do you understand?"

The boy nodded eagerly.

"After you have cleaned, take the bag to your house. Burn it in one of the barrels, burn it hot, like I have shown you. Roll the barrel inside the building so it is out of the rain. Burn the patrón's clothes and boots and all this filth until there is nothing left but ash."

Enrique nodded back at him, the boy was gone again, invisible in the rain and the dark.

"You two," he said to the middle brothers, "are you ready for your tasks?"

The two boys shook their heads vigorously to show that they were.

"Go to May's. You know where she lives. May will be there waiting.

246

There will be another woman also, una hermana de la iglesia. They will give you packages of clothing and food. Wrap the packages so they do not get wet. Come here and get back in this truck. Do you understand? Good, then go."

Enrique watched the boys slide from the seat and disappear like the youngest. He told the oldest boy to check that the man was still alive, to find the four bats, to wash them in the rain and put them in the truck next to the man and the dog, and to get into the driver's seat when he was finished.

When the last boy was out of the truck, Enrique bent down, he pulled Chug's wallet from the blue jeans. He found thirty, wet, one hundred dollar bills, his money, he guessed. He placed it on the seat beside him. He searched the pockets of the patrón's pants, he found Chug's other cash. That money was wet also, and folded, held together by a gold clip. He put the wallet back in the jeans, dropped them to the floor. He picked up the checkered cowboy shirt and found a soggy mess of black and white pills. He threw the shirt back down. He opened the glove box. He saw the thirty-eight. He carefully lifted the pistol from the glove box, he placed it on the pile of wet clothing. He twisted in the seat, he removed Chug's rifle from its holder. He opened the door and let the rifle drop outside the truck in the rain and wet weeds. He picked up all the money and put it where the thirty-eight had been. He turned on the overhead light. Trash, cans and bottles littered the floor of the truck. He reached under the seat, found the forty-five automatic. He pulled out the clip to see that the fat bullets were still inside. He put the forty-five back in its holster, put it back under the seat. There was a tap at the window. Enrique handed the oldest boy the smaller pistol, he told the him to pick up the rifle, and throw the weapons as far as he could into the water of the lake. There was another tap at the window, it was the youngest, dripping wet, smiling in the rain. Enrique could see how white, how square the boy's teeth were. He scooted himself over on the seat and allowed the boy to clean the truck. The boy used his hand and his arm as if they were a broom, he swept the truck free of the detritus.

When the boy was finished and the floor of the truck was much cleaner, Enrique told him to burn the trash and clothing, to bathe himself very thoroughly, use soap, he said, and wait for the others to bring him his new clothes. The youngest ran off, the oldest returned to the truck. He opened the driver's door and got behind the steering wheel.

"You have driven the small tractor," Enrique said to the boy, "this will be almost the same."

Enrique told him where to reach and the boy bent over, found the handle under the seat, and scooted it forward so he could more easily reach the pedals.

"When I was in the army, I taught many boys how to drive trucks, and how to care for them, how to listen to the engine and the gears. Most of them were not as smart as you. Now," he said, "push in the pedal nearest the door, put your hand on the knob. I will teach you the sequence," said the man. "One, two, three, four. Press, shift, release, accelerate. One... two... three... four."

The middle boys returned, the rain had changed to drizzle. It was possible, Enrique thought, that the moon might yet come out. He looked at his watch, it was nearly ten o'clock.

He rummaged through the packages until he found the pants, the shirt, and the shoes that Anita had marked as his. He handed the rest back to the boys.

"Is there food?" he asked.

One of the boys reached into a wet sack. He pulled out a big hamburger sandwich wrapped in wax paper so it would be dry. Enrique thanked him, and put the hamburger on the seat.

"Go to The Quarters, your brother is waiting," he said. "Burn the clothes you are wearing. Burn any papers that have a name for you on them, burn anything that says who you are. For now it is better that you have no names. After you have finished burning, wash yourselves. Do a good job. My stomach is very uneasy. I am afraid I will be sick if I smell smoke. Dress yourselves in your new clothes. Wrap your money in something, we will hide it here in the truck. Should something happen to some, the others will know where to look. When you are dressed, I need you," he pointed again to the oldest, "to come back to me. We will drive this truck away from here. I want the rest of you to wait in the packing house until you see us. Put ten cement blocks and a roll of wire in front of the barn, in the shadow. Fill a container with diesel, but be very careful not to spill it on yourselves. The smell of diesel, I am sure it will make me sick."

The boys' faces were pressed closely together outside the opened window. Enrique turned to the one who sat behind the steering wheel. He continued to practice, he depressed the clutch, shifted the gears, and let the clutch out again. His brothers watched him with plain admiration.

"It will be different when the truck is running," he told the boy, "more exciting. Go now," he said, " all of you. We want to leave here soon."

Chapter Forty Three

Chug was alive under the quilt but his breathing was labored, it happened only with great effort. His broken nose was crusting with blood so he drew in his air through his open mouth. He concentrated on filling and emptying his lungs, one breath at a time. He worked his tongue around, he flinched with a new pain when the tip of it touched the exposed nerves of his broken teeth. He did not consider calling out. A strange calmness came over him, his pains suddenly lessened. He smelled Hitman's bloody coat, he felt the coarse hair of the dog next to his face, his shoulder, his bare leg. The bristle scratched him where it touched his flesh. Hitman's body was hot, fouled, matted. Blood had flowed from where the dog's hide had been split, vomit and bile and piss and shit had been voided during his death throes. Chug sensed that he and Hitman were joined together, but he could not determine how.

His wrist and arm, and where his ear had been were the worst of it. Those wounds kept him from worrying about his ribs and his ankle, and he tried to keep his tongue away from where his front teeth had been. He was naked under a blanket. He felt ants walking over him, he noticed a little when one stopped to bite. He drifted between reality and dream. When he was awake he could not focus on anything very long besides getting more air past his lips and into his lungs. He had no idea who had hit him. He had seen the baseball bats up close when they were coming at his head, coming at him out of the sun. He guessed maybe it was a kidnap, somebody tryin to get the old man to give up some big money. But he couldn't figure out why whoever they was, they had fucked him up so bad. He thought about Marvin, maybe he'd shot his mouth off in front of the wrong crowd, some old boys reckless enough to go after the cash. Whoever it was, Chug decided, they was plenty mean, takin on him an Hitman, puttin him in a blanket beside his dead dog. Whoever done this to him was especially rough. No way it could have been the greaser, he guessed. That old boy was in no condition to hurt him like this. Chug hoped it was kidnap.

His memory had shut down with his first rum and coke. He could recall nothing else of the day except the bats coming at him. He blinked his eyes rapidly, he drew in air as deeply as he could, to sustain his suffocating body.

When the rain started, Chug was cooled at first, then quickly, violently chilled. He shook beneath the blanket, the big teeth on the sides of his mouth clattered together. He moved his head from side to side, trying to bite down, to get them to stop, to keep the jagged ends of the ones in front from touching. That pain was unbearable. His body became rigid with trembling. The rain moistened the dried blood around his nose, it became red water. He swallowed against drowning, he gagged at the metallic taste of it, he struggled to breathe through his open mouth.

He slipped away from consciousness and was enveloped in nightmare. He was underwater in the creek. The water was dark, as dark as it could be. He shivered in the slow moving tide, he'd never known the creek to be so cold. He felt a sensation, a rush of movement against him. The current became unsettled, frenzied. Shapes that moved too quickly to be recognizable as single things brushed against him. Blunt-nosed, bug-eyed, they began to bump into him, some paused, and peered into his face. He believed the creatures was mullet, they was having a turn lookin into his eyes. They began to circle him, surround him. He was overwhelmed by the whirls and velocities of the underwater creatures. He felt rubbery lips tug at his own. He felt them tickle his naked body, they nibbled away at the blood that covered him. They came in tandems to his hurts, bumped at them over and over again. He watched in

251

amazement as the wounds began to close and heal but still he could not breathe. The mullet were ministering to him, but they were smothering him as well. He felt that the smallest of them were filling his nose and mouth. They was so many and they was so close. He blinked, then opened wide to stare into the black water. Mullet, thousands of them, swam directly at him, caught his eyes for an instant, and were past. The fish's tails slapped at his face and body as they navigated the outgoing tide. One fish passed another to advance in the line that looked into his face. They darted and twisted and propelled themselves at him and beyond him except for the little ones that filled his head. He wondered where they had all come from. It seemed that there were more than the oceans could hold. He wondered what was chasing them up the creek. Maybe, he hoped, maybe it was fishermen come up to catch the mullet, gather them up in nets. Maybe the fishermen could save him.

He pushed off the silt bottom, thrust himself upward, got his head out of the water. He screamed as loud as he could but his mouth was filled with fish heads and scales and guts and roe. He spit the vile things out. He screamed again. He was certain that he'd made a sound but he could hear nothing over the noise of the mullet as they splashed a million thick in the narrowest curve in Hendry Creek. He felt like Hitman, like his cords had been cut. He could scream all he wanted but it wouldn't do any good. His eyes were open when he went back under. The fish continued to come at him. They seemed like giant drops of a silver sideways rain.

Chug groaned sadly. He was drawn from his vision by the sound of new thunder. The storm had passed over Iona and settled on top of the beach. He snickered, choked, remembered what he'd told Marvin about predicting the rain. He listened for Mesican talk but couldn't be sure, his hearing wasn't so good, he guessed. He blinked quickly several times. His eyes rolled back into his head. He passed into a deep sleep induced by the booze, the morphine, the deadly beating the boys had delivered. His lungs were filling with fluids. He did not stir until he felt the vibrations of the truck, smelled the diesel fumes floating up from beneath him.

252

Chapter Forty Four

Enrique had swung himself heavily, painfully from the truck. He stood beside it, leaning on his crutch. The boy had done a good job, the inside of the big Ford was free of trash and garbage. He remembered a year before, Chug had just come to the farm. The old man's son had told him to sweep out and wash his truck, Enrique had refused. Chug had become angry, they had exchanged ugly words over it. Things had started badly between them and only gotten worse. Well, Enrique thought, now I have cleaned it for you.

He bent back into the cab, put his hand under the seat. He found a can of insect spray. The rain had just stopped, mosquitoes were already at his ears. He felt them sting his bare arms and leg. He sprayed himself everywhere, unhurriedly, thoroughly. He reached over the high side of the truck and sprayed the bloody blanket that covered the dog and the man bundled together. He put the can back under the seat. He reached in further, found Chug's lead-filled baton. He hefted the thing, felt its solid, dangerous weight. He threw it into the pepper hedge.

Enrique stripped himself of his wet shirt, he used it to rub at his chest, stomach, arms. He used the crutch to push his shoes off, unbuckled his pants, and let them fall in a pile at his feet. His bad leg pulsed with pain, inflammation, infection. He bent over, sniffed at the red and yellow bandage. He recoiled in alarm and nausea when he smelled the soggy wrap, the festering wound beneath it. He would have to hurry through the next day, he decided, and get to a doctor. He dressed as best he could in the new clothes Anita had bought for him. He held his bad leg out stiff and straight, balanced on one foot and the crutch until he had the pants pulled up and the shirt on. He sat against the seat, leaned forward as far as he could, he slipped the new black shoes over his feet. He left the shoes unlaced, his feet were badly swollen. He picked up his old things, dropped them onto the floor of the truck and swung himself back inside. He closed the door behind him against the mosquitoes. He sat very still and chewed slowly at his sandwich.

He had closed his eyes and was near sleep when the oldest boy returned to the truck and tapped at the window. Enrique gestured to him. The boy opened the driver's door and sat behind the steering wheel. When he was set, he looked at Enrique who nodded back. The boy started up the truck.

He drove slowly around the clearing, Enrique looked at his little lake for a last time. He knew its character even in the darkness. They were through the pepper hedge and on the perimeter road. The boy was very cautious on the wet sand, he kept the truck in a low gear, he braked it to a soft stop in front of the packing house. His brothers came out quickly from the black interior of the low wooden building to Enrique's side of the Ford. He told them to load the blocks and wire and fuel in the back. He handed one of them the bundle of clothes and the shoes that had been Hidalgo's. He told the boy to run back to The Quarters and make sure they were burned as thoroughly as the other things. The other two moved around the truck like phantoms. They hefted the cement blocks and braided cable and the full can of fuel so softly, he could not hear the things placed in the back. After a few moments the last boy returned. Enrique moved himself as carefully as he could to sit next to the oldest, he motioned for the others to climb in beside him.

The four boys were very clean, he could smell the soap and the fresh new clothes. They look like altar boys, he thought. The boys' thick black hair was combed. They were dressed in short-sleeved white shirts, black slacks, white socks and black shoes. They had been burnished by exposure to the southern sun of the summer, the white shirts seemed to glow in contrast. It was crowded in the cab, the youngest boy sat on the legs of his brothers. Deep inside each boy's pocket was a new handkerchief, inside each of those was that boy's money, taken from the jar where it had been saved. The cash was tightly rolled, each boy's pockets bulged with it. Each had brought his flower knife. Besides the new clothes and the stiff shoes and the money and the flower knives they left with nothing. Remnants of old clothes and identities smoldered in the bottom of a rusted fifty-five gallon barrel.

The oldest boy steered the truck from the yard, he followed the curve of the driveway through the mango trees.

"Go to the chain," Enrique said to the youngest. "When there are no cars coming, drop it from its hook. When we are on the other side, fasten it back to its place. As quickly as you can."

The youngest boy jumped from the truck. In another minute they were on Gladiolus Drive, the road that carried motorists west from 41 toward the beaches. The headlights illuminated the wet pavement. Royal Glads was left behind.

They rode in silence. Enrique was uneasy, he had joined the boys to him. The boys wondered where they were going with the man and the dog. The oldest boy drove well, he shifted the gears so smoothly, the change was imperceptible. They passed the entrances and driveways to the other farms. Enrique looked for the Australian pines that loomed on the left, he knew of a narrow path through the trees that led to the rock pits. The boy turned the Ford from Gladiolus onto the sand trail, Enrique reached over and cut the lights. The boy drove the truck very slowly under the towering pines. Enrique told the boys to roll down the windows. They caught glimpses of giant agaves, yucca, and Spanish bayonet, growing where yard men had dumped them.

Lightning broke across the sky. The air was charged with the coming of another heavy rain. The oldest boy was glad for the lightning, it helped him steer the truck through the pines.

The sand trail ended in a circle. Enrique told the boy to stop the truck, to shut off the engine. It would rain any minute, the lightning and thunder seemed to be on top of them. A sharp breeze picked up, the wind whistled through the trees. Enrique shook with a sudden chill, from the coolness of the air, from the sickness of his wound. He motioned for the boys to get out of the truck. He followed them. They looked up at the tops of the pines that bent with a wind that had started to scream. The rock pits were forty feet away.

"Get them out and carry them one at a time to the edge of the water," he said. "If the man moves do not strike him, it will be all right. Put them on the rocks at the side of the water, then come back for the blocks and the cable."

The four boys climbed into the back of the truck. They shifted the heavy bundle of man and dog, one boy opened the tailgate. They jumped down, grabbed the quilt together, dragged it, set it on the ground. They used the flower knives to cut the rope that bound the prisoner to the corpse. They carried Hitman first, then they returned for Chug. He moaned, called out. When they rolled him up in the blanket, he was silent again. The boys grabbed the edges of the quilt together. They carried Chug with their wrists and forearms to the side of the quarry, over the slippery rock and slick sand, careful not to drop him. They held the quilt away from their new clothes, they were anxious to keep the red away. They set Chug next to his dog on the rim of the deep water. Enrique limped on his crutch to where the man lay, then stood beside him. The boys were back in another minute with the concrete blocks and braided wire.

"Undo that cable," he said, "wrap it around the patrón and through the concrete blocks. Then do the same for the dog."

The youngest boy spoke, he was difficult to hear in the howling arrival of the new storm.

"How shall we cut the cable?"

"Cut it with these," said Enrique. He held up Chug's bolt cutters. He had found them behind the seat of the truck.

Chug remained faint. The boys wrapped the cable and the concrete and the man together. They coiled the cable around him again and again then cut it. They anchored Hitman the same way.

"Roll the dog into the water," said Enrique. "Throw in that last block and what is left of the wire and the cutters."

The boys dragged Hitman to the edge and pushed him in. The dog, the block, and the cable fell several feet. There was a great splash, the heavily laden creature went down fast.

Lightning flashed. The boys were surprised as they looked after the dog, dark shapes did hurried turns just below the surface of the water. The gar made the water roil, they were following the Hitman to the bottom.

"What were those things?" asked the youngest.

"They are garfish, alligator gar, they are like barracuda," Enrique answered. "They are murderous, evil. They are not like the fish you caught behind the farm. The water that you smell, this place, it belongs to them."

The boys stepped back from the ledge.

"Wrap up the blanket, tie it up tightly. Put it in the back of the truck, we will need it again. All of you go now," the man said. "Wait for me inside the truck. Do not touch anything, just sit and wait. I will be there in a few minutes, then we will leave."

When the boys were gone, Enrique knelt on his good knee beside Chug. He reached into his pocket, he pulled out a small bottle of lotion that May had sent with the other things. He poured the lotion on Chug's hands, to oil the dying man's fingers. In a moment he had removed two big rings from Chug's good hand, but when he tried to do the same to the hand where the arm had been broken, he found that the patrón's fingers were very swollen, the rings would not come off. He put the two into his pocket. He jerked the gold chains from Chug's neck, unlocked the clasps to the bracelets and the gold watch. Chug's eyes were open, he blinked at the rain drops. He tried to breathe through his mouth, there was not enough air.

"You do not need this gold, patrón."

Enrique held his face near to that of the man on the rocks.

"I will use the money I get from the jewelry to buy a tractor for my new farm in Mexico."

Enrique gulped at the air through his open mouth, he was nauseated by the smell of the sulfur.

"No one will be sad you are gone," he said, "no one. It was stupid of you to take my money, ruin my leg, threaten my wife and my children, then let me live. Both of you, incredibly stupid, even for gringos, even for pendejos."

He squinted his eyes at the rain drops. They were falling steadily now,

257

the downpour would begin very soon.

"The chrysanthemums will be happy tomorrow," he said, "They will enjoy the rain tonight, they will stand up straight in the sunshine tomorrow. I am not like you, patrón, I do not let my enemies live to fight me another day. We are not always a peaceable people, as your grandfather thought. You should not have fucked with me. I was going away, the farm would have been there for you to steal, to destroy. I only use that filthy word because it is one of your favorites. I have heard you say it often enough."

The rain came down, Enrique was soaked clear through. He was not happy to be wet, but the truck had a heater. The rain would be good cover for the ride to Punta Gorda. He was anxious to find the deputy.

The rain was filling Chug's nose and mouth, he was drowning anyway, he figured, an busted up inside. He'd heard the Mex givin orders, he'd heard the splash when Hitman's body hit the water. Even through his broken nose, he could smell the sulfur. He had a good idea where he was. He opened his eyes and looked for Enrique but he couldn't see his executioner's face.

"Come close," he hissed.

Enrique placed his ear next to Chug's lips.

"You got lucky, fucker. I shoulda killed ya when I had the chance."

Enrique put his hands under the man's middle. Chug and the blocks and the cable were heavy together. He rolled him off the rocks. Chug bounced on an outcrop, then went straight down into sixty feet of water. The trail of bubbles from his open mouth was interrupted by the logs with teeth that had turned downward. The gar followed down what had come along.

Enrique pushed himself up. He contemplated the spatter of the rain on the water.

Chapter Forty Five

May and Anita tried the keys until they found the right one, it unlocked the door to Chug's apartment. Inside the air was stale, foul, immediately so present that Anita began to gag. She turned back through the carport door and vomited in the weeds along the concrete pad. May's stomach was more hardy, but she had to force herself to breathe through her mouth so the smells from rotting garbage, spilled beer and whiskey, cigars, cigarettes, cloying, heavy perfumes, and the rank body scent of the dog would not enter her nose.

Chug owned the duplex. He had never rented out the other side. He preferred his privacy, and the opportunity to move back and forth without much effort when the side he had been in became uninhabitable even for him. After some months empty he would have the apartment he'd left sprayed down for ticks, fleas, and roaches, have it cleaned and restored, then move back in after some months more. The duplex was heavily shaded by three big mahogany trees. In the winter the old leaves dropped. In the spring, when the tree was flush, soft, light green, tent caterpillars filled the canopies until they too fell, as abundantly as the leaves. A Corvette Stingray rested on its frame in the carport, its wide wheels were flat and cracked, the paint was chipped, flaking. The stucco needed cleaning, the weeds were the tallest in the neighborhood. An old Sarlo rusted in the middle of the yard, where it had stopped and been abandoned.

The apartment was very dark, very cold. May found a light switch. Heavy drapes were pulled across the windows in the living room, a dark curtain shut down the kitchen. In the sink there were grease encrusted frying pans, dirty dishes and glasses. The linoleum floor was filthy. They left the door open, they looked into the living room together. The carpet was stained, and burned in places. Clothes and records, full ashtrays and empty beer cans and liquor bottles and nasty magazines were strewn about the room.

"I wonder where the pigs are?" said May. "I thought they kept them in pens."

"My God," Anita whispered, "why would a man who could live better want to be like this?"

"He doesn't care about this place," May said. "He comes here after there is nowhere else to go, no place else to drink, and he can't find a woman, or he has one with him."

"You have not been with him here, May? You have not been intimate with him in this place?"

"No," May said grimly, "I made him take me to the clean side. You go out to the car, it won't be good if you get sick. You're our driver, we need you to get us away from here. I'll look for your money. Go outside," she said, "where you can breathe."

May pushed Anita out the door, brushed past her, and went to the big Dodge. She took the flashlight from the front seat. She went back inside, left the door open, shut off the kitchen light and began to go through the cold dirty cave that was Chug's apartment. She went down the narrow hallway, into a bedroom. She let the light spill around the room then took it into the closet. The toolbox was on the floor, under a pile of rancid towels. May dragged it into the hallway, bent down, lifted the top, and shined her light inside. There was more money than she would have believed was possible. She didn't know, she guessed, what almost forty thousand dollars should look like. The metal box was full of bundles of money, big bills, crisp, clean, new, sealed by Barnett Bank, specially packaged for the Garzas according to the directions of the manager. She grabbed up the toolbox and carried it through the apartment, out the carport door. Anita stood between the Dodge and the Stingray, keeping watch on the quiet street.

"Here, Anita," said May, "here is what you wanted. Quickly, put it in the trunk."

Anita let May hand her the metal box. She made a sound, like she was choking, caught her breath then turned with the toolbox in her hands. She walked the few steps to the unlocked trunk and set it down inside. Tears rolled down her face. She lifted the top of the box and peered inside while May held the light for her. Anita's lips moved rapidly in prayers of thanksgiving and contrition. The money had been restored to them, she believed, but it would not be without great cost.

"Get in the car, Anita, and wait for me. Leave the trunk unlocked. I'm going back inside."

Anita was startled, she brushed at her eyes with trembling hands.

"Why? This is what we came for, your money is in there with ours," she said, she gestured to the toolbox. "We must get away from this man's house, we must go to Tampa."

"Enrique told me to go back in," May said.

Anita nodded her head slowly, several times, slowly comprehending. Her lips were pressed together for a moment. She lowered the door to the trunk. She told May that she would be waiting for her in the car, she would drive them away when May was finished.

May went back into the bigger bedroom, back into the closet. She brushed through the hanging clothes then bent down to the floor. She shook out a pair of red cowboy boots, she picked up the white bundle that fell out. Inside the sock she found a roll of used bills the size of a big man's fist. May thumbed through the solid wad of old money, it was unsorted, fives next to twenties next to tens. She stuffed the cash back into the sock and looked further into the closet. Nothing. She moved the flashlight across the room again, she was disgusted by the disorder and dirt. She saw little else that attracted her attention, the room was mostly bed. She walked back down the hallway into the kitchen, she found a half-empty bag of dry dog food. She dumped the stuff in the sink, over the stinking pans and dishes, shook the inside clean. She dropped the sock into the bag. She walked into the other bedroom. On the dresser was a sack of marijuana. May opened the bag, held it to her nose, it smelled very strongly of a ripe barnyard. She looked closely at the fine hairs that glistened red and gold. She folded the bag, licked the flap, and

261

dropped it in with the money.

She went through the drawers fast. There were two other bags, one had black capsules and the other white pills. She left those alone. She found a box of rolling papers and an ornate brass hash pipe, those she took. She found two pistols, one was a derringer. She grabbed a clean shirt from the closet, wrapped it around the miniature pistol, slipped it into the bag as well. In the bottom drawer she found Chug's jewelry. It was thick, deep, brilliant in the beam of the flashlight. The jewelry was arranged in a velvet lined box that barely fit in the drawer.

Chug loved gold, she knew, she had never seen him without it. He had become hooked on its specious allure. Everyone watched him, people at the farm, white people downtown, colored people on The Hill. Everyone watched him, she remembered, to see what he was wearing.

He bought his jewelry at the pawn shops on Palm Beach Boulevard, or Anderson Avenue when he was checking on his girls or picking up gambling money, or on his way to LaBelle or Immokalee to hunt. He hammered hard deals at the pawnbrokers, they were never glad to see him coming. Late at night, on the same streets, he'd sit in the bars, spot a drunk Mexican sporting a big gold chain with a gold saint hanging from it, or a Puerto Rican or a colored wearing a diamond ring or a fancy bracelet. Chug would insist that the man sell the thing to him, he would threaten him if he resisted. Chug doubted that the gold had sentimental value, he assured himself it had probably been stolen, fenced, pawned several times over, that the men were better off with the money. If they wouldn't sell, if they wouldn't pay attention to him, then he would simply follow the man he wanted to rob to the next bar, or home. Before the drunk could stumble into either, Chug would have Hitman take him to the ground. The man would be in the sand, screaming, pleading with Chug to have the dog let go of his arm or leg or ass. Chug would walk up behind Hitman, smack him in the head with his lead-filled club, and tell him to back off. He carried the thirty-eight stuck in his belt in case the old boy on the ground had a shooter of his own. Niggers, he believed, was known for it.

"You stupid fuck," he would say, "I tole you I pay you somethin for you bauble. Now you ain't gettin dick. Give it here, boy, or I say the

262

magic word to my pit bull."

If the man looked pouty, Chug advised him against calling the law, or hoping to extract revenge. The sheriff, he'd say, was his buddy, and he, Chug, would think nothing about killing the man's aunts and cousins. Whoever the fuck I can find, he'd say, if he heard through the grapevine that the man was talking shit.

"You think you can sneak past my dog?" he'd ask the man. "Have at it."

Chug had been strong-arming drunks for a year, a lot of jewelry had been added to the stash he had brought from Gainesville. He had started stealing when he was a boy, from his mother and the old man. He pinched silver dollars from his mother's dresser and rare pennies and dimes from Mister Sinclair's library. He bought more silver dollars and gold coins whenever he heard that they were about. He threatened, insulted antique dealers and estate people until they surrendered the goods, just to be on the safe side, just to be rid of him. He made the fences feel like pigs on the run, so brutally did he hound them.

May found the leather bag full of hard money in the hall closet. She had opened the door, set aside rifles and shotguns and fishing rods with big treble hooks, she saw the bag on the floor. When she bent to pick it up she was surprised at how heavy it was. She dragged it into the hallway and untied the leather boot lace.. The sight of all that gold, sparkling, dense, caused her to let out her air and curse at the same time. She retied the leather lace around the leather bag and pulled it to the door. She left it there beside the jewelry box and the big paper sack.

She went through the cabinets in the kitchen. Nothing. She looked under the sink, in the stove, everywhere she could imagine a lazy man would hide his money. She believed there was more, that there was something else, but she was anxious to leave too. She had no idea how much she had already placed by the door, plenty she guessed, maybe it was time to go. She grabbed the dog food bag and the jewelry box and carried them to the car. Anita got out as soon as she saw her, they set the things inside the trunk. May went back into the apartment and dragged out the leather bag, they lifted it in together. May pulled the paper sack back out, she folded it tightly and wedged it behind the spare tire. She worried a little about the dope and the pipe and the pistol. It was raining hard again, the rain came sideways under the cover of the flat roof of the carport.

"Is that all of it?" Anita asked her.

"I don't know," said May. "I don't think so, but I don't know where else to look."

"He told you to get everything? That's what he would say."

"Yes," May answered, "he told me to find it all. But I don't know what more to look for, and I'm ready to get away from here. Chug would kill us both if he knew we had even seen what is in that bag and that box."

"You must go back, you must make sure we have it all," Anita told her. "Take a few more minutes, then we will go."

May went back inside, she was determined to discover. She walked hurriedly through the dank apartment, through the bedrooms and the bathroom and the hallway. Suddenly she was back in the kitchen. She went directly to the refrigerator. Chug was a drunk, he was just like the borachos, younger, richer, meaner, she knew, but he had been a drunk for a long time. Her alcoholicos, kept anything they had of value, singly or collectively, in an old refrigerator that was hidden in the leaves of a passion vine. She opened the door, the light came on inside. Beer. A half-filled bag of cocaine. The remnants of a package of hamburger. A cut onion. A bottle of milk. Chocolate cookies. Pall Malls. Mustard. Catsup. Sliced pickles. She closed that door and opened the one above it, the smaller door for the freezer. More beer, the tops burst with the pressure of the frozen mass inside. A bag of ice. A bottle of vodka. A shoebox hidden behind the rest. She grabbed the shoebox. She opened the lower door again so she would have light. The money was frozen inside. Iced money, wrapped like the Garzas had been, but the seal was from another bank. She held one bundle close to her face and read the lettering on the seal. Edison National Bank. She pulled all the bundles out, set them side by side on the counter. There were twenty bundles. She picked one up, she saw that they were twenties, fifty to a stack, she guessed, twenty thousand dollars. It was Chug's take from the bolito, from Precious and Baby, from the vegetable stand, added to often, wrapped every time there was another thousand by a bank named for the man who had made Fort Myers famous.

May scooped the stiff money back into the shoebox, she shut the doors to the refrigerator. She hunched her shoulders at the sound of her loafers trampling crumbled dog food as she passed through the kitchen to the carport. She checked the trunk to make sure it was latched, she brushed her free hand at the mosquitoes that went for her ears and cheeks, and got in the car. She held up the box for Anita to see, nodded her head, and set the frozen money between them on the seat. Anita put the car into reverse, switched on the headlights and the windshield wipers and backed the Dodge from Chug Sinclair's driveway. She drove slowly up Iona Road, turned left at McGregor, and they were on the way to Tampa. As they crossed over the bridge at Whiskey Creek, where old-time smugglers had hidden rum and whiskey, May rolled down her window. She tossed Chug's keys into the black night, into the black water.

Chapter Forty Six

*T*he oldest steered the truck from the sand trail. He turned on the headlights. He managed the Ford carefully in the sheeting rain. They passed Winkler Road and Bass Road. Enrique told him to turn at A and W, it joined McGregor at a mile. The boy stayed savvy to the slick asphalt. They went by the ramp of the bridge to Cape Coral. Enrique was taking them north, they could cut through the Cape, drive Pine Island Road to Burnt Store, come into Punta Gorda from the west. He was not familiar with the maze of streets, roads, lanes, and terraces that chopped the four hundred square miles of palmetto and sand spurs into dead-end blocks and canals that couldn't be crossed. It would be confusing in Cape Coral, Enrique had decided, especially at night.

They passed the driveway to Everglades Nursery. The first old man had asked him to buy bougainvillea and gardenias from Mister Hendry and young Helen. He asked him to plant the bushes at his house, Enrique had been glad to do it. They crossed Whiskey Creek, they passed the *God Is Love* sign.

McGregor Boulevard was lined with royal palms, sixty, eighty feet tall. Thomas Edison had caused the first of them to be planted. Mister Hendry, Mister Kelley, Mister Pottinger and the city had planted the rest. The palms were very straight, formal, massive, with gray trunks that framed the Spanish stuccos and ranch houses along the two lane road by the river. It was raining very hard, the wind was blowing violently against the leafy tops of the palms. Enrique watched for the big fronds and boots that could come crashing down, to land on the road in front of them, or catch and hang on a power line or a telephone line. He did not want his driver distracted.

The truck rolled smoothly through the last curve on McGregor. The Henry Ford Estate and The Edison Home were on the left. Edison had called his house "Seminole Lodge" but Enrique had asked, when he had gone to visit the house and museum after the war. The guide had told him he didn't think any Seminoles had ever been there. He had the boy turn the truck sharply to the left just past the house and museum. They were on West First Street, very close to the river. Enrique looked to the right as they went by the yacht basin and the big boats, he ignored the water and the lights and cabin cruisers on his left. He looked at the little library that had been the USO club. They stopped at a lonely red light, then crossed the Caloosahatchee on The Edison Bridge. It opened up in the middle, to let boats pass going upriver to the big lake, or coming down it to enter the Gulf. Enrique turned his head to look through the rear window, he caught a glimpse of a light in the Burroughs' home. He had pruned aralias for the ancient sisters who lived in the old yellow house.

The bridge was flat, close to the water, especially with all the rain. It was lined with lamp posts. The light bulbs were forty years old. In spite of the storm, there were fishermen hunkered down in raincoats and ponchos, waiting for the in-coming tide to wane, waiting for a big snook or a red to hit at a pinfish or a live shrimp. None of the men looked up as the truck passed by, they stared down at the water, watching each other's lines.

They were across the river, in North Fort Myers. The road made a great long curve through accidentally placed buildings and businesses, the lights thinned out to almost none. They passed the Shell Factory. The narrow national highway straightened out, they were on the way to Punta Gorda. The boys got to see the lights of the train, the Seaboard Coast Line. It was coming south for potatoes. They saw it cross the wood trestle at Alligator Creek.

It was not lost on Enrique that he had been on this road at the same time only two nights before, on his way to Mexico. He could not

267

remember exactly the place they had been ambushed, it was very dark. The sides of the road looked the same for miles. Dense myrtle and saltbush framed the water-filled ditches. The rain began to lessen. When he saw the place he was watching for he had the boy turn from the highway. They parked behind an abandoned store and restaurant. When he and Anita and the children had traveled to Tampa, they had always stopped here. The place sold sodas, salt water taffy, pralines, coconut patties and pecan rolls. Enrique remembered all of it, the bins full of stiff, stuffed caimans, sea shells, sunglasses, postcards and maps. He would get gasoline here, he recalled, and eat a grilled cheese sandwich. It was where Chug and Marvin had brought them first.

They had ridden out from under the rain. He told the boys to walk, to stretch their legs, to give him some room to stretch his. He had to make water, he told them, he asked the boys for privacy. He didn't think he could swing himself from the truck to stand. The boys dipped ice and sipped water from the cooler, they would have liked hot coffee. They wandered about the dark parking lot, whispering together, startled by the sounds of stray cars on 41. Enrique, twisting, uncomfortable, managed to empty his bladder on the pavement. He drank a cup of water the oldest brought to him, he laid his head back against the seat. The moon emerged from the clouds.

It was very late at night, very early in the morning, downtown Punta Gorda was empty. The only building with a light on inside was the sheriff's office. The boy coasted the truck to a stop across the street, in the shadow of a warehouse. He shut off the headlights and shut off the engine. The street was made of brick. The truck rested at an angle where the brick curved down to meet the storm curb. Twenty five feet away, the light from a streetlamp caused the wet bricks to shine, but it was very dark where the truck was parked. They had filled the Ford with diesel when they stopped. The empty can, the baseball bats, the wet quilt and the cooler were in the bed of the truck.

The four boys exited the cab. Enrique moved himself to the driver's place. He reached underneath the seat for the forty-five. He rolled his window down a fraction. He looked in the direction of the sheriff's

268

office and tapped the horn. The four boys had hidden themselves behind the big tires after the youngest had passed them the baseball bats. When Enrique sounded the horn the second time, they were not startled by the sound against the silence and its echo in the empty street. The door to the jail opened. Marvin stepped out, looked up and down the block then across the street. He saw Chug's truck, waved, stepped back inside and came out with his deputy hat on. His pistol and holster and belt and badge stayed where they were on his desk. In one of the cells against the back wall, where Hitman had been, an old white drunk lay as still as death on the narrow cot. The man smelled of fish and whiskey.

Marvin was real glad to see his buddy. He was surprised that Chug had come up to bring him his half of the money so soon. He had worried Chug was maybe gonna fuck him over. It wasn't like Chug, he thought, to be so timely when he had somethin to share.

"Hey, boy," he said, "where's you fuckin dog?"

Enrique waited until Marvin was just a few feet from the truck. He rolled down the tinted window, followed it with the forty-five, leveled it on the edge of the window. The big bore was lined up with the center of Marvin's chest.

Chapter Forty Seven

"Come very close," Enrique said.

When Marvin stood a foot from the truck, Enrique tapped the horn again with his free hand, gently, almost imperceptibly. The sound was very faint but the boys heard it. In three seconds they were from behind the truck, swinging bats at Marvin. He hadn't seen them or heard them, his eyes were wide, and focused on the gun pointing at his heart. The oldest swung his Duke Snider at the deputy's fat stomach, Marvin lost his wind with a great whoosh. Two of the boys went at his head. The sound of the bats connecting in the silent street was louder than Enrique expected. Marvin was instantly out, his scalp had been split at the top of his head, the wound gushed hot blood when he fell to the wet brick. The youngest boy was last. He had waited for the others to strike, then to give him room. He slid between them, but Marvin was unconscious, already at his knees with his face sideways in the street. The youngest boy put his new shoe on Marvin's big ass. He pushed against it hard until Marvin was flat on the pavement. His deputy hat was beside him.

"Give me that sombrero," Enrique said.

He started up the Ford, pulled it forward a few feet so the tailgate was close to where Marvin lay.

"Put him in sideways, against the cab. Wrap the blanket around him. Make sure the bats are with you," he told them. "Cover him well, tuck the ends of the blanket around him and you three sit on him. If he makes a movement, hit him hard with your weapon."

The oldest boy took his place behind the wheel after Marvin was secured. He drove the truck through the sleeping little town. Lights came on in the bakery. They crossed another low concrete bridge, over Charlotte Harbor where the Peace River joins the Gulf.

The highway was straight and flat. They passed through pine woods, uninterrupted except for fishing camps and bait shops at the little bridges, housing schemes that had gone bust. They passed the Policeman's Hall of Fame and Basketville. The truck was running smoothly, powerfully, they were making miles. Enrique read the faded letters on a big wooden sign. He told the boy to slow down. They turned off 41 a few minutes later into the entryway of a deserted development. They passed under a concrete archway. Stretched out before them in the beams of the truck was a wasteland of tall weeds. The boy turned off the headlights, he followed the light of the moon. He turned sharply left and sharply right, the weeds and grasses crowded the asphalt. He worked the truck further back into the maze of the forsaken streets. Finally he stopped, Enrique had him cut the engine.

Enrique was feverish, his leg was badly infected. The pain was very bad, he wished he had kept the morphine. He had held the pistol all the way from Punta Gorda. He had pressed the handle of the forty-five against his head and tapped himself, not so gently, several times. He opened the door, he turned himself sideways on the seat. He put his crutch in front of him and leaned forward on it.

"Tie him up," he said to the oldest. "There is rope under the seat. Bring him here."

The boys lassoed Marvin, then dragged him on his wobbly legs to stand in front of Enrique. The loud, incessant noises of insects and frogs were the only sounds the men heard except for each other. Marvin was heavy, the boys were breathing hard. Marvin's head lolled forward, Enrique could see it was badly cut. He looked at the side of it, saw that blood had run into his ears, down his fat neck. Enrique put his hand out and lifted Marvin's chin, he held it there until the man focused. Marvin gagged, reflexed like he would be sick, then was. He vomited down his shirt and on his cowboy boots. When he was finished he spit to clear his mouth. The retching made tears come to his eyes, he blinked against the salt.

"You come back. Lordy, Lordy. We tole you never to come back an you did anyway. An now here we is."

Enrique was surprised that the man's head wounds had bled so badly. Marvin's face was covered in red.

"Do you have any of my money? Do you have any of the money you and your friend took from me?" Enrique asked him. He already knew the answer. He tapped his head again with the butt of the pistol.

"Chug's got it all," Marvin said. "He might have give me five hundred outta his wallet. That's all. He was gonna count it an then we was gonna split it. I thought you was him, come to give me my share." Marvin shook his head sadly from side to side. "I guess I ain't gonna get no boat."

"Your friend is dead," Enrique told him. "You are more stupid than you look, he would have given you a little, or nothing."

"What you gonna do with me, sir? You ain't gonna kill me. I didn't do nuthin to be killed for, I don't guess."

"You are going in the deep water, deputy, like your friend did."

He turned to the oldest.

"Take the money from his wallet. Tear everything else into tiny pieces and toss them in the weeds. Wrap him up one more time, lay him against the front of the bed. I want the others to sit on him like before."

Enrique reached out, he touched Marvin's shirt with the pistol.

"You be very quiet. Do not make any sounds or it will be much worse for you, if that is possible. I am thinking about you, deputy. It would be good if you gave us no trouble. Is it possible you could change? You are a young man, and now your life, one way or another, is over. Think about that for when I speak with you again."

Marvin let his head hang, he shook it back and forth.

"I'm already changed," he said at the ground. "Only I got a terrible feelin it's too late."

Enrique dropped the pistol into his lap, his shoulders slumped. He leaned heavily against the seat. The boys loaded Marvin into the truck.

The oldest boy gave Enrique the few hundred dollars he had taken from the deputy's wallet, then resumed his place behind the wheel.

The boys leaned on Marvin, they had drawn their legs up, they clasped their hands around their knees. They were cold, the air was damp from the rain and the truck was moving quickly up the highway, the oldest boy kept his speed at fifty. Enrique told him where to turn. They skirted Sarasota on 301, passed warehouses, industrial buildings, junkyards, stove-in boats, and the Sarasota airport. They had been stopped by red lights in Murdock, Nokomis, and Osprey. Red lights made Enrique nervous so they went around Sarasota rather than through it. A few cars began to be on the road, dawn was an hour or so away. Enrique was anxious to be further north, anxious to be finished with his business. He was not sure about Marvin, although he had been since the inception of his plan. There had been two of them, he recalled. If it had been four, it would not have been different, he would have treated them all the same.

At Palmetto Enrique got the boy on 19. In a few minutes they were on a wide four lane that was the approach to the Sunshine Skyway. The boy came to a good stop at the toll booth. The Skyway had just been completed. It carried cars and pick-ups and buses to a great height over Tampa Bay, from St. Petersburg, to Palmetto, Bradenton, and Sarasota. It was a very tall bridge, almost two hundred feet above the water, it allowed big ships and tankers and even navy vessels to pass in and out of the bay without interference. There were no other cars at the toll booth. The oldest boy rolled down his window, he handed the man five dollars. The attendant gave the boy back his change and a receipt. He looked closer at the boy, then looked in the back of the truck. He saw the three brothers shivering in the dark and the cold, sitting on a pile of blankets. He peered into the front window, saw Enrique across the seat. The man nodded to him and spoke.

"What are those in the back?" he said. "They don't look like regular Mesicans."

Enrique forced a chuckle.

"They are Indians," he told the ticket taker. "I am taking them to Georgia to pick corn."

"You mean they're Seminoles?" the man said. "They don't look like Florida Indians."

Enrique looked at the man very seriously.

"They are Apache," he told him. "They are from the mountains in Mexico. They are very good at picking corn."

"My God," the man said, "Apaches. I never have seen one. How come, you being a Mesican too it looks like, how come they ain't sittin up front with you?"

"They smell," Enrique said, "very strongly. Like smoke."

"Must be from their campfire," the man said. "I can believe it. I've stood next to lots of Mesicans, not clean ones like you all appear to be, but field Mesicans, and they smell. Whew," he said, "they smell bad."

"What is the tide like across the bay?" Enrique asked.

"Man, it's a rip. That tide moves in and out of here like nothin you've ever seen. The big ships have trouble steering in it. One day," he said, "some ship is gonna run into a piling."

"When is the next high tide?"

The man looked at his watch, then at Enrique, curiously, like why did he want to know.

"I'm a fisherman," Enrique said, "I just like to know about the tides."

Well," the man said, "it's high now. In about thirty minutes it'll start goin out, just at sunup."

Enrique looked at his own watch. It was six o clock. He was very tired, he thought, so tired that the pain in his leg had receded, but that was not a good sign.

He leaned down, said thank-you, waved with the hand that did not hold the forty-five.

The truck moved away from the toll place and the man in the uniform. The three huddled against the cab did not raise their heads to look at the attendant, but when they felt the truck shift to match the steepening grade, they opened their eyes. They saw that they were leaving the land behind.

The causeway had been built on giant boulders and millions of yards of shell and sand and cement. It had replaced an older bridge, flat, like the others they had crossed. Remnants of the first bridge remained until the very deep water. Fishermen could walk out from both sides, drive even, and drop a line into Tampa Bay. The new bridge was not heavily traveled. People who were used to the flat land were afraid of it, most drove the long way around the great harbor to get from north to south. There were no cars behind them, a single delivery truck passed the Ford, coming from St. Pete. The causeway began to curve and rise. When they were on the bridge itself, the elevation became dramatic. It rose very quickly, higher and higher and higher. The salt-water was far below. The night was loosening its grip, the sun was just a few minutes away from showing itself in the east. Far in the distance, where land would be, Enrique could make out smoke columns from the phosphate plants that crowded the shore of the bay. The water of the harbor was flat and dark in the dim light, as far as a man could see. The rise had become very steep. The oldest boy accelerated the truck to keep up its speed, he did not let his eyes wander from the center of his lane. The incline of the bridge went up and up and then the concrete changed to steel. The truck tires hammered loudly on the bars and bolts that made the grid. Enrique told the boy to slow down, they passed the highest point of the bridge, he told the boy to stop. The distant lights of St. Petersburg sparkled in the half-light of the passage of night to day, the bay was two hundred feet below them. The boy put the truck in neutral. He pushed hard on the emergency brake and stared straight ahead. Enrique gagged, he was sick to his stomach. He opened the door and retched yellow bile. When he was finished he shook his head to clear it and wiped his eyes with the back of his hand.

"Get the deputy out and stand him next to the railing," he said.

The oldest boy left the truck very cautiously, he held onto it as he made his way to the back. Enrique moved himself to an upright position. He was six feet away from the side of the bridge.

The boys in back were trembling violently from the cold and the wet and the impossible height. They were at a place they had never imagined, in the throes of hypothermia and shock. Enrique supported himself on his arms as he worked his way to the tailgate. The oldest stood ready, the others could not move.

"Get him out, I said. Right now. Get him on his feet," he barked.

The boys uncoiled themselves, they slithered down the bed of the truck. The oldest boy opened the tailgate and they lowered themselves to the grid. They crouched, anchored themselves against the wind, shook in misery from the tops of their heads to their black shoes. They were very cold and paralyzed with fear.

Enrique pulled the forty-five from his belt. He motioned with the gun to the oldest. The boy climbed into the truck, threw the blanket to the side, grabbed Marvin by his shirt and dragged him to the back. The other boys reached in to help. They stood Marvin up, leaned him against the tailgate, then backed away.

Marvin was reconciled. He saw the pistol in the Mexican man's hand and looked down through the steel grid. He could not see what was below it. He too had felt the steep rise of the bridge. He guessed this was what the man meant about going in the water.

"Untie him, then throw the bats over the side," Enrique said to the boys, "and the blanket and the rope."

In an instant the bats were flung over the bay. The blanket opened when the oldest boy tossed it, no one saw it float and flutter down, moved by the stiff winds between the bridge and the water.

"All of you, get in front. Turn on the heater. Go quickly," he said, "there are cars coming."

From the north and the south, far-off lights had appeared.

The boys moved very stiffly to the front of the truck. They climbed in. Except for the oldest, who sat behind the wheel and again stared ahead of him, they put their arms around each other, put their heads in their laps, and closed their eyes.

Enrique looked at Marvin, he raised the forty-five, then threw it over the railing.

"I have decided you should live," he said. "Killing you does nothing for me. It would make me worse than I want to be. I knew young men like you when I was in the army. They started badly but became good soldiers. You change your life, deputy, or it will only be a matter of time before someone else has you on a high bridge with a loaded gun in his hand."

The sun was up. Marvin had never seen anything more wonderful.

276

"You gonna let me live? Ain't you afraid I'll make trouble?" Marvin's voice was choked and emotional. He felt he would jump anyway, if the man asked him.

"Those boys in front are warriors. There are hundreds, thousands more of them coming to do the work here. I can send one to cut off your head with a machete. No one knows I have been back. No one knows the names of the men in the truck. No one knows where Chug has gone."

"Mister, I ain't gonna do nothin bad again. An I ain't gonna nothin, ever, to get back at you. I did me a lot a prayin under that blanket. I ain't gonna miss Chug. He scared me. I'm gonna say I had me a run-in with him. He left me here an took off for Gainesville. That's the best I can come up with so far. But I tell you this, they won't be no Mesican people in my account of what happened to me."

"What's your full name?" Enrique asked him.

"Sir, it's Marvin Johnson."

"You remember, Marvin Johnson, how close you came to death. Now lay down there," he pointed to the outside of the railing, " for an hour. Then you can come out and probably someone will help you."

"I'm sorry for what we done," Marvin said. "I been sorry for stuff I done all my life, I just kept on doin it. Not no more though, Mister Garza, I ain't gonna sin no more. Tell your Missus I apologize."

Enrique watched Marvin move to the railing, climb over it, onto the workman's ledge. He hobbled as fast as he could to the cab and boosted himself in. The boys climbed on top of each other to give him room for his leg.

The oldest boy disengaged the emergency brake, shifted down expertly and pushed hard at the accelerator. The truck tires squealed when they caught the cement, the big Ford hurtled downhill from the high center of the great bridge. The boy had put the heater on and the cab warmed quickly. In a moment they were on another long causeway, bringing them back to the land.

277

Chapter Forty Eight

Enrique told the boy to stop at a convenience store. He told them to go inside, to buy what they wanted and get back in the truck. The boys were happy with hot coffee and rolls. In a few moments the truck was moving north, working its way deeper into the city.

Enrique looked at blocks of low buildings, he leaned his head against the window. He was relieved that he had not killed Marvin, that he had not made the boys part of something very ugly. Chug's death did not bother him, he decided, anymore than he would have been bothered by killing a rattlesnake or water moccasin.

The oldest boy shut off the truck at a Trailways bus station in Clearwater. In the parking lot and the terminal building there was a Saturday morning riot of activity. People were coming and going, loading and unloading, standing and sitting and milling around. Enrique was quiet. One Saturday morning before he had been in his little boat on Hendry Creek. He turned to speak to the four young men. It was strange, he thought, the truck shut down, quiet after the sounds of the diesel engine and the tires on the pavement all the long night. It was a bright September morning. He was surprised, the air felt cool. It was cooler than it would have been at the farm or on the creek, although they had traveled only a hundred miles north.

"You have saved my life, made it worth living," he began, "and my wife's and my children's. I could not have managed the patrón and the

278

deputy without you. We are in your debt."

"What else would you have us do, Enrique?" asked the oldest. "Why are we here?"

"I am going to walk in there," he pointed to the terminal, "if I can," he smiled, "and buy you tickets for the bus to Miami. I will give you the tickets, tell you the number of the bus and when it will board. You must sit there," he pointed again, "where those benches are, and wait."

"What will we do in Miami?" asked the youngest. "It's a very big place, like Mexico City."

"I have a plan for you," the man said. "I will tell you when I come back with the tickets."

"No, Enrique," said the oldest. "We do not want to go to Miami. Isn't that so, brothers?"

The other three nodded in agreement, they looked expectantly at Enrique.

"Where do you want to go?" he asked them. "Why don't you want to go to Miami? There are good farms there, plenty of work, mas companeros de Mexico."

"We have seen enough of Florida," said the oldest. "There is no reason to expect it will be different in Miami. If it is like Mexico City it will be worse."

"Then where? Where do you want to go? You will be men of means. I will have my money back today. You can go anywhere you choose. I will find you and be able to reward you. Where is the place that you will be happy?"

The boys were silent, they stared at the floor of the truck until the youngest one spoke.

"We want to go with you back to Mexico," that one said. "You intend to grow flowers? That is what the ladies at the barn said. Yes? That is what we want to do. We want to work for you, and grow the flowers for the people."

Enrique would have spoken to Hidalgo. With the priest's patrónage, the boys would have good jobs, a safe place to live, near the big city, not in it. He expected they would do well. They worked and battled, he thought to himself, as one. He anticipated there would be a great deal of

279

money. It would buy them a truck, a house, a decent life.

"Miami is Miami, that is true, it is a very big city. I was thinking about Homestead, it is nearby. There are many farms, many Mexican people. I know a priest who would help you. I am not sure what will happen in Mexico. I want to have una finca, but I don't know about the land, what the ground is made of, the rainfall, who will buy my flowers."

"Those things are important," said the oldest, "but they cannot be so different from here. It is the same Gulfo de Mexico. Vera Cruz is on the edge of it, like here. What is most important to us is that we are together and that we have honorable work."

Enrique believed the boys were a blessing. He believed they would have the finest flowers in Vera Cruz.

"You are very wise," he said. "You are right. Wherever there is a big city there is corruption, and temptation for young men, for everyone. I thought I knew what was best for you, but you have changed my mind. We will do well together. Wait here," he said, "I will be back."

He lowered himself painfully from the seat to a standing position in the parking lot. He used both hands to hold the crutch. He made his way carefully across the stained, pitted concrete to the bus building. He was gone several minutes. The boys let themselves out of the truck, they leaned against it, watched the crowd move back and forth in the brilliant sunshine. When he returned they gathered to him. He gave the oldest boy four tickets to Brownsville. He pulled out his wallet and carefully counted the ten one hundred dollar bills. The oldest boy placed his hand across Enrique's.

"What?" he asked. "What is wrong?"

"We have no use for that money," the boy said. "It will make our journey more dangerous, it will give us too much to worry about. Keep the money for the farm, and here," he pushed four big wads of cash into Enrique's pockets, "take our savings with you. We have enough in our pockets for the bus ride, we have more than we will spend. Our money will be safer with you. We are Mexicans. We are not yet gone from los Estados Unidos."

"It is not the United States that is bad," Enrique said, "men like the patrón are everywhere. There are many in Mexico who are worse, we will

280

have to watch for them. These tickets will get you to the border," he said. "Take this much," he handed the oldest boy two of the hundreds, "in case one of you loses a ticket or becomes sick and needs a doctor. Men of means do not travel without money."

"How long will we be on the bus?" asked the youngest.

"It will be a long ride," said Enrique. "Today is Saturday, you will be in Brownsville by Monday afternoon. There are many stops along the way, and the bus changes drivers. Pay attention when you get off. Go no further than the bathrooms and the restaurant. Stay together."

"We will have no trouble. We want to talk about the flowers, and sleep. We are going to eat and sleep and talk," the oldest said. "When will we meet you in Brownsville? When will you be there?"

"I will be there Tuesday night," said Enrique, "I will find you Wednesday. We will buy identifications for you. Burning the cards you had was a precaution, I did not know how this would end. I thought you would be going to Miami, where no one is who his card says he is. We will buy you new ones. The police at the border are not so interested in young men coming into Mexico as they are in the ones trying to get out. I will meet you in the plaza in front of the biggest church. All of you," he said, "let us sit in the truck one more time."

When they were in the cab, Enrique tied the wads of bills together with a last piece of string.

"Run for a bag of ice and some sodas," he said to the boy perched nearest the door.

Enrique had the boy dump the ice on the concrete. He shook the bag free of moisture, wrapped the cash inside, set it in the cooler. He placed a few cans of soda over the money and covered the cans with the ice.

"You saved all that from the work?" he asked.

"As much as we could," said the oldest. "There are things we wanted to have someday. But that money in there," he pointed at the cooler, "is for the new farm. We are your partners, we share the responsibility as well as the profits. There is one thing we want to have, though, sooner instead of later."

"You are the owners," Enrique said, "what would you buy for yourselves?"

281

"We want a house that belongs to us, a new house on the same land where the flowers will be grown."

"And we want a lake so we can fish," said one of the middle boys.

"That house will be the first thing we build together," said Enrique. He shook the hands of each of the four brothers. He told them he would buy a boat when they got to Vera Cruz, he would teach them to fish the mangroves and the sand bars along the coast. They were finished fishing in small ponds, he said.

Enrique looked at his watch.

"I have called for a taxi cab," he said. "It is time for us to vanish. I will wait for the taxi at the front, you must go to your bus in the back. It will depart in thirty minutes. The beautiful flowers we will grow will be reflections of our lives. I am not sorry for what we have done together. I am very glad the deputy is not dead. Leave what we have had to do behind us in this truck. There has been no moral offense on your parts. Those men... it was only a question of time. Probably we have saved other people from the tendencies of the patrón. I don't know. I do not think he will be missed. I will take care of your money," he said. "Go now amigos, wait for the bus. I will meet you in Brownsville on Wednesday."

He watched them walk to the terminal. For the last time he let himself down from Chug's pick-up. He reached in for his crutch, the cooler, and Marvin's deputy hat. It had been flattened and dirtied by the shoes of the boys. He pulled the key from the ignition. He moved himself with his arms and one leg to the storm drain for the parking lot. Water rushed beneath the iron grate, rain-water that would spill into the bay. He dropped the key and the cowboy hat through the bars. He made his way slowly to the front of the bus station, the crowd gave him room. In a few minutes a cab arrived. When he was settled in the back, he asked the Cuban driver if he could take him to a doctor that spoke Spanish and would not ask many questions. The man was courteous, and said that he could. If the man would wait while he saw the doctor, Enrique told him, and then take him to Ybor City, he would pay him well for his time.

282

Chapter Forty Nine

They sat in the atrium of The Columbia in Ybor City. It was the finest Spanish restaurant in the state, it had been there many years. Enrique and Anita had visited the place with the children. They had enjoyed the food, the setting, and the flamenco dancers. Immaculate Cuban waiters scurried from the shadows and the archways and stone corners. They filled water glasses, took orders for meals and soups and desserts, delivered warm bread and cold butter and cleared the dishes without being summoned. Enrique sipped at a cup of strong black coffee, Anita and May drank red wine from fluted goblets.

The Cuban doctor had told Enrique that the first people to treat him had done a good job. He would not lose his leg, but he would forever limp. His leg would probably draw itself up to protect the knee, the doctor said. While the infection would be arrested by his own treatment, the doctor advised him to go to a hospital in Mexico and have the knee properly repaired. He would need surgery, the doctor had told him, and much time spent sitting down so the flesh would mend.

People were talking and eating and drinking. They were enjoying the Saturday afternoon. Father Hidalgo's dark blue Dodge, freshly washed, the oil checked, the tires checked, the gasoline tank filled, was parked in the shade of a great oak tree. There was nothing on the seats of the car but the trunk was full. There was cash, coins, jewelry and books inside, and May's alligator suitcase. May had told Anita about the reefer and the pipe and the derringer. They were things that were just for fun, she had said, she would put them in her suitcase before she got on the plane.

It would be cool in Monterey, she was telling them, she would live next to the ocean. May was dressed to the nines. Her long hair was shiny, a little bit of makeup reddened her lips and darkened her eyes. Every waiter, young and old, sought to give her attention. They hovered over that table, none were thinking about the tip. May smiled at all of them. She sat up straight in the chair. Her perfect ass was just a little wide for the narrow seat, the waiters noticed that also.

They sipped at the coffee and the wine, they spoke softly together. Each thought to himself and to herself that they did not look like whores and murderers and robbers and thieves.

The driver had helped Enrique from the taxi, at the red doors of The Columbia. Enrique waited on an iron bench. When she saw him, Anita drove the Dodge around the corner, parked, and hurried to where he sat. May took the cooler back to the car and locked it in the trunk. The Garzas were alone for a moment, then the women helped him into the restaurant.

"You say those boys are gone to Texas," said May, "they are good boys."

"They have decided they do not like the way things are done in Florida. They will be partners with Anita and I at the farm."

"I was afraid that Chug would hurt one of them," she said.

"If he had, the rest would have made him regret it. What has been done, it would not have been possible without them." He thought for a moment. "They were like soldiers."

Two waiters arrived with the food. The elegant, dark haired men set big flat plates with yellow rice and black beans and pork cooked in secret sauces before them. They returned with more Cuban bread and white, whipped butter on smaller dishes.

When they were finished, and the covey of waiters and servers had cleared the plates and brushed the tablecloth, May lit a dark Cuban. She puffed at it with enjoyment, she was amused at the stares of the men that were astounded at the way she smoked the cigar.

284

"The patrón was not redeemable," he told them. "He will never be found. The deputy, I could not kill him. I almost did," he said, "but I believe he has enlisted."

"It is over," Enrique told them. "We will go for a drive after a little more coffee. I want to ride to the harbor and look at the big ships. We will park in the shade. I want to see what you have in the trunk."

May and Anita exchanged quick glances. They guessed he would be very surprised at how wealthy they had all become, at what they had found in Chug's apartment. They had talked about it almost the whole way to Tampa. They wondered how much it was all worth, wondered at the things it would enable them to do, in Vera Cruz, in Monterey, wherever. Enrique had known wealth was there but they did not believe he had known how much.

"Then," he said to May, "we will take you to the airport. Are you happy that you are going to California?"

May blew a smoke ring and another after that, then leaned forward on her chair, her eyes were bright with excitement.

Oh yes," she said, "I am going to live next to the Pacific Ocean. It has cold water and sea lions. I am going to meet a man, maybe a doctor like the one in the books who studies fish and ocean creatures. I want to meet a nice man, a strong man. I will have money to share with my man. I have something else too, that I have been saving for him."

Anita sputtered and coughed. Her lip was nearly healed. She looked young again in the new sundress. They had stopped at a drugstore for things and May had done her hair.

"I do not like fishing," she said when she recovered. "I do not like to eat them," was all she could think of to say.

Enrique looked at his wife. She did not have to like fishing, he thought, he liked it enough for both of them. The boys would make sure the catch was eaten. He thought about the old captain.

"We are going to live by the Gulf," he said. We are going to grow the best flowers in the city, but I am going to fish whenever I can. Those boys can work seven days a week," he said, "I am finished with that. I will catch more snook and redfish than anyone. They are the same waters," he recalled what the captain had told him, "perhaps I will catch a snook that swam in Hendry Creek."

He looked at Anita, she nodded her head at his pleasure. She was a good wife, he thought, his blessings were not countable. He was a good husband, she thought, she would help him with the flowers. There was an incredible sum of money and riches in the Dodge, they had capital. They would share it with Hidalgo and the sisters.

May spoke.

"Enrique, I did not know you very well. I did not know Anita either. Where did your courage come from? You could have gone to Mexico. If he had surprised you instead he would have killed you and Anita. How did you know what to do?" She paused, the cigar had gone out. "You have always been a farmer."

Enrique's eyes welled with tears. He was becoming emotional too often, he thought, it was a sign of aging. He took a moment to calm himself. He remembered resting there in The Quarters, under the sour orange tree, his visions and the cadences. He cleared his throat, he looked directly at the woman.

"I had a great enthusiasm to see that man punished. I have not always been a farmer," he said. "In Buckingham I was a sergeant. I was a soldier," he said, "during World War II. Maybe when we are in the car you will let me tell you a little of what I remember."

Epilogue

Gladiolus Drive still connects U.S. 41 to McGregor Boulevard and San Carlos. 30,000 cars a day pass under the traffic lights at Gladiolus and the highway. Six lanes provide motorists speedy access up and down Gladiolus, to Summerlin Road and the beaches. The rock pits were changed to Lakes Park, the big garfish are gone from the sulfurous waters. They starved to death probably, after they had eaten everything that swam there, or fell in. The rest had been caught and killed by murderous fishermen and fisherboys. Near the bottom of one of the lakes, hung up on an outcrop of limestone rock, there are two little piles of concrete blocks and several feet of braided cable. Blue crabs hide there from bass and turtles. There is a parking lot where abandoned agaves and yucca grew, the Australian pines remain.

Harlem Heights is about the same as it was in 1971, except for the new houses that Habitat has built for deserving people. The sand trails that led from Gladiolus are paved streets with names. Harlem Heights passed through a bad time in the Eighties. Gangs of mad black boys crowded the corner at Gladiolus and Concourse and waved down cars to sell crack. The boys grabbed at the purses and gold necklaces of the people stupid enough to stop. The coconut palms have died from lethal yellowing, no one has cared for the mangos and avocados, the green canopy that shaded the cottages and shacks is mostly gone.

The Potter Estate and the orchid house, the little red cypress build-

287

ing and Mister Congdon and the old fishermen are departed. The worst treatment was given to the once beautiful grounds of the old lady doctor. She died. The house, the orchids and bromeliads and the terra cotta maidens were abandoned, then abused. The reclinatas grew into each other, they crowded out the light. The trunks of the royals and Alexander palms grew thin, the tops were spindly without fertilizer, without water in the winters and springs. Birds dropped Brazilian pepper seed, those bastards grew thick, they choked out the crotons and gingers. The reflection ponds became green with scum and algae. The house was broken into, windows were smashed, paint was sprayed on the walls, empty wine bottles and beer cans littered the inside where bright sunshine had once made the wood floor glow. Finally, the house was destroyed, the bougainvillea was bulldozed with the stucco and tiles and windows and doors. The moat that rose and fell with the tide was filled in with rock and sand. A new owner tried to build a modern house for himself but he ran out of money. The house he started is vandalized, trashed, ruined. Presently the grounds are in upheaval.

There are no flower farms left in Lee County, which once called itself the *Gladiolus Capital Of The World*. A plat map of 1968 shows that Gladiolus was all farms. A few men still graze cattle, there are a couple of U Picks for strawberries and tomatoes. That's done to keep the agricultural zoning, to keep the property taxes low, until the right developer comes along who can't afford to live without owning more land, who can't live without owning more houses, hospitals, apartments, and shopping centers.

Mullet still swim in Hendry Creek. They are made of smaller groups, usually five or seven of the gentle fish swim together in lazy circles just below the surface of the whiskey colored water. They don't jump like they used to, when the old captain and Enrique cast homemade wooden plugs under the mangroves.

Brady Vogt is a Florida nurseryman and a rare book dealer. Visit his website at www.evergladesbooks.com. He has lived in Fort Myers most of his adult life. *Gladiolus Drive* is his first book. He is presently at work on a story about shrimpers at Fort Myers Beach.